Praise for the Mercy Thompson novels

BONE CROSSED

"Briggs makes a well-deserved move into hardcover with the rousing fourth adventure for kick-ass werecoyote auto mechanic Mercedes Thompson." —*Publishers Weekly*

"Mercy is not just another cookie-cutter tough-chick urban fantasy heroine; she's got a lot of style and substance and an intriguing backstory. Series fans will appreciate the resolution of some ongoing plotlines, and the romantic tension is strong." —*Library Journal*

"[Mercy is] one of the best of the kick-ass heroine crop." —*Locus*

IRON KISSED

"The third book in an increasingly excellent series, *Iron Kissed* has all the elements I've come to expect in a Patricia Briggs novel: sharp, perceptive characterization, nonstop action, and a levelheaded attention to detail and location. I love these books." —Charlaine Harris, #1 *New York Times* bestselling author

BLOOD BOUND

"Once again, Briggs has written a full-bore action adventure with heart . . . Be prepared to read [it] in one sitting, because once you get going, there is no good place to stop until tomorrow." —*SFRevu*

"Plenty of action and intriguing characters keep this fun. In the increasingly crowded field of kick-ass supernatural heroines, Mercy stands out as one of the best." —*Locus*

continued . . .

MOON CALLED

"An excellent read with plenty of twists and turns. Her strong and complex characters kept me entertained from its deceptively innocent beginning to its can't-put-it-down end. Thoroughly satisfying, it left me wanting more."

—Kim Harrison, *New York Times* bestselling author

"Patricia Briggs always enchants her readers. With *Moon Called* she weaves her magic on every page to take us into a new and dazzling world of werewolves, shapeshifters, witches, and vampires. Expect to be spellbound."

—Lynn Viehl, *New York Times* bestselling author

Praise for the novels of Patricia Briggs

DRAGON BLOOD

"It goes without saying, I suppose, that I'm looking forward to seeing what else Patricia Briggs does. If *Dragon Blood* is any indication, then she is an inventive, engaging writer, whose talent for combining magic of all kinds—from spells to love—with fantastic characters should certainly win her a huge following, and a place on many bookshelves."   —*SF Site*

DRAGON BONES

"I enjoyed *Dragon Bones* . . . This is an enjoyable, well-written book, with enough plot twists and turns to keep the reader's attention. This book is sure to appeal to lovers of fantasy."

—*The Green Man Review*

"[Briggs] possesses the all-too-rare ability to make you fall hopelessly in love with her characters . . . It's good stuff all the way . . . You find yourself carried away by the charm of the story and the way Briggs tells it."   —*Crescent Blues*

THE HOB'S BARGAIN

"This is a 'Beauty and the Beast' story but unlike any I've ever read. Ms. Briggs blends adventure, romance, and innovative fantasy with a deft hand. [I] highly recommend this one to all my readers."   —S. L. Viehl, national bestselling author

"[A] fun fantasy romance . . . There's plenty of action, with battles against raiders and magical creatures, a bard who isn't what he appears, and an evil mage—but there's also plenty of humor and some sweet moments of mischief and romance."   —*Locus*

"Briggs has a good ear for dialogue and pace, and a marked talent for drawing complex characterizations . . . If you're looking to while away some time with a good story full of magic and wonder, you might find it worthwhile to accept *The Hob's Bargain*."   —Rambles.net

"It is easy to like Patricia Briggs's novels. Her books are perfect for a Friday evening or a late Saturday afternoon when you don't want to have to work to enjoy your reading. Her books are clever, engaging, fast-moving, and with plots that manage to be thought-provoking without being heavy-handed. A warning, however—make sure you don't start the dinner cooking or the lawn watering before you curl up with one of her books, because you'll end up with a burnt dinner and a soggy lawn and an enjoyable few hours lost in another world."
                            —*Romantic Science Fiction & Fantasy*

WHEN DEMONS WALK

"An interesting cross between a murder mystery, romance, and fantasy . . . There are enough twists and turns in the plot to keep most readers' interest."   —*VOYA*

"Patricia Briggs proves herself a rare talent as she devises a clever mystery with appealing characters in a fantasy setting . . . top-notch reading fare."   —*Romantic Times*

Titles by Patricia Briggs

The Mercy Thompson Novels

MOON CALLED
BLOOD BOUND
IRON KISSED
BONE CROSSED
SILVER BORNE
RIVER MARKED

The Alpha and Omega Novels

ON THE PROWL
(with Eileen Wilks, Karen Chance, and Sunny)
CRY WOLF
HUNTING GROUND

MASQUES
WOLFSBANE
STEAL THE DRAGON
WHEN DEMONS WALK

THE HOB'S BARGAIN

DRAGON BONES
DRAGON BLOOD

RAVEN'S SHADOW
RAVEN'S STRIKE

MASQUES

PATRICIA BRIGGS

ACE BOOKS, NEW YORK

THE BERKLEY PUBLISHING GROUP
Published by the Penguin Group
Penguin Group (USA) Inc.
375 Hudson Street, New York, New York 10014, USA
Penguin Group (Canada), 90 Eglinton Avenue East, Suite 700, Toronto, Ontario M4P 2Y3, Canada
(a division of Pearson Penguin Canada Inc.)
Penguin Books Ltd., 80 Strand, London WC2R 0RL, England
Penguin Group Ireland, 25 St. Stephen's Green, Dublin 2, Ireland (a division of Penguin Books Ltd.)
Penguin Group (Australia), 250 Camberwell Road, Camberwell, Victoria 3124, Australia
(a division of Pearson Australia Group Pty. Ltd.)
Penguin Books India Pvt. Ltd., 11 Community Centre, Panchsheel Park, New Delhi—110 017, India
Penguin Group (NZ), 67 Apollo Drive, Rosedale, North Shore 0632, New Zealand
(a division of Pearson New Zealand Ltd.)
Penguin Books (South Africa) (Pty.) Ltd., 24 Sturdee Avenue, Rosebank, Johannesburg 2196,
South Africa

Penguin Books Ltd., Registered Offices: 80 Strand, London WC2R 0RL, England

MASQUES

An Ace Book / published by arrangement with Hurog, Inc.

PRINTING HISTORY
Ace mass-market edition / December 1993
Ace mass-market revised edition / October 2010

Copyright © 1993 by Patricia Briggs.
Copyright © 2010 by Hurog, Inc.
Excerpt from *Wolfsbane* copyright © by Hurog, Inc.
Map by Michael Enzweiler.
Cover art by Mélanie Delon.
Cover design by Annette Fiore DeFex.
Interior text design by Laura K. Corless.

ISBN: 978-0-441-01942-7

ACE
Ace Books are published by The Berkley Publishing Group,
a division of Penguin Group (USA) Inc.,
375 Hudson Street, New York, New York 10014.
ACE and the "A" design are trademarks of Penguin Group (USA) Inc.

PRINTED IN THE UNITED STATES OF AMERICA

10 9 8 7 6 5 4 3 2

With love to my parents:

Harvey C. Rowland
1917–1989

Betty J. Rowland
1920–1992

INTRODUCTION

One day, in the middle of my senior year of college, I decided to write a book. I'd written a few things before. Nothing so complex as an actual short story (aside from a few five-hundred-word shorts for various high-school assignments and one memorably bad story I'd written in German in lieu of a report), but scenes and scraps of dialogue. I'd never met an author, never gone to an SF convention, when I set out to write this book. And for the next few years I wrote, and rewrote, the first ten pages of my novel. Those ten pages, I might add, are the first thing I cut for this edition. Sometimes I wake up in the middle of the night and find myself muttering those lines: *The great hall of the castle was his favorite room . . .*

With our newly minted degrees, my husband and I set out for the wilds of Chicago, where Mike had taken a job as an aquarist with the John G. Shedd Aquarium (we do seem to have had a lot of interesting if not lucrative careers, my husband and I) and I began working at an insurance office. The Greater Chicago area had seven and a half million people. My home state of Montana (in the 1990s) had eight hundred thousand people—in the whole state. Suddenly my manuscript represented more than a challenge—it was an escape. Don't get me wrong, I loved Chicago—I just didn't love living with seven and a half freaking million people.

We stayed a full year before culture shock sent us racing homeward, and about that time, somewhat to my surprise, I had finished the book.

I knew that I knew nothing about writing a book when I started it. So I took those things I did know and stuck with them. The plot, my patient husband pointed out, had been done before—but I was okay with that. The important thing to me was that I'd actually finished the book. It shocked and amazed me when the book actually sold.

Masques, when it came out, was what my husband likes to call an extremely limited edition. That's husband speak for "It sold very poorly." Fortunately, before my publisher figured out just how poorly it had done, they'd bought *Steal the Dragon* as well. My second book, blessed by a terrific Royo cover and a writer who had figured out a little more about writing, did a lot better than the first. *Masques* went out of print the month *Steal the Dragon* came out back in 1995, and hasn't been in print since.

Years passed by, my career started to pick up, and *Masques* started to command higher prices on the secondary market. If I had a box of twenty-four copies left, I could sell them on eBay for more than I sold the publication rights for the original novel.

With that in mind, I took out the unpublished sequel, *Wolfsbane*, blew off the dust, and did an extensive polishing run. I sent the result to my editor and asked about reprinting *Masques* and publishing *Wolfsbane*. She agreed and asked me if I wanted to revise *Masques* before they released it. Absolutely, I said. Please. And that was about the time I got a call asking me if I'd like to try my hand at an urban fantasy first. With the subsequent success of the Mercy Thompson and Alpha and Omega novels, *Masques* and *Wolfsbane* got put on the back burner for a few years.

Finally, I had a bit of breathing room and sat down for the first time in a decade or so to start reading *Masques*. I had intended to do a brief polishing run. I read the first chapter (squirming uncomfortably all the way through) and turned to my husband. "By golly," I said (or words to that effect). "Why didn't someone tell me I needed to use a few descriptions?"

When I wrote *Masques*, I was in my twenties and hadn't even finished a short story worthy of the name. I knew nothing about writing. The only tool I had in my craftbox was that I loved the fantasy genre and had read a lot of books. Twenty years later, I've written more than fifteen books, discussed/argued writing with a number of enormously skilled craftspeople—and learned a lot in the process. But that same experience also means I could not write *Masques* now.

Thus, fixing the book and still allowing it to be the same story, my first story, became quite a problem.

In the end, *Masques* and I have come to a compromise. Though I have added a bit to the beginning, I have not taken away any of the original pieces of the story (much as it sometimes pained me). I just fit those pieces together a little better. I left in most of the clichés and the oddities that, if I were editing an unpublished work, I would have removed. Thus, I hope that those few of you who read the original and remember it fondly will feel as though this is an expanded version of the same story. And that those of you who are only familiar with my later, more polished work won't be disappointed.

PROLOGUE

The wolf stumbled from the cave, knowing that someone was searching for him and he couldn't protect himself this time. Feverish and ill, his head throbbing so hard that it hurt to move, he couldn't pull his thoughts together.

After all this time, after all of his preparations, he was going to be brought down by an illness.

The searcher's tendrils spread out again, brushing across him without recognition or pause. The Northlands were rife with wild magic—which is why other magic couldn't work correctly here. The searcher looked for a wizard and would never notice the wolf who concealed the man in its shape unless the fever betrayed him.

He should lie low, it was the best defense . . . but he was so afraid, and his illness clogged his thoughts.

Death didn't frighten him; he sometimes thought he had come here seeking it. He was more afraid he wouldn't die, afraid of what he would become. Perhaps the one who looked for him was just idly hunting—but when he felt a third sweep, he knew it was unlikely. He must have given himself away somehow. He'd always known that he would be found one day. He'd just never thought it would be when he was so weak.

He fought to blend better with the form he'd taken, to lose himself in the wolf. He succeeded.

The fourth sizzle of magic, the searcher's magic, was too much for the wolf. The wolf was a simpler creature than the mage who hid within him. If he was frightened, he attacked or ran. There was no one here to attack, so he ran.

It wasn't until the wolf was tired that he could gather his humanity—that was a laugh, *his* humanity—well then, he gathered *himself* together and stopped running. His ribs ached with the force of his breath and the tough pads of his feet were cut by stones and an occasional crystal of ice from a land where the sun would never completely melt winter's gift. He was shivering though he felt hot, feverish. He was sick.

He couldn't keep running—and it wasn't only the wolf who craved escape—because running wasn't escape, not from what he fled.

He closed his eyes, but that didn't keep his head from throbbing in time with his pounding pulse. If he wasn't going to die out here, he would have to find shelter. Someplace warm, where he could wait and recover. He was lucky he'd come south, and it was high summer. If it had been winter, his only chance would have been to return to the caves he'd run from.

A pile of leaves under a thicket of aspen caught his attention. If they were deep enough to be dry underneath, they would do for shelter. He headed downhill and started for the trees.

There was no warning. The ground simply gave out from under him so fast he was lying ten feet down on a pile of rotted stakes before he realized what had happened.

It was an old pit trap. He started to get up and realized

that he hadn't been as lucky as he thought. The stakes had snapped when he hit them, but so had his rear leg.

Perhaps if he hadn't already been so sick, so tired, he could have done something. He'd long ago learned how to set pain aside while he used his magic. But, though he tried, he couldn't distance himself from it this time, not while his body shivered with fever. Without magic, with a broken leg, he was trapped. The rotting stakes meant no one was watching the pit—no one to free him or kill him quickly. So he would die slowly.

That was all right because he didn't want to be free so much as he didn't want to be caught.

This was a trap, but it wasn't *His* trap.

Perhaps, the wolf thought, as his good legs collapsed again, perhaps it would be good not to run anymore. The ground was cold and wet underneath him, and the flush of heat from fever and the frantic journey drained into the chill of his surroundings. He shivered with cold and pain and waited patiently . . . even happily, for death to come and take him.

———————

"If you go to the Northlands in the summer you might avoid snowstorms, but you get mud." Aralorn, Staff Page, Runner, and Scout for the Sixth Field Hundred, kicked a rock, which arced into the air and landed with an unsatisfactory splut just ahead of her on the mucky trail.

It wasn't a real trail. If it hadn't led from the village directly to the well-used camping spot her unit was currently stopped at, she'd have called it a deer trail and suspected that human feet had never trod it.

"*I* could have told them that," she said. "But no one asked me."

She took another step, and her left boot sank six inches down into a patch that looked just like the bit before it that had held her weight just fine. She pulled her foot out and shook it, trying unsuccessfully to get the thick mud off. When she started walking again, her mud-coated boot weighed twice what her right boot did.

"I suppose," she said in resigned tones as she squelched along, "training isn't supposed to be fun, and sometimes we have to fight in the mud. But there's mud in warmer places. We could go hunting Uriah in the old Great Swamp. That would be good training and *useful*, but no one would pay us. Mercenaries can't possibly be useful without someone paying us. So we're stuck—literally in the case of our supply wagons—practicing maneuvers in the cold mud."

Her sympathetic audience sighed and butted her with his head. She rubbed her horse's gray cheekbone under the leather straps of his bridle. "I know, Sheen. We could get there in an hour if we hurry—but I see no sense in encouraging stupid behavior."

One of the supply wagons was so bogged down in mud that it had broken an axle when they tried to pull it out. Aralorn had been sent out to the nearest village to have a smith repair the damage because the smith they'd brought with them had broken his arm trying to help get the wagon out.

That there had *been* a nearby village was something of a surprise out in the Northlands—though they weren't very deep into them. That village had probably been why the mercenary troops had been sent to practice where they were instead of twenty miles east or west.

The mended axle was tied lengthwise onto the left side of Sheen's saddle, with a weighted bag tied to the opposite stirrup to balance the load. It made riding awkward, which was why Aralorn was walking. Part of the reason, anyway.

"If we get to camp too early, our glorious and inexperienced captain will be ordering the wagon repaired right away. He'll send us out from a fairly good campsite to march for another few miles until the sun sets—and we'll be looking for another reasonable place to camp all night."

The captain was a good sort, and would be a fine leader—eventually. But right now he was pretty set on proving his mettle and so lost to common sense. He needed to be managed properly by someone with a little more experience.

"If I don't arrive with the axle until it's dark, then he'll have to wait to move out until dawn," she told Sheen. "With daylight, it won't take long to fix the wagon, and we'll all get a good night's sleep. You and I can trot the last half mile or so, just enough to raise a light sweat and claim it was the smith who took so long."

Her warhorse jerked his head up abruptly. He snorted, his nostrils fluttering as he sucked air and flattened his ears at whatever his nose was telling him.

Aralorn thumbed off the thong that kept her sword in its sheath and looked around carefully. It wasn't just a person—he'd have alerted her to that with a twitch of his ear.

The scent of blood might have called her horse's battle training to the fore, she thought, or maybe he sensed some sort of predator. This was the Northlands, after all; there were bear, wolves, and a few other things large enough to cause Sheen's upset.

The gray stallion whinnied a shrill challenge that was likely to be heard for miles around. She could only hope that her captain didn't hear it. Whatever Sheen sensed, it was in the aspen grove just uphill from where they stood. It was also, apparently, in no hurry to attack them since nothing answered Sheen's call: no return challenge, not even a rustle.

She could go on past. Likely, if it hadn't come out yet, it wasn't going to. But what was the fun in that?

She dropped Sheen's reins on the ground. He'd stand until she came back—at least until he got hungry. Aralorn drew her knife and crept into the thicket of aspen.

———

He heard her talking and smelled the horse without moving. He'd heard them come by earlier, too—or he thought so anyway. The horse put up a fuss this time because the wind that ruffled the leaves of the aspen would have brought him the wolf's scent.

He waited for them to leave. Tonight, he thought hopefully. Tonight would be the third night he'd spent here, maybe it would be the last. But part of him knew better, knew just how long it took for a body to die of thirst or of hunger. He was too strong yet. It would be tomorrow, at the soonest.

He'd distracted himself with the hope of death, and only the sound of the woman's feet told him that she'd approached. He opened his eyes to see a sturdily built woman, plain of face except for her large sea-green eyes, leaning over the edge of the pit. She wore the uniform of the mercenaries, and there were calluses and mud on her hands.

He didn't want to see her eyes, didn't want to feel interest in her at all. He only wanted her to leave him alone so he could die.

"Plague them all," she said, her voice tight and angry. Then her voice softened to a croon. "How long have you been here, love?"

The wolf recognized the threat of the knife she held as she slid down the far side of the pit to stand, one foot on either side of his hips. He growled, rolling off his side in preparation to get up—because he'd forgotten he wanted to die. Just for a moment. He shook from exertion, sickness, and from the pain of moving his leg. He lay back down again and flattened his ears.

"Shh," she crooned, inexplicably sheathing her knife in the face of his aggression. "Not so long as all that, apparently. Now what shall I do about you?"

Go away, he thought. He growled at her with as much threat as he could, feeling his lips peel back from his fangs and the hair rise along his spine.

The expression on her face was not the one that he'd expected. Certainly not one any sane person would turn on a threatening wolf she was standing over. She should fear him.

Instead . . . "Poor thing," she said in that same crooning tone. "Let's get you out of this, shall we?"

She dropped her gaze away from his and knelt to examine his hips, humming softly as she moved closer.

She didn't stink of fear, was all he could think. Everyone feared him. Everyone. Even *Him*, even the one who searched. She smelled of horse, sweat, and something sweet. No fear.

He snarled, and she wrapped one hand over his muzzle. Sheer astonishment stopped his growls. Just how stupid was she?

"Shh." Her voice blended into the music she was making, and he realized that her humming was pulling magic out of the ground around and beneath them. "Let me look."

He was as surprised at himself as he was at her when he let her do just that. He could have torn out her throat or broken her neck while she examined every inch of him. But he didn't—and he wasn't quite certain why not.

It wasn't that killing her would bother him. He'd killed a lot of people. But that was before. He didn't want to do that anymore. So perhaps that was part of it.

He knew she was trying to help him—but he didn't want help. He wanted to die.

Her magic swept over and around him, cushioning him. The wolf whined softly and relaxed, leaving the mage in him fully in charge for the first time since the illness had hit. Maybe even longer ago than that.

Her magic didn't work on the mage because he knew what it was—and, he admitted to himself, because it wasn't coercive magic. He was mage enough to read her intent. She didn't want the wolf to become a lapdog but only to relax.

But the woman's helpful intent wasn't why he didn't kill her. Not the real reason. He hadn't been interested in anything in longer than he could remember, but she made him curious. He'd only ever met a practitioner of green magic, wild magic, once before. They hid from the humans in the land—if there were any still left. But here was one wearing the clothes of a mercenary.

She could pick him up—which surprised him because she didn't weigh much more than he did. But she couldn't hoist him high enough to reach the edge of the trap, so she set him down again.

"Going to need some help," she told him, and clambered to the top. She almost didn't make it out of the pit herself; if it had been round, she wouldn't have.

When she departed and took her magic with her, it left him bereaved—as if someone had covered him with a blanket, then removed it. And only when she left did he realize that her music had deadened his pain and soothed him, despite his being a mage on his guard against it.

He heard the horse move and the sound of leather and something heavy hitting the ground. The horse approached the pit and stopped.

When the mercenary who could do green magic hopped back into his almost grave, she had a rope in her hand.

He waited for the wolf to stir as she tied him in a make-shift harness that somehow managed to brace his bad leg. But the wolf waited as meekly as a lamb while she worked. When he was trussed up to her satisfaction, she climbed back out.

"Come on, Sheen," she told someone. Possibly, he thought, it was the horse.

The trip out of the hole was not pleasant. He closed his eyes and let the pain take him where it would. When he lay on the ground at last, she untied him.

Freed at last, he lay where he had fallen, too weak to run. Maybe too curious as well.

ONE

Aralorn paced, her heart beating with nervous energy.

It had seemed like a good idea at the time. She intended to sneak in as a servant—she was good at being a servant, and people talked in front of servants as if they weren't there at all. But then there had been that slave girl, freshly sold to the very Geoffrey ae'Magi whose court Aralorn was supposed to infiltrate and observe . . .

Maybe if the slave girl hadn't had the gray-green eyes of the old races, eyes Aralorn shared, she wouldn't have given in to impulse. But it had been easy to free the girl and send her off with connections who would see her safely back to her home—proof that though she had lived in Sianim all these years, Aralorn was still Rethian enough to despise slavery. It was even easier to use the magic of her mother's people to rearrange her body and her features to mimic the girl and take her place.

She hadn't realized that slaves could be locked away until they were needed; she'd assumed she'd have work to do. It was well-known that the Archmage's passions were reserved for magic, and he seldom indulged in more fleshly pleasures. She'd figured that the girl had been purchased to *do* something—not sit locked in a room for weeks.

Aralorn had been just about ready to escape and try again using a different identity when she'd been brought up to the great hall of the ae'Magi's castle four days ago and put into the huge silver cage.

"She's to be decoration for the ball," said the servant who put her in the cage, in response to another servant's question. "It won't be for a week yet, but he wanted her here so he could see the decorations and her at the same time."

Decoration. The ae'Magi had purchased a slave to decorate his great hall.

It had seemed out of character for the Archmage, Aralorn had thought. It took more than power to become the ae'Magi. The man or woman who wore that mantle of authority was, in his peers' eyes, a person of unassailable virtue. Only such a one could be allowed the reins to control all of the mages—at least all those west of the Great Swamp—so there was never again a wizard war. Purchasing a person in order to use her as decoration seemed . . . petty for such a one as the ae'Magi. Or so she'd thought.

Four days ago.

Aralorn shivered. Her shoes made no sound on the marble beneath her feet, not that anyone would have been able to hear them over the music.

Beyond the silver bars of her cage, the great hall of the ae'Magi's castle was resplendent. By reputation, if not fact, the room was nearly a thousand years old, kept beautiful by good maintenance and judicious replacement rather than magic.

Though this room was the heart of the ae'Magi's home, by tradition no magic was to be done here. This was the place the rulers of men conducted business with the ae'Magi, and the lack of magic proved to one and all that there was

no magical coercion taking place. Aralorn now knew that
the current ae'Magi didn't particularly care about following tradition, and coercion was something he used . . . on
everyone.

That first day, she'd been shocked when the stone beneath
her feet vibrated with magic. She looked out at the room.
Ten centuries old, or at least ten centuries of care and careful preservation by the finest craftsmen available. And the
ae'Magi had saturated the stone with magic. No one would
think to check, would they? And if they did, they'd just
suspect another ae'Magi, an earlier one, because Geoffrey
ae'Magi would never defy tradition.

This evening it was lavishly decorated for the pleasure
of the people who danced lightly across the floor. Late-
afternoon rays of sunlight streamed through the tear-shaped
crystal skylights etched on the soaring ceilings. Pale pillars
dripped down to the highly polished ivory-colored marble
floor that reflected the jewel-like colors of the dancers'
clothing.

Aralorn's cage sat on a raised platform on the only wall
of the room that lacked a doorway. From that perch, she
could observe the whole room and be observed in return.
Or rather they could see the illusion that the ae'Magi had
placed on the cage.

Instead of the tall, white-blond woman that the ae'Magi
had purchased to decorate his great hall with her extraordinary beauty, observers would see a snowfalcon as rare
and beautiful, the ae'Magi had told her, as his slave, but not
so controversial. Some people, he'd told her, licking blood
off his hands, disliked slavery, and he disliked controversy.

He'd decorated the room around his slave for his own
amusement. Disguising her as a rare predator was simply a joke played upon the people who'd come here for
entertainment.

A chime sounded, announcing new visitors. Aralorn
hugged herself as the ae'Magi greeted his guests with a

warm smile. He'd smiled that same smile last night while he'd killed a young boy and stolen his magic.

The stone floor had been red with blood, but it wiped up cleanly, and only someone able to sense magic might notice the pall that unclean death had left. Or not. The ae'Magi was the lord of mages, after all, and they could only use their powers to the extent he allowed.

She was scaring herself again—that was really not useful at all. Biting her lip, Aralorn gazed at the dancing nobles in an effort to distract herself. She matched names and countries to the dancers' faces with the ease that made her the valuable spy she was.

The ae'Magi had killed an old man, an old man without a spark of magic—human or green—about him and used the power of the death to turn the walls of the great hall a sparkling white. "An illusion," he'd told her. "It takes some power, and I don't like to use my own when I might need it at any time."

That had been the first night. On the second, he'd brought a man—one of his own guardsmen. With that blood, the ae'Magi had worked some magic so foul that the taste of it lingered on Aralorn's skin still.

The boy had been the worst. Only a child, and . . .

Dozens of the rulers of the kingdoms of the Anthran Alliance were present. Some of them had been members of the Alliance for centuries, others were newer than that. The Empress of the Alliance wasn't here, but she was six, and her guardians kept a sharp eye on her lest any of her subjects decided to make her cousin the new empress instead. Just because they were allied didn't mean they were loyal subjects. The squabbles among the Alliance helped keep the coffers of Sianim full.

Gradually, she managed to replace the boy's dead eyes with dates and politics, but she still paced her cage restlessly. It wasn't just the horror of her discovery of exactly what kind of man held the power of the ae'Magi that kept

her from sitting down—it was fear. The ae'Magi scared
her to death.

There was a kaleidoscopic quality to the dance: the brilliant colors of the rich fabrics twisting around and around
only to stop, rearrange themselves, and swirl into motion
once again. More like a clockwork than a dance populated
by real people. Perhaps it was a side effect of all the magic.
Or maybe it was deliberate, the ae'Magi amusing himself.
He liked to make people unwittingly do his bidding.

She saw the Duchess of Ti and the Envoy of the Anthran
Alliance dancing cordially with each other. Ten years ago,
the Envoy had had the Duchess's youngest son assassinated, sparking a bloody feud that left bodies littering the
Alliance like a plague.

The Envoy said something and patted the Duchess's
shoulder. She laughed gaily in return as if she hadn't had
the Envoy's third wife killed in a particularly nasty manner only a month ago. She might have thought it a clever
ruse designed to put the other off guard, but the Envoy was
not particularly politic or clever. Aralorn wondered if the
effect of whatever spell the ae'Magi had apparently cast
upon his guests was specific to them and whether it would
last beyond this evening. Just how powerful was he?

When the musicians paused for a break, people crowded
around the Archmage, Geoffrey ae'Magi, drawn to his
twinkling eyes and mischievous grin the way butterflies
surround the flowering coralis tree. When a butterfly landed
on the sweet-smelling scarlet flower of the coralis, the petals closed, and the flower digested its hapless prey over a
period of weeks.

There were some times when her penchant for collecting trivia wasn't an asset.

Like the coralis, Geoffrey ae'Magi was extraordinarily
beautiful, with blue-black hair, high cheekbones, and the
smile of a child with his hand caught in the cookie jar.

Aralorn had been in his presence before. The Spymaster

liked to use her in the rarefied society of which the ae'Magi was a part because she knew how to negotiate it without betraying herself. She'd attributed the wave of magic that surrounded him to his being the most powerful mage in the world. His beauty had stunned her at first, but it hadn't taken her long to decide that the attraction lay in his gentle warmth and his self-deprecating humor. Four days ago, Aralorn, like every other woman who'd ever laid eyes upon him, had been more than half-enamored of him.

Aralorn turned her gaze away from the ae'Magi and back to the room. While she'd been watching the Archmage, someone had stopped next to the pillar nearest her cage.

Leaning lazily against the polished pillar, a short, square-built young man wearing the colors of the royal house of Reth also observed the throng: Myr, Prince—no—King now, of Reth. His face was strong-featured, even handsome in other company. There was a stubborn tilt to his chin that he'd inherited from his paternal grandfather, a formidable warrior and king.

It wasn't his appearance that caught her attention; she'd expected that he was the person from whom the ae'Magi had been hiding his slave. It was the expression of distaste that briefly crossed his face as he looked at the crowd, remarkably different from the vacuous smiles that everyone else wore.

He shifted unexpectedly and met her gaze. He looked quickly down, but then began to make his way through the edges of the crowd toward her cage. When he reached the platform, he tilted his head down so that no one could read his lips, and asked in a low tone, "Do you need help, Lady?"

Shocked, she glanced quickly at the mirror that covered the back of the cage. The ae'Magi's illusion of a snow-falcon stared back at her indifferently.

She knew that Myr was no mage—he wouldn't have been able to conceal that from her, not with her mother's blood in her veins. Green magic could usually hide from the tamed stuff that the more human mages used, but the reverse was not true. Still, there was no doubt that he saw a woman and not the rare bird the ae'Magi showed his guests.

Rethians believed they were the descendants of an enslaved people who had risen up to kill their masters. They were taught at their mother's knee that to take another human and own him was evil beyond comprehension.

Even so, even for the King of Reth, it was a bold move to offer to help one of the ae'Magi's slaves to escape. There were a lot of mages in Reth who owed obedience first to the ae'Magi and second to the king—obedience enforced by their own magic. To move against the ae'Magi could spark a civil war in Myr's kingdom. His offer was heartfelt and showed just how young this new king was.

Perhaps it was his rash offer that appealed to her or that she had been born Rethian and part of her still thought of Myr as her king. In any case, she answered him as herself, and not the slave that she played for the ae'Magi.

"No," she answered. "I'm here as an observer."

There were rumors that the ruling family of Reth had occasionally produced offspring who were immune to magic. There were stories, and Aralorn was a collector of stories.

"A spy." It wasn't a question. "You must be from either Sianim or Jetaine. They are the only ones who would employ women to spy in as delicate a position as this." Women were important in Reth, and they were far from powerless politically. But they didn't go to battle, didn't put themselves in danger.

With a half smile, Aralorn clarified, "I get paid for my work."

"Sianim mercenary."

She nodded. "Pardon me for asking, but how did you see past the illusion of the snowfalcon that the ae'Magi placed on the cage?"

"Is that what you're disguised as?" His smile made him look even younger than he really was. "I wondered why no one said anything about the beautiful woman he had in the cage."

Interesting. He saw through the ae'Magi's illusion but not her altered shape. No one had ever called Aralorn beautiful. Not in those tones. Maybe it wasn't only altruism on his part that had him offering to free her. That made sense, though; when she'd taken the likeness of the slave girl, magic had altered her—not just other people's perceptions of her as the ae'Magi's illusion did.

She felt eyes on her and glanced up under her lashes to see the ae'Magi not ten paces away, staring at Myr in fascination.

Myr might have been young and impetuous, but he wasn't dumb. He caught the subtle tension of her body.

"Aren't you a pretty thing," he murmured softly, though a little louder than he'd been speaking before. "I wonder if you are trained to glove and jess?"

"Ah, I see you admire my falcon, Lord." The deep, resonant voice of the ae'Magi could have belonged to a musician. Not only was the Archmage physically beautiful; he even sounded beautiful.

Myr straightened abruptly, as if taken by surprise, and turned to look at the ae'Magi, who strolled up to stand next to him in front of the ornate cage.

"She is extraordinary, isn't she?" the ae'Magi continued. "I purchased her a month or more ago from a traveling merchant—she was captured somewhere in the Northlands, I believe . . . I thought she would go well with this room." He waved a casual hand that managed to indicate the rest of the hall.

Aralorn had grown adept at reading the ae'Magi's voice, and his tone was just a little too casual. She wondered if he'd also heard the stories of the odd talent said to crop up in the Rethian royal family.

Reth was a small country in size but rich in minerals and agriculture. It also had a well-trained army, left as the legacy of Myr's grandfather. Its army had served to keep Reth independent every time the Anthran Alliance had periodically tried to swallow it over the past few centuries. Myr was a very new king, and certain conservative political factions would have been happier had he been the same kind of puppet as his father. But there were enough houses who would support him against all comers that Myr should be safe even from the Archmage. She didn't know why she thought the ae'Magi might harm Myr. Maybe it was because part of her still believed she owed fealty to the royal house of Reth, and it made her overprotective. Maybe it was the way the ae'Magi reminded her of a cat watching a mouse hole.

The sweet interest in the ae'Magi's face gave Aralorn cold chills. *Be careful,* she silently urged Myr.

Myr turned to the magician with a smile and more confidence than a boy his age should have had. "Yes, the ivory tinge is the same as the color in the marble here. It's unusual to see a snowfalcon this far south; you must have paid a great deal for her."

The two men talked at length about falconry, something that Aralorn happened to know interested neither of them. When they had exhausted the subject, the ae'Magi abruptly changed topics.

"My dear Myr," said the ae'Magi, "please accept my condolences upon the untimely death of your parents. I had no opportunity to talk to you at the funeral. I sent a note, of course, but I wanted to speak to you face-to-face."

Myr started to speak, but the ae'Magi laid a long-fingered hand on Myr's shoulder, effectively forestalling what the younger man might have said.

"If you have need of anything, feel free to turn to me. I have connections and substantial power as the ae'Magi, and you may need what aid I can offer. It has never been easy to ascend the throne, especially now with the Uriah restless in the eastern forests. Not to mention that there are always opposing factions or"—he hesitated, waving his hand expressively—"other enemies."

With professional interest, Aralorn heard the slight edge of guilt in his voice. It was masterfully done and reminded her that the former rulers of Reth had been killed after leaving one of the ae'Magi's elaborate parties. No one had ever implied that the accident might have had more sinister causes. She wouldn't have thought about it on her own— but, given what she now knew, Aralorn would have been astonished to discover the Archmage *didn't* have something to do with the king's death.

She wondered if Myr knew why the ae'Magi apparently had such interest in him. She could all but smell the wizard's intent. She just couldn't tell why he was so intent. Myr suspected something; his distrust was obvious from his little charade.

Myr bowed his head quickly to acknowledge the offer without accepting it. "I know my parents counted you their friend. I appreciate your offer." He smiled apologetically. "I have enjoyed our conversation, but I must excuse myself. You see"—he leaned in closer, as if confessing an embarrassing secret—"I just bought a new stallion, and I'm not sure I trust him on the trails after dark." His face lost its eagerness for a moment. "After what happened to my parents, sir, I feel a need to be overly cautious."

Had that been a dig? *Don't bait him,* she thought urgently. *Don't bait him.*

The magician smiled understandingly. "I'll summon your servants for you."

Myr shook his head. "I left them outside with orders to meet me an hour before dark."

"The gods follow you, then." The Archmage paused. "I hope you know that your father was so proud of your courage and strength—you do credit to your lineage. I wish that my own son had been more like you."

To Aralorn's sensitive ears, the magician's voice held just the right amount of pain. She wondered why she hadn't noticed before she'd been assigned here that his emotions were always perfectly calculated.

"Lord Cain could not be termed a coward or weak, sir." Myr's voice held a matching amount of sympathy, as false as the ae'Magi's. He should have just thanked him and left, gotten out of his sight and hoped the ae'Magi forgot all about Reth and its young king.

"No," the ae'Magi agreed, "I think that it would have been better for all of us if he were a coward. He would have done less harm."

The ae'Magi kept his dark magics secret, but his son had performed them in the broad light of day.

Aralorn had never met Cain: He'd disappeared before she'd become involved in her present occupation. She'd heard the rumors, though—they got worse with each telling. But Myr would have known him; the ae'Magi and his son had been frequent visitors to his grandfather's court.

The stories put the ae'Magi in the role of a grieving father, forced to strip his son of magic and exile him. Aralorn suspected that the boy had died rather than been exiled. It would have been inconvenient if someone had questioned where the ae'Magi's son had learned so much about forbidden magic. As he'd told her himself, the ae'Magi preferred to avoid controversy.

"Be that as it may"—with apparent effort the ae'Magi dismissed the thought of his son—"your servants will probably be awaiting you even now."

"Yes, I should go. You may be sure I shall remember your gracious offer of assistance if ever I need help." With that, Myr bowed once more and left.

Watching Myr's broad back as he strode through the

room, the ae'Magi smiled—the slight imperfection of one crooked eyetooth lending charm to the more perfect curve of his lips. "What a clever, clever child you have grown to be, Myr." His voice purred with approval. "More like your grandfather every day."

It was late before the crowd began to thin and later still before everyone had gone. Aralorn couldn't control her apprehension as each person left, knowing that the meager protection their presence offered would soon be gone. After seeing the last couple out, the ae'Magi walked slowly over to the cage.

"So," he said, swaying gently back on his heels, "the Rethian doesn't see my lovely Northland bird."

"My lord?" she said neutrally. Having had most of the night to reflect upon the incident, she'd been pretty sure that the ae'Magi had figured that much out. She'd also had time to come to the conclusion that if he thought Myr was immune to magic, the ae'Magi's primary power, Myr would die.

The Archmage smiled and flicked a silver bar of her cage with his forefinger chidingly. "When he looked at you, he looked where your eyes are, not where the eyes of the falcon would have been."

Plague it, Aralorn thought. The ae'Magi put one hand through the bars and caressed her neck. She leaned against him and rubbed her cheek on his hand, forcing herself to obey the vague compulsion of the charismatic spell that had kept his guests happy instead of throwing herself backward and huddling in the far corner of the cage.

The ae'Magi tilted her face so that her eyes met his, and said in a leading tone, "I wonder how he broke through my illusion."

He couldn't expect a slave to understand what had happened, he was talking to himself. But he'd given her an opening—this was going to hurt.

"But he didn't break through your spell, Master," she answered in bewildered tones.

He looked down at her expressionlessly, and she quit fighting the urge to curl into a ball on the floor of the cage. He made a small motion with a finger, and she screamed as her body twisted helplessly under the fire of his magic.

Each time he did this to her was worse than the time before. Aralorn watched as the tendons pulled and stretched, protesting the sensations they endured. When it finally stopped, she didn't fight the tremors that shook her, telling herself that she was playing her part—but wondering deep inside whether she could have stopped had she tried.

After she lay still, the ae'Magi said softly, "I don't like to be contradicted, child. He knew you were not a falcon."

It was over. Over. He probably wouldn't do that again tonight. Or if he did, he'd at least give her some time to recover. She could tell herself that anyway.

"Yes, my lord," she said hoarsely, from her position on the floor of the cage. "Of course he knew, I didn't mean to contradict you—how could I? I misunderstood what you meant. You knew his magician broke the spell for him, how else would he have known?"

"What magician?" The ae'Magi's voice was sharp, almost worried.

"He was standing over behind that pillar." She pointed to someplace vaguely on the far side of the room, and the mage turned swiftly as if to look for someone still there.

"What made you think that he was a magician?"

"He made gestures like you do sometimes. He left with the young king." Aralorn kept her voice to a whisper such as a frightened girl might use. No anger. No protest. People in his thrall felt pain all right, but they adored him even while they shuddered in fear of what he could do. She'd seen them.

"What did he look like?"

"I don't know, he stayed in the shadows. He was dressed all in blue, my lord." Blue was the ae'Magi's favorite color—a good third of the people in the room had been wearing some shade of blue.

"What did the boy say to you?" He held the word "boy" just a little longer than necessary, apparently liking it better than "king."

"I don't remember . . ."

Whatever he did with his spell didn't work only on her body—though her muscles cramped hard enough that she thought she could hear the bones begin to break. The pain weakened Aralorn's natural resistance to his other spells and gradually the newly familiar feeling of shame crept over her. *She should try harder to please him. Why wasn't she more obedient? Look at what she made him do to her.* As suddenly as it had begun, it stopped, leaving her shuddering and crying helplessly.

"When I ask you something, I expect an answer." The ae'Magi's voice was gentle.

"He asked if I wanted to be freed. I told him I wanted to be here. I live only to serve you, my lord. It is my honor to serve the ae'Magi . . ." She let her voice trail off. *That's it,* she cheered herself silently, placate him, stay in character; the gasps as she fought against crying and the whimper at the end were a nice touch; artistic really—it was too bad that she hadn't thought to do them on purpose.

He reached a hand out to her, and she pressed against it, getting as close to him as she could though the pain had gone and, with it, the full effect of his magic. She almost wished that the magic he used to increase his charisma stayed as effective on her as it was when he hurt her. Instead, she experienced an overwhelming desire to bite the manicured fingers—or throw up. The cold, metal edge of the cage dug into her side.

"What else did you say to him, little one?"

Aralorn pulled back from him and gave him a wide-eyed, somewhat confused look, even as she felt herself regain some clarity of thought. "Did you want me to say something else to him? I didn't because I wasn't sure if you would want me to." She deliberately widened her eyes as if she were pleading with him to be pleased with her, trying to keep herself from tensing in anticipation of the wild, twisting pain.

"No. You did well." He absently patted her cheek. "I've been working on other things lately and haven't had the time to do more with you. Tomorrow, when I've completed this spell, I've got a use for you."

If she were in any doubt about what he was talking about, the hand that ran lightly down her breast would have clarified it for her. The ae'Magi seemed satisfied that the shudder that ran through her at his touch was in response to desire. He smiled warmly at her and, humming a sweet tune, walked lightly through an archway.

Aralorn stared at herself in the mirror at the back of her cage. The ae'Magi must have dispelled his illusion, because she didn't see a bird anymore. The flickering light from the torches gave a dancing appearance to the fine, blond hair. The fragile face that stared expressionlessly back at her was extraordinarily beautiful. A thin sheen of sweat glistened on her forehead, and the misty, sea-green eyes looked dazed and vulnerable.

Abruptly irritated with that vulnerability, Aralorn stuck her tongue out at her reflection. It didn't make her feel any better.

She wrapped both arms tightly around her legs. Head bowed on her knees, she listened to the sounds the servants made as they banked the fireplaces and snuffed the torches, trying to think over the uncontrollable panic that the thought of his intimate touch brought on.

"Patience, Aralorn, patience," she warned herself, speaking almost soundlessly. "If you leave now—granting that you *can* leave—he is going to doubt what you told him about Myr, which may not matter in the long run anyway." She tilted her head back and addressed her words to the reflection, summoning up a tone of bleak humor. "But if I don't get out of here, I'm going to break and tell him everything I know, from the name of my first pony to the bald spot on the top of Audreas the Vain's head."

It was the truth. Four days—she didn't count the time she'd spent locked up alone. A fifth day here would break her. And someone needed to let the Spymaster know what dwelled in the ae'Magi's castle.

Decision made, she waited while the sounds of the castle diminished and the moon hung high in the sky, revealed by the clear panels in the ceiling.

When she was more or less satisfied that the people who were going to sleep were asleep, she knelt in front of the cage door. Grasping each edge, she began to mutter quietly, sometimes breaking briefly into song or chant to help focus her magic. She pushed aside the doubt that kept trying to sneak in: Doubt would cripple the small gift that she had. She was grateful to the ae'Magi's vanity that her cage was made of precious silver rather than the iron that would have kept her prisoner until her bones crumbled to dust.

First her fingers, then her hands, began to glow a phosphorescent green. Gradually, the light spread to the metal between her hands. When all the metal of the gate held the soft, flickering glow, she stepped through, leaving the spells on the locks intact. Her body ached from the ae'Magi's magic, but nothing that wouldn't fade in a day or two. It wouldn't slow her down much, and that was all she was worried about.

The light of her magic died, leaving the great hall black as pitch. She stood still and waited for her eyes to start adjusting before venturing out into the room.

The only light in the room came from the skylights high above, only a faint reflection of the moon, which made it difficult to find the doorways. She took the first doorway that she could find, hoping that it was one of the two that traversed the outer wall of the castle.

She bent low, occasionally putting a hand on the ground to help keep her balance. It was awkward, but people generally look at eye level, so from her lower vantage point she should be able to see any guards before they saw her. Her position also had the secondary benefit of making her a smaller target if she was seen.

The corridor was lighter than the great hall had been, although not by much. The stone of the floor was dry and cool, and she ran a hand lightly over the walls. It took her longer than she thought that it should to find the small opening she was searching for.

Panic clawed at her, and the temptation to run blindly down the hallway was almost overwhelming. *This,* she thought with wry humor, *must be how a pheasant feels just before it jumps out of hiding and into the path of the arrow.* She bottled up the panic and stored it away where it wouldn't get out until this was all over.

She had almost decided to look for another way to leave when she found what she was looking for. Just above the bottom row of blocks, her fingers scraped over one end of a pipe cut flush with the wall. Silently, Aralorn blessed the old man she'd met at a bar one night who told her the story.

Centuries ago, an apprentice to one of the ae'Magis discovered an old rain spell in a book he was reading while the master was away. Three weeks later, when the Archmage came back, the castle was flooded, and the apprentice was camped outside. The Archmage drained the castle expediently by placing a drainpipe every sixteen stones in the outer corridors.

One such drainage pipe was under her fingers. It was bigger than she'd hoped for; being about four fingers in diameter. It cut directly through the thick stone wall of the castle to the outside. The air coming through it smelled like a moat. Like freedom.

She took a deep breath and concentrated. The familiar

tingle spread though her body until it was all the sensation she could absorb, leaving no room for any of her other senses. Unable to see or feel, Aralorn focused on each part of her body shifting into one part of the mouse at a time; nose first, then whiskers. It took her only as long as it took to breathe deeply three times before a very small mouse crouched where she had stood.

The mouse who was Aralorn shrank against the wall underneath the pipe for a minute and waited for the ae'Magi to investigate the magic she'd used—but he didn't come. Human magicians weren't usually sensitive enough to detect someone else using magic, but the ae'Magi was a law unto himself.

The mouse shook herself briskly, twitched her whiskers, and scratched an itchy spot where the tingle hadn't quite worn off yet; then she climbed up into the pipe.

It was dark, which didn't bother her much, and smelly, which did. Centuries of sludge had built up in the opening, and if several other bold rodents hadn't foraged through (perhaps to escape a castle cat), she wouldn't have made it. As it was, she was belly deep in slimy stuff. Busy not thinking about the composition of the muck, she almost fell out of the pipe and into the moat some distance below—only saving herself by some ungraceful but highly athletic scrambling.

Poised on the edge of the old copper pipe, Aralorn shivered with nervous energy. Almost. Almost out. Just this one hurdle, and she would be away.

The little slime-coated mouse leapt. The air blurred, and a white goose flapped awkwardly over the water, one wing dripping goo from the moat. There were plenty of birds who could fly better than a domestic goose—most birds, actually, since the goose could manage little better than a rough glide. But the goose was the only bird Aralorn knew how to become.

Hampered by the wet wing, Aralorn was unable to gain

any altitude and came to a flapping halt several hundred yards beyond the moat, in front of the bushes that signaled the beginning of the woodland surrounding the castle. She straightened her feathers and waddled toward the woods, carefully leaving the ooze-covered wing stretched away from the rest of her body.

A black form erupted from the shadows, its ivory fangs catching the light of the moon as it halted directly in Aralorn's path. The goose squawked and dodged backward, resuming a human form just in time for Aralorn to fall on her rump rather than her tail.

Her own rump, too. She was back in her own skin: short, brown-haired, and plain-faced. Her anger fueled the speed of her transformation.

"Allyn's blessed toadflax!" she sputtered, using her father's favorite oath. There had been no need for drama, and she'd been scared enough for ten lifetimes in the past few days. "Wolf, what are you trying to do to me?" Mindful of the proximity of the castle, she lowered her voice to a soft tone that didn't carry but did not lack for force either. But anger faded into sheer relief, and the abrupt transition left her giddy.

"I could have died of shock"—she put her hand theatrically over her heart—"then what would you have done? Why didn't you warn me you were here?"

The wolf stood over her, fey and feral, with the stillness of a wild thing. The snarl had disappeared at her furious whispers, and he waited for a moment after she finished, as if he wanted to make certain she was done.

His macabre voice, dry and hoarse, was passionless when he spoke—he didn't answer her question. "You should have told me that you intended to spy on the ae'Magi—if I had known that you were contemplating suicide, I would have killed you myself. At least it would be a cleaner death than any *he* would bestow." Fathomless golden eyes gazed at her coolly.

A green mage could speak in animal form—though it required practice and a great deal of uncomfortable effort. Wolf wasn't a green mage, though, not as far as she could figure him out. And those few human mages who could transform themselves to animals were lucky if they remembered to transform themselves back again. Wolf was an endlessly fascinating puzzle who didn't fit into any category she could find for him.

A reassuring puzzle, though.

She watched him for a moment.

"Do you know," she said, after weighing his words, "that is the first time I have ever heard anyone say anything against him? I even asked why I was being sent to spy there—and none of it struck me as strange at all."

She nodded at the dark shape of the castle where it stood on the top of the mountain, its silhouette almost blacking out the sky to the east. "The Mouse said that there were rumors of an assassination plot, and I was to investigate it and warn the ae'Magi if necessary." Her customary grin restored itself, and if it felt a little stiff, that was all right.

Safe. She was out, Wolf was with her, and she was safe. "If there is such a plot, I can only wish them luck in their endeavors."

"It has always amazed me how well he can blind people, even when he is not using magic to do it," replied the wolf. He glanced at the castle, then away. His yellow eyes glistened, glowing with a light that might not all have been a reflection of the moon. He looked back again, as if he could not resist the impulse. A growl rose low in his throat, and the hair on his neck and back stiffened.

Aralorn cautiously set a hand on his fur, smoothing it down. In all the time she'd known him, he'd always been slow to warm from his customary reserve, and though she'd seen him kill several times, she'd never seen him quite this upset. "What's wrong?"

The wolf quieted and lowered his head for a moment.

Then he shook himself, and said softly, "Nothing. Perhaps it is the moon. I find that it sometimes has this effect on me."

"The moon." She nodded solemnly. "That must be it." She caught his gaze and raised one eyebrow. The wolf stared back at her. Aralorn gave up the contest without a fight, knowing that he was perfectly capable of continuing the stare-down all night. "Shall we go, or do you want to wait for the ae'Magi so we can destroy him and win the world back for goodness and light?"

The wolf grinned ferally. "If we killed him, the world would be more likely to draw and quarter us than praise us as saviors. So by all means, let us make haste so as not to be forced to destroy the ae'Magi." The sarcasm in his voice clearly dismissed any chance he thought they'd have of destroying the Archmage.

He turned and made his way back through the brush, leaving Aralorn to follow.

Several hundred yards from the edge of the woods, her gray stallion was tied to the trees. At their approach, he whickered a greeting. Aralorn laughed as the animal lipped the plain tunic she wore, then drew back in obvious disgust at the taste.

"Why how did you find your way here, Sheen?" She slanted a look at the wolf, and said to him, "Thanks, I wasn't looking forward to walking back."

Over the years, she'd learned not to question him too closely—mostly because he wouldn't answer her. If he wanted to be a wolf, who was she of all people to question it? Still, the knot that attached the colorful cloth reins to the tree would have been difficult for someone with no fingers to tie.

Aralorn untied the reins and mounted, only to dismount and shorten the stirrups. She sighed loudly as she untied the leather strings that were woven into the saddle to keep the stirrups at one length. Someone with much longer legs than hers had ridden the horse last.

"Sheen, how many times have I told you not to give strangers a ride? You never know where they might take you."

She might not question him out loud, but she liked to make it obvious that it was cooperation and not stupidity.

The wolf tilted his head to one side, and there was a hint of amusement in his eyes. She laughed and continued to unweave the strings. He'd even remembered to bring her sword and knives.

Sometimes she thought that he might be a renegade shapeshifter, one of her mother's people—though he lacked the gray-green eyes that were characteristic of the race. Someone more skilled than she and able to hide what he was from her. It shouldn't be possible, but nothing he was should have been possible.

That he was a human magician was very unlikely because human magic didn't lend itself well to shapeshifting. Instead of blending in with the forces of nature, it sought to control them and required immense concentration that was impossible to maintain for extended periods of time. To turn oneself into an animal for a prolonged period would require the strength of the ae'Magi . . . or his son.

Her normally deft hands faltered at their familiar task, so she stopped and gazed almost impersonally at her hands, which trembled without her consent. The mindless babbling fear threatened her as she worked her way through her suspicion. It was very unlikely that Wolf was a human mage, she reminded herself again. She glanced at the wolf and then back to her saddle. The ae'Magi's son had disappeared six years ago. There were other green-magic users than her own people, and she'd never heard of a human mage who could take and keep an animal's shape so long, not in all the stories she'd ever collected, ae'Magi or not. Still, her body would not release the panic it insisted on; terror was a difficult emotion to reason with. She'd noticed that before.

She looked at him again, and he caught her gaze and held it, his gold eyes no more readable than a pair of amber gemstones. She remembered the fever-bright agony that had been in them when she first met the wolf.

It had taken only a week for her to heal his leg, but he'd fought the fever for almost a month. He'd left as soon as he could stand up, at least for a while. One day she'd looked up to find him watching her with his uncomfortably canny eyes. After that, he came and went, sometimes staying away for months at a time, then appearing as suddenly as he had left.

She remembered how long she'd worked to gain his trust. It had taken time to get him to let her touch him, more time before he would eat food she gave him, and almost a year before he trusted her enough to reveal for certain that he was more than just a wild animal. She compared his remoteness to the ae'Magi's easy smile and beautiful voice. If she ever met a corpse that talked, she imagined that its voice would be similar to her wolf's.

———

The wolf watched her and saw the wear of her time with the ae'Magi. He saw the tremor of her hands and smelled the sweat of her fear. He saw that she'd used the cheerful demeanor that was her habit as a mask, and he lost the hope that she had by some miracle escaped unscathed from the ae'Magi's games. The desire to kill the Archmage rose in his throat and was set aside for future use. He saw the fear in her eyes, but until he stepped closer to comfort her, he didn't realize that she was afraid of him.

Instantly, he halted. This was the one thing that he hadn't expected. Four years, and never had he seen the fear that he'd inspired in everyone else he'd ever met. Not even when she'd had reason to fear.

The old ache of bitterness urged him to flee. If they had been somewhere else, he would have left without a backward glance, but here, near the castle, she was still in desperate danger; already he could smell the excitement of the ae'Magi's "pets." She wouldn't be able to lose them on her own despite her training and surprisingly formidable combat skills—she wasn't very big to be so dangerous. After three weeks in confinement, she was hardly at her best, so he waited.

———

Whoever he was, whatever he was—he was not anything like the ae'Magi. She was jumping at shadows. But that certainty had come too late; she could see it in the stillness of Wolf's body.

She crouched down to look him in the eye; she didn't have to lower herself far—he was tall and she wasn't. "I'm sorry. I'm . . . just a little shaky"—she gave a half laugh and held up an unsteady hand—"as you can see. He's got me doubting everything I know." She moved the hand to touch him, and he quietly moved just out of reach.

She knew that she had hurt him, but before she could fix it, the stallion snorted softly. She turned back to him and saw that he was twitching his ears back and forth and shifting his weight uneasily.

"Uriah," commented the wolf, looking away from her. "If they are getting close enough that even Sheen can smell them, we'd best be on our way. There are riding clothes in the saddlebags. Put them on, we may have a long ride ahead."

She wiped herself off as best she could on the simple cotton slave tunic she wore. Ten years of being a mercenary had destroyed any vestige of ladylike modesty she might once have felt, but she hurried into the clean clothes anyway, as they could use every second to avoid a confrontation with the Uriah.

She swung into the saddle and let the wolf lead the way at the brisk trot dictated by the rough country and the dark.

Had the Uriah been closer, she would have risked a fall with a faster gait, but for now there was no need for panic.

When she had scrounged for her clothes, Aralorn found that the saddlebags also contained oatcakes. She pulled a couple out and ate one as she rode, feeding the other to the horse, who knew how to eat and move at the same time. When she offered one to the wolf, he refused. She let him pick the way, trusting him to do his best to rid themselves of the Uriah.

The Uriah were vaguely human-looking creatures that appeared more dead than alive though they were almost impossible to kill. The insatiable hunger that drove them gave them a berserker's ferocity. They were normally found only in the far eastern regions that bordered the impassable Marshlands, but in the last decade or so they'd begun to turn up in unexpected places. But to find them this far west was almost unheard of. Especially since the ae'Magi could certainly . . .

"Stupid!" she exclaimed out loud. The warhorse, slightly spooked by the nasty smell behind them and miffed by the slow pace they were taking, took exception to the sudden sound and bucked hard. She didn't fall off, but it was a near thing, and it took a while to stop the curvetting completely. "The sudden upswing in Uriah attacks, their appearance in places where there have never been Uriah before—that's all him, isn't it?"

The wolf waited until the show stopped, then said, "They belong to him." Without commenting further, he continued on, leaving Aralorn to follow as she could.

The sun began to rise on the silent travelers. Aralorn was quiet at first because she didn't know how to undo the damage she'd done to him with her distrust; after a while, it was fatigue that kept her silent. Three weeks with no exercise left her feeling as if she were recovering from a prolonged illness. Despite her tiredness, when the wolf halted and told her they were stopping for the afternoon, she protested.

"If we don't stop and let the horse graze and get some rest, you'll be walking tomorrow." He spoke slowly and clearly, and his voice managed to pierce through her exhaustion.

She nodded, knowing he was right, but the urge to run away from the castle was stronger than her common sense, so she didn't dismount. The horse arched his neck and blew, as if ready for battle, responding to the invisible signals of his rider.

Wolf was silent until he saw her sway in the saddle from sheer tiredness. "I will stay on watch, Lady. I know when the ae'Magi or his playthings are near, and I won't let them take you back." His voice softened.

Again she nodded, but this time she dismounted and, with more instinct than willpower, began to untack the horse. The light saddle seemed to weigh more than she remembered, and it was an effort to reach high enough to get the bridle off—but she managed. Sheen needed no restraint to keep him close.

She untied the sleeping roll and climbed in it without even dusting off her clothes. The wolf stretched out beside her, his big warm body warding off the chill of lingering fear even better than her blankets. The last thing she noticed before sleep claimed her was the comforting sound of the stallion munching grass.

TWO

Aralorn breathed in ragged gasps and rubbed a shaky hand across the wetness on her cheeks. Sweating, and still half-caught in her nightmare, she curled under her blanket and covered her ears with her hands to shut out the soft seductive voice of the ae'Magi.

She'd fought in the regular troops and knew that nightmares were part of the territory. They'd get better, but for right now, every time she drifted to sleep, her dreams all led back to the Archmage's fine-boned hand holding the ornate silver dagger he used to butcher his sacrifices. The young brown-eyed boy, no older than some of her brothers the last time she'd seen them, was so caught by the spell that he smiled as the ae'Magi drew his knife. At least it was daylight when she opened her eyes—and the dirt under the leather comprising the outer layer of her bedroll felt a lot different from marble.

She sat up abruptly and wiped at her wet cheeks. Sheen stood nearby, dozing with one hind foot cocked and his convex nose lowered almost to knee level. Near Sheen,

Wolf lay still, his muzzle on his paws. He was looking away from her. Aralorn knew that he must have heard her when she woke up, so his inattention was deliberate. Her momentary fear had hurt him—she hadn't realized he worried about her opinion. She hadn't thought he worried much about anyone's opinion of him.

She addressed his back. "That place—it . . . twists everything. There is so much magic in the castle, it makes the air heavy, and when I breathed it . . . He loves it, you know—playing games and making people into his puppets. Power."

She shuddered slightly, and continued, "I watched him drink the blood of a child he'd just killed, and I found myself thinking how beautifully the light of the candles reflected off his hair. It's . . . not pleasant not to know whether your feelings are your own." She brought her legs up until she could wrap her arms around them.

She'd begun in an attempt to explain herself to Wolf—to show him that it wasn't him she'd distrusted but her own perceptions. Once she'd started talking, she couldn't stop. "I have never been so frightened in my entire life," she whispered. "I always thought that I was strong-willed, but even with my mother's blood to help me resist the spells, I couldn't completely block the feeling that I wanted to please him." Her voice died.

For a long time there were only the sounds of the forest—the wind in the trees, a creek nearby, and a cricket singing.

She sighed. "I might have been able to block it entirely toward the last—when I knew what the spells were and how he worked them; but I couldn't, because I had to act as if the spell were having its effect on me. Sometimes I think . . . that maybe I didn't want to block the spell because it made me feel so much better . . ." She knew that she would have bruises in the morning from gripping herself so hard. She took a shuddering breath and put her forehead down on her knees. "I can't get him out of my mind.

I think some of it is still his magic, but I see his face every time I close my eyes."

Slowly, Wolf stood up and left his place. He sat down and leaned against her. She loosed her grip on her legs and ran a hand in the thick pelt.

A cold nose worked its way under her arm, and his warm, wet tongue licked at her chin until she squealed and pulled away with a quavering laugh, wiping at her face with her sleeves.

The wolf smiled, as wolves do, and rolled over against her on his back. She rubbed his stomach (something that he *didn't* allow in public) and one back leg snapped rapidly back and forth as she caught just the right spot.

After he felt he had cheered her up, he said in his usual cool voice that sounded wrong coming out of a wolf getting his stomach rubbed, "Don't worry about it, Lady. Living in that place for any length of time will twist your thoughts and feelings until what you feel and what he wants you to feel are tangled together in a knot that would baffle a sailor." His voice was gentler, sounding like velvet on gravel. "Time will help."

"I know," replied Aralorn, then continued in a lighter tone, "but I'm not looking forward to the next decade or so."

Wolf rolled over with improbable quickness and nipped her lightly on the hand in response to her quip, tacitly agreeing with her unspoken decision that the discussion was too serious.

Aralorn tilted her head to the side, a slow grin twisting her lips. "So you want to fight, do you?" She tackled him and began a wrestling match that left them both flat on the ground and panting.

"Will you be able to sleep now?" he asked, rather hoarsely, even for him. "I'll wake you up when it's time to go."

She nodded and rolled over until she was on the bedding,

unwilling to use enough energy to get up and walk. She mumbled a good night that lost most of its consonants. He touched his nose to her cheek and woofed softly before curling up against her.

————

In the end, it was the stallion that woke them both. The high-pitched whistle split the night.

Aralorn leapt to her feet and had the bed rolled up almost before she opened her eyes. Bridling and saddling took somewhat longer as the obstinate beast wouldn't stand still. As she worked, she kept an eye on the wolf as he stared into the night. At his signal, she left what was not already attached to the saddle and mounted the stallion, who was already trotting. Although not built for running, Sheen managed a very credible speed as he followed the wolf's lead. The Uriah were close enough behind them that they could hear the howls the beasts made when they found their camp.

Aralorn had fought the Uriah before, and she knew that they were faster than any horse—certainly faster than Sheen. The creatures were too close behind and gaining quickly. She drew her sword and slowed the stallion in preparation for facing them.

Noticing that Sheen was slowing, the wolf darted back and nipped at the stallion's heels, nimbly dodging the war-trained horse's well-placed kick.

"No," Wolf snarled at her. "You don't stand a chance against the number that we have behind us. If you keep going, I can lure them away." With that, he began to veer off, but Aralorn guided Sheen to block his path.

She shook her head and shouted over the sounds of the Uriah, "It's me that they want. They won't follow you, and even if they did, it would mean that you would have to face them alone. Together, we might stand a chance."

"You know better than that, Lady." His tones rang with

impatience. "Against two or three maybe, but there are many more than that. You needn't worry about me, I can keep ahead of them on my own." Here the wolf paused a moment, as if he were choosing his words carefully. "They will follow me if given a choice between the two of us."

"What do you mean by that?" Then, before he could answer, she said, "Cursed obscure Wolf. Never mind. We don't have time to argue." It was getting difficult to talk and keep Sheen from bolting as the howls grew nearer.

He flashed his fangs at her in a mock smile as only a wolf can do. "Lady, this isn't the first time I've dealt with them. Nor will it be the last."

She didn't want to leave him. If she hadn't known he was no ordinary wolf, she wouldn't have even considered leaving. But, against so many Uriah, she would have been more of a hindrance than a help. She heard the wails of the Uriah increase exponentially as they sighted their prey.

"Right," she said abruptly. "I'll see you in Sianim. But, plague it, Wolf, take care not to let them ruin your fur coat." With that, she turned Sheen in their original direction and urged him on. The wolf stayed in the path of the Uriah and watched with yellow eyes as they came closer. When the tone of their calls changed and became even more frantic, he broke into a swift run, leading them away from the path taken by his companions. Aralorn, looking back, saw that Wolf had been correct: All of the grotesque, humanoid forms followed the wolf's trail, ignoring her entirely.

She wondered, this time without last night's panic, exactly who Wolf really was. It wasn't a new puzzle, by any means. She had a list somewhere of possible identities for Wolf. Some of them were vague, others were names of specific people—today she added another name to it: Cain, the ae'Magi's son. Cain was younger than she'd placed Wolf's age, and she'd never caught a whiff of human magic off Wolf. She'd be surprised if Cain wasn't buried with the other people the ae'Magi had been killing, whose magic he had been stealing to use for himself. But wasn't it interesting the way the ae'Magi's creatures took off after the wolf?

Aralorn traveled during the dark and slept, or at least tried to rest, during the day—not because it was safer that way but because she couldn't stand to wake from her nightmares alone in the dark. Sometimes she traveled for miles without seeing anything. Being alone didn't bother her; she'd done a lot of traveling on her own.

She had nothing of value except her warhorse and her sword—and both were as much a deterrent as a prize. On the evening of the third day, she left the forested mountains behind for the gentler hills and valleys of the lowlands. Traveling was faster, and it was only another day until she caught sight of Sianim.

The fortressed city stood on the top of an artificial plateau in the middle of a large valley. Nothing but grass was allowed to grow within a half mile of the hill, and even that was kept short. The plateau itself was steep-sided, and the road that led to the only gate into the city was narrow and walled, so that only three people could ride side by side through it. Although it was good for defense, the narrow path made it a nightmare to get large groups of soldiers in and out of Sianim.

The origins of the city were buried in the dust of ages past: Even the oldest known manuscripts mentioned it as a thriving city. Originally it had been a center of trade, but the small armies hired by the merchants to accompany their wagon trains drew mercenaries from all over. People looking for groups of mercenaries to hire began to go to Sianim. Gradually, the mercenaries themselves became the center of Sianim's economy. A school for teaching the arts of war was founded, and eventually Sianim became a city of professional warriors.

Mercenaries of Sianim were some of the finest fighters

in the world. With the only other military school at Jetaine, which had the minor drawback of allowing no males entrance within its walls, Sianim had little competition. In addition to training its own mercenary troops, Sianim also trained fighters for various kingdoms and principalities for a healthy fee. The elite guard for most of the rulers were Sianim-trained.

Because politics and war go hand in hand, Sianim also had a spy network that would have amazed an outsider. It was run by a slender, short academian. It was to his small office tucked away in the rabbit warren that was the back of the government building in the center of town that Aralorn went after stabling Sheen.

Someone needed to know as soon as possible the danger that Geoffrey ae'Magi presented.

Stairs and narrow hallways connected little rooms occupied by bureaucrats necessary to the successful and profitable running of the mercenary city: taxes and licenses and all. And buried away down a stairway behind a worn door that nonetheless opened and closed tightly and soundlessly was a large, airy room with a window (she'd never managed to figure out which window it was from the outside) that housed the man whose fingers dipped into the well of rumors and politics that drove the world.

She slipped through the worn door without knocking— if the Spymaster had wanted privacy, the door would have been locked. She closed the door, sat on a ratty-looking chair, and waited patiently for Ren, known semiaffectionately as the Mouse, to acknowledge her.

He was perched on top of his battered-but-sturdy desk, leaning back against a bookshelf and reading aloud from a collection of poems by Thyre. He was only a little older than Aralorn, but he appeared as though someone had put him out to dry and forgotten to take him back in again.

His hair had faded and thinned until it no longer concealed the scalp beneath. His hands were ink-stained and soft, free of calluses, though she knew he was an excellent swordsman and for a time, before he came to Sianim, had made a living as a duelist in several of the Alliance cities. Only his sharp eyes distracted from the impression of vagueness, and at that moment they were hidden from her as he kept his attention on the lines he read.

Thyre wasn't one of her favorites; he reached too hard for his rhyme. Usually, she would have fished out a book from Ren's impressive library and read until he decided to question her; but today she just sat quietly, listening, finally stretching out on the padded bench and closing her eyes. Since Thyre was notoriously long-winded, she had plenty of time to rest.

When Ren finished, she was snoozing peacefully, and the soft sound the book made as Ren stuffed it into one of the many bookcases made her jump to her feet. He offered her a glass he filled from the bottle on his desk.

Aralorn accepted it but sipped cautiously. Bottles on Ren's desk could contain anything from water to Wyth, more affectionately known as Dragonslayer. This time it was *fehlta* juice, only a mildly alcoholic drink, but she set it down on the end of his desk. She had the rueful feeling that it would be a long time before she would take anything that could cloud her thoughts. She sat back down on the bench and waited . . . and waited.

When Ren finally spoke he sounded almost nervous to her sensitive ears. "I trust that everything went smoothly as usual, hmm? Got in, got out, came here."

"Yes. I—" He cut her off before she could speak.

"Did you talk to him about the assassination attempt?" Ren strolled around his desk and resumed his seat.

"No, the—"

"Good," he said, breaking in once again before she could continue. "I would hate to have him upset with us, or think that we were spying on him—although I doubt that he would mind. I'm sure he would have understood that we gather information whenever we can. I trust that you were either able to put a halt to the assassins or discovered that the rumor I sent you to investigate was just a rumor."

Aralorn tapped her fingers on the arm of the chair and contemplated Ren. His babbling didn't bother her, he always talked like that. He once told her that it distracted people, and they said things that they wouldn't normally have said—just to get him to shut up. She'd used the technique herself upon occasion and found it effective.

What did bother her was that he wasn't listening. Usually, he listened carefully to everything she said, then quizzed her for hours about what she'd heard and seen. It just wasn't like him to gloss over anything or stop anyone from speaking. He never, not ever, interrupted. The bright black, somewhat beady eyes shifted restlessly.

She had never seen him embarrassed before, so it took her a while to identify the emotion that brought a red tinge to his face. Ren was ashamed that he had sent her to spy on the ae'Magi—the same Ren who had once sent her to spy on his own brother.

None of her disquiet showed on her face. She didn't want to heed the intuition that was hinting that something was awry. She wanted to give her report with no more than the usual lies: Not even Ren knew that she could alter her shape. Shapeshifters used wild magic—and this was a world that had learned to fear magic used without strict limits.

She wanted to ignore the insistent disquiet that the Mouse's unusual reactions spawned, but she couldn't. With visions of the docile people in the ae'Magi's ballroom in her head, she bowed her head and waited.

She'd never heard anyone say anything against the ae'Magi—only Wolf. The people the ae'Magi had brought out to sacrifice to his magic had come willingly. Only Wolf knew what he was—and he hadn't really told her until he was certain she knew what she'd gotten herself into.

While Ren talked, she carefully edited what she was going to tell him, waiting as he drifted from topic to topic until he got around to asking her about her mission.

Aralorn gave him a brief description of her method of entry, incorrect, of course. Someday Ren would find out just how poor she was at picking iron locks and would be deeply disappointed.

Ren needed to know about the ae'Magi, but somehow she found herself rattling on at length about the various heads of state at the dance the ae'Magi had held and obligingly going into as much detail as she could when Ren requested it. Evidently, he was only upset about her spying on the ae'Magi—otherwise, he wanted to know everything. He could pull surprising conclusions out of the smallest thing.

"Wearing a red cape?" he said, after she'd described what one of the Anthran demiprinces was wearing. "It was a gift from his sister's husband—looks like peace talks between their territories might be on again. We'll be able to pull those troops out and use them elsewhere."

She hedged when he asked her about Myr, saying only that she'd seen him talk with the ae'Magi but hadn't been near enough to hear what was said. Time enough to inform Ren of the young king's interesting talent after she discovered what was making the Spymaster behave so out of character.

To distract him from Myr, Aralorn continued to the main reason for her mission and said with some caution, "I couldn't find any information on an assassination attempt. If there is a plot, it doesn't originate from within the castle. I did get the impression that if there was such an attempt, the ae'Magi would be perfectly capable of handling it without need for our aid."

She paused, to give herself time to choose just the right words. "I left early, I know. But I felt so *uncomfortable*." Uncomfortable was true, uncomfortable enough to curl into a quivering ball of jelly at the bottom of that cage. "I thought that I had better get out before he figured out who I was and took offense. If it were widely known that Sianim spied upon the ae'Magi, half the world would be angry at us."

"Ah yes, I quite understand." Ren nodded and picked up another book—his habitual method of dismissal.

If she needed confirmation that something was awry, she had it then. Ren would never, ever accept "uncomfortable" as a reason for leaving an assignment early without picking the vague term into pieces. Unhappy, and baffled by what to do about it, she exited the room.

————

Alone, Ren put his book down and rubbed his hands together with great satisfaction. If that performance didn't cause Aralorn to start thinking, then nothing would. He needed her to be suspicious and questioning, but also cautious.

He'd had a feeling about her—she got out of too many situations that should have been fatal—and those eyes. He'd seen that color of eyes before. He had wizards who worked for him, but they'd have been useless. The office of ae'Magi existed to control them.

She'd come right to him, and she was well and truly spooked, he thought, though he flattered himself that no one else would have been able to read that in her.

He couldn't afford to come out and warn her; the ae'Magi had his own ways of learning things . . . and if anyone would be subject to the Archmage's watchful eye, it would be the Spymaster of Sianim.

He rubbed his chest, pressing into his skin the charm he wore on a thong. A gift from a friend, another mage, it was supposed to be able to dispel magic aimed at its wearer. It dated from sometime around the old Wizard Wars and, his friend had told him, was unlikely to still have the power to block a spell directed specifically at him. It had been given as a curiosity—from one collector to another.

He still wasn't absolutely sure it worked, but he'd been wearing it day and night for the past few months. So far he seemed to be immune to the odd fervor that had taken most of the usually sensible people he reported to when he chose. He patted his chest again and worried, though his ma had taught him that worry did no one any good.

———————

If Aralorn's footsteps were quiet, it was out of habit rather than intent: She was deep in thought as she wandered down the cobbled street. She absently waved at acquaintances but didn't stop to talk. She shivered a little, though it was warm enough out. Why was Ren acting as if he'd never had a suspicious thought about the ae'Magi? Ren was suspicious of *everybody*.

More by chance than design, she found the dormitory where she stored her few possessions, and retreated through the halls to her room.

It was musty after her prolonged absence and in desperate need of dusting. There were only a few pieces of worn furniture placed here and there, but the room was small enough that it still seemed cluttered. She spent so little time in it that size and clutter didn't matter.

Aralorn sneezed once, then, ignoring the much-abused chair, she sat on the rough stone floor that was unrelieved by carpet or fur.

Never before had Ren seemed worried about where he sent her to spy. He cared little for politics, leaving that to the statesmen to whom he gave selected bits of information. Instead, he thirsted for knowledge the way that some men thirst for food or sex. It was from him that she had gleaned many of the folkstories she collected.

He was no respecter of persons, not ever. When she had protested her assignment with the ae'Magi, he had laughed at her and quoted her his favorite saying: "He who does no wrong need not fear perusal." He used it so often and said it with such pride that she suspected that he had made it up himself.

When he sent her to the castle, he'd made it clear that although nominally she was investigating the "assassination attempt," her main objective would be to gather information on Geoffrey ae'Magi. Why else would he send her when a simple note of warning would have done the same thing? She had, even at the time, suspected that there was no assassination plot except in the Mouse's busy labyrinthian mind.

All of which led her back to her original question: Why was Ren troubled about her spying on the ae'Magi? Had the ae'Magi bespelled Ren? If so, why? And worse, who else had he taken?

Aralorn sat for a while and came to no brilliant conclusions. It was better than worrying about the wolf—though she did that as well. Fretting about one was about as useful as fretting about the other—so she, being a believer in using her resources properly, gave equal time to each.

Finally, tired in mind and body, she stripped off her clothes and threw them on the floor. She stretched out carefully, slowly working each muscle until it was relatively limber. She pulled off the top covering of her cot, careful to leave most of the dust on it. Then she collapsed onto the bed and slept.

The nightmare came back—it wasn't as bad as it had been the first few days, but it was bad enough. She was only half-awake when she touched the wall that her cot sat against and thought for a minute that she was back in the cage.

She rolled away from it quickly and landed with a thump, fully awake and surrounded by a cloud of dust from the blanket on the floor.

She sneezed several times, swore, and wiped her watering

eyes. It was obvious that she wasn't going to get any more sleep for a while, so she lit a small lamp and dressed, pulling on her practice garments—knee-length leather boots, loose breeches, and tunic.

Night had fallen, but the nice thing about being home in Sianim was that even in the busy summer season, there were always people in the practice arenas willing to go a few rounds; mercenaries tended to keep strange hours. She strapped on sword and daggers and slipped out the window and onto the narrow ledge just below.

Gingerly, she traversed the narrow pathway until it was possible to drop onto the roof of the building next door. From there it was only a short jump to the ground. It would have been easier to exit by normal means, but she took opportunities to practice wherever she could get them.

Outside, the street torches were already lit for the night, but people were still wandering around. There was a friendly brawl going on at one of the pubs, with bystanders betting on the outcome.

She inhaled deeply. The smell of Sianim was a fusion of sweat, horse, dust, and . . . freedom.

Aralorn had grown up stifled by the restraints placed on women of the high aristocracy, even bastards like her. Reth might have outlawed slavery, but women of high estate were surrounded by a wall of rules strong enough to confine any drudge. If it hadn't been for her father, she might have been forced into a traditional role.

When the Lyon of Lambshold's illegitimate daughter came to him and stated her objections to the constant needlepoint and etiquette lessons that his wife imposed on his daughters, he'd laughed—then taught her to ride like a man. He also taught her to fight with sword and staff. When she left home, he sent her off with his favorite warhorse.

She had tried Jetaine but found that the women there were enslaved to their hatred of men. Aralorn had never hated men, she just hadn't wanted to sit and sew all her life.

She'd often wondered what it would have been like for her if she'd been born a merchant's daughter, or someone who had to work for a living, instead of an aristocrat, who was expected to be decorative.

The thought of herself as decoration was absurd. Even before she'd become battle-scarred, she'd been short, plain, and too willing to speak her own mind.

Two big men in the rough, hooded garb favored by the farmers who serviced the town had been following her for the past few blocks, and now they were getting close enough to be worth paying attention to. Sianim might be used to women in its ranks, but outsiders could be bothersome, expecting a woman wearing pants and a sword to be a woman of loose morals who would sleep with any man who asked. A simple refusal could end in a nasty fight.

Out of the corner of her eye, she noticed the pair slink behind a cart she'd just passed. Her left hand went automatically to her sword. Her right already held a dagger. One of the thugs said to the other in a stage whisper meant to carry to her, "Squelch you, Talor, you lumbering ox. She saw us again. I told you to change those shoes. They make too much noise."

She laughed and spun around to face them, her dagger tucked invisibly back into her sleeve sheath. "You're getting better, though. This time I honestly thought that you were just a couple of outsiders looking for prey."

The second one pushed the first sideways with a playful punch. "See, Kai? I told you that we'd do better blending in with the environment. Who pays attention to a couple of hog lovers in this place?"

Kai twitched one eyebrow upward, managing, despite the dirt on his clothes, to look aristocratic. "However, if you had worn the shoes I told you to . . ." He let his voice trail off and flashed the wicked grin he shared with his twin brother.

With practiced ease, he slipped out of his assumed

character and flung an arm around Aralorn's neck. "Well, my dear, it looks like I have you at my mercy." Or at least that's what he meant to say. Actually, thought Aralorn, the last word sounded more like "eyah" than "mercy."

She turned to Talor, and said, "I need to bathe in muck more often. It seems to work better than throwing him on the ground and making him look silly like I did the last time he tried to kiss me, don't you think?"

Old friends—the perfect answer to the frightening feeling that she was all alone. She'd served with both of them right up until the Spymaster had pulled her to his office and informed her she was changing jobs. Her gift of manipulating her superior officers had been noted as well as her ability to act without direct orders. Ren had been right—she was far better suited to spying than to warfare. Still, it was a lonely profession and she treasured her friends from the old days. Especially the ones smart enough that she didn't have to lie. Talor and Kai were sharp and knew how not to ask questions.

Talor assumed a serious demeanor, but before he could say whatever he intended to, Kai broke in. "Tell me, Lady, what villain gave you that perfume? Surely it must be cursed. Let me slay him for you that you may once again be your sweet-smelling self."

"I'd almost gotten used to smelling like this," she said truthfully. She'd slept like this on her bed, she remembered. She'd have to pull off all the bedding and take it to the laundry for cleaning. "I was going to go to the practice ring, but I think that I'll head to the baths first. Interested in a little fun?" Kai brightened comically until she added, "In the ring."

Kai bowed low. "To my sorrow, I have a previous engagement." He slanted her a grin. "Do you remember that redhead in the Thirty-second?"

"Uhm-hmm." She raised an eyebrow, shook her head, and in an exaggeratedly sorrowful tone said, "Poor girl, doomed to a broken heart." She grinned, and added, "Have a good time, Kai." He waved and sauntered away.

Aralorn looked at Talor, and inquired, "Does he really have a date with Sera?"

He laughed. "Probably not, but he will. Mostly, I think, his skin is still too thin from the last time you put him down. The whole squad ribbed him about being beaten by a woman for weeks. I, on the other hand, have no pride and, after you rid yourself of the unfair advantage you now hold"—he grabbed his nose with a hand to show her what he meant—"I will be awaiting you at the Hawk and Hound."

"Done." She gave him a mock salute and headed for the baths.

———

In one of the sparring rings that, like many of the taverns around town, the Hawk and Hound provided, Aralorn faced Talor warily with a single body-length staff held lightly in her hands.

Normally, they were evenly matched with the long staff, Talor being a better fighter than his brother, but Aralorn was still stiff. They fought together often because no one else wanted to face either of them with staves, long or short, in serious sparring.

As a warm-up, they played with variations on the training dances, and rather than aiming for body shots, the object was to hit a small metal plate, which dangled from a belt. Normally, there would be a third to call shots fair or foul and award points at the sound of wood striking metal, but she and Talor were veterans and cared more for the sport than for the winning or losing.

The ring that they had chosen was in the basement of the tavern rather than the one on the main floor, so they had no spectators. By mutual consent, they stopped for a bit to rest before they proceeded out of the standard patterns for some real sparring.

"So, what was that smell anyway? It seems somewhat familiar, but I just can't place it. Something like a cross between an outhouse and a pig barn." Talor's voice was a bit unsteady because he was stretching out as he talked.

Breathing ridiculously hard from such light exertion, Aralorn leaned unashamedly against one of the waist-high walls that surrounded the ring. She was paying for her confinement and the long ride home with her lack of stamina.

She started to think up a reason for the moat smell but decided that there was no harm in letting him know what she'd been doing. Kai and Talor didn't ask questions, and they also knew when to keep their mouths shut. There was nothing secret about what she had done, now that she was out of there. And it would be good to talk to Talor about what she'd found. She wouldn't go so far as to tell him about Ren, though. She needed to think about what had happened.

"Unless you've been visiting the ae'Magi's castle lately," she said, "it probably wouldn't be too familiar. I only wish the ae'Magi was half as honest and sweet-smelling as his moat . . ." Conditioned reflexes were the only thing that brought her staff up to deflect his from her face. The sheer force of the blow numbed her hands, as she hadn't been holding the staff in a proper grip.

She ducked underneath his arm to come to the center of the arena and give herself some room for maneuvering. The move also gave her a chance to talk. "What are you doing?"

Talor's face twisted with wrath as he came after her. "How dare you, worthless bitch? How dare you sharpen your tongue on the ae'Magi?"

It was his rage that saved her, interfering with the timing and precision of his attacks. Time and time again, she was able to block or turn aside his furious blows.

This unchecked anger was unlike him: A good warrior strives above all for control. She knew something was terribly wrong, but his ruthless barrage left no more time for speculation or analysis. She cleared her mind and concentrated on staying alive.

Finally, one of his swings caught her hard behind the back of her knees and she fell backward, letting his staff carry her legs up with it. She turned the fall into a roll, going over onto her shoulders and coming up on her feet. As soon as she was upright, she raised her staff to guard position, trying to protect her face and torso.

The roll had forced her to take her eyes from her opponent, and she barely saw the flicker of movement as his staff came under her defenses. Rather than the standard sweep-strike, Talor had chosen to thrust. The end of the staff caught her low in the chest and drove the breath out of her body. Without the protective padding she wore, it would have broken ribs. Had his staff struck just a few finger-widths higher, it would have been fatal, padding or not.

She twisted frantically to the side, trying to dive out of striking range. It was a desperate maneuver, exposing her vulnerable back to her opponent, and after the blow she'd just received, she knew she was moving far too slowly. Even as she moved, she waited for his strike—knowing that there was no way for her to evade the impact of the metal-shod staff.

The blow didn't come. She completed the diving roll and snapped to her feet, staff poised and lungs working desperately for air.

Talor stood in the middle of the ring, leaning against his staff. He shook his head like a wet dog, then looked up at her in dazed bewilderment. "I don't know what came over . . . Are you all right, Aralorn?"

"Fine." She gasped the word out, her diaphragm not operating quite correctly yet. "Don't . . . worry about it. No harm done, and I . . . needed a workout. Your stick work has improved, but you're still a little slow on your returns . . . Watch your hands. You hold on too tightly when you're mad, and it makes it easier for your opponent to force you to drop your staff."

As she got her breath back, she made her tone more baiting, trying to get him to forget what had happened. If she was correct about the cause, then it would do him more harm than good to worry about it. It scared her that the ae'Magi's magic was able to do what it was doing. It was just possible that he would have chosen to turn Ren into one of his puppets—but Talor had no political power. If he was affected, then she had to believe that most people in Sianim would be touched by the ae'Magi's magic: They all belonged to him. The thought of how much power that would take terrified her.

Talor took the refuge she offered. "You need to pay more attention to your opponent's eyes. You watch the body too much, and that doesn't give you much advance warning. If you'd been watching more closely, you could have avoided that last hit."

She dropped her staff and waved her hands out in the traditional surrender, and said, "Okay, you beat me. My reputation is in tatters. Just do me one favor and don't tell your brother about it. Last time you beat me, he challenged me, then I had to put up with his sulks for a week." It was important to act naturally.

"You only got it for a week because we had to go out on maneuvers. He sulked for almost a month. Okay, I won't tell him. Besides"—here he struck up an obviously false pose and looked down his nose at her—"it ill becomes a man to brag about beating a woman."

For all of his humor, Aralorn could tell that he was feeling uncomfortable. She wished she was only uncomfortable. She wasn't surprised when Talor excused himself though they generally would have drunk a couple of rounds before they left. When she turned to watch him leave, she noticed the wolf lying just inside the doorway, his head on his front paws. Talor stooped and patted him on the back, which Wolf answered with a small movement of his tail, but his clear yellow eyes never wavered from Aralorn's face.

Aralorn waited until Talor was gone before dropping exhausted to the floor, her back against the barrier. She patted the space beside her in invitation. The wolf obligingly got up, trotted over, and resumed his relaxed pose, substituting Aralorn's shins as his chin rest.

They sat like that for a while, Aralorn running her hand through the thick fur—separating the coarse dark hair from the softer, lighter-colored undercoat. When her breathing had returned almost to normal, she broke the silence.

"It's good to have you back," she commented. "I take it that they didn't kill you."

"I think that is a safe assumption to make." His voice was more noncommittal than it usually was.

She gave him a halfhearted grin.

"How long had you been watching?"

"Long enough to see you put your foot in it and almost let that clumsy young fool remove you from this life."

She obligingly rose to his bait. "Clumsy? I'll have you know that he is the second-best staffsman in Sianim."

"You being the first?" Amusement touched his voice.

She cuffed him lightly. "And you know it, too."

"It looked to me as if he had you beaten. You might have to step into second place." He paused, and said in a quieter voice, "Finally noticed that people are a bit touchy concerning the ae'Magi, have you?"

She gave him an assessing look. "Has it been going on for a long time?"

He grunted an affirmative. "I first saw it about a year ago, but recently it has gotten much more intense."

"It seems to be some sort of variation of the spells that he had at his castle, but I didn't think that anyone could create a spell of this magnitude alone." Aralorn's tone was questioning.

"He's not doing it alone," replied the wolf. "He started small. The villages near the ae'Magi's castle have quite a few inhabitants who are strong in magic. The side effect of having so many young virile magicians apprenticing at the castle for several hundred generations." His tone was ironic. "The adults that he couldn't subdue he killed because their deaths provide more of a kick to his power than people with no magic at all. But the ones he craves are the children, who have raw power and no training . . ."

Aralorn shuddered and rubbed her arms as if chilled.

"You've seen what he does with the children." Wolf's tone gentled. "Fifteen years ago, if you made a negative remark about the ae'Magi, only the reaction of the villagers just outside the castle would be as strong as Talor's. Now the streets of that village are empty of all but old men and women because the rest are dead. He has taken them and used them. As far away as Sianim, people are affected by the ae'Magi's spell. He needs still more prey to continue to increase the strength of his magic, so he's looking elsewhere. Sianim, I think, is merely getting the backlash of the main focus."

"What is the main focus?" she asked.

"Where is magic at its strongest? Where do many of the common villagers have the ability to work charms? Where has magic flourished, protected by strong rulers from the persecution that magic-users were subject to after the great wars?"

"Reth," she answered.

"Reth," he agreed.

"Crud," she said with feeling.

THREE

———⊗⊗⊗———

The inn lay about halfway between the small village of Torin and the smaller village of Kestral. It had been built snugly to keep out the bitter cold of the northern winters. When the snow lay thick on the ground, the inn would have been picturesque, nestled cozily in a small valley between the impressive mountains of northern Reth. Without the masking snow, the building showed the onset of neglect.

The inn had had many prosperous years because the trappers of the Northlands were bringing down the thick pelts of the various animals that inhabited the northern mountain wilds. For many years, merchants from all over flocked to Kestral each summer because it was as far south as the reclusive trappers would travel. However, over the last several years, the trappers had gradually grown fewer, and what furs they now brought to trade were hardly worth owning—and the inn, like the villages, suffered.

The Northlands had always been uncanny: the kind of place that a sensible person stayed away from. The trappers who came to stay at the inn had always brought with them stories of the Howlaas that screamed unseen in front of the winter winds to drive men mad. They told of the Old Man of the Mountain, a being who was not a man, no matter what he was called, who could make a man rich or turn him into a beast with no more than a whisper.

But now there were new stories, though the storytellers were fewer. One man's partner disappeared one night, leaving his bedding and clothes behind although the snow lay thick and trackless on the ground. A giant bird hovered over a campsite where four frozen bodies sat in front of a blazing fire. One trapper swore that he'd seen a dragon, though everyone knew that the dragons had been gone since the last of the Wizard Wars.

Without the trappers or the merchants who came to buy the furs, the inn depended more heavily on the local farmers' night out and less on overnight guests. The once-tidy yard was overgrown and covered with muck from horses and other beasts, some of them two-legged.

Inside, greasy tallow candles sputtered fitfully, illuminating rough-hewn walls that would have lent a soiled air to a far-more-presentable crowd than the one that occupied the inn. The chipped, wooden pitchers adorning the tables were filled with some unidentifiable but highly alcoholic brew. The tabletops themselves were black with grease and other less savory substances.

Rushing here and there amid the customers, a woman trotted blithely between tables refilling pitchers and obviously enjoying the fondles that were part of any good barmaid's job. She wasn't as clean as she could have been, but then neither was anyone else. She also wasn't as young as she claimed to be, but the dim light was kind to her graying hair, and much was forgiven because of her wholehearted approval of the male species.

The only other woman in the room was wielding a mop across the uneven floor. It might have done more good if both the water and the rag mop she used weren't dirtier than the floor. The wet bottom of her skirt did as much to remove the accumulated muck as the mop.

As she passed close to the tables, she deftly avoided the casual hands that came her way. Not that many did. Most of the customers were regulars and were aware that if someone got too pushy, he was liable to end up with the bucket over his head for his troubles.

Dishwater blond hair was pulled into an irregular bun at the back of her neck. Her plain face was not improved by the discontented expression that held sway on her thin lips as she swung the mop. "Discontented" was a mild word for how Aralorn was feeling.

A month after she'd returned from the ae'Magi's castle, Ren had called her into his office and told her that he was sending her to the middle of nowhere to keep an eye on the local inhabitants. The only reason that she'd been able to think of for her demotion to this kind of assignment was that Ren no longer trusted her; something that he had in common with most of the rest of Sianim. The story of what she had said to Talor had somehow become common knowledge, and even her closest friends avoided her as if she had a case of the pox. Ren hadn't been interested in discussing it one way or the other.

She had spent almost a full month cleaning floors, scrubbing tables, and serving poor man's ale. Profits might be down, but business at the inn was still fairly brisk because of a high rate of alcoholism and infidelity among the people of both villages. If the tavern had been located in the middle of a busy town, she might have picked up some useful bits of information for Ren. However, the inn was mostly frequented by tinkers, drunken "family men," and occasionally by one very impoverished highwayman—the more skilled and ruthless of his kind having left for richer pastures.

The most monumental thing that had happened since Aralorn started there was when the daughter of the Headman of Kestral ran off with somebody named Harold the

Rat. When the highwayman came in next time looking more miserable than usual, accompanied by a female who was taller than he by a good six inches and harangued him from the time they sat down until they left, Aralorn concluded that he was the mysterious Harold and offered him her silent condolences.

Normally, she'd have been relatively content with the assignment, especially since she'd added a few new tales to her collection of stories—courtesy of the few trappers she'd seen. But she had the doubtful privilege of knowing that the ae'Magi was striving to re-create the power the wizards had held before the Wizard Wars—and hold that power all by himself.

She *should* be doing something, but for the life of her she couldn't think what. If she left without orders or extreme necessity, being banished from Sianim was the very least of the punishments she was likely to suffer. It was more likely she'd be hung if they caught her.

Tonight, her restlessness was particularly bad. It might have had something to do with the innkeeper's wife being sick, leaving the innkeeper doing all of the cooking—rendering the food even less edible than it usually was. That led to more than the average number of customers getting sick on the floor—because the only thing left to do at the inn was drink, and the alcohol that they served was none of the best and quite probably mildly poisonous judging by the state of the poor fools who drank it.

As the newest barmaid, the task of cleaning up fell to Aralorn. With the tools she'd been handed, this consisted mostly of moving the mess around until it blended with the rest of the grime on the floor. The lye in the water ate at the skin on her hands almost as badly as the smell of the inn ate at her nose.

She dipped the foul-smelling mop into the fouler-smelling water in her bucket and occupied herself with the thought of what she would do to Ren the next time she saw him. As she was scrubbing—humming a merry accompaniment to her thoughts, a sudden hush fell into the room.

Aralorn looked up to see the cause of the unusual quiet. Against the grime and darkness of the inn, the brilliant clothing of the two men in court attire was more than a little incongruous.

Not nobles surely, but pages or messengers from the royal court. They were usually used to run messages from the court to a noble's estate. What they were doing at this little pedestrian inn was anyone's guess. Unobtrusively, Aralorn worked her way to a better observation post and watched the proceedings carefully.

One of the messengers stayed near the door. The other walked to the center of the room. He spoke slowly so that his strange court accent wouldn't keep the northerners from understanding his memorized message.

"Greetings, people. We bring you tragic news. Two weeks ago—Myr, your king, overset by the deaths of his parents, attacked and killed several of his own palace guard. Overwrought by what he had done, His Majesty seized a horse and left the royal castle. Geoffrey ae'Magi has consented to the Assembly's request to accept the Regency of Reth until such time as King Myr is found and restored to his senses. The ae'Magi has asked that the people of Reth look for their king so that a cure may be effected. As he is not right in his mind, it may, regrettably, be necessary to restrain the king by force. As this is a crime punishable by death, the Regent has issued a pardon. If the king can be brought to the ae'Magi, there is every possibility that he can be cured. As loyal subjects, it is your duty to find Myr.

"It is understood that a journey to the royal castle will be a financial hardship, thus you will have just recompense for your service to your king. A thousand marks will be paid to the party that brings King Myr to the capital or restrains him and sends a message to the court. I have been authorized to repeat this message to the citizens of Reth by the Regent, Geoffrey ae'Magi." He repeated his message twice, word for word each time, then he bowed and left the inn with his companion.

A thousand marks was more than a farmer or innkeeper would make in a lifetime of hard work. *Recompense, my aching rump,* thought Aralorn, it was merely a legal way to put a bounty on Myr's head.

Wandering between tables, she caught bits and pieces of conversation and found that most people seemed to feel the ae'Magi had done them a great service by taking the throne. They didn't all agree on what ought to be done for the king. She heard an old farmer announce that everything should be done to see that Myr was captured and taken to be cured, poor lad. He was answered by agreeable muttering from his table.

Olin, the tanner from Torin (and more than slightly drunk), spoke up loudly. "Anyone who cares about Reth should kill Myr and ask for Geoffrey ae'Magi to take the kingship of us. Who needs a king what is going to attack his own folk out of the blue like that? Just think what'd be like havin' the Archmage for a king. We'd not worry 'bout those Darranians, who're claiming our mines over in the west borderlands." He paused to belch. "'N with the most powerful magician in the world, we could even drive those Uriah spooks outta the wilds. We could claim the North-lands altogether. Then we could be rich again."

The patrons of the inn shifted uncomfortably and chose another topic to speak on; but they didn't disagree with what he'd said.

Proof, if she'd needed it, that what Wolf had warned her of was actually taking place. The whole of Reth had adored their handsome prince, who was promising both as a warrior and a statesman—and it didn't hurt that he was the spitting image of his grandfather, who had been a great king by any reckoning. Two years ago, the last time

Aralorn had worked a job in Reth, Olin's words would have gotten him into a rough argument or even a beating.

Moving unobtrusively, Aralorn took the slop bucket outside to dump it. That done, she strolled to the stables, where Sheen was.

She received a lot of harassment from Ren when she took the warhorse with her on assignments, because he was too valuable to go unremarked. Talor carried an old coin for luck when he went into battle: It must be much more convenient than a horse.

She did what she could to disguise his worth. He'd long ago learned to limp on command, which helped somewhat. She also left him ungroomed, but anyone with an eye for horses could see that he was no farmer's plug.

At the inn, she'd let it be known that he was the only legacy left to her when her elderly protector died. The innkeeper didn't ask her too many questions—just retained the better part of her weekly salary in payment and half the stud fees Sheen had been earning.

Aralorn scuffed her foot lightly in the dirt as she leaned against the stall door. Sheen moved over to her and shoved his head against her shoulder. Obligingly, she rubbed his jaw.

"The last time I saw Myr, he was hardly distraught enough to go berserk," she confided. "Convenient that the Assembly decided to place the ae'Magi as Regent. I wonder how he managed that—only in Reth would a mage of any sort be welcome to help himself to the throne. But there are some really strong mages in the Assembly. Hard to believe he could use his magic on them, and no one even noticed."

The stallion whickered softly, and Aralorn fed him the carrot she'd taken before it would have gone to its death in some greasy pot of stew. She tangled her hand in Sheen's coarse gray-black mane as he munched. "I could go to Ren with this, but given his present attitude toward the ae'Magi, I don't know what he would do—and doubtless he knows about it anyway. Probably supports it the same way those fools in the inn do—and for the same reason." She tightened her hands in the horsehair, and whispered, "I think we should go looking for Myr, don't you? Myr is immune to magic—he's the ideal hero to stand against the ae'Magi. An outcast spy from Sianim isn't enough to make a difference, but maybe I can help with strategy. At the very least, I can tell Myr why everyone is suddenly against him."

There was a noise—she froze for a moment, but it was only the wind rattling a broken board on one of the stall doors.

Even so, she lowered her voice further. "I only wish I had some way of contacting Wolf. Knowing him, he probably could tell us exactly where Myr went." Wolf was full of useful information when he chose to share it. "It could take us quite a while to find Myr." She paused, then smiled. "But if I'm going out to engage in hopeless tasks, I'd rather look for Myr than struggle to clean that floor another day. We'll start with those messengers and see what they know."

Finished with the carrot, Sheen bumped her impatiently—asking for more. "Well, Sheen, what do you say? Should we abandon our post and go missing-monarch hunting?" The gray head moved enthusiastically against her hand when she caught a particularly itchy spot: It looked for all the world as if he were nodding in agreement.

The restlessness that had been plaguing her was gone. Like a hunting dog let off the leash, she had a purpose at last. She snuck into the kitchen and blessed her luck because no one was there—she could hear the innkeeper arguing with someone in the common room. It sounded as though he might be occupied for a long time, which suited her just fine.

She located a large cloth that was almost clean and folded it to hold such provisions as would keep on a journey: bread, cheese, dried salt meat.

Cautiously, she made her way upstairs without meeting

anyone and snuck into the room that had belonged to the only son of the innkeeper. He'd died last winter of some disease or the other, and no one had yet had the heart to clean out his room. Everything in the room was neat and tidy—and she had the sudden thought that perhaps it hadn't been the change in customs that caused the inn to fall on harder times. She murmured a soft explanation of what she was doing and why in case the young man's spirit lingered nearby.

She opened the chest at the foot of the bed and found a cloak, a pair of leather trousers, and a tunic: tough, unre-markable clothes well suited to traveling. At the bottom of the trunk, she found a pair of sturdy riding boots and a set of riding gloves. She wrapped all of her ill-gotten goods in the cloak and hurried out of the room and up the ladder to her attic room.

She retrieved her sword from its hiding place inside the straw mattress (she generally slept on the floor, it being less likely to be infested by miscellaneous vermin). Before sliding the sheath onto her belt, she drew the sword from habit—to make sure that the blade needed neither sharp-ening nor cleaning. It was a sword she'd found hidden in one of the many cubbyholes of her father's castle—the odd pinkish gold luster of the metal had intrigued her. It was also the only sword in the place that fit her, her father's blood tending toward large and muscle-bound, which she was not. Aside from Sheen, it was the only thing she'd taken from her home when she left.

She wasn't a swordswoman by any means. Practice and more practice had made her competent enough to make it useful against things like the Uriah, creatures too big to be killed quickly with a dagger and not easily downed with a staff—creatures not holding swords of their own.

She gratefully rid herself of the filthy maidservant's dress and dropped it on the floor, donning instead the stolen garments and found that, as she expected, they were very tight in the hips and chest and ridiculously big everywhere else. The boots, in particular, were huge. If the innkeeper's son had lived to grow up, he would have been a big man.

Her mother's people could switch their sex as easily as most people changed shoes, but Aralorn had never been able to take on a male's shape. Perhaps it was her human blood, or perhaps she'd never tried hard enough. Fortunately, the boy whose clothes she'd appropriated had been slender, so that it was an easy thing to become a tall, angular, and androgynous woman—with big feet—who could pass as a man.

Once dressed, she was satisfied she looked enough like a young man neither rich nor poor, a farmer's son . . . or an innkeeper's. Someone who wouldn't seem out of place on a sturdy draft horse.

Most of the items in the room she left behind, though she took the copper pieces that she'd earned as well as the small number of coins that she always kept with her as an emergency fund.

She shut the door to her room and made sure that the bundle that she was carrying wasn't awkward-looking. As she made her way down the stairs, she was met by the other barmaid. Aralorn gave the woman a healthy grin and swept past her unchallenged.

In the stable, Aralorn saddled Sheen. The cloak and the food she packed into her copious saddlebags. She filched an empty grain sack from a stack of the same and filled it with oats, tying it to the saddle. From one of the saddlebags, she took out a small jar of white paste. Carefully, she painted the horse's shoulders with white patches such as a heavy work collar tends to leave with time. Farmer's plug no, but he could well pass for a squire's prize draft horse.

On the road, she hesitated before turning north toward Kestral. That was the direction that the messengers had been traveling. If she could find them, in the guise of a young farmer, she could question them without anyone's taking too much notice—as the barmaid could not have. A second reason for looking north was that the mountains were the best place for someone seeking to hide from a human magician. Human magic didn't work as well in the Northland mountains as it did elsewhere. She knew stories of places in the mountains where human magic wouldn't function at all. Conversely, green-magic users, her mother's brother had told her, found that magic was easier to work in the north. She'd experienced that herself.

As Myr was from Reth, Aralorn felt that it was safe to assume that he was aware of the partial protection the Northlands offered. There were very few other places as easily accessible that offered any protection from the ae'Magi. Unfortunately, the ae'Magi would also be aware that the Northlands were the most likely place for Myr to go, hence the messengers to the otherwise-unimportant villages that dotted the border of Reth.

Although it was still late summer, the air was brisk with the chill winds. They retained their bite this far north year-round, making Aralorn grateful for the soft leather gloves and warm cloak she wore.

Several miles down the road, she turned off to take a trail she'd heard the highwayman describe when, half-drunk, he bragged about getting away from an angry merchant. The shortcut traversed the mountain rather than wandering around its base. With luck and the powerful animal under her, she could cut more than an hour off her travel time.

Sheen snorted and willingly took on the climb, his powerful hindquarters easily pushing his bulk and hers up the treacherously steep grade. His weight and large hooves worked against him on the rocky, uncertain ground, though, and Aralorn held him to a slow trot that left Sheen snorting and tossing his head in impatience.

"Easy now, sweetheart. What's your hurry? We may have a long way to go yet this evening. Save it for later."

Always mindful that someone could overhear, she kept her voice low and boyish.

One dark-tipped ear twitched back. After a small crow hop of protest, Sheen settled into stride, only occasionally breaking gait to bounce over an obstacle in his way.

As evening wore on, the light began to fade, and Aralorn slowed him into a walk. In full dark, his eyesight was better than hers, but in the twilight, he couldn't see the rocks and roots hidden by shadows. They had a few miles before the sun went down completely, then they could pick up the pace again.

Being unable to see clearly made the seasoned campaigner nervous, and he began to snort and dance at every sound. There was a sudden burst of magic nearby—she didn't have time to locate it because that was the last straw for Sheen, who plunged off the trail and down the steep, tree-covered side of the mountain.

She sank her butt into the saddle and stayed with him as he dodged trees and leapt over brush. "Just you behave, you old worrywart, you. It's all right. Nothing's going to get us but ghosts and ghoulies and other nice things that feed on stupid people who ride in the woods after dark."

The dark mountainside was too treacherous to allow her to pull him up hard, especially at the pace he was going, so she crooned to him and bumped him lightly with the reins—a request rather than an order.

He sank back on his haunches to slide down a steep bit instead of charging down it, and stopped when the ground leveled some. He took advantage of the loose rein to snatch a bit of grass as if he hadn't been snorting and charging a minute before.

Aralorn stretched and looked around to catch her bearings. As she did so, she heard something, a murmur that she just barely caught. Sheen's ears twitched toward the sound as well. Following the direction of the stallion's ears, she moved him toward the sound. When she could pick up the direction herself, she dismounted and dropped his reins.

She crept closer, moving as slowly as she could so as not to make any noise. Several yards from Sheen, she picked up the smell of a campfire and the residue of magic—it tasted flat and dull: magic shaped by human hands despite the nearness of the Northlands. Probably the remnant of the spell that had startled Sheen into charging down the hill, toward danger, just as any good warhorse would have done.

She followed the sound of men's voices and the smell of smoke through a thicket of bushes—she had to use a tendril of magic to keep quiet going through that—and around a huge boulder that had tumbled down from a cliff above. Peeking around the side of the boulder, she saw a cave mouth, the walls of the entrance reflecting light from a fire deeper inside.

The voices were louder, but still too far away to be distinguishable.

The wonderful thing about mice, Aralorn reflected as she shifted forms, was that they were everywhere and never looked out of place. A mouse was the first shape she'd ever managed—and she'd since worked hard on a dozen different varieties and their nearest kin. Shrew, vole, field mouse, she could manage any of them. The medium-sized northern-type mouse was just the right mouse to look perfectly at home as she scampered into the cave.

Two men stood by a large pile of goods that ranged from swords to flour, but consisted mainly of tarps and furs. The scent of fear drifted clearly to her rodent-sharp nose from the more massive (at least in bulk) man as he cowered away from the other. He bore the ornate facial tattooing of the merchant's guild of Hernal, a larger city of Ynstrah, a country that lay several weeks' travel to the south on the west side of the Anthran Alliance. He was wearing nothing but a nightshirt.

The second man had his back to her. He was tall and slender, but something about the way he moved told her that this man knew how to fight. He wore a hooded cloak that flickered red and gold in the light. Underneath the hood of the cloak he wore a smoothly wrought silver mask in the shape of a stylized face.

Traveling players used such masks when they acted out skits, allowing one player to take on many roles in a single play without confusion to the audience. Usually, these masks were made out of inexpensive materials like clay or wood. She'd never seen one made of silver, not even in high-court productions.

Each mask's face was formed with a different expression denoting an explicit emotion that mostly bore only a slight resemblance to any expression found on a real face. As a girl from a noble house, Aralorn had spent many a dreary hour memorizing the slight differences between concern and sympathy, weariness and suffering, sorrow and defeat. She found it interesting that the mask this man wore displayed the curled lips and furrowed brow of rage.

In one hand the slender man held a staff made of some kind of very dark wood. On the lower end was the clawed foot of a bird of prey molded in brass, and its outspread talons glowed softly orange in the darkness of the cave as if it had been held in hot coals. The upper end of the staff was encrusted with crystals that lit the cave with their blue-white light.

The staff made it obvious that this man was the mage responsible for the magic that had so startled Sheen. If he had spirited the merchant and his goods from wherever he'd been to here—she assumed the man hadn't been traveling in his nightshirt—then he was a sorcerer of no little power.

Hmm, she thought, *maybe this mouse idea wasn't such a good one.* A powerful mage on alert might find a nearby mouse that wasn't really a mouse, and he wasn't likely to be

very pleasant about it. Even as she started to back away, the
mage looked over his shoulder and gestured impatiently.
She didn't even have time to fight the spell before she was
stuffed into a leather bag that smelled strongly of magic.

She tried once to shift back into her human shape, but
nothing happened. He'd trapped her, and until she figured
a way out, she was stuck.

"How much, merchant?" the mage asked in Rethian.
His voice was distorted with a strange accent—or maybe it
was just the leather bag.

"Fourteen kiben." The merchant, too, spoke good
Rethian, but his voice was hoarse and trembling. Still,
Aralorn noticed, the price he'd quoted was at least twice
what the items were worth, unless there was something
extremely valuable among them.

"Six." The magician's voice may have had an odd slur to
it, but it was still effective in striking terror into the heart
of the merchant—who squeaked in a most unmanly fashion. Aralorn had the feeling that it wouldn't take much to
achieve that result.

"Six, I accept," he gasped. There was the sound of
money changing hands, then a distinctive pop and an
immense surge of magic, which Aralorn decided signaled
that the merchant had been sent back to wherever he'd
come from in the first place.

There was a moment's pause, then a third person's voice
spoke.

"It worked." He sounded as if he hadn't expected it to.
He also sounded young and aristocratic, probably because
Myr was both.

She hadn't planned on finding him quite so soon, not a
half day's ride from the inn. It was too convenient. Had Ren
known that something was going on here? Was that why
he'd sent her out to the backside of nowhere? She might
have to take back months of heartfelt curses if that was so.

"Hopefully our mutual enemy will not think to question

all of the merchants traveling in Reth." There was something about the tone of the magician's voice that was familiar, but the odd accent kept throwing her. She should be
able to figure out what kind of an accent it was, she *knew*
languages—which was why Ren had pulled her out of the
rank and file in the first place.

"He wouldn't learn much even if he did. The merchant
doesn't know where you brought him to."

The magician grunted. "He knows that it was in the
north because of the cold. He knows that it was in the mountains because of the cave. That is more than we can afford to
have the ae'Magi know."

Myr gave no vocal reply; but he must have nodded,
because when he spoke again, it was on a different topic.
"What was that you grabbed off the floor?"

"Ah yes. Just a . . . spy. Small but effective nonetheless."
Was that amusement she picked up in his tone?

The bag was opened, and she found herself hanging by
her tail for the perusal of the two men. She twisted around
and bit the hand that held her, hard. The mage laughed, but
moved his hand so that she sat comfortably on his palm.

"My lord, may I present to you the Lady Aralorn, sometime spy of Sianim."

She was so shocked she almost fell off her perch. How
did he know who she was? It wasn't as if she were one of
the famous generals that everyone knew. In fact, as a spy,
she'd worked pretty hard to keep her name out of the spot-
light. And no one, *no one* knew that Aralorn could become
a mouse.

Then it hit her. Without the additional muffling of the
bag she recognized the voice. It was altered through the
mask, a human throat, and that odd accent—but she knew
it anyway. No one else could have that particularly macabre timbre. It was Wolf.

"So"—Myr's voice was quiet—"Sianim spies on me
now." Aralorn turned her attention to Myr. In the short

time since she'd seen him, he'd aged years. He was thinner, his mouth held taut, and his eyes belonged to the harsh old warrior who had been his grandfather instead of the boy she'd met. He wore clothing that a rough trapper or a traveling merchant might wear, patched here and there with neat stitches.

Deciding that the mouse was no longer useful—and it was easier to talk as a human—Aralorn jumped nimbly off her perch and resumed her normal shape, which was not the one that he would recognize. "No, my lord," she answered. "Or at least that wasn't my assignment. Sianim has spies on *everyone*. In fact, this is a rather fortunate meeting; I was looking for you to tell you that the ae'Magi's messengers have reported your fit of madness to all the nearby townsfolk." She spoke slowly and formally to give him a chance to adjust to her altered state.

Rethians were not less prejudiced against shapeshifters, just more likely to admit their existence. Since her mother's people lived in the northern mountains of Reth and paid tribute yearly to the King of Reth in the form of exquisite tapestries and well-crafted tools delivered in the night by unseen persons, the Rethians had a tougher time dismissing them as hearsay.

Folktales warned villagers to stay out of the forests at night, or they would be fodder of the shapeshifters or other green-magic users who might still be lurking in the impenetrable depths of the trees. Given the antagonism that the shapeshifters felt toward invading humans, Aralorn was afraid that the stories might not have it all wrong. But the royal family tended not to be as wary, probably the result of the yearly tribute they received—and the fact that they lived in southern Reth, far from any possible outpost of shapeshifters.

Myr glanced at the mage, who nodded and spoke. "That she means you no harm, I will vouch for." The slurred quality was not a product of the muffling of the pouch;

if anything it was stronger than it had been. Maybe it was the mask.

"She has a gift for languages," Wolf continued. "I need someone to help me in my research. If she is not occupied with other things, it would do no harm to bring her to camp with us. She can fight, and the gods know we have need of fighters. Also, she stands in danger from the ae'Magi if he should discover who it was that spied on him."

"You spied on the Archmage?" Myr raised an eyebrow at her.

Aralorn shrugged. "It wasn't my favorite assignment, but definitely one of the more interesting." She let her face shift quickly to the one he'd seen in the ae'Magi's castle, then went back to normal.

Myr looked a little sick—watching someone's face move around could do that—then he blinked a couple of times. Finally, he smiled. "Yes, I see. Welcome, then, Lady. I invite you to join our small camp."

Myr gave a short bow of his head, which she appreciated as exactly the correct height for a male sovereign to give in polite invitation or acceptance to a female who was neither his subject nor fellow royalty.

She in her turn, dressed in the clothes of the dead son of the innkeeper, gave him the exact curtsy she would have given him as her father's daughter. Rethian nobility overdid manners, so she knew he'd catch the subtle difference.

He did. "*Who* are you?"

She gave him an apologetic smile as she pulled at the uncomfortably tight front of the tunic. "Lady Aralorn of Lambshold, at your service."

"One of Henrick's daughters." Myr's voice carried a hint of incredulity.

Aralorn nodded, smiling apologetically. "I know, I don't look much like him, do I? He didn't think so either. I was quite a disappointment to him." She rolled up the sleeves until she could see her hands again.

"No, that's not what I mean," said Myr. "I've seen you in court—a long time ago. You're his oldest child?"

She laughed. "You must have been all of ten. I'm the oldest daughter, but I have a brother a year older than I am. We two are the illegitimate get of youthful folly. My older brother's mother was a household maid, and my mother was a shapeshifter who seduced poor Father in the nearby woods. With fourteen of us, I can see where you could have trouble keeping us straight. My siblings are all copies of our father, rather unfortunate for my sisters, but my brothers are all considered quite handsome."

She startled a laugh out of Myr at her descriptions of her family. Her sisters were all quite beautiful, golden like their father—and like their father, they overtopped most men by a good handspan.

"How did you end up in Sianim?"

She tilted her head, thinking about how best to frame a reply. "I am too much my father's daughter to be content with sewing a dress or learning how to converse. He taught me swordplay with my brothers because I asked him. When it came time for me to go to court, it was obvious to both him and me that as a Lady I was hopeless. He gave me his own horse and sent me on my way."

It had been a lot more complicated than that, but that had been the heart of the matter. The rest of it wouldn't matter to the King of Reth. As she talked, she worked at rolling up her pant legs. Finally, she cut the bottom off with her dagger. There was nothing to be done for the boots.

"Somehow that sounds like the Lyon of Lambshold. He's the only man I know who is unconventional enough to do that." Myr shook his head.

Straightening up to her unimpressive height, Aralorn continued, "He said, if memory serves, that if no one had the nerve to laugh in his face when he was addressed as the 'Lyon of Lambshold,' no one would say anything about an absent daughter."

"If you are through talking, it might be best if we left for camp." The harsh voice was distracted, and Wolf's eyes focused on some distant point.

"Someone coming?" Myr changed in an instant from courtier to warrior.

Wolf grunted, then said, "Not here, but near enough that we ought to move out. So much magic was bound to attract attention."

Aralorn left them to their packing and ducked through the trees to grab her horse. As she checked the girth, she muttered to Sheen, "I wonder what mischief our friend Wolf has been up to?"

FOUR

When Aralorn awoke to face her first full day at Myr's camp, it was still dark. She slipped out through the tent opening, moving quietly to avoid disturbing the two women who had shared their quarters with her. She retied the crude flap so the cold early-morning air would stay outside.

Most of the tents in the camp were makeshift. Several were little more than a rug stretched over a stick or rope in true field-soldier style. The only tent she'd seen that had been worthy of the name belonged to Myr, who shared it uncomplaining with a number of the smaller children.

As she passed Myr's tent, near the fire pit, she gave the royal dragon embroidered on the side a respectful nod, but it glared balefully at her anyway. The flickering light of the fire gave the illusion of life to the green-gold eyes.

Also near the fire pit was one of the few wooden structures in the camp. The kitchen was little more than a three-sided shed, but it kept the food dry. The camp cook was already up, chopping something by lantern light, but he stopped long enough to give Aralorn a look no more friendly than the dragon's had been. Aralorn grinned cheerfully at him and kept on her way.

The camp was located in a small dale, no bigger than the largest of the riding arenas in Sianim, that lay half a day's ride north of the Rethian border. It was long and narrow, with a stream in the middle that she suspected would cover a much larger area in the spring, when the top layer of snow melted off the mountain peaks. As it was, the ground near the stream was marshy and made soft, slurping sounds when she walked over to take a drink and throw water on her face.

The tents were all in the eastern end of the valley near the only obvious trail down the steep, almost clifflike sides. Those sides, heavily covered with brush on the top, were the strongest defense the camp could have, rendering it almost invisible to anyone not already in the valley.

By the simple expedient of running a split-rail fence across the valley the narrow way, the western end had been turned into a pasture for most of the livestock—two goats, four donkeys, several horses, and a scrawny cow. It was toward this part of the valley that Aralorn headed.

Knowing how well Wolf liked people, she thought that he would be as far from the tents as he could get—although she couldn't see him anywhere in the dale. As she neared the pasture, she was welcomed with a soft whinny. Sheen, only slightly inconvenienced by the soft leather hobble that bound his front legs, bounced up to her to get his nose rubbed. She'd hobbled him outside the pasture so that the owners of the two mares didn't end up with unwanted foals. He followed her for a while before wandering off to forage.

It took her a little time to find the faint trail running up the steep slope near the fence. The terrain was rough and treacherous with loose stones, and she thought ruefully that a person would have to be part mountain goat to try this very often—or part wolf.

Grabbing a ragged piece of brush, she pulled herself up a particularly steep area and found herself unexpectedly in a hollow that hadn't been visible from below. A small smokeless fire burned near a bedroll. The rather large, lank wolf turned amber eyes to her and swayed his tail in casual welcome.

Since he wasn't using it, she seated herself on the bedroll and rested her chin on her raised knees. Casually, she threw a few more sticks onto the fire, leaving it for him to break the silence. Typically, he explained nothing but questioned her instead.

"Tell me about the camp." His voice was mildly curious.

"Why? You've been here much longer than I have."

He shook his head. "I just want to know what you see— how much I need to explain to you."

"Well," she began, "there has been a camp here for several months, probably starting in the spring. Originally, the person or people who started it didn't know much about camping in the woods, so I'd guess that they weren't locals. It looks like someone is in the process of reorganizing camp. If I were a gamester, I would place gold that Myr is the reorganizer—since I suspect you wouldn't bother." She looked to the wolf for confirmation.

Wolf nodded, and Aralorn continued to speak.

"From what I can tell, most of these people came with not much more than the clothes on their backs. There are what, maybe fifty people here?"

"Fifty-four with you," Wolf replied.

"Then over a third of them are children. There is no common class among them. I've seen peasants, townsfolk, and several aristocrats. The children are, as far as I've seen, without family. They are almost all Rethian." Aralorn lay back and made herself comfortable. "They have all the earmarks of refugees, and I'd lay my last gold that they are running from the ae'Magi."

Wolf grunted an affirmative.

"How did they all get here, though? I could see northerners finding this valley, but I heard southern Reth accents, too."

"You, of all people, should know the reputation of the northern mountains," replied Wolf.

Aralorn frowned at him. "I saw you transport the merchant, and my understanding is that teleportation is a difficult, high-level spell. And you managed it in the Northlands."

Wolf shook his head. "I wouldn't have tried it this far north even if we weren't worried about the ae'Magi finding the valley. Small spells seem unhampered here, but more delicate spells are harder to control. Some people it affects more than others—the ae'Magi won't travel even as far as the northern lands in Reth. It doesn't seem to have much effect on my magic"—he nodded at the fire, which flared up, dancing wildly with purple and gold flames—"but I wouldn't have bet even the merchant's life on it; so we traveled south."

"The stories about that aspect of the Northlands are common enough, even in southern Reth," agreed Aralorn. She gave him a look. "I suppose that this area would be a good place to run to if you were trying to hide from a human magician."

"I"—he hesitated a minute, and Aralorn got the distinct feeling that he changed what he was going to say—"previously located this valley as a possible refuge although I never intended to set up a camp of this size here."

He gazed with an air of bemusement over the camp. "I don't know how these people found this valley in particular. You can ask, but everyone has a different story. It is unreasonable that fifty people, most of whom have never been a mile away from their own front doors, would wander blithely into a hanging valley that would be hard for a forester or trapper to find."

After a slight pause, he continued, "As you speculated, they are all running from the ae'Magi in a manner of

speaking—the way that you would have been fleeing from
Sianim if you had made a few more negative comments
about the ae'Magi. Most of them were driven from their
villages by the townspeople.

"Except for Myr, everyone in camp can work a little
magic. The adults didn't have enough ability to be trained
as magicians and escaped the ae'Magi's control that way.
The children are young enough that they had not yet been
sent for training."

"How far does that control go?" she asked him. "Are
they his puppets?"

"No more than Ren or any of the other nonmages who
do as he wants. He just takes away the advantage their
magic gives them, and so they only see what he wants them
to see."

Aralorn turned until she faced him. "Why aren't you
under his control?" She expected him to avoid answering
as he usually did when her questions became too pointed.

But Wolf moved in a lupine version of a shrug. "I either
broke the ties of the binding, or I wasn't in training long
enough. I am not sure which."

Aralorn and Wolf sat in silence, watching the camp stir
in the valley below them. Aralorn stretched her feet out to
the fire, which still flared uneasily, as if waiting for another
command.

Watching the red play of flame reflected on her feet in
the dim light, she ventured another question. "How long
have you been helping Myr?"

She noticed with self-directed amusement that her tone
was disinterested, revealing none of the jealousy she felt.
It had surprised her to feel resentful of Myr, but Wolf was
hers. When she found out that not only was there someone
else close to him but that Wolf had revealed himself as a
human mage to him—it bothered her.

Wolf spoke slowly. "I have been looking for a way to
move against the ae'Magi for a long time. It came to my

attention that Myr didn't hold the ae'Magi in the same esteem that most people do: Apparently, Myr is not susceptible to magic. I am still not sure what use he will be against the ae'Magi, but it seemed prudent to watch him. At first I did little more than observe, but after Myr's parents were killed, I introduced myself and offered my help. For the most part, all that I did was offer advice and block a few spells that might have resulted in fatal accidents."

"Accidents like a carriage overturning unexpectedly," offered Aralorn, remembering Myr's parents.

Wolf nodded. "Or an archer's arrow going astray, things that immunity to magic does not shield against. I am not sure if I helped much in the end. The last attack that the ae'Magi set against Myr was more subtle. Did you hear what happened?"

Aralorn shook her head. "The first thing that I heard about it was back at the inn, when some messengers from the capital rode in and spouted nonsense. Myr was supposedly crazed with grief and attacked one of his own men."

Wolf snorted. "Myr was in his private courtyard in the palace when he was attacked by an elemental—a lucky choice for Myr, as most of an elemental's ability to harm is magical." So maybe she'd convinced the ae'Magi that Myr wasn't immune to magic, or maybe he was testing it.

Wolf continued with the story. "They made enough noise that I went out to investigate. I think that Myr would have won even if I hadn't been there." Wolf shrugged. "When it was dead, the demon transformed into a more mundane creature—one of Myr's personal guards. We were still standing over the body when the better part of the castle guard ran into the courtyard. They attacked, and we managed to flee. Here is where we've been ever since."

"What now?" asked Aralorn, drawing pictures in the dirt near the blankets.

Wolf let out a sound that passed as a laugh. "Now, Myr is trying desperately to prepare this camp for winter,

and I am trying to find a way that I can move against the
ae'Magi." He paused, then said in a tone that reeked of
frustration, "It's not that I don't have the power. It is the
training I lack. Most of what little I do know I've learned
myself, and it's not enough. If I could find just one of the
old magicians not under his spell, I could find something
to use against him. Instead, I have to wade through piles of
books that may be utterly useless."

"I will help with the books," offered Aralorn. He wasn't
worried about power? Against a mage strong enough to
turn Sianim into his worshipping congregation? "But this
is the ae'Magi you're going up against, Wolf. He's not just
some hedgewitch."

He ignored her worries about the ae'Magi. Instead, he
said, "If I have to read through the dusty old relics, you
might as well suffer, too." He was teasing her; she could
tell by his tone of voice. He knew she would devour every
time-scarred tome with a zealot's passion—she loved old
books. "How many languages do you read? I've heard you
speak three or four."

Aralorn shrugged. "Including dialects? Ten, maybe
twelve. Sometimes I can pick out the essentials in a related
language. Father was a fanatic about it—he got caught in
a battle one time trying to negotiate a surrender, and the
only person who spoke both languages had been killed.
So he started us all when we were children. After I came
to Sianim, I learned a lot of others. Anything very old,
though, will be in the Ancients' tongue. I can pick my way
through that, but I'm not fluent."

He gave her a wolfish grin. "And they always said that
collecting folktales was a useless hobby." He continued
more seriously, "The two of us can get through more material than I can alone. If I even had the name of a magician
with a spell that could stop him, I could save time. I have
a library near here, and if you can go through the secular
books, it would leave me free to work with the grimoires."

Aralorn made a point of looking around at the mountain wilderness that surrounded them. "You have a library nearby?"

"Yes."

"Yes," she repeated.

Gravely, he met her eyes. If she hadn't known him as well as she did, she might not have seen the faint humor in the amber depths.

"I did notice that you ignored me earlier," she said. "This is the ae'Magi you are talking about facing. Do you really think you can take him?"

"No," Wolf answered softly. "But I'm the only chance we have, aren't I?"

From the valley rose the distant sound of a metal spoon hitting a cooking pot—the time-honored call to gather for a meal.

Wolf rolled lithely to his paws, changing almost as he moved into the tall, masked figure that was his human form. Courteously, he extended a hand to help her to her feet.

Aralorn accepted the hand a little warily, finding that Wolf in his human form was somewhat more intimidating than the wolf was. As a human, he maintained the grace that he had as a wolf. She watched with envy as he easily negotiated the slope that she scrambled and slid down.

A stray thought caught her. At the valley bottom, she touched his arm to stop him.

"Wolf, I think that I may have caused a problem for you." Anxiously, she bit her lip.

"What's that?" he asked.

"During the ball at the ae'Magi's castle the night I left, Myr saw me in the cage where he should have seen only a bird. The ae'Magi saw him talking to me and questioned me about it. I told him that I'd seen a magician help Myr break the illusion spell, hoping to keep Myr's immunity to magic from the ae'Magi." She kept her eye on the contrast her hand made against the black silk of his sleeve: It was hard to remember that the masked figure was Wolf. "Did I cause you any trouble?"

He shook his head. "I don't think so. That was probably why he progressed beyond straying arrows to an elemental—the timing is about right. But since we survived it, there was no harm done."

———

Myr was up and arranging breakfast with a dexterity that Aralorn, who liked to arrange people as well, found fascinating to watch. She let herself be organized with a bowl of cooked grain that made up in amount what it lacked in flavor. After the food she'd eaten at the inn, she felt no inclination to complain. Wolf neither ate nor removed the mask, a situation that seemed an established pattern since no one commented on it.

As she ate, Aralorn took the time to observe the people. The introductions she'd received the night before had been needfully brief, and many of the people had been asleep. She could only place the names to a few of the faces.

The sour-faced cook was a smith from a province in southern Reth. A large snake tattoo wrapped itself around one massive forearm, disappearing into his sleeve. She noticed that for all of his gruffness, his voice softened remarkably when he was talking with the children. His name was Haris.

Edom sat a little apart from the rest. He had the dark straight hair and sallow skin typical of parts of western Reth, the legacy of interbreeding with the dark Darranians. His hands were the soft, well-cared-for hands of an aristocrat. He was an oddity in the camp. Too old to be a child, yet younger than any of the adults. He was a recent arrival and still looked as if he felt a little out of place.

All but two of the children had been sleeping when she'd arrived at the valley. Those two who she'd met were now seated as close to Myr as they could get. Stanis had the red hair and freckles of the Southern Traders and the flamboyant personality to go with it. The second boy, Tobin, was a quiet shadow of his friend. Stanis tugged impatiently at Myr's shirt until he had the young king's attention. Then he settled back on his knees and started talking with grand gestures of his arms that looked a little odd on a boy of ten or eleven summers.

Aralorn was just about to look away when she saw Myr's expression sharpen with alert interest. He looked around for Wolf and waved him over. Aralorn followed.

"Stanis, tell Wolf what you just told me."

Stanis hesitated for a moment, but the enjoyment of being the object of attention manifestly won out over any shyness that he felt around the intimidating magician.

"Yesterday afternoon, when it was time to eat lunch, nobody could find Astrid. Me and Tobin thought that she might have been playing up near the old caves. So we all went up there to see if she still was. Edom was too scairt to go in, but I wasn't. We looked for hours and hours. Then when we all got back out together, she was waiting with Edom.

"She said that she was lost in the dark. She cried and a nice man who knew her name found her and took her out of the caves. Edom says that he didn't see no one with her when she came out. And Haris said that he thinks that she wandered into the mouth of one of the caves and fell asleep and dreamed about the man. But I think that she met a shapeshifter, and Tobin does, too. Only he thinks that it could have been a ghost."

Aralorn suppressed a smile at the boy's delivery—he'd gotten most of that out in one breath.

"What do think, Wolf? Astrid doesn't tell stories, for all that she's but a child. Who do you think she saw?" Myr's tone was quiet, but it was evident that the thought of someone living in the caves (wherever they were) bothered him.

Wolf said, "It's entirely possible that she did meet some-one. Those caves interconnect with cave systems that run throughout the mountain chain. I have seen many strange things in these mountains and heard stories of more. I know for a fact that there are shapeshifters in this area." He didn't even look at Aralorn as he said that, nor did Myr, though the young king twitched. "I'll keep an eye out—but if he were going to harm us, I'd think he'd have already done so."

Myr relaxed a little, relying on the older man's judg-ment. Stanis looked pleased with himself—Wolf had agreed with *him*.

After breakfast, Aralorn found herself cornered by Myr, and before she knew it, she was agreeing to give lessons in swordsmanship. Myr divided the adults into four groups to be taught by Aralorn, Myr, Wolf, and a one-armed ex-guardsman with an evil smile and the unlikely name of Pussywillow. The other three teachers were, in Aralorn's estimation, all much better with a sword than Aralorn was, but luckily none of her students were good enough to real-ize how badly outclassed she was.

The first part of any low-level lesson was a drill in basic moves. Haris Smith-Turned-Cook handled the sword with the same strength and sureness that a good smith uses in swinging a hammer. He learned rapidly from a word or a touch. Edom had the normal flaws of adolescence—all elbows and awkwardness. The others were in the middle range. Given three or four years of steady sword work, they would be passable, maybe.

It didn't really matter, she thought. If it came down to hand-to-hand fighting, they were all doomed anyway. But it was something to keep the people busy and make them feel as though they were working toward a common goal.

She fought her first bout with Haris, deciding to face the

best fighter first—when she was fresh. It was a good idea. He might not have had much experience with a sword, but he had been in more than one dirty fight. If she'd had to rely on only her swordsmanship to fight him, she might have lost, but she'd been in a few dirty fights herself.

When she finally pinned him, Haris gave her the first genuine smile she'd seen on his face. "For a little bit of a thing, you fight pretty well."

"For a hulking brute, you're not too bad yourself," she said, letting him up. She turned to the observers. "And that is how you fight on a battlefield. But not in a training session on swordsmanship. The sword got in his way more than it helped him. If he were fighting in a battle today, he'd be better off with a club than with a sword. That will not be true in a month, for any of you—I hope."

The others were easier, so she lectured as she fought. By the time she was facing the last student, Edom, she was short on breath. Cleaning the inn had been good for keeping in shape, but a two-hour workout with a sword was enough to test her powers of endurance.

She opened with the same move that she'd used in all the other fights—a simple sidesweep that all the others had been able to meet. Edom fell, which should have shown him to be an utter idiot with a sword. She heard a few suppressed sniggers from the audience. But something about the fall struck her as a little off; if he had fallen from the force of the blow, he shouldn't have fallen quite as far as he had. She wasn't big enough to push him that distance without more leverage than a sidesweep allowed for.

She helped him up and handed him his sword. Grasping his wrist, she showed him the proper block and swung again. He met it that time, clumsily. She worked slowly with him at first, gradually speeding up. He progressed slowly, with nothing more odd than ineptness showing in his fighting.

She worked with him on three blocks, aiming different

attacks at him and showing how each block could be used. She was getting tired, and made a mistake that a better swordsman would never have made. She used a complex swing, difficult to execute as well as counter, and misjudged it. Horrified, she waited for her sword to cut into his leg.

He blocked it.

He shouldn't have been able to, not at his level. She wasn't sure that she could have blocked it. She certainly couldn't have executed the combination that he used. She stepped back and met his eyes. Softly, so that no one but she could hear, he said, "Can I explain in private?"

She considered a minute and nodded. Turning back to the others, she dismissed them, sending them to watch Myr, still fighting nearby.

Alone, Edom met her gaze. He shuffled a foot in the dirt. "You . . ." His voice cracked, and he cleared his throat and tried again. "You know that I'm not quite what I appear to be. I'm not even Rethian; I'm from Darran. I don't know if you know it, but Darran is under the ae'Magi's influence, too."

"Darran?" Darranians hated magic. People who could work magic left, or risked being killed. Impossible to imagine Darranians approving of the ae'Magi.

He saw her expression.

"Yes. It was pretty obvious when it happened," he said. "Scary. I said the wrong thing, and I had to run for my life." He shrugged. "I don't know why I came here. Something . . . drew me here, I guess. It seemed as good a place to go as any. I found the valley full of people like me, hiding from the ae'Magi. But they were all Rethians. Given current feelings between Darran and Reth, I could hardly tell them that I was a noble-born Darranian.

"So I told them that I was the son of a Rethian merchant. I thought that it was a good idea, I speak Rethian with a faint enough accent that I could pass for any number of western provinces—and it explained the richness of my clothes.

"Then Myr came and started this swordsmanship training. Where would a merchant's son get trained in Darranian-style swordsmanship? So I faked it."

Aralorn looked him over. "Quite a problem, I agree. What you will do is tell this all to Myr. You do it, or I will." She put a bite into her last sentence. She'd trained her share of new recruits before she became a spy—some of them needed orders that sounded like orders.

Edom balked; she saw it in his eyes. Whether it was the order, the idea of telling Myr his secret, being told what to do by a woman, who was also obviously Rethian (prejudice went both ways between Reth and Darran), or all of the above, she didn't know. Though she suspected all three. She waited while he worked it out, saw him swallow his pride with an effort.

"I've heard he's not as prejudiced as most Rethians." She waved a hand in the vague direction of the rest of the camp. "And with the lack of trained fighters here, Myr can't afford to be too picky."

Edom stared at her a moment. "I guess I'll go do that now, then." He gave her a small smile, took a deep breath, and seemed to relax. "If he doesn't kick me out, I guess it might be nice to be useful, instead of sitting on the sidelines all the time." After a brief bow to her, student to teacher, he ran off to where Myr was fighting.

Aralorn stretched wearily. Tired as she was, it had felt good to work out with a sword rather than a mop—it was almost as good as playing at staff.

The exercise had made her hot and itchy, so she wandered over to the creek. It took her a while, but she found a place deep enough to wash in, with a large flat rock that she could kneel on and avoid the worst of the mud. She ducked her head under the water—its icy temperature welcome on her overheated skin.

As she was coming up for air, she heard a newly familiar voice say, "See, I told'ja she had a funny-looking sword. Look, the handle's made out of metal."

Aralorn took her time wiping her face on her sleeve and smoothing her dripping hair away from her face. Stanis and his silent-but-grinning companion, Tobin, stood observing her. She hid a smile when she recognized Stanis's solemn-faced, feet-apart, hands-behind-his-back pose. She'd noticed that Myr did that when he was thinking.

"Have you killed anyone?" Stanis's voice was filled with gruesome interest.

She nodded solemnly as she rolled up the long sleeves of the innkeeper's son's tunic again. Maybe she should cut them, too. The boots were giving her blisters.

"You're not supposed to fight with swords that don't have wooden handles," said Stanis worriedly. "If you kill a magician with your sword, his magic will kill you."

She could have explained that any mage powerful enough to be problematical that way would certainly not need a sword to kill her. But she didn't want to scare them any worse than they already were.

"That's why I only *wound* magicians with my sword," she explained. "When I kill magicians, I always use my knife. It has a wooden grip."

"Oh," said Stanis, apparently satisfied with her answer.

They were silent for a moment, then Stanis said, "Tobin wanted to know if you would tell us about killing someone?"

"All right," agreed Aralorn. Far be it from her to give up the chance to tell stories. Her friends rolled their eyes when she started one, but children were always a good audience. She looked around for a good place. She settled on a grassy area, far enough away from the stream so that the ground was relatively dry, and sat down cross-legged. When her audience joined her, she cleared her throat and began the story.

That was where Wolf found her. Her audience had grown to include most of the camp, Myr's raggle-taggle army as enthralled as any bunch of hardened mercenaries at her favorite tavern. He walked quietly closer until he could hear what she was saying.

". . . so we snuck past the dragon's nose a second time. We had to be careful to avoid the puddles of poison that dripped from the old beast's fangs as it slept."

She had just thrown away her career and her home—no matter what the outcome of this, she had disobeyed orders. If she returned to Sianim, it would be as a criminal and a deserter. She knew that. Knew that Myr's little band of refugees was doomed unless they had the luck of the gods—and he didn't believe in luck, not good luck, anyway. Yet here she was, entertaining this grim and hopeless bunch with her relentless cheer.

"Dragon's ears"—she spoke in such serious tones that several people in her audience nodded, including, to Wolf's private amusement, Myr—"though you can't see them at all, are very acute. There we were, the four of us, loaded down with all sorts of treasures, sneaking past this huge beast that could swallow us all in one gulp. We held our very breath when we neared it. Not a sound did we make, we stepped so soft." Her voice dropped to a carrying whisper. "Now you remember those bejeweled golden goblets Wikker'd liked so well? Just as we crossed in front of the dragon . . . that great beast, he breathed out, and it was as if we were caught in a spring storm the wind was so bad. It grabbed one of Wikker's goblets, and it landed right on that giant fiend's scale-covered muzzle." She closed her eyes and looked sorrowful for a moment, waiting . . .

"What happened?" asked a hushed voice from the crowd.

Aralorn shook her head and spread her arms. "What do you expect happened? It ate us."

There was a short silence, then sheepish laughter as they realized that she'd been telling them a tall tale from the beginning. Wolf was close enough to hear Stanis's disgruntled, *"That's* not how it should have ended. You're supposed to kill the dragon."

Aralorn laughed, hopped to her feet, and ruffled the boy's hair as she passed by him. "There is another ending to the story. I'll tell you it later. Now, though, I think that I hear someone calling us for lunch."

———

Aralorn ate the last of the bread and cheese that was lunch, and Wolf touched her on the shoulder. She dusted off her hands and followed him without a word. They slipped out of camp and scaled one side of the valley. Once on the top, they followed a faint trail through the trees that led to a cliff with several dark openings, including a large, shallow-looking cave.

Wolf walked past that and took her into a smaller opening twenty paces farther along. As he entered the dark tunnel, the crystals on his staff began emitting a pale blue light. Aralorn hadn't noticed that he was carrying the staff while they were walking, but she supposed that it was just part of being a mysterious mage . . . or maybe it was just Wolf.

"These caves would make a much better shelter than the tents. Why aren't you using them?"

Wolf motioned to a small branch and halted her with a hand on her arm. He tilted the staff slightly until she realized that directly in front of them was a dark hole. "Aside from the problem of lighting them—which could be managed—there are several of these pits. That one goes down far enough to kill someone, and there are some holes deeper than that. If there were no children, you might risk it, but it's too difficult to keep them from wandering. We are storing a lot of the supplies in a few caves near the surface, and I drew up a map for Myr of a section that is pretty isolated from the main cave system. If it becomes necessary to move the camp into the caves, we can. But it is safer in the valley."

Aralorn looked at the blackness in front of them and nodded. She also stayed close to Wolf the rest of the way through the caves.

They came to a large chamber that he illuminated with a flick of a hand. The chamber was easily as spacious as the great hall in the ae'Magi's castle. Carved into all the walls were shelves covered with books. Wooden bookcases were packed tightly with more books and stacked in rows with only a narrow walkway between them. Here and there were careful stacks of volumes waiting to find places on the crowded shelves.

Aralorn whistled softly. "I thought that Ren's library was impressive. We're going to read all of these?"

Wolf shrugged. "Unless we find something before we have to read them all." As he spoke, he led her through one of the narrow pathways between bookcases to an open area occupied by a flat table that held an assortment of quills, ink, and paper. On either side of the table were small, padded benches.

Aralorn looked around, and asked, "Where do you want me to start?"

"I'll take the grimoires. Normally, I know, you can tell if something is magic, but for your safety let me look at the books before you open them. There are spells to disguise the presence of magic, and some of the grimoires are set with traps for the unwary. I'd prefer not to spend valuable time trying to resurrect you," he said.

"*Can* you resurrect people?" She kept her voice mildly curious though she'd never heard of such a thing actually happening. He'd brought all of this here from somewhere, just as he'd transported that merchant and the supplies. She was ready to believe he might bring people back from the dead.

"Let's not find out," he said dryly.

"So, what do I look for, I mean other than a book titled *Twenty-five Foolproof Ways to Destroy a Powerful and Evil Mage*?"

He gave a short laugh before he answered. "Look for the name of a mage who fought other mages. Some of these books go back a long ways, when dueling was allowed between mages. If I have a name, I might be able to find his grimoire. You also might note down any object that could be of use. Magical items are notoriously hard to find—even if they're not the creation of some bard's overactive imagination—and we don't have the leisure time to go on a quest."

She could go though the books methodically. Doubtless that was what Wolf was doing. But sometimes . . . She blew on her fingers and thought hard on how much a little luck right now would be of use. She didn't pull more than a breath of magic for it—luck magic could backfire in unexpected ways. It was best to keep such things small. Then she walked to a random shelf and took out the first book that caught her eye. She ran her fingers lightly over the metallic binding of the book. Originally, it had been silver, but it had tarnished to a dull black.

She could read the title only because she once coaxed Ren into teaching her the words inscribed on the old wall mosaics in some of the older places in Sianim. Reluctantly, she put it away without opening it, knowing that it wouldn't have anything of use. The people who used that language had disliked magic to such an extent that they burned the practitioners of it. They had been a trading people, and merchants in general were not overly fond of mages. She thought about the chubby merchant she'd seen in another cave and smiled; maybe merchants had good reason to dislike magic.

It took several more tries before she found a book that suited her and passed it by Wolf for inspection. He handed it back to her with a perfunctory nod and went back to his work.

This book was, in her estimation, about three hundred years old and told the history of a tribe of tinkers that used to roam the lands in great numbers. They were scarcer now and tended to keep to themselves. Whoever wrote the book she was reading still believed in the powers of the old gods, and he intermixed history and myth with a cynicism that she thoroughly enjoyed. Taking a piece of blank paper, she kept careful note of anything that might be potentially useful.

Her favorite was the story of the jealous chieftain whose wife was unfaithful. Frustrated, he visited the local hedge-witch, who gave him a fist-sized bronze statue of the demi-god Kinez the Faithful. When his wife kissed a man in its presence, it would come to life and kill the unlucky suitor. The chieftain had the statue placed in his wife's wagon, and after several of her favorites died, she sinned no more. Or, noted the author of the book, at least she found another place to sin.

At last satisfied that his wife would be faithful, the chieftain entered her wagon to engage in his husbandly duties. He forgot to remove the statue first. His widow became chieftain, enjoyed her widowhood, and ruled for many prosperous years.

———

Wolf wondered why it was that mages had such wretched handwriting. The fine motor skills prerequisite to spell-casting should be reflected in decent writing: His own was very nearly flawless. He painstakingly cross-checked the word he was trying to decipher with several others to compare the letters. As he was writing the actual word neatly in the space above the original in case he ever had to read the book again, he heard Aralorn laugh softly.

Safe behind the mask, he smiled at the picture she made with her quill scritching frantically along the paper. Her handwriting wasn't any better than what he'd just been attempting to read. The hand moving the quill was callused and ink-spattered. Ink also resided in blotchy patterns across her face where she'd pushed back her hair.

Reluctantly, he returned to his reading.

———

Aralorn finished her book and replaced the slender volume on its shelf. When she found another likely-looking candidate, Wolf was deeply engrossed in his grimoire, so she sat to wait.

"Wolf," she said suddenly, startled by a strange thought.

He held up a hand to ask her to wait while he finished, which she did with some impatience. Finally, he looked up.

"What is the difference between standard and green magic to you? I have always been told that human mages draw the magic from themselves while green-magic users draw power from the outside world, but didn't you say that the ae'Magi had found a way to link to outside power? That that's how he manages to push his influence all the way out to Reth and Sianim? Does that make him a green mage, too? His magic doesn't feel like green magic to me."

In typical Wolf fashion, he started his answer with a question. "How much training have you had in magic?"

She grinned at him. "Not much. You mages are not especially open to sharing knowledge even among yourselves, and the shapeshifters are not exactly fascinated by intellectual pursuits. The only thing I know even about green magic is how to use it, and in that I'm by no means an expert. I spent enough time with my mother's people to learn how to shapeshift and a few minor magics. I can feel the difference between the types of magic"—she put a fist against her heart—"here, but I don't know exactly what it means."

He grunted in acknowledgment and paused to choose his words. "I've heard that explanation, too. I would even venture that most mages believe it. That human magic is more powerful than green magic." He tapped his fingers on the table a couple of times, which surprised her. He was so shut down, so self-controlled, that to see him make a movement for no other reason than that he was collecting his thoughts was unusual.

Finally, he said, "The Ancients believed magic existed in a secret pool in the castle of the goddess of nature, and she used this magic to make the seasons change and the grass grow. One day, a clever man found a way to steal some water out of the pool without the goddess's knowing about it. He was the first human magician.

"Picture magic as a pool of raw, unshaped power that gradually seeps into the natural world to act as nature would have it—making the trees grow and the sun rise. My understanding of green magic is that it is the magic already harnessed by nature the green magician uses, persuading it with nudges here and there to take a different course. The magic that he uses is nature's magic already shaped to a purpose. It is safer and perhaps easier to use, but it is not as flexible as the raw stuff.

"If you accept that story—even just as imagery—then normal . . . *human* magic . . ." He hesitated. "At least for most magicians, it works in steps. First, the human magician must tap into the magical pool. It is like drinking through a straw—when one runs out of breath, the liquid stops flowing. The magician then takes the raw power he has gathered and uses it to form a spell or pattern that he shapes himself. The more magic the magician can pull, the stronger he is, but he needs to know the patterns into which to shape the magic and begin the shaping immediately, while he is still drawing it out, so it doesn't overwhelm him."

He looked over her head. Aralorn took a quick look, too, but didn't see anything that would hold his attention.

"If he cannot shape the magic, he must release it as raw power. Raw magic let loose in the world will take the form of fire and burn itself out. Few mages can call enough power that their uncontrolled magic will do much more than start a campfire. Because for most mages, it is the gathering of magic that is the most difficult. Containing it and making it follow one's will is generally a matter of memorizing a spell or two, although a large amount of raw magic is more difficult to shape than a smaller amount."

"Are you going to get kicked out of the secret society of mages for telling me all of this?" asked Aralorn, feeling a little breathless at the amount of knowledge he'd just given her.

"Secret society of mages?" His voice was amused, but it wasn't happy. "If there were such a society, I ripped myself free of that a long time ago. Trust me, sharing a few stories is the least of my crimes."

He looked down at the book in front of him, but she didn't think he was reading it.

"The ae'Magi, powerful as he is, could not do *this*—" His whole body was tight, and he flung a hand outward— she supposed toward outside, though she'd have to think about it for a minute before she could be sure which direction was "outside." "Could not take over the minds of a whole people without turning to older ways."

"Older ways?"

He slumped, his hands petting the book as if it gave him comfort. "There is a lot of knowledge stored in the ae'Magi's castle. They brought the things—books, artifacts, and the like—that could not be destroyed there, where they would be safely guarded against misuse. In the forbidden books, the ae'Magi found a way to leach energy so that he could use it to hold open the magical channels longer than he otherwise could have. He has greatly increased the amount of power that he can capture at any one time, making him stronger than any wizard living."

She looked at him and thought again about Cain, the ae'Magi's son. But the ae'Magi, by his actions, betrayed a lot of people. The personal knowledge that Wolf had could have come from any of the wizards who'd been close to the ae'Magi. One of his apprentices maybe. There were several who had "died" or disappeared five years or more ago—the study of magic at the higher levels wasn't any safer than being a mercenary.

"Earlier, you said that human magic works this way for most magicians, not for you?" asked Aralorn carefully.

His yellow eyes caught hers like a bird of prey's. He seemed a stranger to her, hostile almost.

Aralorn set her chin and stubbornly refused to let herself feel threatened. "How does it work for you?" she rephrased her question.

Suddenly, he relaxed and loosened his shoulders. Mildly he said, "I forget sometimes, how difficult it is to intimidate you. Very well, then; yes, it is different for me. When I started working magic, it wasn't obvious just how different I was. Not until I started working the more powerful spells did the difference make itself felt. Most magicians are limited by the magic they can draw into themselves; I am limited more by the amount of magic I can shape into a spell."

A lot, Aralorn thought, remembering the merchant he'd transported.

"I suspect that the ae'Magi"—he paused and touched her hand lightly—"who was my teacher, as you suspect"—he'd learned to read her, too, over the past few years—"knew long before I did, and separated me from the rest of his apprentices. From then on, I lacked anyone with whom to compare myself. When I was fifteen, the ae'Magi decided to try to use me to gather more power. He had me gather all the magic that I could so that he could use it."

Wolf fell silent. Aralorn waited for a minute, then asked, "Something happened?"

Wolf made a sound that could have been a laugh. "Yes, something happened. Either the method that he was trying to use wasn't successful, or he wasn't ready for the amount of power I drew; but before he could do anything, I destroyed most of the tower we were in. The stones were melted. I don't know how he managed to keep us alive, but he did. It was three months before I could bring myself to collect enough magic to light a candle." He paused for a minute, collecting his thoughts or dealing with the memory.

Aralorn waited patiently for him to continue or not, as it suited him. He had told her more about himself in the last five minutes than he'd told her in the four years she'd known him. If he chose to stop, she wasn't going to push him.

In time, he began again. "That was when he turned to the older texts. He began to experiment with drawing power from others. Not with me, because that first experiment had proved such a disaster. It was during these experiments that he found that with the aid of certain rituals—rituals forbidden even before the Wizard Wars, if you can imagine anything those wizards would have forbidden—he could use the power of untrained magic-users, especially children. They don't have the defenses that others do." He stopped again, his golden eyes bleak.

———

I should stop here, he thought. She knew what he did now about the ae'Magi. If something happened to him, she might be about to find another mage—surely some of the more powerful mages could work themselves free, if the half-trained wreck that he'd been had managed it. But he was consumed by the desire, the *need* to let her glimpse the monster that he was, to destroy her belief that Wolf, her wolf, was some kind of paladin for right and justice.

"For a long time, I helped him," he continued. To his surprise his voice was still its sepulchral self, cool tones that gave no hint of the volcano of emotion that seethed within him. It sounded as though he were telling the story about someone else. "You need to know that." *I need you to know that.* "Even though I knew what he was. I used dark magic, knowing it was evil. I worked his will and gloried in the power and the madness of it. Knowing what he was, I tried to please him."

His hands gripped the table until they were white-knuckled, he noticed, but he couldn't force them loose. Maybe she wouldn't see them. Maybe he didn't care if she did.

"What happened?" she asked. As if she were pulling information for an assignment, something that had nothing to do with her.

When he didn't speak, she did. "What happened? What changed?"

Didn't she understand what he'd told her? Where was her fear? Her disgust? Then he remembered—she was a green mage, not a real one. She wouldn't know exactly how bad it was, how evil the things he'd done. The screams of the innocent and the not-so-innocent—he could still hear them sometimes when he permitted himself to.

He released his grip on the table abruptly. He didn't want to hurt her, he reminded himself, and if he let himself get . . . She wanted a story, something pleasing, something hopeful. Something he could talk about without touching on things best left alone.

He started almost at random. "When I was young, the passages of the ae'Magi's castle fascinated me." That was good, he could feel something settle down. "I wandered through them for hours, sometimes days." When he could.

While the ae'Magi traveled, or had to attend to others who couldn't know what he did. "There are places in the passages that haven't seen human hands for generations." The discovery of those safe, dark ways had saved him, he thought. "About a year before I left the castle, I found an abandoned library. A whole library that no one but me had been in for a very long time." A private library, he thought later. Some ae'Magi had picked out favorite books and tucked them away where he could keep them to himself.

"It fascinated me. Almost everything that I had read before I found the library was grimoires and the like. Books I had been told to study." Endless lists, useless, weak, or broken spells, he figured out later. Things to keep him busy without really educating him. "There were books in the little room of another ilk entirely. Someone had collected books about people—histories, biographies, myths, and legends. I learned from what I read." He hesitated, understanding for the first time that he'd actually been answering her question—what had happened to change his path. He looked at her, but her face was still, intent on picking through every word he gave her. Impossible to tell what she was thinking, when she was just listening.

"What I learned made my current occupation . . . more distasteful. So I left." Those were Aralorn's words when she told people why she was no longer filling the role of daughter to one of the best-loved heroes in Reth. He wondered if those words covered up as much for her as they did for him.

She smiled at him and touched her finger to her temple in salute. She'd heard the echo.

The smile let him end his story as lightly as he'd tried to begin it. "Departing the castle was easy enough; but changing what I am has proven to be more challenging."

"If you change into one of those zealots who give everything they have to the poor and go around all the time telling everyone else to do the same, I will feed you to the Uriah myself."

She startled a laugh out of him, and he shook his head in mock reproof. "*You* ought to watch what you say around me. I might forget that I have repented of my evil ways and turn you into something really nasty."

FIVE

Myr, Aralorn decided approvingly, had the soul of a sergeant where a king's should have been. Sometime during the night, he had apparently decided that the camp needed improvement more than the refugees' weapons skills did.

After breakfast, anyone who could ply a needle was sent to turn yards of fabric into a tent. The design of the tent was Myr's own, based loosely on tents used by the northern trappers.

When the project was finished, there would be three large tents that could house the population of the camp through the winter. The tents would be stretched over sturdy frames, designed to withstand the weight of the snow. The exterior of the tent was sewn with a double wall so it could be stuffed with dry grass that would serve as insulation in the winter. A simple, ingenious flap system would make it possible to keep a fire inside the tent.

Those who could not sew, or who were too slow to grab the needles Myr had also procured, were put to work building what Myr termed "the first priority of any good camp"—the lavatories.

The risk of disease was very real in any winter camp, and any military man knew stories of regiments destroyed by plagues because of the lack of adequate waste facilities. Myr's grandfather had been a fanatic on the subject. Myr, thought Aralorn with private amusement, was more like his grandfather than some people in the camp could appreciate.

Aralorn, needleless and worried that Myr would notice, searched futilely for Wolf and noticed Edom looking frustrated as he was trying to stop the tears of a little girl in a ragged purple dress.

"I want Mummy. She always knows how to fix it so her hat doesn't come off." Clutched in the child's grubby hand was an equally grubby doll.

"Astrid, you know that your mum isn't here and can't help you," said Edom impatiently. This was the child who'd been rescued by a stranger in Wolf's caves. Aralorn looked at her with interest. How had a girl as young as Astrid made it to the camp safely without kin? Maybe someone had brought her—she'd ask Wolf. In the meantime, she couldn't leave Edom so obviously over his head.

"Hello, Astrid," Aralorn said, and got a suspicious look in return.

After a wary second, the girl said, "Hullo."

"Boys don't know how to dress dolls," said Aralorn, squatting down until she was at eye level.

Astrid looked at her distrustfully for a minute before slowly holding out doll and hat.

Years of being the oldest daughter of fourteen gave Aralorn the experience to twist the hat on at just the right angle so that it slipped firmly over the doll's wooden head and caught on the notch that had been carved to hold it in place. Astrid took the doll in one hand and smeared her tear-wet cheeks with the other.

"Can you see if you can get all of you young ones over here?" asked Aralorn. Astrid nodded and ran off.

Turning to Edom, Aralorn said, "I take it that you are supposed to be keeping an eye on the children?"

Edom rolled his eyes. "Always."

"I can relieve you for a while if you like."

He nodded and took off with a grin before she could take it back. She wondered if he'd be as pleased when Myr cornered him for latrine duty.

She had the children sit in a semicircle around her. Some of them did it with a sort of hopelessness that broke her heart. Astrid was the youngest by several years. Most of them were ten or eleven, with a few older and a few more younger. There were more girls than boys. Wary eyes, eager eyes, restless eyes, children were a much more difficult audience than adults because no one had yet had a chance to teach them that it was better to be polite than honest.

Before she began, she looked at their faces to help her select a story. At breakfast, Stanis had told her that most of them hadn't been there much over a month. None of them had any family at the camp, and judging by Astrid's tears, they were all feeling lost.

She sat cross-legged and looked at them. "Do you have a favorite story? I won't claim to know every story anywhere, but I know most of the common ones."

" 'Kern's Bog'?" suggested one girl. "Kern's Bog" was a romantic story about a boy and his frog.

" 'The Smith,' " said Tobin in a rusty little voice. Everyone looked at him, so Aralorn guessed that it wasn't just in her company that he was mute. "My pa, he told me it. Right before I had to leave."

It wasn't a gentle story, or, really, a children's story. But, she supposed, sometimes a story isn't about entertaining.

"All right," she agreed. "But you will have to help me if I get parts wrong or forget things. Can you do that?"

She waited until they agreed.

"Very well," she said, sitting back and settling into the proper frame of mind. "Once upon a time, when the old gods walked the earth and interested themselves with the affairs of men, there lived a smith in a small village. The smith was skilled, and his name was known far and wide. Although he was a gentle man, he lived in a time of war and so spent most of his day shoeing the great warhorses of the nobility, mending their weapons, and creating and repairing their armor."

A hand went up.

She stopped and tilted her head, inviting a dirty girl with two mismatched braids to speak.

"He didn't do it to get rich," she said. "It was because the war made food expensive. And if he didn't make swords and stuff, his family would have starved."

Aralorn nodded. "These things he did so that he would have money to live, for food was scarce and dear. But at night, in the privacy of the forge, he created other things. Sometimes they were practical, like rakes and hoes or buckles. Sometimes, though, he made things whose only purpose was to be beautiful."

"The war god," said a boy, one of the younger ones, jumping to his feet. "The war god comed. He comed and tried to take the beautiful thing for himself."

"Hands, please," said Aralorn.

The boy's hand shot up.

"Yes?"

"The war god comed," he said in a much more polite voice.

"So he did," she agreed. "Temris, the god of war, broke his favorite sword in battle. He heard of the smith's skill and came to the village one night and knocked upon the smithy door.

"The smith had been working on a piece of singular beauty—a small intricately wrought tree of beaten iron and silver wire bearing upon each branch a single, golden fruit." It had always sounded to her like something a gold-smith or silversmith might make, but it was an old story. Maybe back then a smith did all those things: shod horses, made armor and jewelry. "Temris saw it and coveted it and, as was the custom of the gods when they wanted some-thing from a mortal, demanded it."

"'Cause he was greedy," someone said.

She looked around, but no hands went up, so she ignored the comment. They were all old enough to know proper protocol for storytelling. "The smith refused. He said, 'You who are creator of war cannot have something that is rooted in the hope of peace.'"

Stanis raised his hand. "How come a tree with fruit is rooted in the hope of peace?"

Tobin said, "My father said it was because during a war there aren't any fruits on any trees."

Aralorn looked at the solemn little faces and wished Tobin had chosen a happier story. "The smith cast the statue to the ground, and such was his anger, he shattered it into a thousand thousand pieces. Temris was angered that a lowly smith would deny him anything." Aralorn dropped her voice as low as she could and spoke slowly, as befitted a god of war. "'I say now, smith, that you will forge only three more pieces, and these will be weapons of destruc-tion such as the world has never before seen. Your name will be forever tied to them, and you will be known forever as the Smith.'

"The smith was horrified, and for many days he sat alone in the forge, not daring to work for fear of Temris's words. During this time, he prayed to Mehan, the god of love, ask-ing that he not be forced to build the instruments of another man's destruction. It may be that his prayer was answered, for one day he was seized by a fit of energy that left all the village amazed. For three fortnights he labored, day and night, neither eating nor sleeping until his work was done."

"My ma said that if you spent six weeks not eating, you'd starve to death," said one of the older girls.

"Not if the gods don't want them to," said Tobin fiercely. "Not if they have things to do that are important."

"Quiet, please," Aralorn told them. "Raise your hand if you have something to help me."

They settled down, so she resumed the story. "The weapons he created could only be used by humans, not gods. He made them to protect the weak from the strong. He built Nekris the Flame, which was a lance made of a strange material: a red metal that shimmered like fire."

A hand was raised. "It kills sea monsters," Aralorn's newest helper informed her.

Aralorn nodded. "It was Nekris that King Taris used to drive the sea monster back into the depths when it would have destroyed his city.

"The second weapon was the mace, Sothris the Black. The weapon that, according to legend, was responsible for one of the nine deaths of Temris himself. It was used during the Wizard Wars to destroy some of the abominations created in the desperate final days.

"The last weapon was the sword, Ambris, called also the Golden Rose. There are no stories about Ambris. Some say that it was lost or that the gods hid it away for fear of its power. But others, and I think they are right, say it was hidden until a time of great need."

"Donkey warts!" exclaimed Stanis wide-eyed. "Your sword is a rosy color and kind of gold."

She raised her eyebrows and pulled it out so all the children could see it. "Well, so it is."

"It's kinda puny, though," said one young boy a year or two older than Stanis, after careful inspection.

She nodded seriously. "I think you're right. Ambris is big enough that only a strong warrior could hold her. This sword was built for a small person—like me or you."

The boy gave her a little grin of solidarity.

"A big strong warrior like our King Myr?" asked someone else.

She sheathed her sword before someone decided to
touch it and got cut. "Exactly like our King Myr."

Stanis, evidently deciding the topic of Ambris had been
covered enough, said, "Do you know any other stories?
Other ones about swords an' gods an' stuff? I like 'em
with blood an' fight'n, but Tobin says that it might scare
the young'uns."

Aralorn grinned and started to reply, but noticed that
Wolf was waiting nearby. Beside him was Edom. "It looks
like I'll have to wait and tell you a story another time.
Remind me to tell you the one about a boy, his dog, and a
monster named Taddy."

Edom came up to her. "Thank you for the break," he
said with a short bow. "I am most grateful. But Wolf says
he needs you more than Myr needs another hand at the
trenches."

"Watching the children is better than digging?" she
asked.

He grinned. "Absolutely. Hey, Stanis, how about you
help me get a game of Hide the Stone going?"

And a moment later they were all running for the bushes
to search for just the right stone.

"So you wield Ambris now?" Wolf commented, walking toward her when Edom and the children were gone.

She hopped to her feet. "Of course. I am Aralorn, Hero
of Sianim and Reth, didn't you know?"

"No." She heard the smile in his voice. "I hadn't heard."

She shook her head and started for the caves. "You need
to get out more, have a few drinks in a tavern, and catch up
on the news."

"I think," he said, "even as isolated as we are here, I
should have heard of the woman who wields Ambris."

Aralorn laughed. "Half the young men in Sianim
paint their maces black. And at the Red Lance Inn of the

Fortieth's favor, just a few blocks from the government building, there's a bronze ceremonial lance on the wall that the innkeeper swears is Nekris. I guess we don't have to worry about the ae'Magi, you and I. We'll just take Nekris and Ambris to destroy him."

After a few silent steps, she said, "I will admit, though, that when I found it in the old weapons hall at Lambshold, when I was a kid not much older than these, I used to pretend I'd found Ambris."

She drew the sword and held it up for his inspection. It gleamed pinkish gold in the sunlight, but aside from the admittedly unusual color, it was plain and unadorned. "It was probably made for a woman or young boy, see how slender it is?" She turned the blade edgewise. "The color is probably the result of a smith mixing metals to make it strong enough not to break even if it is small enough for a woman. Even the metal hilt isn't unusual. Before the population of magic-users began to recover from the Wizard Wars, there were many swords made with a metal grip. It has only been in the last two hundred years that metal hilts have become rare." As if he needed her to tell him that. "Sorry," she said sheepishly. "That's what happens when I've been storytelling to the children."

"How long did you pretend she was Ambris?" asked Wolf.

"Not long," she said. "No magic in her. Not human, not green, not any. And I was forced to concede that the Smith's Weapons would be rife with magic." She gave him a rueful smile. "Not to mention bigger, as is fitting for a weapon built to slay gods."

"She might not be Ambris, but"—Aralorn executed a few quick moves—"she's light and well balanced and takes a good edge. Who can ask anything more than that? I don't need a sword for anything else, so she suits my purposes. I don't use a sword when a knife or staff will do, so I don't have to worry about accidentally killing a magician." She sheathed the sword and gave it a fond pat.

The route that they took from the cave mouth to the library was different this time. Aralorn wasn't sure whether it was deliberate or just habit. Wolf traversed the twisted passages without hesitating, ducking the cave formations as they appeared in the light from the crystals in his staff, but she had the feeling that if she weren't there, he wouldn't need the light at all.

The library was as they had left it. Aralorn soon started skimming books rather than reading them—even so, the sheer volume of the library was daunting. Once or twice, she found that the book that she arrived at the table with wasn't the one that she thought she had picked up. The fourth time that it happened, she was certain that it wasn't just that she had picked up a different book by mistake: The book that she had taken off the shelf was unwieldy. The one that she set in front of Wolf to look over was little more than a pamphlet.

Intrigued, she returned to the shelf where she'd gotten the book and found the massive tome she thought she'd taken sitting where she'd found it. She tapped it thoughtfully, then smiled to herself—wizards' libraries, it seemed, had a few idiosyncrasies. It certainly wasn't her luck spell—that had dissipated a few minutes after she cast it.

Wolf had taken no notice of her odd actions but set the thin, harmless book on her side of the table and returned to what he termed "the unreadable scribbles of a mediocre and half-mad warlock who passed away into much-deserved obscurity several centuries before: safe from the curses of an untrained magician, however powerful."

Aralorn, returning to the table, listened to his half-voiced mutterings with interest. The mercenaries of Sianim were possessed of a wide variety of curses, mostly vulgar, but Wolf definitely had a creative touch.

Still smiling, Aralorn opened the little book and began reading. Like most of the books *she* chose, this one was a collection of tales. It was written in an old Rethian dialect that wasn't too difficult to read. The first story was a version of the tale of the Smith's Weapons that she hadn't read before. Guiltily, because she knew that it wasn't going to be of any help defeating the ae'Magi, she took quick notes of the differences before continuing to another story.

The writer wasn't half-bad, and Aralorn quit skimming the stories and read them instead, noting down a particularly interesting turn of phrase here and a detail there. She was a third of the way through the last story in the book before she realized just what she was reading. She stopped and went back to the beginning, reading it for information rather than entertainment.

Apparently, the ae'Magi (the one ruling at the time that the book was written, whenever that was) had, as an apprentice, designed a new spell. He presented it to his master to that worthy's misfortune. The spell was one that nullified magic, an effect that the apprentice's two-hundred-year-old master would have appreciated more had he been out of the area of the spell's effect.

Aralorn hunted futilely for the name of the apprentice-turned-ae'Magi or even any indication when the book was written. Unfortunately, during most of Rethian history, it had not been the custom to note the date a book was written or even who wrote it. With a collection of stories, most of which were folktales, it was virtually impossible to date the book reliably within two hundred years, especially one that was probably a copy of another book.

With a sigh, Aralorn set the book down and started to ask Wolf if he had any suggestions. Luckily she glanced at him before a sound left her mouth. He was in the midst of unraveling a spell worked into a lock on a mildewed book

as thick as her hand. She'd grown so used to the magic
feel of the lighting, she hadn't noticed when the amount of
magic had increased.

He didn't seem to be having an easy time with it, although
it was difficult to judge from his masked face. She frowned
at his mask resentfully.

"Doesn't that thing ever bother you?" she asked in an
I-am-only-making-conversation tone as soon as the lock
popped open with a theatrical puff of blue smoke.

"What thing?" He brushed the remaining blue dust off
the cover of the book and opened it to a random page.

"The mask. Doesn't it itch when you sweat?"

"Wolves don't sweat." His tone was so uninterested
that she knew that it was a safe topic to push even though
he was deliberately avoiding her point. And he did, too,
sweat—when he was in human form, anyway.

"You know," she said, running a finger over a dust pattern on a leather book cover, "when my father took me to
visit the shapeshifters, I thought that it would be really
fun to be able to be someone else whenever I wanted. So I
learned and worked at it until I could look like almost any
person I wanted. My father, though, had an uncanny knack
of finding me out, and he was a creative genius when it
came to punishments. Eventually, I got out of the habit of
shapechanging at all.

"The second time that I visited with my mother's people, I was several years older. I noticed something that
time that I'd missed the first time. If a shapeshifter doesn't
like something about himself, she can just change it. If her
nose is too long or her eyes aren't the right color, it is easily altered. If she did something that she wasn't proud of,
then she could be someone else for a while until everyone
forgot about it. They, all of them, hide from themselves
behind their shapes until there isn't anything left to hide
from."

"I assure you," commented Wolf dryly, "that as much as

I would like to hide from myself, it would take more than a mask to do it."

"Then why do you wear it?" she asked. "I don't mean out there." She waved impatiently in the general direction of camp.

"It's that way," Wolf said, moving her hand until it pointed in a different direction.

"You know what I mean," she huffed. "I am sure that you have your reasons for wearing a mask out there. But why do you use it to hide from me, too? I am hardly likely to tell everyone who you are if that is what you're hiding."

He tensed but answered with the same directness that she had shown. "I have reasons for the mask that have nothing to do with trust or the lack of it."

She held his eyes. "Don't they? There are only the two of us in this room."

"Cave," he interjected mildly.

She conceded his correction but not the change of subject. " 'Cave,' then. A mask is something to hide behind. If I am the only one here to look at your face, then you are hiding from me. You don't trust me."

"Plague take it, Aralorn," he said in a low voice, stealing her favorite oath. "I have reasons to wear this mask." He tapped it. There was enough temper in his eyes, if not his voice, that a prudent person would have backed down.

Not even her enemies had ever called Aralorn prudent.

"Not with me." She wouldn't retreat.

He closed his eyes and took a deep breath and opened them again. The glitter of temper had been replaced by something that she couldn't read. "The mask is more honest than what is beneath it." There was emotion coloring his voice, but it was disguised so it could have been as mild as sorrow or as wild as the rage portrayed by the mask.

She waited, knowing that if she commented on his obscure statement, he was fully capable of sidetracking her into his peculiar philosophical mishmash until she forgot her purpose.

When he saw that she wasn't going to speak, he said softly, "I find that trust is hard for me to learn, Lady."

There was nothing obvious holding the mask on his face, no hidden straps to hinder him when he put his hands up and undid the simple spell. He gripped the mask and took it off smoothly. She probably only imagined the slight hesitation before his face was revealed.

She'd been certain it was his identity that he hid. If she had been another person she might have gasped. But she had seen burn victims before, even a few who were worse—most of those had been dead. The area around the golden eyes was unscarred, as if he'd protected them with an arm. The rest of his face matched his voice: It could have belonged to a corpse. It had that same peculiar tight look as if the skin was too small. His mouth was drawn so tightly that he must have trouble eating. She knew now why his voice had sounded muffled, the words less clearly enunciated than they had been when he took wolf shape.

She looked for a long time, longer than she needed to so that she could think of the best way to react. Then she stood up and walked around the table, bent over, and kissed him lightly on the lips.

Returning to her seat, she said quietly, her eyes on his face, "Leave your mask off when we are here alone, if you will. I would rather look at you than a mask."

He smiled warmly at her, with his eyes. Then he answered what she didn't feel free to ask. "It was that spell of which I lost control. I told you that uncontrolled magic takes the shape of flame." As he spoke, he clenched his fist, then opened it to show her the fire it held. "Human flesh burns easier than stone, and the ae'Magi wasn't able to extend his shield to me fast enough."

When he was fifteen, he'd said. It took effort, but she

sensed that he was still uncertain, so she grinned at him and playfully knocked his hand aside. "Get that out of here. You, of all people, should know better than to play with fire." She knew by his laugh that she had taken the right tack, and she was glad for the years of acting that allowed her to lighten the mood.

Obediently, he extinguished the flame, and with no more ceremony than he usually exhibited, he turned back to his book. Aralorn went to the nearest bookcase and picked out another book.

After it had been duly inspected for traps and pitfalls, she opened it and pretended to read as she pondered several other questions that popped up. Things like: Why couldn't a magician, who could take on the form of a wolf indefinitely, alter his face until it was scarless? The most likely answer to that was that he didn't want to. *That* led to a whole new set of questions.

She was so engrossed in thought that she jumped at the sound of Wolf's voice as he announced that it was time to leave. She set the book she'd opened on the table, on top of the book she'd forgotten to tell Wolf about. Tomorrow was soon enough for both books. As she started after Wolf, she caught a motion out of the corner of her eye; but when she turned, there was nothing there. Nonetheless, she felt the itch of being watched by unseen eyes all the way through the caverns. Places where magic was worked often felt like that, so she didn't say anything.

As they left the caves, Aralorn noted that there were faded markings just inside the entrance. Some sort of warding was her guess because they had been drawn around the cave mouth. There had been people here long before them, she thought while touching the faint pattern lightly. Under her fingertips, she felt a sweet pulse of green magic.

Outside, the gray skies carried the dimness of early evening. Reluctant drops of rain fell here and there, icy and cold on her skin. There was no wind near the caves but Aralorn could hear its relentless spirit weaving its way through the nearby trees. She looked apprehensively at the sky. It was still too early for snow, but the mountains were renowned for their freak storms, and the icy rain boded ill.

Seeing her glance, Wolf said, "There will be no snow tonight at least. Tomorrow, maybe. If it hits too soon, we might have to move them into the caves. I would rather not do it; it's too easy to get lost, as has already been demonstrated. Next time there might not be a rescue." She saw that he had replaced the mask without her noticing when he did it.

———

Though it did not snow, it might as well have. The storm that hit that night was violent and cold. The wind carelessly shredded the makeshift tents that still comprised most of the camp. Everybody huddled in the tents that leaked the least and waited out the storm. It left as abruptly as it had struck. With the wind gone, the body heat from the huddled people warmed the remaining overpopulated tents. Tired as they were, everyone, with the exception of the second-shift night watch, was soon fast asleep.

Aralorn woke to the sound of a stallion's whistle. There was probably a mare in heat. She swore softly, but when Sheen whistled again, she knew she had to go quiet him before he woke the camp. It probably would be a good idea to check on the horses after the storm anyway.

She reached under the furs she slept on—not an easy feat with so many others sleeping on the furs, too—and strapped on her knife. Carefully, she stepped over the slumbering bodies and threaded her way to the door.

Once outside, she jogged toward the corral. Sheen's light gray underbelly was easy to see against the darkness. Just as he was about to cry out again, he saw her and came toward her, hopping because of the hobble. She looked him over, but saw nothing unusual.

He shifted abruptly, as if the wind brought a scent to his nose. His attention was focused high on the ridge surrounding the valley. Every muscle tensed, and only a quick word from Aralorn kept him quiet.

It could have been only the scent of one of the two guards Myr posted every night in shifts or, more probably, a wild animal of some sort. For her own peace of mind, Aralorn decided to trek up the side of the valley and see if she could locate whatever was disturbing the stallion. She commanded him to silence again, told him to wait, and started the climb.

The terrain was more cliff than anything else. There was an easier trail over more-exposed ground, but she chose to stay in the sparse cover of the tough brush that grew here and there. Once on the crest, crouched in the dense thicket of young willows that surrounded the valley, she glanced back down to see if Sheen was still upset.

His attention was still focused, but he could have just been watching her. Swearing softly to herself, she crept through the brush. If it had been a wild animal, it was probably long gone, or waiting for a nice tasty human to join it for its evening meal—wasn't it dragons that were supposed to enjoy feasting on young women?

She tripped over it before she saw it—or rather him. He was very dead. She called a dim light ball that would allow her to get a better look at the corpse without drawing attention to herself.

It was one of the guards—Pussywillow, the one-armed veteran. He had been killed recently, because the body was still warm, even in the chill of the wet foliage. What really bothered Aralorn was the way he'd been killed. He'd probably been knocked out, judging by the lump on his head. With him unconscious and unable to struggle, it had been an easy matter to cut his heart out of his chest and carve the skin of his chest with runes. The same runes she'd seen the ae'Magi cut into living skin.

Impulsively, she traced a symbol over one of the bloody runes. She knew that certain symbols and runes held a power of their own, independent of green or human designation. Once when she and Wolf had been traveling, she had seen him trace the symbol with a stick held in his jaws (he'd been in his wolf guise). Curious, as always, she asked him the meaning of it. Wolf told her that it was a symbol that simply promoted good rest and taught it to her at her request. She hoped it would help.

She started to run around the edge of the valley without worrying about cover. She almost hoped to draw the attention of the killer; she was able to take care of herself better than almost anyone else in the camp. From the signs around the body, there had been only one person, but he was skillful.

Heart pounding, and not from effort, she searched the darkness for some clue as to his whereabouts. Less than halfway around the camp, she found the other guard. The woman's heart lay, still hot, on the grass that was too dark even in the night.

She had probably been killed after Aralorn found the first body. The killer, safe in his knowledge that there was no second guard to worry about, had taken his time and done the ritual more properly, though still without active magic use that might have alerted Wolf (or anyone else in the camp, for that matter). The guard had been awake for the ceremony, gagged so that she could make no sound. A small pewter drinking glass lay near the body, stained dark with blood.

Gently, Aralorn closed the open eyes.

Taking stock of her position, Aralorn realized that she was no more than a hundred yards from Wolf's camp. It would be wiser to have two people looking for the killer. Finding the camp from her position on top of the rim was not as easy as finding it from the bottom, though; there were no trails to lead her to it.

Just as she decided that her time would be better spent trying to locate the enemy, she saw the light from the meager campfire Wolf preferred. With a sigh of relief, she made her way down the steep slope, taking the path slowly to avoid twisting an ankle.

Without warning, a violent surge of magical backlash drove her to her knees. She waited until the wash of magic dulled to a point that it was no longer painful before struggling back to her feet. Forgetting caution, she grabbed a stick and used it for balance as she slid down the hill, announcing her presence with a modest avalanche of stones and dirt.

She slid to a stop just above the small, flat area that Wolf had appropriated as his camp. Wolf, in human form, lay unmoving on his back, eyes glistening with rage. Narrow luminous white ropes lay across his legs, chest, and neck.

Edom stood over him, his attention momentarily diverted to Aralorn. Half-raised in his right hand, he held a sword that was *not* the sword he'd been using in the sparring match. It glowed gently, with a pulsating lavender light.

The sight of it sent a cold chill up Aralorn's back as she recognized the weapon for what it was: a souleater. The last of them was supposed to have been destroyed centuries ago—but, she reminded herself grimly, that was storytelling for you: You could only trust it so far.

Even minor wounds from a souleater could be mortal.

The section of the ledge that she stood on was just far enough above Edom to be out of the sword's reach. Crying out an alarm to the camp, she drew her knife and shifted it lightly by the blade in a thrower's grip. At this distance she didn't even need to aim, so she had it in the air before he would have been able to see what it was she threw. He certainly shouldn't have been able to dodge it, but her blade landed harmlessly on the ground behind him.

The speed of his move told her that he was a much better fighter than he had shown himself to be. Easily good

enough that he could have fooled her into thinking him
unskilled if he'd wanted to. Darranians being singularly
prejudiced against women, she thought, Edom probably
simply hadn't bothered.

His face, revealed more by the light of the souleater than
the modest campfire, appeared older—although that could
simply have been an effect of the light. He smiled at her.

She was unarmed against him. Normally that wouldn't
have worried her, but the souleater made the situation
anything but normal. She could only hope to hold out
until someone from the camp got there. Preferably lots of
someones.

All the shapes that she could take quickly were suited
to her chosen trade as a spy: the mouse, several types of
birds, a few insects. Nothing that would hold off an experienced swordsman for long enough to keep both her and
Wolf alive.

She took an apparently involuntary step sideways, away
from Edom, and lost her footing. She made sure that the
fall carried her past Wolf's ledge and on down the hill into
some brush.

Edom had two options, either he would follow her
down, getting more distance between that sword and Wolf,
or he would turn to finish Wolf off—giving her the extra
few seconds that she needed. She planned for either—and
he turned back to finish his business with Wolf.

She chose the first form that she could think of; it was
deadly, though small. The icelynx had no trouble with the
steep climb and launched herself at Edom's back before he
even had his sword raised at Wolf.

Warned by the brief shadow she caused when she ran
in front of the fire, Edom turned—sweeping aside her
rush with his sword arm, but not before she raked his back
with her formidable claws. Hissing, she faced him as she
crouched between him and Wolf, still held captive on the
ground.

Pale sword and paler cat feinted back and forth: she, just out of reach of the lethal blade; he, careful not to expose himself to the poisonous fangs of the icelynx.

Suddenly, Edom spoke softly as if not to antagonize the cat, though his tone carried anxious desperation. "It's Aralorn. She's a shapeshifter, don't you see it? She's here to destroy us, betray us. I came up to ask Wolf about something, and I found her here, with Wolf like that. You've all heard of the arcane practices of shapeshifters. Help me before she kills him. Quick now."

Aralorn didn't have to look to see what her nose had belatedly informed her. A half dozen armed people from camp had just shown up to rescue the wrong person. They were too far to do anything—yet. It wouldn't take them long to reach her.

She couldn't speak when in animal form without more preparation—which she was too busy to do—and so was without her most formidable weapon.

Edom continued, even as he tried to maneuver closer to Wolf. "I've heard that shapeshifters need to kill when the moon is full. I guess that Wolf, out here alone, seemed an easy victim. I found this sword near, it must be Wolf's. She seems afraid of it."

Aralorn knew that she had to do something before the time to act was gone entirely. If he succeeded, Wolf would be dead. Disregarding the sword, she leapt at his throat while Edom was still distracted by the sound of his own voice.

She missed as he threw himself flat on the ground. However, Edom managed to nick her with the sword as she passed him. Her rear leg became icily numb and folded underneath her, but worse was the strange sucking sensation that consumed her. The sword was alive, and it was hungry.

Edom quickly regained his feet. On three legs, fighting the pull of the sword, she didn't have much of a chance. Aralorn watched as the sword descended.

Abruptly, it was jerked out of its intended path. Aralorn could feel the sword's intense disappointment as Edom was suddenly consumed in flames. The smell of burning flesh offended her feline-sensitive nose almost as much as the light bothered her nocturnal eyes.

Apparently, someone—she found out later that it was Stanis—had finally thought to remove the ropes holding Wolf down. The spells that allowed the ropes to hold him unable to move or work magic didn't keep someone from simply pulling them off.

Wolf did a more thorough job of burning Edom than was absolutely necessary, but then it must have been maddening to lie there and know what was going on without being able to do anything about it.

She yowled at him demandingly. With her leg numb and the odd dizziness that accompanied the wound, she was stuck where she was—too close to the flames. He also made her nervous, putting so much effort into burning a dead body. He needed a distraction. When the yowl didn't do it, she rolled until she could bite him on the ankle, hard enough that he could feel it, but not hard enough to release the venom in the glands underneath her fangs.

Abruptly, she was gathered up and set gently down on his bedroll. Wolf grabbed his staff from wherever he put it when he wasn't using it and balanced it on its feet so that he could examine her wound in more certain light. She noticed with interest that the rest of the camp was staying well away from them. Well, Wolf's pyrotechnics had been pretty impressive.

Wolf traced a quick design over the wound with a finger; Aralorn decided that it was to break the sword's hold rather than close the wound, since human magic-users were not the best healers. Nothing seemed to change. He frowned and traced it again, and this time she could feel the power that he used. Still nothing happened. She meowed at him nervously. He ignored her and chanted a few words.

Abruptly he stood and looked toward the crispy skeleton that was all that was left of Edom. Aralorn rolled to stand shakily on her three good legs to see what he was looking at. At first she didn't see it, but a flicker of movement caught her eye. It was the sword. Edom, or the thing that was Edom, had kept its grip on the sword. Now it lay a good foot away from the body. Except for the flicker that caught her eye at first, she hadn't seen it move again—but it was undeniably closer to her than it had been when she'd first seen it.

The coldness that numbed her leg seemed abruptly to be spreading. It could have been her imagination, spurred by the thought that the sword was coming for her. Aralorn lost her precarious balance and fell, missing exactly what Wolf did.

With a harsh, almost human cry of anguish that she heard only partly though her ears, the sword broke. Abruptly, the numbness ceased, and for a brief moment the pain made her wish it back; then it was only a small cut that bled a little.

The icelynx twitched its stubby tail and exploded to its feet with legendary speed. When she was sure all her legs were working, Aralorn arched purring against Wolf, who was still kneeling beside the blankets.

When she'd stood, she heard someone cry out, reminding her that there was an audience. Looking at all the fear and hostility in the surrounding faces, Aralorn decided that it might defuse matters if they weren't being reminded that she was a shapeshifter. She transformed herself into her usual shape and dusted off the innkeeper's son's tunic that was looking the worse from her roll down the wet hillside. Surreptitiously, she kept a close eye on the others. She'd expected them to be worried about her, but they were all staring at Wolf.

He had furnished an excellent display of what happens when a wizard with his strength lost his temper. They all must have known that he was powerful, but knowing something and seeing it were different matters.

Most people also lacked the casual acceptance of gore that mercenaries had. It didn't help that Wolf didn't wear his mask to sleep in, and his horribly scarred visage had been clearly revealed in the flaring light. He wore his mask now, but the knowledge of what lay underneath it was with them all. What was really needed at that moment was someone to take control.

Aralorn looked around to see if she could find Myr, but he was conspicuous by his absence. There was always the possibility that he was still asleep, unaffected by the magic disturbance that had waked the rest of the camp; but, given what she knew about him, Aralorn thought that unlikely. The noise alone should have brought him out.

As the thought crossed her mind, Myr—his clothes covered with bits of brush and blood—took the same path down the side of the hill that she had. *Plague it.* She must have woken him up when she went to check on the horses. If he'd been following her around, there was a good chance that he thought that she'd been the one who murdered the guards. As she had not been trying to hide anything, her footprints would be much more conspicuous than Edom's.

Myr ignored the commotion in favor of investigating the blackened corpse. Aralorn wondered how much he hoped to learn from the scorched, skeletal remains, and suspected he was using the time to think. When he stood up, he seemed slightly paler, though it could have been a trick of the light.

Composedly, he directed his question at Wolf. "Who was it?"

"Edom," answered Wolf, his chilling voice even rougher than usual. If Wolf's hand hadn't been locked on her shoulder with a bruising grip, Aralorn would have thought him unaffected by the events of the night. It was obvious from

the incredulous looks they directed at Wolf that most in the
little gathering were disturbed by his calmness.

"Is he the victim or the attacker?" asked Myr, voicing
the question that was on almost everyone's mind.

"The attacker and the victim, though he didn't intend
to be the latter," answered Aralorn, deciding to take part
in her defense. Myr, at least, had already known what she
was. She continued to tell them what she had done and
the discovery of the dead guards. "I came to see if Wolf
wanted to help track him down and found Edom with his
nasty little sword drawn, standing over Wolf."

An unfamiliar voice asked, "How do we know she's
telling the truth? She could have laid a spell on Master
Wolf so that he thinks that she has the right of it. Shapeshifters can do things like that. Edom was just a boy. Why
would he attack Wolf? As for magic rituals, I spent three
days teaching him how to move a stick without touching it.
He didn't have hardly any magic at all."

Wolf spoke, and even the most unobservant could see
that he was not in control of his temper yet. "I assure
you"—he looked at the man who'd spoken, and the man
took a quick step back and stumbled over a rock—"I am
certain of what took place tonight."

Silence fell.

Wolf's gaze found the ropes that had been left tangled on
the ground. He gestured and the ropes burst into flame so
hot it was blue and white rather than orange. The three or
four people nearest them flinched, even Myr.

"Also," growled Wolf in a voice like a coffin dragged
over rock, "the sword Edom fought with was a souleater. It
did not belong to me. Aralorn, with her shapeshifter blood,
could not have held anything so unnatural for long enough
to draw it."

Good to know, Aralorn thought. In the unlikely event of
her running into another one.

Myr said, "Our guards were dead before Aralorn found them."

Tobin spoke up from his position as Stanis's shadow, his eyes on the blackened bones. "Edom had a lot of books in his tent written in Darranian."

There was a brief silence. Aralorn almost smiled as she saw the meaning of Tobin's words echo in the minds of all present. It was Tobin's testimony that bore the most weight. A shapeshifter, being, after all, native to the Rethian mountains, was better than a Darranian. If Edom was a Darranian, it put an entirely different light on the events of the night.

All the same, nobody but Myr met her eyes as they left to collect the bodies.

They buried the guards in rough graves dug in the night, as Wolf said that it was the best. He had counteracted the runespell as best he could, but the runes enacted on the living flesh of dying people were stronger than they might otherwise be. He never made clear the exact purpose of Edom's runes, but he said that burying the bodies would give strength to his own spells.

When the last shovelful of dirt had been spread Wolf raised his hands and spoke words of power and binding. It was coincidence, Aralorn knew if no one else did, that it started pouring rain at the moment Wolf finished speaking.

The huddled group of people stood uneasily for a minute under the rain. The sting of death was no new thing to any of them, but that didn't make it any more pleasant. They all shared guard duty, and it could have been any of them. None held any illusions that they would have escaped better than Pussywillow had. The magic they had witnessed this night had its effect as well. Most of them were not quite comfortable with magic even though they could work a touch of it themselves.

Gradually, they drifted back to their tents until Aralorn, Myr, and Wolf were the only ones left by the new graves.

Myr hit the stone he was standing near with a clenched fist, hard enough to break the skin. He spoke with quiet force. "I am tired of feeling like a cow waiting for slaughter. If we didn't realize before this that the ae'Magi is just biding his time until there isn't something more interesting to turn his attention to, we know that now. Edom is . . . was too young to be anything but a minor servant, and we almost didn't stop him in time. When we face the ae'Magi, we don't stand a chance."

"Edom was older than he looked, and more than a minor servant if he worked the runes that were on the bodies," commented Wolf calmly, having recovered most of his usual control. "Carrying and hiding a souleater from me is not much easier. Don't make the same mistake that the ae'Magi is: He is not invincible."

"You think that we have a chance against the ae'Magi?" Myr's tone was doubtful.

"No, but we can bother him for longer than he thinks that we can," said Aralorn briskly. "Now, children, I think that it is time for us to go to sleep. Don't forget that we have the sanitary facilities to dig in the morning. Wolf, if you don't mind, I think that everyone would be a little more comfortable if I sleep in your camp rather than the tent I've been sharing." *Me, too,* she thought, *I'll be much happier here.* "Let them meet their shapeshifter in the light of day."

SIX

Somewhere in the darkness, a nighthawk cried out in defeat, and the mouse escaped for another night. Aralorn sympathized with the mouse, as she knew exactly how it felt.

Edom's remains had been gone when she'd arrived back at Wolf's camp with her belongings. Nothing remained of the blackened body except a slight scorched smell, as if someone had left the stew on the fire too long. She supposed that Wolf had disposed of the body somewhere; she hadn't been inclined to ask.

Now that the excitement was over, it was time to rest, but she couldn't do it. When she closed her eyes, she could all but feel the not-quite-cold metal cutting her and tearing at more than the flesh of her thigh. Every time she managed to doze off, she had nightmares about arriving too late to help Wolf or the sword's bite cutting all the way to her soul and leaving her bleeding to death from a wound that no bandage could stem.

As she lay awake in the chill air of early morning, the

blankets she used seemed too thin to protect her from the cold and damp. She pulled her legs up and wrapped her arms around them in an effort to get warm, but even that didn't seem to help. She shivered convulsively and knew that some of it was due to fear rather than the night air.

She sat up and rested her forehead on her knees. She closed her eyes, but that didn't stop the jumbled images from presenting themselves to her.

If she hadn't decided to find out what was bothering Sheen, or Edom had been just a little swifter in his work, Wolf would be dead. Not only would that have meant the end of any chance of defeating the ae'Magi, but she would have lost her enigmatic companion. Some part of her was amused that of the two results, it was the second that bothered her the most. Ren would not approve.

She was so intent on her thoughts that she didn't notice that Wolf had gotten up until he sat down beside her.

"Are you all right?" he asked softly.

She started to nod, then abruptly shook her head—without lifting it from her knees. "No. I am not all right. If I were all right, I would be asleep." As she spoke, still without looking up, she scooted nearer to him, until she was leaning against his shoulder.

There was a pause, and then he slid an arm around her shoulder. "What's wrong, Lady?"

He was so warm. She shrugged.

"Is there something I can do?"

She let go of her legs and snuggled closer until she was almost sitting in his lap. "You're already doing it, thanks. I'm sorry. Just jittery after the fight."

"I don't mind." He sat still, holding her almost awkwardly—but his warmth seeped in and alleviated the cold that blankets hadn't been able to dispel.

Aralorn relaxed but felt no pressing need to move away. "I must be turning into one of those women who moan and wail at the first chance they get—just so a handsome man will take them into his arms." Yes, she was flirting. It didn't seem to bother him.

"Hmm," he said, apparently considering what she had said. "Is that why they do it? I have always wondered."

"Yup," she said wisely, noticing that he wasn't holding her as stiffly. As if he wasn't used to someone so close. She'd snuggled down with the wolf sometimes—although rarely. He seldom invited touch. "Then," Aralorn continued, keeping it light, "she has her way with him, and he has to marry her. It's nice to know that I haven't fallen to that level . . . yet."

"So that's not why you're here?" He seemed intrigued rather than unhappy, she decided.

She paused, then said, "I was just getting a little chilled and thought to myself, 'Aralorn, what is the easiest way to get warm?' 'Well,' I said, 'the fire is nice, but moving requires *so* much effort.' 'Ah yes,' I answered, 'why didn't I think of it before? There is all of that heat going to waste on the other side of the fire.' All it took was a few broad hints, and, presto, you're here: instant heat with very little effort upon my part."

"Yes," he said, tightening his grip and releasing it a moment later. "I can see how that works. Nicely underhanded of you."

She nodded happily: The tension caused by the nightmare dissipated with the familiar banter. "I thought so, too. It's Ren's fault—he teaches us how to be sneaky." She yawned sleepily, closing her eyes. "Oh, I meant to ask—who is keeping watch on the camp?"

"Myr took care of it," he answered her. "The ae'Magi won't have planned two attacks in the same evening, and he won't find out about Edom's failure until he doesn't report. Magical communication isn't all that it could be in these mountains."

"Report." She sat up a little straighter. "Wolf, if Edom was his creature, the ae'Magi knows where we are. Are

you sure Edom wasn't acting on his own?" It was unlikely,
but it was possible.

"Edom belonged to the ae'Magi," Wolf answered. "I recognized the sword. As far as the ae'Magi knowing where
we are . . . Aralorn, there are only so many places we could
hide from the ae'Magi. Eventually, he'll find us, whether
or not Edom had a chance to tell him." He shrugged. "If it
helps any, I would have noticed anything Edom could do
magically to communicate. He'd have had to use mundane
means."

It did make her feel better. Her temporary alertness faded
into exhaustion. As she wiggled into the generous warmth of
him, she decided that Wolf was more comfortable to sleep
on when he was wearing human shape; he smelled better,
too.

———

Wolf waited until she was asleep before he set her back
down on her blankets. He added his blankets to hers and
tucked them carefully around her. He brushed a hand
against her cheek. "Sleep, Lady." He hesitated, but she was
truly asleep. "My Lady," he whispered.

He shifted into his wolf shape and stretched out beside
her and stared into the night. Being human so much made
him nervous after all the time he'd spent as a wolf. The
wolf would have heard Edom coming.

The wolf wouldn't have felt so awkward taking what
she'd given him.

———

As she had expected, Aralorn was alone when she woke
up. Wolf's longest absences were the result of a display of
affection on his part, as if it was something with which he
was not comfortable or, in light of what she'd been learning
about him, felt he didn't deserve.

To her surprise, her reception at camp was cordial. She

collected a few wary looks, and that was all. Mostly, she thought, Myr was keeping them too busy sewing and digging to worry about her one way or another.

If the adults showed little reaction, the children were fascinated by the shapechanger in their midst. They wanted to know if she could change into a rock (no) or a bird (they liked the goose, but would have preferred an eagle or, better yet, a vulture), and if shapeshifters really had to drink blood once a year, and . . . She was grateful when Wolf came to get her. For once she was tired of telling stories.

"I hope," she said, as they reached the caves, "that they don't believe half of what I tell them."

"They probably don't," Wolf replied. "Your problem is that they will believe the wrong half."

She laughed and ducked into the opening in the limestone wall.

When they reached the library, she noticed that her notes had been scattered around. One of the pages that she had been writing on the previous day was conspicuously situated in the space where Wolf worked. Looking closer at it she saw that it was the one that she'd been using to jot down the stories she'd found in the last book she'd read the day before. She never had gotten around to telling Wolf about the apprentice's spell that negated magic.

Wolf took up the paper and read her closely written scribblings with interest—or maybe, she thought guiltily, her handwriting was bad enough it required his whole attention. Aralorn straightened the rest of her papers, then glanced around the library. What kind of a breeze could pull a sheet of paper out from under the books that were still neatly stacked where she had left them? If she hadn't been here with Wolf, she'd have been worried; as it was, she was merely curious.

"I assume that if the apprentice who developed a way to negate magic were given a name, you would have told me." Wolf set down the paper.

She nodded. "I don't remember ever seeing that story before, so it can't be very well-known."

Wolf tapped the paper impatiently with a finger. "I *have* read that story somewhere else, a long time ago. I know that the one that I read gave his name. I just need to remember which book I read it in." Wolf stood silently a minute before shaking his head in disgust. "Let's work on this mess"—he waved his hand vaguely at the bookcases—"and hopefully I will remember later."

They sat in their respective chairs and read. Aralorn waded through three rather boring histories before she found anything of note. As she was reading the last page of the history of the Zorantra family (who were known for developing a second-rate wine) the spine of the poorly preserved book gave way.

While inspecting the damage, she noticed that the back cover consisted of two pieces of leather that were carefully stitched together to hide a small space inside—just big enough for the folded pages it contained. Slipping the sheets out of their resting place, she examined them cautiously.

———

By this time Wolf was used to Aralorn laughing at odd moments, but he had just finished deciphering a particularly useless spell and so was ready to relax for a minute.

"What is it?"

She grinned at him and waved the frail cluster of parchment in his general direction. "Look at this. I found it hidden in a book and thought that it might be a spell or something interesting, but it looks as though someone who had the book before you acquired it was quite an artist."

He took the sheets from her. They were covered with scenes of improbably endowed nude figures in even more improbable positions. He was about to give it back to her when he stopped and took a closer look.

He crumpled the pages and flamed them. Someone had set protection and hide-me spells, doubtless the reason Aralorn hadn't felt its power, but the old magic wasn't up to withstanding his will. The drawings—on sheets of human skin, though he wasn't about to tell Aralorn—flared deep purple and silver before settling into gold-and-red fire. He dropped the flaming bits, and they fluttered to the table, burning to ash before touching down. If it smelled like burning flesh, she'd probably just assume they had been made of goatskin.

"Wolf?"

"You were right on your first guess." He couldn't look at her. "It is a spell. It's a rather crude representation on how to summon a demon."

"Demon?" asked Aralorn, sounding interested without being eager. "I didn't think that there was any such thing, or do you mean an elemental, like the one that tried to kill Myr?"

Wolf tilted his head and laughed without humor. He should just drop it, but felt the self-destructive urge that had been such a huge part of who he'd once been take hold of his tongue. "This from a shapeshifter? Yes, there are demons, I've summoned them myself. Not many magicians are willing to try it. Mistakes in the spellcasting can be dangerous, and it's getting difficult to find a virgin who can be forced to submit to the process. The ae'Magi never had a problem with it, though; his villagers could always produce some sort of victim.

"The depiction was not entirely accurate. It isn't necessary for the magician to participate in the sexual activities unless he wishes to. He can use a proxy if he wishes."

───────────

Wolf continued to outline the practices of summoning demons. It wasn't something she'd want to listen to on a full stomach, and if Aralorn hadn't been a mercenary, she wouldn't have been able to sit coolly through it all—but a reaction was what he wanted, and she'd be plague-stricken before she gave it to him. So she maintained a remote facade while she listened. This, she decided, was his way of driving her away after the closeness of last night.

". . . so afterward, it is necessary to dispose of the focus, or the demon will be able to use her again to return without summoning. The blood of a woman used in such a fashion is valuable, as are the hair and several other body parts. The most useful method of killing the girl is to slit her throat." His voice was clinically precise. His glittering eyes never left hers.

She listened to his detached description of the horrors he'd committed and decided that she must be in love because what she really heard was the self-directed hatred that initiated his lecture. Doubtless he'd participated in the twisted ceremony of demon summoning and probably worse. Aralorn was even more certain that it now revolted him as much as he intended it to appall her. Possibly it had revolted him even then.

She waited until he was starting to run out of details, cupping her hand under her chin in feigned boredom. When he stopped speaking, she said, "Fine. I understand. You've done things that a normal human being would find abhorrent. All right. You've stopped doing them . . . I hope. Now can we get back to work?"

There was a long pause, then Wolf commented in the same dry tones he'd been using before. "You are frustrating at times, aren't you?"

She grinned at him. "Sorry, Wolf. I can't help it; melodrama has that effect on me."

"Pest," he said, his tone not at all affectionate, but then his voice seldom showed what he thought.

"I try," she said modestly, and was pleased when his eyes warmed with humor.

Deciding that the crisis was over, she bounced up and

strolled to a bookcase several rows away from the table, out
of sight of Wolf to give them both time to calm down and
sort things out. Absently, she plucked a book from a nearby
shelf. She had started to open it when it whisked itself out
of her hands and leapt back on the shelf with a loud thud.

She stared at it for a minute, then took two quiet steps
backward until she could see Wolf, seated half of the room
away with his back toward her, muttering to himself as he
wrote. There was no one else in the library.

Carefully, without opening it, she picked up the book
again and examined it. Now that she was paying attention,
she could see the faint magical aura that was just barely
visible woven into the cotton that covered the thin wood
that lent the cover its hardness.

Just to be sure, she took the book to Wolf for inspection.

"Trapped," he confirmed, and sent a flash of magic
toward the book. A pop, a sharp scent, and a bit of dust
floated up and returned to the surface of the book. He
opened it and glanced through. "Not a grimoire. Looks
like it might be a diary."

She sat down with the book—for lack of anything better
to do. Rather than a diary, it contained the autobiographi-
cal history (exaggerated) of a mediocre king of a long-
forgotten realm. As a distraction from the gory details of
Wolf's discourse that kept trying to play themselves out in
her head, it ranked right up there with sewing and digging
holes in the dirt. She had no idea why anyone would have
thought it valuable enough to trap.

"Wolf," she said, staring at open pages. Time to ask him
rather than trying to figure out what was going on herself.

"Hmm?"

"Is there someone besides us in your library?" She kept
her tone carefully nonchalant.

"Hmm," he said again, and there was a quiet thump as
he set his book on the table. Aralorn did the same. "What
prompted you to ask?"

She told him of her odd experiences, leaving out the last incident to spare herself his censure. When she was through, he nodded.

"These mountains have a reputation for odd happenings, like Astrid's guide through the cave. A ghost or spirit of some sort would not be out of place." He paused. "Though I brought these with me from the ae'Magi's castle, I suppose something could have come over with them."

It didn't sound like it bothered him too much.

He looked over at her, read her face, and shrugged. "So far whatever is here has been relatively helpful. It could just as easily have hidden your papers or led Astrid to fall into one of the pits. With the ae'Magi to deal with, it is surely the least of evils."

———

When they left the caves it was still light outside. The skies were slightly overcast, but the wind was from the south, so it was warm enough.

Aralorn took a deep breath of air and Wolf's arm at the same time. "Have I thanked you yet for rescuing me from the tedium of mopping the floor of the inn for another six months or however long Ren decided to leave me there?" she said to distract him from her touch.

His stride broke when she took his arm, and he stiffened a little. She'd have backed off, but he put his hand on hers where it hooked into his elbow.

"I am certain"—he said gravely—"I will find the proper way for you to express your gratitude. I noticed just today that the library floors are starting to get a bit dusty."

Aralorn gave an appreciative snort and quickened her pace a bit to keep up with him. He noticed what she was doing and slowed his stride until her shorter legs could keep up.

They were traveling in comfortable silence until Wolf stopped abruptly and snapped his fingers.

"I just remembered where I read that story about the apprentice who killed his master. It will take me a few days to get the book. Tell Myr that I've gone seeking a clue. Between the two of you, you should be able to handle anything that happens." He stepped away from her, then turned back. "Don't go to the library without me, I'd rather lose a few days' work than have you turned into a rock if you opened the wrong book."

Aralorn nodded. "Take care of yourself."

He took the wolf's shape and disappeared into the woods with all the stealth of a real wolf. It wasn't until he was gone that she thought to wonder how the camp would take the fact that she was returning without Wolf after the events of last night. Edom's death would not have vindicated her of all suspicion. With a wry smile, she resumed her course.

At the camp, Aralorn skulked around until she found Myr organizing a hunt for the next day, as the camp supplies were getting low. She caught his attention and waited for him to finish. Listening to him work was unexpectedly fascinating.

He reassured and soothed and organized until he had a small, skilled party who knew where to go and how to get back—without any of those who were not chosen feeling slighted or overlooked. With everybody as edgy as they were, this was a major accomplishment. If Myr survived to regain his throne, he would be a ruler that Reth would not soon forget.

"What did you need, Aralorn?" Myr asked, approaching her after he sent the others to their appointed tasks.

"Wolf is going to be absent for a few days. He is looking for a book that might be able to help us fight the ae'Magi."

She kept her voice neutral, not certain how he would take it. He had no reason to trust her except that Wolf did—and Wolf was gone.

"All right," he said. When she didn't take that as a

dismissal, he paused and considered what she'd said again. "I see your problem. You think people are going to wonder if you were really the villain last night and have completed your nefarious plot today."

Aralorn nodded, relieved that he seemed not the least bit leery of her. "I didn't think of it until Wolf was already gone, or I would have made him come back to camp before he left. I thought that you might want to break the news."

Myr nodded. "I'll tell them that he left and leave out the details. There are enough things to worry about—we don't need a lynching."

Abruptly, like an extinguished candle, the taut energy that generally characterized him was gone. He just looked very tired. He needed to pace himself better.

"You need to let them look after themselves for a while," she told him. "They don't really need you to tell them what shoe they should put on which foot or how to make stew."

Myr laughed involuntarily. "You saw that one, huh? How should I know how much salt to put in? I've never cooked anything in my life—that was edible, at any rate."

"I wish I could help you more; but even if they aren't terrified of me, I'm not someone they can trust. You have my sympathy—for what it's worth."

"Thanks, anyway." He glanced up at the cloudless evening sky. "I wish all the tents were done and we had twice as much food. The winter comes in the blink of an eye this far north. My old groom could predict the weather. He told me that the air had a tartness to it before a snowstorm, but I could never smell it." He was talking to himself more than Aralorn. Abruptly, he turned on his heel and headed toward the center of activity.

Aralorn watched as he stopped and laid a hand on the shoulder of an older woman plying a needle. Whatever he said made her smile.

He looked as if he'd seen ten years more than she knew

he had, and she wondered if he would live to see the year out. He'd probably wondered about that, too.

Since Wolf had asked her to stay out of the library, Aralorn did her best to keep busy. It wasn't difficult. Without Pussywillow or Wolf, only she and Myr had the training to teach the motley band of rebels how to fight.

Haris was easily the best student. The muscles he'd developed swinging a smith's hammer lent an impressive strength to his blows. Like most big men he was a little slow, but he knew how to compensate for it. In unarmed combat, he could take Aralorn but not Myr.

The rest of the camp varied from bad to pathetic. There was a squire's son who had at one time been quite an archer, but he was old, and his eyesight wasn't what it had been. One of the farmers could swing a scythe but not a sword. Then there was the big carpenter whose greatest asset as a fighter was his size, which he more than made up for by his gentleness.

"Okay now." With an effort, Aralorn kept her voice from getting snappy. "Keep your sword a bit lower and watch my eyes to see where I'll move. Now, in slow motion, I'm going to swing at you. I want you to block overhanded, then underhanded, then thrust."

The carpenter would have been a lot better off if he could have forgotten she was a woman. The only way that she could get him to strike at her was if she did it in slow motion. But when they sped things up, he wouldn't use his full strength. She was about to change that if she could.

"Good," she said when he had completed the maneuvers. "Now at full speed."

He blocked just fine, but his strike was slow and careful, lacking the power that he should have been able to put behind the blow.

Aralorn stepped into it and inside. With a deft grip and twist she tossed him over her head and into the grass.

Before he had a chance to move, she had her knee on his chest and his sword arm twisted so that it would hurt him; maybe enough that he would fight her when she let him up.

There had been a collective gasp from her audience when she tossed the big man on his back. The move looked more impressive than it was, especially since he easily outweighed her by a hundred pounds.

Stanis, who was watching with his faithful shadow and a couple of other children, said, "I wouldn't pin 'em that way, Aralorn. Two coughs from a cat, and I'd be out of it if it'd been me you caught."

Aralorn raised an eyebrow and let her victim up. Stanis, she'd learned, had been born to a group of Traders, traveling clans no better than they should be. It was very possible that he had a few good tricks up his sleeve.

"Right, then. Come on, Stanis," she invited.

He did. She must have pinned him a dozen times, but he kept slipping out of her grasp. Drawn by the noise, Myr quit his bout to come and watch, too. Soon the whole crowd was cheering for Stanis as he broke away again and again. Aralorn quit finally and raised her hands in surrender.

"You're using magic to do that," she said quietly as she shook his hand. No one but Stanis could hear her—she wouldn't give away his tricks without permission. "I've never seen anyone do that."

Stanis shook his head, gave her a wary look, then grinned and nodded. "Most of 'em are easier with magic, but there's a few tricks that the Clansmen know if ya wanna learn 'em."

So Stanis took a turn at teaching. He must have been a very good thief, and doubtless there were a few magistrates who were looking for him. They'd have had a hard time keeping him.

When it was time to dig latrines, sew, or hunt, Aralorn watched over the children. It was nice to have a ready audience who believed every word that came out of her mouth—at least until they got to know her better. Keeping the mischievous, magic-toting hellions out of trouble kept her from getting restless while Wolf was away. It also kept her from latrine duty.

The storm struck without warning two nights later. Within moments, the temperature dropped below freezing. Without a tent to cover her, since she was still sleeping in Wolf's camp, Aralorn woke as the first few flakes fell. Instincts developed from years of camping had her gathering her bedding before she was really awake. Even so, by the time she left Wolf's chosen spot and made it into the main camp, most of what she carried was already covered with snow.

At the camp, Aralorn found that Myr, efficient as ever, was shuffling people who had occupied inadequate tents to the few that looked like they would hold up in the storm. Seeing her trudge in, Myr motioned her toward his own.

She found it full of frightened people. The storms of the Northlands were rightfully legendary for their fierceness. Although their camp was protected from the brunt of the storm by the steep walls of the valley, the angry howl of the wind was so loud that it made it difficult to hear when someone spoke.

Evaluating the situation, Aralorn casually found a place for her blankets, lay down, and closed her eyes, ignoring the slight dampness left on her bedroll after she had brushed the snow off. Her nonchalance seemed to work because everyone settled down and were mostly asleep when Myr returned to his bed.

By morning the worst of the storm was over. The snow was knee deep everywhere, and in places it had drifted nearly waist high.

Aralorn was helping with the fire when Myr found her and pulled her aside. "I'm no mage, but I do know that this is a freak storm. Feel the air. It's already getting warm, the snow is starting to melt. The storms come suddenly here, I know—but this is more like the spring storms. The winter storms hit and don't ease for weeks. Did you notice anything unnatural about it?"

Aralorn shook her head and sneezed—sleeping in damp bedding wasn't the best thing for one's health. She wasn't the only one coughing. "No, I wondered about that myself so I tried to check. I couldn't find any trace of magic"—human magic, anyway; there was always green magic in a storm—"in the storm, although there was something strange about it, I'll grant you." She shrugged. "If the ae'Magi was causing that storm, he was trying to hide it, which is something he could probably do—at least from me. Weather isn't something that mages like him are generally good with. The trappers who hunt these parts for furs would tell you that it was the Old Man of the Mountains who caused the storm."

There was a brief silence, then Myr, who was beginning to know her, smiled slowly. "I'll take my cue, storyteller. Who is the Old Man of the Mountain?"

She grinned cheerfully at him. "The trappers like to tell a lot of stories about him. Sometimes he is a monster who drives men mad and eats them. Other times he is a kindly old man who does things that kindly old men can't do— like change the weather." *Maybe he might guide a child to safety,* she thought. *Given that there's a thread of truth in any story. Sometimes just a piece as big as spider silk.* She'd run it past Wolf when he returned. "The Old Man of the Mountain is invited to every trapper's wedding or gathering, and a ceremonial place is laid for him when the trapping clans meet in their enclave each year to decide which trapper goes where."

"Which mountain?" he asked.

Aralorn shrugged. " 'The Mountain,' " she said. "I don't know. I've met trappers who swear that they have met him. But I've never seen the story in any book."

"Do you think he could be one of the shapeshifters?"

"The Old Man who drives men mad and eats them, certainly," she said. "But I've never met a full-blood shapeshifter who'd help a human find water in the middle of a river."

"Could one of them have brought the storm?"

Impossible to explain fully how taboo it was for a green mage to mess with the greater weather patterns. Taboo implied ability, and she didn't want the King of Reth to know that her mother's kin had that kind of power. Eyes as clear and innocent as she could manage, she said, "Absolutely not." Truth, but not quite the truth he'd think it.

His curiosity satisfied, Myr changed the subject. "I wish I knew how long this weather was going to last. We need to get more meat, and I can't send the hunters out in this. They don't have the skills to hunt in the snow. Only two or three of them have the skills to hunt at all, and none are experienced with northern weather." As he spoke, he paced back and forth restlessly. "And mud. We're going to have mud everywhere, then we'll have ice."

"Don't borrow trouble." Aralorn's tone was brisk. "If we starve, there is nothing that you can do about it. However, Sheen's not been getting much exercise lately, and I'm not too bad with a bow. I also know how to set traps if we need to. Keep your hunters home, and I'll see what I can do for our larder."

Myr's face cleared. "Are you sure? This isn't good riding."

"Sheen's no stranger to snow, and he's big enough to break through this with no trouble."

She hadn't intended to leave just then, but the relief on his face kept her from putting it off until afternoon. She recovered her gear from the storage tent, commandeered a pair of boots, and borrowed a crossbow and arrows from one of the erstwhile hunters.

Sheen snorted and danced while she saddled him, and took off at a dead run when she was only half in the saddle;

a dramatic departure that was met with ragged cheers and good-natured laughter. When she was able to pull him up and scold, they were already headed up the main trail out of the valley.

It wasn't as difficult to travel once they were out of the valley as the harsh winds had swept the snow away from many places. As long as she stayed out of the gullies and valleys, the deep snow was usually avoidable.

There were few tracks in the snow. Hunting usually wasn't her job; she didn't know the habits of deer after the first good snowfall. She'd have expected them out once the snow started to melt—on the sun-exposed slopes if not the valleys—to eat the revealed greenery before winter came for good. But perhaps they were just staying sheltered. Maybe they knew something about the weather she didn't.

She stumbled upon tracks that she'd never seen before. The prints were several hours old and smeared hopelessly by the melting snow. Whatever had made them was big—she found a branch as big around as her leg that the animal had snapped off a tree. She looked at the branch a minute and guided her nervous mount away from the thing's trail.

"Anything that big, Sheen, is bound to be too tough and stringy to make good eating. Besides, it would be a pain to drag the body back to camp." Sounded like a good excuse to her. The big horse snorted at her and increased his speed.

Several hours later, Aralorn wiped a gloved hand across her nose and squinted against the glare of the sunny snow-covered meadow. The oiled boots that she'd found in Myr's stockpile worked well to keep out the water. She appreciated them all the more for the fact that all of the rest of her was wet.

The brush was so laden with heavy wet snow that even riding she got drenched. There was a lot of undergrowth on the steep slope behind them. The sun had melted enough of the snow that water ran down everywhere, making the

ground muddy and slick. The light sneezes of the morning
had turned into a full-blown plaguing cold.

"You know, Sheen"—she patted his glossy neck, also
somewhat damp—"I think that I would prefer it if it were
really cold. At least that way we would be just chilly and
not wet, too."

She pushed a soggy strand of hair out of her face with a
sigh. The sun was starting the trek toward its evening rest,
and they hadn't seen so much as a rabbit. It was unusually bad luck. The camp was far enough off from com-
monly hunted areas that the game animals were unafraid
of people. Just on the walk from the camp to the caves,
Aralorn generally saw traces of deer. Today, even the birds
were scarce.

Maybe whatever large beastie left its traces for her to
find had scared off all of the prey. She hoped not. That
would mean that it was probably something that people
should be running from, too. She wished Wolf were here
to tell her what it was.

A grin caught her lip as she thought about what his
response to being viewed as a rescuer of Ladies in distress would be. The picture of herself as a Lady in distress
caused her smile to widen a bit. She still wished for his
comforting presence.

Absently she looked at the meadow and admired the
pristine beauty of the untouched snow that gleamed subtly
with all the colors of a rainbow, more startling because
of the dark, dense forest surrounding it. She was deciding
whether it was worth crossing the meadow to the river that
ran on the other side or if she ought to head up the steep
and muddy side hill and circle around back to camp when
she noticed that there was something odd about the peaceful meadow.

She stiffened at the same time that Sheen noticed them.

"Yawan," she whispered.

The filthy word described exactly the way she felt. Stupid,

stupid to have missed them when in front of her the whole meadow was moving slowly. The covering of deep snow completely masked their scent, or maybe the cold kept them from rotting. Whatever the case, not two feet in front of her a Uriah rose from its snowy bed. It wasn't the only one. There must have been at least a hundred of the defiled things, and though none of them was on its feet, their heads were turning toward her. She had never in her life seen so many in one place—or even heard of such a thing.

The path behind was no escape. The slick mud would slow Sheen much more than it would the Uriah. Cold slowed them, but not enough. The best ways to stop them were fire and running water. There were no fires around that she could see, but running water there was aplenty.

All this took less than a second to run through her head. She squeezed Sheen with her knees, and bless his warrior's heart, he plowed right into the meadow filled with moving mounds of snow. The Uriah howled, and Sheen redoubled his speed, leaping and dodging the creatures. One of them stood up reaching for the reins. Aralorn shot it in the eye with a bolt from the crossbow. It reeled back but recovered enough to catch Aralorn's stirrup. Desperately she hit it hard with the butt of the crossbow, breaking the arm off the body at the shoulder. Sheen struck it with his hind feet as it fell.

The cold must have had a greater effect on their speed than she thought it would, because—much to her surprise—Aralorn made it to the ice-edged river while the Uriah were still sluggish. Sheen protested the cold water with a grunt when he hit, but struck out strongly for the other side. Aralorn took a good grip on Sheen's mane and lay flat on the fast-running surface, letting the water take most of her weight.

The river was deep and swift, but narrow. The horse towed Aralorn to the far bank without mishap. The current had swept them far enough downstream that the Uriah were no longer in sight, but she thought that she could hear them above the rush of the water. When she turned back to mount again, she noticed that the arm she'd severed from the Uriah still held fast to her stirrup.

There was a story about a man who kept a finger from a Uriah's hand for a trophy of war. Ten years later the Uriah who owned the finger showed up on the man's doorstep. Aralorn didn't believe that story, she told herself. Not really. She just wasn't enthusiastic about riding around with a hand attached to her saddle.

Aralorn pried at it with grim haste. The thing was strangely stubborn, so she finally used an arrow as a lever to pull it away. As she worked she noticed that it wore a ring of heavy gold on a raggedly clawed finger—stolen from some poor victim, she supposed. Ren would be fascinated— Uriah were not generally looters; their primary interest was food.

She threw the arm and its ring in the river and watched in some satisfaction as it disappeared in the depths. She reloaded the crossbow from habit; it obviously wasn't much good against Uriah. Mounting Sheen, she headed in the general direction of camp, hoping that there would be a good ford over the river between here and there.

Uriah, normal Uriah, never came where it was cold. Never. But the ae'Magi had Uriah who were—how had Wolf phrased it?—pets. A hundred of them? Ren was fond of saying that it was futile to argue with your own eyes. A hundred of them, then.

The only thing that Uriah who were the ae'Magi's pets could be after was Myr—assuming that Wolf was correct in labeling them servants of the ae'Magi. They had obviously been caught by the storm and incapacitated by the sudden cold. Given when the storm had hit, if the snow hadn't stopped them, they would have reached the camp early this past morning. The storm gave her a chance to bring warning.

Shaking with cold, she urged the stallion to a trot that he could maintain until they made it back to camp. As they went, she sawed at the girth and dumped the heavy saddle and bags to the ground—staying on Sheen while she did so with a trick her old troop's first scout had taught her. The less he had to carry, the better time he could make. She retained her grip on the loaded crossbow.

The Uriah's ring nagged at her more as she rode. That, and how to turn whatever time they had before the Uriah came into a way to survive.

The river was between the Uriah and Aralorn, but it stood between her and the camp as well. She rode as far as she could, looking for a shallow place to ford across, but there was none. The only choice was to swim again. When they came out of the water the second time, Aralorn was blue with cold, and Sheen stumbled twice before he resumed trotting. Warming was one of the easier magics she knew, but, cold and exhausted, it took her three times to get it right.

She rode right into the camp, scattering people as she went. She stopped finally in front of Myr's tent. Drawn by the sound of horse's hooves, Myr ducked outside just as Aralorn slipped off the stallion's back.

"What's wrong?" he asked, taking in her appearance.

"Uriah . . . about a hundred of them. They're coming." Aralorn panted heavily, her voice hoarse with what was turning into the grandfather of all colds. Winter river crossings will do that. "Caves. We can defend the entrance. Leave the tents behind, but take all the food, blankets, and weapons that you can."

He was acting before she finished speaking. The children, under the leadership of Stanis, were sent ahead with such things as they could carry. Myr had the majority of the camp packed and on the trail to the caves before anyone had time to panic.

Aralorn and Myr brought up the rear of the procession.

Aralorn, listening for the Uriah behind them, chafed at the slow pace they were forced to take because most people were on foot—but then again, even a dead run would have been too slow. She walked beside her exhausted horse and hoped that Sheen wasn't so tired that he wouldn't give warning if the Uriah got too close.

By the time they arrived at the caves, Aralorn found herself mildly surprised that they had beaten the Uriah there. Light wasn't a problem—light, like fire, was easy magic. Even the children could form the small balls of light that mages used in place of torches.

Myr followed Aralorn as she led Sheen into a solitary cave a hundred feet from the entrance—one big enough to hold the animals they had. "I've been told they can track a man as well as a hunting dog and travel faster than a man on horseback." Myr spoke in a soft voice designed not to carry to anyone but Aralorn. "I don't have much experience with Uriah. All that I know is that they are very hard to kill and are almost as immune to magic as I am."

Aralorn nodded. "They don't like fire, so make sure that there are torches ready. This lot"—she swung a hand in the general direction of the others in the cavern—"will fight better with torches than swords."

Myr gave her a tired smile. "And no worries about how to light the torches either, with this assortment of amateur magic-users. I think that the only one who can't light a torch with magic is I. Haris!" He caught the attention of the smith, who was organizing the storage of supplies. "I want a bonfire laid in the entrance and someone who can light it from a distance stationed somewhere safe to watch for the Uriah."

Haris waved an acknowledgment, and Myr returned his attention to Aralorn. "There are three or four here who should be able to light the fire from a good distance. I'll station them in relays."

Aralorn shivered in her still-damp clothes. "We could

be lucky. There is some kind of warding near the entrance. You can see the markings if you want to look. I suspect that the warding was the reason that Edom wouldn't enter the caves. Do you remember? When he lost Astrid?" She'd given it a lot of thought and decided they'd have to plan as if the warding wasn't there. But still, a little hope couldn't hurt.

Myr nodded.

Aralorn continued, "If it works like the shapechangers' spells do, the Uriah won't even see the caves unless we are lighting fires and running in and out to attract their attention. The trail that we took up here is virtually a stream from the melting snow, so in a little while there will be no sign that we came this way. With luck, we'll have that time. The cold makes them slower than usual. That's the reason Sheen and I beat them here."

"I'll see that everyone stays inside." Myr started to go—someone was calling his name—then turned around. "Aralorn?"

She pulled off Sheen's bridle and vainly patted her clothing in search of something she could use to dry him off. But he was dryer than her clothing. "Yes?"

"I'll send a couple of the older children in with toweling to dry your horse. You change your clothes, before you catch lung fever. My packs are marked over against the far wall; find something in them."

It made sense. "Thanks."

She made her way to his packs, unmistakable because of the embroidered dragon that glared at her as she riffled through his belongings. A true shapeshifter could probably alter the clothes that she was wearing, but Aralorn had no idea how to go about it. She pulled out a pair of plain trousers and a tunic of a dark hue and, best of all, a pair of dry cotton stockings. With clothes in hand she hunted down an unoccupied cranny and exchanged the wet clothes for the dry ones.

The oil coating on the boots worked better in snow than in rivers. The water had run in from the top and been prevented from leaving by the oil on the outside so that they were marshy inside. Aralorn dried them out as best she could and pulled them on over her newly acquired socks. She had hoped for better results.

She surveyed herself wryly when she was done. Myr was not tall—for a man—which left him only a head or so taller than she. He was, however, built like a stone wall.

Well, she thought, tugging at the front of the tunic, at least she wouldn't have to worry about its being too tight.

The camp was starting to look organized again. Aralorn went back to check and found Sheen had been dried. He stood quietly with head lowered and one hind foot cocked up—a sure sign that he was as tired as she was.

Stanis found her there, her head resting against the horse's neck, more asleep than awake.

"Aralorn, I think Astrid went back to camp."

It was enough to wake her up. "What?"

"I can't find her anywhere, an' neither can Tobin, we searched an' searched. She was crying all of the way up here because she left the doll her mother made her at camp. We tried to tell her that it would be all right, everyone knows that Uriah don't eat dolls, just people. But I haven't seen her since you came in, and neither has anyone else."

"How many people have you told this to?" She fitted her bridle to the fastest of the camp horses. Sheen was too tired to run.

"Lots of people know I'm looking for her, but you're the only one I told what I thought happened to her. I tried to tell Myr, but Haris was talking to him and lots of other people."

"Here's what we're going to do. I'm going to sneak out of here and go look for her. I don't want you to tell anyone that I've gone." There was no use sending out more than one person. She was more than enough to bring back one little girl if the Uriah hadn't found her yet. If they had made it to camp, then there was no sense in sending more people to die. "Keep looking for her here. She was pretty excited about the man who helped her find her way out of the caves. She may have just wandered deeper into the cave to see if she could find him. Wait until Myr isn't busy, then tell him where I've gone. That should take long enough that I'll either be back or I'm not coming back. Tell him that I said not to send anyone else after me. There aren't enough people to spare. I'm just going to sneak down to our camp and see if I can spot her. If I don't see her, I'll ride right back up."

She paused only long enough to get her sword. As she belted it on, the thought occurred to her that if she were going to have to keep using it against Uriah, it would behoove her to get more proficient at using the plaguing thing.

It wasn't easy, with her limited magical powers, to sneak through a cave filled with magic-users, albeit weak ones. The gelding, sulky at leaving the other horses munching dinner, didn't make matters any easier. She almost left him behind, but although he made it a little bit more difficult to escape undetected, he also gave her an edge if the Uriah were there.

Once out of the occupied caves, she gave up trying to remain unseen. The guards didn't challenge her as she took the horse past them. They were looking for Uriah coming in, not people going out.

The camp gelding was a lot skinnier than Sheen and not so well trained. She stayed off the trails and followed a creek bed to the far side of the valley near Wolf's camp, so the Uriah couldn't easily follow her back trail to the caves. It wasn't until she got to the valley that she realized that Astrid would have followed the main trail down and back.

Tired and cold and stupid.

It was quiet and peaceful, so she turned the horse directly

toward camp. He took three strides forward, stiffened, and spooked wildly. She clung to his back, cursing silently, as the animal's distressed cry and crashing branches gave whatever had scared him no doubt that there was someone riding on the mountainside above them.

Apparently the ae'Magi's pets were capable of stealth.

She'd just gotten the horse under control when she heard a whistle from down below.

She would have known it anywhere. Talor had always been tone deaf—giving his signals a peculiar flat sound all their own, as well as making it unclear exactly what he was signaling. In this case it could have been either "all clear" or "help." Given the circumstance, Aralorn picked the latter.

Without hesitation, she urged the horse down the slope. The only excuse that she had for her action was that she was exhausted and reacting from instinct. Gods bless them, was all she could think, somehow Ren had known. Somehow he'd sent them help from Sianim.

Her borrowed horse was not as sure-footed as Sheen and fought her all the way down. The horse made a lot of noise and ended up sliding most of the way on a small avalanche of his own making.

The gelding was still sliding uncontrollably when she ran into a small group of Uriah. As they easily pulled down her mount, Aralorn jumped clear, hoping that the horse, poor thing, would distract most of them and give her a chance to find either Talor or Astrid.

Her jump took her clear of the feeding frenzy and earned her only a scraped shin and modest bruises. By the time she regained her feet, there were two Uriah nearly upon her. She used the split second before they attacked to search for a possible escape, but everywhere she looked there were more of them converging.

Bleakly, she thought of another of Ren's homilies— rashness eventually exacts a full, fell price. She used her sword in a useless attempt to defend herself and waited to die.

It seemed like it took forever. She swung, and limbs fell, still writhing as if unwilling to accede to death with somber dignity. She swung until her arms were heavy and her tendons burned like slow acid in her shoulders. Her body was covered with myriad scrapes.

Surprisingly, none of her wounds was in itself serious; but collectively, they sapped her strength and dulled her reflexes. The Uriah just kept coming. The horse's screams had stopped, for which she was profoundly thankful. It had been stupid of her to come running; any human who had been here was beyond anyone's ability to help. The gelding had died for her foolishness, and she would soon follow.

She had little talent as a mindspeaker, but she sent a distress cry on a thread of magic to Wolf or any gods who happened to be listening anyway. Then she bit her lip and grimly hacked away.

Her arms were numb by the time that it dawned on her what was going on. She timed her strokes to the refrain in her head: *stupid, stupid, silly bitch.*

They could have killed her anytime they wanted to, but they didn't want to. They were trying to capture her to take back to the ae'Magi for questioning. The thought of that redoubled her efforts. If she could win herself enough space, she could draw her knife and eliminate the chance of being questioned by the ae'Magi again. Her sword, although shorter than normal, was still too awkward to kill herself with before they stopped her.

She spun around, slicing a creature open across the belly when she heard some disturbance behind her, more a lack of attackers than a noise. She caught a quick glimpse of Talor's face before she struck. Frantically, she avoided hitting him by a narrow margin, leaving her sword in an awkward place for defense. But that was all right, because it was Talor.

She blinked sweat out of her eyes. Something was wrong with him. Bile rose in her throat as she brought the sword back up again, but before she could strike she was caught from behind and held helpless.

What happened next was enough to top her worst nightmares. Talor smiled—and it was Talor despite the rotting flesh—and it said in Talor's teasing voice, "I told you to always follow through on your strokes, or you would never make a swordmaster."

She thought that she screamed then, but it might have been just the sound of a Uriah lucky enough to feast on the horse.

SEVEN

The wolf leapt neatly over the small stream that hadn't been there the week before, and landed in the soft mud on the other side. The moon's light revealed other evidence of the recent storm—branches bent and broken from the weight of a heavy snowfall, long grass lying flattened on the ground. The air smelled sweet and clean, washed free of heavy scents.

Knowing that the camp was near, Wolf increased his speed to a swift lope despite his tiredness. He reached the edge of the valley and found it barren of people. He felt no alarm. Even if the storm hadn't driven them to the caves, the meltwater from the heavy snow that turned most of the valley bottom to marsh would have.

With a snort, he started down the valley side nearest where he had made his private camp. He decided to stop there and get his things before going on to the caves. Aralorn's bedroll was gone, but his was neatly folded and dry under its oilcloth cover.

He muttered a few words that he wouldn't have employed

had there been anyone to hear and took on his human form. Wearily, he stretched, more than half-inclined to stay where he was for the night and join the others in the morning.

He'd always been solitary. As a boy and while an apprentice, he'd spent time alone as often as he could manage. He had become adept at finding places where no one would look.

When he left his apprenticeship behind him, he'd taken wolf shape and run into the wilds of the Northlands, escaping from himself more than the ae'Magi. He had avoided contact with people at all costs. People made him uncomfortable, and he frightened them—even Myr, though that one hid it better than most. He had a grudging respect for the Rethian king but nothing that approached friendship.

For Wolf, the only person who mattered was Aralorn.

Absently, Wolf moved his bedroll with the toe of his boot. He made a sound that was not humorous enough to be a laugh. He'd been running away from and back to Aralorn for a long time. She had caught him in a spell, and he hadn't even known that she was weaving one.

Four years ago, he'd told himself that he followed her because he was bored and tired of hiding. Maybe it had even been true at first. She was always *doing* something. But then he'd heard her laugh. Until then, laughter had never made Wolf feel anything but repulsed (the ae'Magi laughed so easily).

He needed to see her.

Needing someone made him *very* uncomfortable. He didn't remember ever needing anyone before, and he hated the vulnerability of it almost as much as he . . . as he loved her.

It wasn't until he'd found out that Aralorn was spying on the ae'Magi that he knew how much she meant to him. Even the thought of her there made him shake with remembered rage and fear.

He wasn't quite certain when his interest had turned to

need. He needed her to let him laugh, to be human and not a flawed creation of the ae'Magi. He needed her trust so that he could trust himself. Most of all, he needed her touch. Even more than laughter—he associated touch with the ae'Magi—a warm hand on his shoulder (cut it so, child), an affectionate hug (it won't hurt so much next time . . .).

Aralorn was a tactile person, too, but her touch didn't lie. It still made him uncomfortable to feel her hands on him, but he craved it anyway. He picked up the bedroll and went down into the valley since it was the shortest way to the caves. When he arrived at the valley floor, even his dulled human nose caught the scent.

Uriah.

Not panicking, he took a good look around him and noticed the signs of hasty packing as well as the fact that the tents (including the one that Myr had worked so hard to get finished) had been torn into pieces by something other than the wind. He also noticed that there were no obvious bones.

He walked briskly though the camp to get a closer look. Here the scent was stronger, and everywhere were signs of anger vented on inanimate objects. That was good, he assured himself. Anger meant they had missed their prey.

There was a small bone—chicken. Haris would be unhappy about that. Human bones were conspicuously absent, and he felt a faint sense of relief. Myr must have had enough warning to get the camp into the caves. As long as the Uriah hadn't been within sight when the people entered the caves, the wards would keep the entrances hidden from them.

Wolf had started once more for the caves when he saw something white in the drying mud: a horse's skeleton. Too small to be Sheen.

It was picked clean, with only a wisp of mane to distinguish it. The leg bones had been cracked so that all the marrow could be sucked out. It wasn't until he noticed the distinctive patterns on the silver bit that lay nearby that he knew that Aralorn had been riding the horse.

He found another pile of bones, also picked clean, fifteen or twenty paces away. They all had the peculiar twists of the Uriah. He found several skulls—she'd accounted for three of them. He had hoped that he would find her among the dead—something inside him howled with mocking laughter at the thought. But dead would be . . .

He could have followed her there easily.

He left his bedroll forgotten among the ruins of the camp and took wolf shape to run toward the caves because it was faster. On the way there he found the pitiful remains of a small child—a dirty battered doll lay nearby. Astrid— he remembered the doll. He knew then why Aralorn had confronted the Uriah.

Rage sang in his blood. He restrained it with a pale sense of hope that Myr would know something to help his search. If he let the rage take him, there was no telling who would die. If everyone was dead, he reminded himself, no one could tell him if a search had been made. And Aralorn wouldn't want him to kill her friends.

He planned quickly as he ran so that he wouldn't think too much about the wrong things. He was conscious of a numbness that crept over him, covering hot rage with a thin coating of ice.

The furious arguments were audible even before he entered the darkness of the cave.

"Silence!" Myr's voice cracked with tiredness but its power was still enough that it stopped the bickering. "There is nothing that we can do. Aralorn and Astrid are gone. I will not send out parties to be picked off two at a time by the Uriah. We will wait here until I am satisfied that they are gone. Even if Aralorn and Astrid were still alive, even if our whole party went down to the camp and found them prisoners of the Uriah, it wouldn't matter. We could not take them. A hundred, she said, and she didn't strike me as a person who exaggerated."

Only in her stories, Wolf thought. *Not when it mattered.*

He stopped in the shadows of the entrance to one of the great caverns. Myr stood in front of him, facing the main room so that Wolf had a clear view of his profile. The light from the torch revealed the tired lines of his face. "It wouldn't matter because twenty Uriah could destroy all of us, however we were armed. They would kill us, and we'd be lucky if we killed ten of them. Aralorn knew that when she went out looking for Astrid. She stood a better chance than any of us because she has dealt with them before. Had I known what she was doing, I would have stopped her, but I didn't. I will, however, stop any of you who try to leave now. When the sun comes up, I will look."

"Afraid of the dark, princeling?" A swarthy man stepped out of the crowd. His face was unfamiliar, so he must have arrived after Wolf left. He was an aristocrat, from his clothes—less impressed with the king than the peasants were.

Wolf spoke then from the darkness of the entryway, almost not recognizing his own voice. "As you should be," he said. "If I were he, I would send you out on your own to find out what happens to fools in the dark."

Wolf stepped to the left of Myr, clearly revealing himself in the light of Myr's torch. When he was sure that all eyes were upon him, he took his human form with all the theatrics that even the ae'Magi could have used. Masked and cloaked, he stood with a hand on his glowing staff that made Myr's torch look like a candle.

"As it happens, though, it is unnecessary for anyone to go out. Astrid is dead." Wolf pitched his voice so that it carried to everyone in the room without echoing. "I found her remains as well as those of the horse that Aralorn was riding. I found no trace of Aralorn's body. I suspect that she is a prisoner of the ae'Magi."

He had to quit speaking after those words left his throat. From the reaction of the people facing him, he could tell that they hadn't realized that this attack, too, had been engineered by the ae'Magi. He couldn't work up the effort to care. As long as the ae'Magi didn't know that Wolf was here helping Myr and as long as he didn't know what Aralorn was to him, the Archmage probably wouldn't torture Aralorn himself—he wouldn't consider any information she had to be vital. She had to be important enough that he didn't just kill her for the power he might gain, but not so important that he concentrated on her himself. That would buy Wolf time. It would keep her alive for him to find. It all rested upon how independent Edom had been.

The ae'Magi tended to give his tools more autonomy because he could trust that they had his best interests at heart. So Wolf would believe that he had time to find Aralorn. He had to believe he had time.

Wolf continued in a voice that sounded disinterested even to his own ears, this time speaking directly to Myr. "My advice is for you to stay here for now. It is probably quite safe for you to go out for a while yet. The ae'Magi won't expect you to be this close to the original camp. If I am not back in a fortnight, it would be best for you to move on." Wolf started to leave but turned back. He might not care for them, but Aralorn would want them safe.

"I would find a way to block off the paths that I didn't map for you so that no one is hurt or lost. You could follow these caves for a hundred miles if you wanted to." He left then, as quietly as he had come in.

———

He knew all the ae'Magi's holdings, even those acquired after he'd left. He had made a point of exploring each of them, partially to see if he could do it without getting caught, but also because he might find that he needed the knowledge. Even as he had done so, he'd been amused that

Aralorn's passion for information had passed on to him. Now he was grateful for the habit.

First, he went, traveling by magic, as soon as he was far enough south that his spells worked, to the ae'Magi's castle since it was the ae'Magi's preferred residence as well as the closest one to the camp. He took the time to see if the ae'Magi was in residence, not that it would have kept Wolf out if he had been. He searched the dungeon twice, certain that she would be there—but he didn't see her among the pitiful captives. He looked through the castle, even the stables, but saw no sign of her anywhere. Then he continued to the next hold.

———

He searched through the night and all the next day, even the royal palace of Reth and the small cottage in which the ae'Magi had been born. Finally, he had to admit defeat. He hoped that she had been able to kill herself because he found no trace of her anywhere with which the ae'Magi was remotely connected. For lack of anything better to do, he returned to the caves.

———

Aralorn traveled out of the Northlands flopped over the back of the Uriah who had captured her (she would *not* think of it as Talor). The smell of the thing at such close range was debilitating, and she was glad enough for the cold that stuffed up her nose. She had been stripped of her weapons with ruthless efficiency and bound hand and foot. The constant jostling of the thing's shoulder in her midriff was giving her a headache that made it difficult to think clearly.

They stopped when they were out of the mountains and dumped her ignominiously facedown on the ground. By turning her head to the side, she could see them moving about restlessly, snarling irritably at each other. For the most part they ignored her, but she received enough hungry looks that she tried to make herself as inconspicuous as possible. She tried shapechanging once when nothing was paying attention to her, but the pain in her head kept distracting her.

She was concentrating for another attempt, but this time the distraction came in the form of a thud originating just out of her field of view. One by one the Uriah dropped to the ground; only the glitter of their eyes gave indication that they were not asleep—or dead.

"Sst. Filthy things. Why he uses them I cannot imagine." The voice was a light tenor, speaking Rethian with a high-court accent. Her position on the ground limited her field of view, but she could see the elegant shoes topped by the embroidered stockings of a true dandy.

"So," the soft voice continued, "you are the prisoner the ae'Magi is so anxious to get."

She was pushed over on her side by a magical shove and got her first full look at the mage. His face was handsome enough although overpowered by the purple wig he affected. She didn't know him by sight, but his ability to immobilize an army of Uriah and his dress let her put a name to him: Lord Kisrah, a minor noble whose abilities had been invaluable to Myr's grandfather in the last war.

Her father told her once that he was a competent tactician and diplomat, high praises from a man who despised the courtier type.

"Not very much of you, is there? From all the fuss the ae'Magi is putting up over you, I had expected more—although you would clean up well enough, I suppose. It is too bad that you chose to attack the ae'Magi in such treasonous fashion." He shook his head sadly at her, and she noticed with shock that his eyes were kind. "Get set now. I'm going to transport you to the ae'Magi's castle. I don't like transporting humans, it's too hard on them. But the ae'Magi is concerned about Myr. It's not right to take advantage of a man whose mind is turned by grief, and we need to get to him as soon as possible."

He rubbed his hands together a minute in preparation. "The ae'Magi is much better at this than I am; but he is busy with other matters, so I will have to do."

His magic hit her body with enough force that she almost passed out. She hit a hard stone floor sweating and coughing. If she wasn't careful, she was going to die of lung fever before the Archmage could get his hands on her. She laughed at the thought, bringing on another fit of coughing.

Ungentle hands grabbed her upper arms with bruising strength, but the man grunted as he picked her up—she was a lot heavier than she looked. Muscle would do that.

It had been daylight outside, so the gloominess of the torchlit stone walls and her hair, which had come undone from its customary braid and hung over her face, rendered her effectively blind.

She was stripped with ruthless efficiency. To take her mind off what *that* meant, she tried to recapture a stray thought she'd had just before Lord Kisrah had sent her over. She had a vague notion that it might be important. Her aching head didn't want to cooperate.

"Look here, Garogue, she ain't as small as she looks!" Rough laughter and comments she would have felt better not hearing as a second guard neared.

Think, Aralorn. I was relieved that . . . that I had not met Lord Kisrah before. Her face felt hot and tight, in spite of the coolness of the stone under her feet. *Lord Kisrah would not recognize me as the Lyon's daughter.* She waited a minute before the significance of that thought hit her. *I have, however, met the ae'Magi as the Lyon's daughter. He was intrigued with the color of my eyes—my shapeshifter blood.*

Gods, she thought bleakly. *If he realizes who I am, he can use my father against me.*

While the guards were preoccupied, she tried again to

change. Not a drastic change this time, just an adjustment to her face and eyes. Her features sharpened until they were as common to Rethian peasant stock as her medium brown eyes. The eyes were always the hardest part, for some reason, and she didn't usually bother. But she didn't want the ae'Magi to think that she had even the slightest touch of green magic. It might be important in her escape. With a bit more effort, her skin darkened to add authenticity.

"Too bad we can't do nothin' with her but look." A callused hand ran over her hip.

"Yup, don' you ever think of nothing else. Just you remember what happened to Len. He thought the ae'Magi wouldn't ever know. Besides, we usually get a turn at 'em."

Goody. Something to look forward to.

She was dragged forward again, her exhaustion making her more of a deadweight than before. Her head contacted the stone wall when she was swung over a broad shoulder.

"They sure grow these Northerners heavy!" More laughter, but by then Aralorn was beyond caring.

It was late at night when Wolf returned to the camp. He expected everyone to be asleep. Instead, he came upon Myr seated on a rock in front of the caves and polishing Aralorn's sword by the light of the moon.

"Where did you find it?" Wolf asked.

Startled, Myr leapt to his feet, holding the sword at ready. Seeing Wolf, Myr resumed his former position on the rock.

"Oh, it's you, Wolf. No luck? Damn." Myr held the blade up to the light. "I found it in a small cave off the entranceway this evening. Someone had made an attempt to clean it but didn't do a very good job. I suppose that one of the children found it and left it there when he realized what it was. I couldn't sleep, so I thought I'd clean it—no sense letting a good sword rust."

"No," agreed Wolf, lying down facing Myr with his muzzle on his paws.

Myr wasn't his friend. But Aralorn had liked him.

After a while, Myr asked, "Where did you look?"

So Wolf told him. It took some time. Myr listened, running the soft cloth over the odd-colored blade. When Wolf was done, Myr thought for a minute.

"How did you look for her? I mean did you just look? Couldn't a shapeshifter change her shape and escape?"

Wolf shook his head. "Once she was imprisoned, she wouldn't be able to change. Too much iron in the bars." And she'd have been chained.

"Iron does suppress magic?" Myr said, only half asking.

"Shapeshifter's magic."

The night was still except for the noise the soft cloth made on the sword. Then Myr said, "I'd met her once before, did you know that? It took me a while before I could pin down just where, because I was only a child. A more pompous, self-centered, proper little brat than I was you'd be hard-pressed to find. She was younger then, too, but she had the same mannerisms. Equal with anybody and observing protocol only because it suited her. I was offended, but my grandfather laughed and kissed her hands and said something about counting on her to liven up a dull reception."

There was a brief pause before he continued with his story. "You have to understand that I've been raised reading people's faces all my life. I saw that she really respected the tough old man, and the lack of sincerity in her manners was—dislike for the untruths that protocol demanded. It was a lesson that I took to heart." Myr paused, examining the gleaming blade.

With a sigh, he set it aside. "What I'm getting to is this: The ae'Magi was at court a lot in those days. My grandfather thought the world of him. If I met Aralorn at court, wouldn't he have? She's not . . . pretty, but she is memorable.

And if she wasn't, her father certainly is. If I were going to break someone, the easiest way would be to go after her family. You might check out Lambshold and see if all of the Lyon's family are accounted for."

Wolf caught his breath sharply. "She would be much more conscious of that than you. With that in mind, she would do her best to make herself unrecognizable. How long is it since she was taken?" He'd lost track of time.

"Four days."

Finally, the wolf spoke again. "She's in one of the dungeons obviously—or she's escaped, though that is extremely unlikely." She'd escaped once, but the ae'Magi hadn't been expecting it. "I think she may be in the first place I looked—in the Archmage's castle. When I searched the last few castles I was thorough, and I think that she would have had to hide herself really well—better than she probably could by then. She doesn't have much time, the dungeon masters in the ae'Magi's keeps are not renowned for their gentle treatment of the prisoners—to say nothing of the ae'Magi himself. She should be safe from him, though; he's got other concerns that are more important." Wolf hadn't been subtle the last two places he'd been, and the ae'Magi would know he'd been inside. Three dead men would have told him that someone had been there, and the method of their deaths would have told the Archmage who.

Wolf paused to think before he continued. "If she's not there, I'll come back here to check in with you. If she escapes, this is the only sanctuary that she has to come to." On those words, the wolf melted into the forest shadows, leaving the young king sitting alone on his rock.

"Myr has a mage with him. What does he look like?"

The ae'Magi's voice was really extraordinary, thought Aralorn. Soft and warm, it offered sanctuary—but she knew those tones, and terror cat-footed toward her.

But not even that fear combined with the cuts he was making on her arm was enough to hold her attention for long. The pain from the recoil of centuries of magic woven tightly into the stones of the dungeons made what he was doing to her body seem secondary.

She wondered if she ought to tell him that if he used iron manacles in the torture chamber as well as in the cell, she would be much more aware of what he was doing. The iron effectively blocked her meager talents from picking up on the twisted magic that a thousand years of magicians had left in the stone of the dungeon.

A bucket of cold water brought her attention back to her body. It felt good against her hot skin at first, but then the chill made her shake helplessly. In a rational moment, she smiled; the lung fever would take her soon—in a few days—if she could just hide it from him so that he wouldn't turn her into one of the dead things that hung restlessly in her cell. She'd been grateful when she didn't have to look at them anymore—if only she could do something about hearing them.

He wasn't using magic on her as he had the first time she'd visited his castle. Maybe the dungeon inhibited his magic as well—or maybe he was using all his magic for something else.

———

Baffled, the ae'Magi looked at the pathetic figure hanging in front of him. He had seen her smile while he was cutting her, and it bothered him. She wasn't one of those who enjoyed pain, but she didn't seem to even feel it. Torture wasn't working on her.

She seemed confused sometimes, though. Perhaps stealth could get him what pain could not.

"Sweetheart, sweetheart, listen to me," said the ae'Magi in Myr's voice, his tones gentle, like a young man courting a mate.

Aralorn jerked in reflex at the voice.

"Sweetheart, I know that you hurt. I've come to get you out of here, but you need to tell me where Cain is. We need him to get you out."

She frowned, and said in a puzzled voice, "Cain?"

"Yes," asked Myr again, and she heard a touch of anger in the voice now, "where is Cain? Where is Myr's mage?"

———

Myr wouldn't be angry with her—even though it sounded like Myr, it wasn't him. The certainty came from somewhere. She should know who Cain was, though, and it bothered her that she didn't. That didn't mean that she wanted the person who stole Myr's voice to know that.

"Dead," she said then, with utter certainty in her voice. Somewhere a part of her applauded the edge of melancholy she gave to her voice. "He is dead and gone."

———

That hadn't occurred to him; it simply hadn't occurred to him. The ae'Magi paced the length of the chamber. It wasn't possible. Angrily, he stripped off the gloves he'd fastidiously donned to separate him from her filthy flesh.

It would ruin everything if his son was dead. All his efforts would be for nothing. He raised the knife to her throat, then thought better of it. She still had information for him; he wouldn't kill her for spite.

Turning on his heel, the ae'Magi stalked out of the chamber. As he passed through the guardroom, he left orders to have her moved back into her cell and, as an afterthought, told the dungeon master that if he could find out where the rebels were hiding, he would give him a silver piece.

———

The dungeons were among the parts of the ae'Magi's castle that were very old—the result of those years was not lovely.

The smell made Wolf choke as he snuck into them from the hidden entrance. Magic had taken him to the castle, but he'd been forced to use mundane methods to enter. The ae'Magi was in residence, which gave him hope that Aralorn would be, too—but it meant he had to be very careful about the magic he used.

No one saw him as he emerged into the walkway between the cells. The night guards were in the room that was the only passageway from the main dungeon, other than the hidden ones, of course. There was no need for their presence in the actual dungeon at this time of night, unless they were escorting a captive in or out—or someone was being tortured.

He stood on a wide stone walkway, in human shape. On one side were seven cells, sunken the depth of a grave, in the old style. On the other side was the torture chamber, also so sunken. It was unoccupied at the moment. The only hint of life came from the smoldering coals in the raised hearth in the center of the cell.

There was no light in the dungeon other than Wolf's staff, but it was sufficient. The ring of keys was still kept on its holder near the guardroom door—for convenience's sake.

He slid the nearest door open and climbed down the steep, narrow stairs. The prisoners chained to the wall were too far gone to notice him. He took wolf shape because of the wolf's sharper senses and regretted the necessity. The smells of a dungeon were bad enough to the human nose, but the wolf's eyes were watering as he backed out of the cell. Returning to his human form, he closed the cell back up. She wasn't in there. He found the same at the second cell.

In the third cell, chained corpses littered the floor and hung on the wall like broken dolls, but they moaned and breathed with the pseudolife that animated Uriah. They watched him with glittering eyes as he shifted again to wolf shape to sample the air. But they were too new, too heavily controlled by the ae'Magi's spells, to give alarm.

More people in the fourth cell. When he'd lived here, there had seldom been more than one or two people in the whole dungeon. He shifted to wolf, took a breath—and stopped breathing altogether.

She's here.

He pushed the fierce joy of that aside. Time enough to celebrate when he had her safe.

He found her in the corner of the cell. Her face was different, but she was muttering to herself, and it was her voice, her scent under the filth. Her breathing was hoarse and difficult, breaking into heavy coughing when he shifted her against him to take off the irons—the dungeons held so much magic that short of melting the stone, the ae'Magi wouldn't feel what he did unless he was in the next room. That didn't mean they could afford to stay here long. Wolf swore at the wounds the cuffs left on her ankles and wrists.

No time to look for further wounds. He had to get out of here.

Gently, he picked her up, ignoring the smell of dungeon that clung to her. He stepped over the huddled bodies of her fellow inmates with no more attention than if they had been bundles of straw. Although he had no hands free to carry it, the staff followed him like an obedient dog.

It wasn't until he stood outside the cell that he realized he had a problem. The secret door he'd entered through was a crawl space, too narrow to get through with Aralorn unable to move on her own.

He didn't have time to dawdle.

A touch to the mask with his staff and both disappeared. A brief moment of concentration, and the scars followed. He was no shapeshifter. The face he wore beneath the scars was the one he was born with: It was his as much as the scars were also his.

Trying to avoid causing her any further hurt, he positioned Aralorn on his shoulder, holding her in place with one hand and letting the other hang carelessly free. A ball of light formed over his left shoulder and followed him to the guardroom door.

As he opened the door, the guards scrambled for their weapons until they saw his face. Wolf carelessly tossed the keys on the rough-hewn table, where they left a track in the greasy buildup as they slid. When he spoke, it was with the ae'Magi's hated voice, soft and warm with music. The illusion was simple—he didn't need much to make his face look so near to the ae'Magi's that in the dark they would not be able to tell him from his father.

"I think that it would be wiser from now on," he told them, "for the guard in charge to keep the keys on his person. It is too easy for someone to enter the dungeon by other paths. There is no reason that we should make it any easier to get into the cells than it already is."

Without looking at the men again, he walked to the far door, which obediently opened to let him through and closed after him. The wide staircase that led to the upper floors stretched in front of him, leaving but a narrow space against the wall, supposedly to allow access to the area under the stairs that was sometimes used for storage. It was this path that he took, ducking as he moved under the stairway.

Unerringly, he touched the exact spot that triggered the hidden door. As he stepped through, he whispered a soft spell, and the dust under the stairs rearranged itself until it looked as it had before he walked there.

He put out the light as the stone door shut behind him. The passage was as dark as pitch, and there was little light for even his mage-sensitive eyes to pick out. Tiny flecks of illumination that found their way through openings in the mortar made the towering walls glitter like the night sky. Their presence was the reason he'd put out the light—lest someone in a dark room on the other side of the wall witness the same phenomenon.

Wolf kept one hand against a wall and the other securely

around Aralorn and felt the ground ahead with his feet. He slowed his progress when a pile of refuse he kicked with his foot bounced down an unseen stairway. With a grim smile that no one could see, he continued blindly down the stairs.

There were shuffling noises as rats and other less savory creatures scrambled anonymously out of his way. Once he almost lost his footing as he stepped on something not long dead. A growling hiss protested his encroachment on someone's dinner.

Only when they reached the last of the long flight of steps did he decide they were far enough down that he dared a light. The floor was thick with dust; only faint outlines showed where he had disturbed the dust the last time he'd been here several years before, raiding one of the hidden libraries—there were more than the one he'd made off with completely.

Content that the passage had remained undiscovered, Wolf walked to a blank wall and sketched symbols in the air before it. The symbols hung glowing orange in the shadows until he was finished; then they shimmered and moved until they were touching the wall. The wall glittered in its turn, before abruptly disappearing—opening the way to still another obscure passage, deep in the rock under the castle. He continued for some time, his path twisting this way and that, through passages once discovered by a boy seeking sanctuary.

Twice he had to change his route because the way he remembered was too small for him to take carrying Aralorn. Once, the passage was blocked by a recent cave-in. Several of the corridors showed signs of recent use, and he avoided them as well. They surfaced finally from the labyrinth, several miles east and well out of easy view of the castle.

He shifted her from his shoulder then, cradling her in his arms, though she was harder to carry that way. There was nothing that he could do until they reached safer ground, so he trod swift of foot through the night-dark forest, listening intently for sounds that shouldn't be there.

He wished that he hadn't had to show himself, because now—after all of his caution—it was going to be obvious that he was mixed up with Myr's group. The ae'Magi had been seeking him for a long time. So the attacks on Myr's camp were going to intensify. It was possible that the guards wouldn't mention the incident to the ae'Magi—but it was always better to be prepared for the worst. He was going to have to stage his confrontation with the Archmage soon.

He wasn't looking forward to the coming battle. Old stories of the Wizard Wars—Aralorn could tell them by the hour—spoke of battles of pure power between one magician and another, and the great glass desert, more than a hundred square miles of blackened glass, gave mute evidence of the costs of such battles. If he, with his strange mutations of magic, ever got involved in a battle on those terms, the results could be far worse.

It might be better by far to let the magician extend his power. Even the best magicians live only three to four hundred years, and the ae'Magi was well into his second century. Expending his power the way that he was now, even taking into account the energy he stole, would take years off his life. A hundred years of tyranny was better than the destruction of the earth.

The glass desert had been fertile soil once.

————

He walked until well after the sun rose, following no visible trail—losing the two of them in the wilds as best he might. He stopped when they reached the cache he'd set up on his way to the castle, far enough off the trails that they should be safe for a while. Not safe enough to use magic to transport them—that the ae'Magi might follow. But he could hide them from this distance—he'd found some spells that worked for that since his time hiding in the Northlands. Spells that had allowed him to follow Aralorn around without worrying the ae'Magi would find him.

He opened the bedroll awkwardly, unwilling to set her on the hard ground, and gently placed her on the soft blankets. His arms were cramping and sore from carrying her, so he had to stretch a bit before he did anything else.

Her darker skin hid the flush of fever, but it was hot and dry to his touch. Her breathing was hoarse, and he could hear the fluid in her lungs. He rolled the second blanket up and stuffed it under her head to help her breathe. Efficiently, gently, he cleaned her with spell-warmed water.

On the dark skin it should have been more difficult to see the bruises, but her skin was gray from illness, revealing the darker patches. Some were obviously old, probably from her initial capture. But fresh bruises overlay the old ones.

Three ribs were either broken or cracked, he wasn't well enough trained in healing to tell the difference. The ribs and a large lump on the back of her head seemed the worst of her wounds—both were more likely the result of her initial capture than any torture.

Her fingernails had been removed, swollen knuckles revealed the violence of the method used to pull them. The toes on her right foot were broken, the smallest torn off completely. She had been whipped with efficiency from the top of her shoulders to the backs of her knees. But those wounds would heal in few weeks (except, of course for the misplaced toe). A woman could live without a toe.

He pulled out the bag of simples that he had brought with him. He wasn't a healer, by any means, but he'd picked up enough to bind her wounds.

When he was through cleaning her back, he covered it with a mold paste and wrapped the bandage around tight enough to help immobilize her ribs. He splinted the toes and cleaned and bandaged her ankles, hands, and wrists.

It was while he was working on her wrists that he noticed the large sore where the inner side of her arm had been skinned. He stilled, then very gently covered the sore with ointment and wrapped it as if it hadn't sent chills down his spine.

It was one of the ae'Magi's favorite games. The inner arm was tender, and a man who was skilled with a skinning knife could cause significant pain without incapacitating his victim. The ae'Magi usually did something extremely nasty first to soften his victim.

Carefully, Wolf opened Aralorn's mouth and examined the inside of her cheek, the roof of her mouth, under her tongue, and her teeth. Nothing. He looked inside her ear and said a few soft words of magic. Nothing. As he turned her head to look at her other ear, something sparkled in the sun. Her eyelids.

Carefully Wolf held her face where the sunlight fell on it fully. Both of her eyelids, on careful examination, were slightly swollen, but it was the seepage that told the real story.

He held his open hand several inches over her eye and murmured another spell. When he took his hand away, he held four long, slender, steel needles, each barbed on the end like a fisherman's hook. The needles were sharp enough that they slid in with little pain, but every time the eye moved, the sharpened edges of the needle cut a little more. They were not the expensive silver needles, but the cheaper iron-based steel—made primarily for coarser work.

He looked at them for a minute and they melted, leaving his hand undamaged. As he removed four more from her other eye, he wished passionately, and not for the first time in his life, that he knew more.

True healing was one of the first things taught to a shapeshifter; but for a human magic-user, it was one of the last arts learned. Increasing the efficacy of herbs was the best he knew. He doubted that in this case even a shape-shifter could heal her eyes—he seemed to remember something about wounds made with cold iron being more difficult than others.

He put her in a soft cotton shirt that reached to her thighs. When he was finished, he put a cold-spelled compress over her eyes and bound it tightly in place.

He had reached the end of his expertise. Tiredly, he covered her with another blanket and lay down next to her, not quite touching. He slept.

Her world consisted of vague impressions of vision and sound. She saw people she knew, strangely altered. Sometimes they filled her with horror, other times they drew no emotion from her at all. There was Talor as he'd been the last time she'd seen him in Sianim—then something happened to him, and he was dead, only he was talking to her and telling her things that she didn't want to hear.

Sometimes she floated in a great nothingness that scared her, but not as much as the pain. Her body was a great distance away, and she would pull back as far as she could because she was afraid of what she would find when she returned. Then, like the stretchy tubris rope that children played with, something would snap, and she would find herself back in the midst of the pain and heat and terror. Someone screamed, it hurt her ears, and she wished the sound would stop.

This time her return was different. Besides being hot, she was also wet and sticky. The pain was dimmed to bearable levels; even the ache in her side was less. There was something that attracted her attention and she concentrated—trying to

figure out what it was. It had called her back from her nothingness into a place she'd much rather not be. She decided
in a moment of pseudorationality that she needed to find it
and kill it so she could be free to go away.

She looked for it in her dreams and fragments of impressions touched her. There was something terribly wrong
with her eyes. Cold iron whose wounds were permanent. It
had bitten and chewed and . . .

She shied away and found another piece of memory.
Magic horribly distorted and twisted, making dead men
breathe. It frightened her. There was no safety in death
here, and she wanted the sanctuary that death should offer.
Then the cold iron cut off her awareness of the dead things
that shared her space. She had never felt so helpless; it gave
her a dispirited claustrophobia that made her strain repeat-
edly against the bonds, until she exhausted herself. Bonds
that most well-trained, full-blooded shapeshifters might
have gotten out of, but she had all the weaknesses and too
little power.

There . . . while she was fighting . . . she almost had it.
The thing that had pulled her back and made her hurt again.
It was sound, familiar sound. Why should that bother her?

She was so tired. She was losing her concentration, and
pictures came more rapidly until she was lost in her nightmare memories again.

———————

They'd been camped in the same place for three days.
It worried him because they were much too close to the
ae'Magi's castle, but the thought of moving her worried
him more. Instead of getting better since being out of the
cell, she seemed worse. Her eyes were seeping with the
pus of infection. Her fever was no higher, but it was no
lower either. Her breathing was more difficult, and when
she coughed, he could tell that it hurt her ribs.

As he watched her, he tormented himself with guilt. Had he been quicker to find her, she would have stood a better chance. The needles had been used on her eyes only recently. He could have found her in his first search if he'd only remembered that she might be wearing someone else's face.

As it did when he was angered, the other magic in him flickered fey—nudging him, tempting him. Usually he used it, twisting it toward his own ends, but this time he was tired with worry, guilt, and sleeplessness. The magic whispered, seducing him with visions of healing.

His eyes closed, without conscious thought he stretched out carefully beside Aralorn. Gently, he touched her face, seeing the wrongness there—the slight fracture in the skull that he hadn't been aware of.

As he gave control away to the seductive whispers of his magic, he found that he could feel her pulse, almost her thoughts. Sex notwithstanding, this was closer than he'd ever been to another human being. With anyone else, he would have lashed out, done anything just to get away—to be safe alone.

But this was Aralorn, and he had to heal her, or . . . He caught a flick of the desperation of that thought, but was soon lost in the peace of his magic. He floated with it for what could have been a hundred years or a single instant. Gradually, his fear of the loss of control, so well learned when his searing magic had leapt out burning, hurting, scarring, crept upon him—breaking the trance he'd fallen into.

He opened his eyes and gasped for air. His heart was pounding, and sweat poured off his body. Great shudders racked him. He turned his head enough to look at Aralorn.

The first thing that hit him was that he *was* looking at Aralorn. The guise she'd donned was gone. The bruises on her legs looked much worse on her own relatively pale skin. Fever had brought unnatural color to her pale cheeks.

When he could, he bent over and removed the bandage from her eyes. The swelling had almost completely gone and her eyes appeared normal when he carefully lifted her eyelids. He hadn't looked before—he knew what those needles had done. He felt carefully with his fingertips where he'd seen the break in her skull and could locate nothing.

Almost too tired to move, he pulled her head onto his shoulder and drew blankets neatly around them. He knew he should stay up and keep watch—there was no warhorse to share guard duty with—but he hadn't been this tired since his early apprentice days.

It was morning when Aralorn awoke, still slightly delirious. She'd had dreams of the quiet sounds of the forest before, and she let herself take that comfort now. She knew that all too soon she would have to face reality again. The nice thing was that the times reality crept in were getting farther and farther apart.

She thought about that for a minute before she realized that there was a man beside her. Delirium took over then, and she was drowning slowly. It was very hard to breathe, and she lost track of the forest while she strangled.

The soft sounds of a familiar voice lent her comfort and strength, but there was something wrong with the voice. It was too soft, it should be cold and rough, harsher. She associated unpleasant things with the warmer tones. The voice she wanted to hear should be dead like the Uriah, like Talor. She could hear someone whimpering and wondered who it was.

She ate and it tasted very good, salty and warm on her sore throat. She drank something else and a part of her tasted the bitter herb with approval, knowing that it would help her breathe. *Wasn't there some reason that she didn't want to get better?*—but she couldn't decide why she wouldn't want to get well, and while she thought about it, she drifted back to sleep.

———————

Wolf watched her and waited. Without the unquenchable energy that characterized her, she looked fragile, break-able. Awake, she had a tendency to make him forget how small she was.

He gritted his teeth and controlled his rage when she cried out in terror. Although she babbled out loud, she said nothing that would have been any use to the ae'Magi were he listening.

She was quiet finally, and Wolf sat propped up against a tree, near enough to keep an eye on her but far enough away that he wouldn't disturb her slumbers.

He should never have been able to heal her. Indisputably, he had. Even if he did nothing more than eliminate the paths the needles had cut into her eyes, it was more than human magic allowed for. Less dramatic but even further outside the bounds of magic, as he understood it, was the fact that she now wore the appearance that was hers by birth.

He'd always had the ability to do things beyond the gener-ally accepted bounds of human magic—taking wolf shape for extended periods of time was one of those. Always before he could have attributed this to the enormous power he wielded. Human magic could heal, but it required a more detailed knowledge of the human body than he had acquired—killing required much less precision. Human magic could not recog-nize a shapeshifter's natural shape and restore her to it . . . as he had done.

His magic had blithely crashed through the laws of magic established for thousands of years. What *was* he that he could do such things?

He found no answers. He'd seen the woman who bore him only once that he could remember. She'd seemed

ordinary enough—for a woman who had spent a decade in
the ae'Magi's dungeon. But the ae'Magi had got a son on
her and kept her alive afterward. She must have been more
than she seemed.

Wolf had been the result of an . . . experiment perhaps:
one that had gotten out of hand.

Aralorn stirred, catching his attention. He got to his feet
with relief at being drawn from his thoughts, and went to her.

EIGHT

⟨⟨⟨⟩⟩⟩

Aralorn was in the habit of waiting until she knew where she was and who she was supposed to be before she opened her eyes—a habit developed from frequently being some-one other than herself. For some reason, it seemed more difficult than usual. The warm sun on her face seemed as much out of place as the sound of a jay squeaking from its perch somewhere above her.

She moved restlessly and felt a warning twinge from her side that was instantly echoed from various other parts of her body. As a memory aid, she found it effective—if crude.

The problem was, she had no idea how she had gotten from the ae'Magi's dungeon to where she was.

Deciding that it was unlikely that she would come to any earth-shattering conclusions lying around feigning sleep, she opened her eyes and sat up—an action that she had immediate cause to regret. The abrupt change in position caused her to start coughing—no pleasant thing with cracked ribs. She collapsed slowly back into her prone position and waited for her eyes to quit watering.

Breathing shallowly, she restricted herself to turning her head to examine her current environment. She was alone in a small clearing, surrounded by thick shrubs that quickly gave way to broad-leafed trees. She could hear a brook running somewhere nearby. The sun was high and edging toward afternoon. Mountains rose, not far away, on at least three sides. They were smaller than their Northland counterparts, but impressive enough. Also unfamiliar, at least from her angle.

The blankets in which Aralorn was more or less cocooned were of a fine intricate weave and finer wool. She whistled softly at the extravagance. Just one of them would cost a mercenary two months' salary, and she was wrapped in two of them, with her head pillowed on a third. She should have been too warm, bundled up so heavily—but it felt good.

The bandaging on her hands and wrists was neatly tied and just snug enough to give support without being too tight. Whoever had tied it was better at binding wounds than she was—not a great feat. She didn't bother to examine the other bandages that covered her here and there, preferring not to scrutinize her wounds in case too many body parts were missing or nonfunctional.

It occurred to her then that her eyes should belong to the category of missing and nonfunctional items. The method the ae'Magi had used to blind her had been . . . thorough. Enough so that she had not thought that even shapeshifter magic could heal her.

She shivered in her blankets. She had the unwelcome thought that it might be possible for a strong magician to create the illusion of this meadow. She didn't know for sure, but from her stories . . . Much more likely than someone breaking her out of the ae'Magi's dungeons. Much easier, she was certain, than it would be to heal her eyes.

She looked around, but she was still the only occupant of the clearing.

Deciding that if it were the ae'Magi who was going to

show up, she didn't want to face him lying on her back, she
found a slender tree growing near her head. She pushed
herself back until she bumped into it—the effort it took was
not reassuring. Gradually, so as not to trigger another fit of
coughing, she raised herself with the tree's support until
she was sitting up with her back against it. She waited for a
minute. When she didn't start coughing, she slid herself up
the tree, the bark scraping her back despite the wrapping
job someone had done—that felt real enough. Finally, she
was standing—at least leaning.

She didn't hear him until he spoke from some distance
behind her. His voice was without its usual sardonic over-
tones, but it was still blessedly Wolf's. "Welcome back,
Lady."

Sheer dumb relief almost sent her crashing to the ground.
Wolf. It was Wolf. He, she was willing to believe, could rescue her and heal whatever needed healing. Safe.

She swallowed and schooled her face—he wouldn't
enjoy having her jump on him and sob all over him any
more than she'd have enjoyed the memory of it once she got
her feet safely under her again.

When she was sure she could pull off nonchalant, she
turned her head with a smile of greeting that left her when
she saw his face. Only years of training kept her from giving her fear voice, even that couldn't stop the involuntary
step backward that she took. Unfortunately, her feet tangled in one of the blankets, she lost the support of the tree,
and fell.

Definitely cracked ribs, but not even pain could pen-
etrate her despair.

The Archmage.

Unwilling to let her enemy out of her sight, she rolled
until she could see him, which set off a coughing fit. Eyes
watering from pain, she saw that he, too, had stepped
back, albeit more gracefully. He raised a hand to his face
and then dropped it abruptly. He waited until she finished

coughing and could talk—and there was no expression on his face at all.

Aralorn found herself grateful that she was unable to speak for a minute because it gave her a chance to think. The ae'Magi's face it might be, but Wolf's yellow eyes glittered at her—as volatile as the face was not.

It was Wolf, her Wolf. The still, almost flight of his body told her that more than his eyes. Illusion could reproduce anyone's eyes, but she was unwilling to believe that anyone but her knew Wolf's body language that well.

Cain was the ae'Magi's son, but no one had ever told her how much the son resembled the father. If the ae'Magi's son had shown the world his magic-scarred face, the one she knew best, surely someone would have mentioned the scars. Perhaps the ae'Magi didn't want people to remember how much he looked like his demonized son. She could believe that if he didn't want people to comment, they wouldn't. Her next thought was that Wolf didn't look like a man only a few years older than Myr—a few years younger than she was. Her third thought, as her coughing slowed down, was that she'd better figure out a way to handle this—she didn't want to hurt him again.

Before she could say anything, Wolf spoke. "If I thought that you could make it to safety alone, I would leave you in peace. Unfortunately, that is not possible. I assure you that I will leave as soon as you are back . . ."

She ended his speech with a rude word and assumed as much dignity as she could muster while lying awkwardly on the ground amid a tangle of blankets. "Idiot!" she told him. "Of course I knew who you were." She hadn't been certain—he'd just made her short list, but she didn't need to tell him that. "Just how many apprentices do you think the ae'Magi has had? I know the name of every one of them, thanks to Ren. He seemed to think that information might be valuable someday. How many mages do you think would have the power to do what you did to Edom?" Two or three, she thought, but one of those was Kisrah—who had not been on her list. "Just how stupid do you think I am?" She had to pause to keep from coughing again—but he didn't attempt to answer her question with any of his usual sarcasm, and that worried her. So she turned her defense into an attack. "Why did you hide from me again? First the wolf shape, then the mask and the scars." She let her voice quiver and didn't give in to the temptation to make it just a little too much. "Do you distrust me so much?"

"No," said Wolf, and the hint of a smile played around his mouth—more importantly, he no longer looked like he'd rather be anywhere than there. "I forgot." He waved a hand in the general direction of his face. "The scars are legitimate. I acquired them as I told you. It wasn't until I left there . . ." Left his father, she thought. "I realized that I could get rid of them the same way that I could take wolf shape. But for a long time, it didn't matter because I was the wolf. When I decided to act against him instead of continuing to run—all things considered, I preferred to keep the scars."

Aralorn certainly understood why that would be. "So why change now?"

"When I got you out of the dungeon, it was necessary to appear to be the ae'Magi in order to get past the guards. I was . . . I forgot to resume the scars, the mask." He sat beside her. "I didn't mean to startle you."

Startle. Yes, that was one way to put it.

With an expression that didn't quite make it to being the smile she intended, Aralorn told him, "When I die of heart failure the next time you frighten me like that, you can put that on my gravestone—'I didn't mean to startle her.'"

As she talked, she looked at him carefully. Seeing things that hadn't been apparent at first. His face was without the laugh lines around the eyes and mouth that characterized the ae'Magi's. There was no gray in the black hair, but the expression in his eyes made him look much older than his father had. Wolf eyes, Wolf's eyes they were—with a hunter's cold, amoral gaze.

"So why didn't I know that Cain was scarred?" she asked him.

"My father kept them hidden."

"Does Myr know who you are?" She found that was important to her—which told her that she'd never given up Reth, being Rethian, the way she'd given up Sianim. Myr was her king, and she wouldn't have him lied to.

He nodded. "I told him before I offered my assistance. It was only fair that he knew what he was getting into. And with whom."

There was a slight pause, then Aralorn said, "The ae'Magi asked me about you, about Cain." That much she could remember.

"Did he?" Wolf raised an eyebrow, but he wasn't as calm as he appeared. If he had been in his wolf shape, the hairs along his spine would have been raised: She recognized that soft tone of voice. "What did you say?"

Aralorn raised her eyebrow in return. "I told him that you were dead."

"Did he believe you?" he asked.

She shrugged and started to tug discreetly at the heap of blankets that intermingled with her feet. "At the time he did, but since you chose to rescue me, he'll probably come to the conclusion that I lied to him."

"Let's get you into a more comfortable position"—he indicated her troublesome hobble with a careless hand—"and back under the covers with you before you catch your death, shall we?" His voice was a wicked imitation of one of the healers at Sianim.

Even as he untangled her and restored her makeshift bed to its previous order, she could feel an imp of a headache coming on. "Wolf," she said softly, catching his hand and stilling it, "don't use the scars. You are not the ae'Magi—you don't have to prove it."

He tapped her on the nose and shook his head with mock despair. "Did anyone ever tell you that you are over-bearing, Lady?" That "Lady" told her that things were all right between the two of them.

That knowledge meant that the crisis was over, and she was suddenly exhausted. He resumed his efforts and tucked a pillow behind her head.

"Where are we, and how long have we been here?" It was an effort to keep her eyes open any longer, and her voice slurred as she finished the sentence, ending in a rack-ing cough. As she hacked and gasped for breath, he lifted her upright. She didn't notice that it helped any, but the feel of his arms around her was pleasant.

The hazy thought occurred to her that the greater part of the reason she'd left Reth to go to Sianim in the first place was to get away from the feeling of being protected. Now she was grateful for it. She didn't think that he'd notice that the last few coughs were suppressed sounds of self-directed amusement.

"We're about a day's brisk walk away from the Master Magician's castle. We've been here for three days. As soon as you wake up, we'll start on our way."

He said something more, she thought, but she couldn't be bothered to stay awake for it.

He bent down and whispered it again. This time she heard it. "Sleep. I have you safe."

———

The next time Aralorn regained consciousness, she was ruthlessly fed and dressed in a tunic and trousers she rec-ognized as her own before she had a chance to do any more than open her eyes. She was propped up with brisk efficiency beside a tree and told to "stay there." Wolf then piled all of the blankets, clothes, and utensils together and sent them on their way with a brisk wave of his staff.

"Where did you get my clothes?" Aralorn asked with idle curiosity from where she sat leaning against a tree. Her tree.

"From Sianim, where you left them." With efficient motions, he was cleaning the area they had occupied until only the remains of the fire would give any indication that someone had camped there.

She'd known that. Had just needed him to admit it to her.

She raised an eyebrow at him, crossed her arms over her chest, and said in a deceptively mild tone, "You mean the whole time that I was all but bursting out of the innkeeper's son's clothes, wearing blisters on my feet with his boots— you could have gotten mine for me?"

He grunted without looking at her, but she could see a hint of a smile in his flawless profile. He was, she decided, without it soothing her ire in the least, more beautiful than his sire.

"I asked you a question," she said in a dangerously soft tone she'd learned from him.

"I was waiting for the tunic seams to finally give way . . ." He paused to dodge the handful of grass she threw at him, then shrugged. "I am sorry, Lady. It just never occurred to me."

Aralorn tried to look stern, but the effort turned into a laugh.

Wolf brushed the grass from his shoulders and went back to packing. Aralorn leaned back against her tree and watched him as he worked, trying to get used to the face he now wore.

In an odd sort of way, he looked more like his father than his father did. The ae'Magi's face was touched with innocence and compassion. Wolf's visage had neither. His was the face of man who could do anything, and had.

"Can you ride?" he asked, calling her back from her thoughts.

Aralorn considered the state of her body. Everything functioned—sort of, anyway. Riding was certainly better than any alternative she could think of. She nodded. "If we don't go any faster than a walk. I don't think that I could sit a trot for very long."

He nodded and said three or four brisk words in a language she didn't know. He didn't bother with the theatrics in front of her. The air merely shimmered around him strangely. Not unpleasant—just difficult to look at, much nicer than when she changed shape. The black horse who had replaced Wolf snorted at her, then shook himself as if he were wet. His eyes were as black as his hide, and she found herself wishing he'd kept his own eyes no matter how odd it would have seemed for a horse to have yellow eyes.

She stood up stiffly, trying not to stagger—or start coughing again. When she could, she walked shakily up to him, grateful to reach the support of his neck.

Unfortunately, although Wolf-as-a-Horse wasn't as massive as Sheen, he was as tall, and she couldn't climb up. After her third attempt, he knelt in the dust so that she could slip onto his back.

He took them down an old trail that had fallen into disuse. The only tracks on it were from the local wildlife. The woods around them were too dense to allow easy travel, but Wolf appeared to know them—when the trail disappeared into a lush meadow, he picked it up again on the other side without having to take a step to the left or right. Wolf's gaits, she found, were much smoother than Sheen's; but the motion still hurt her ribs.

To distract herself when it started to get unbearable, she thought up a question almost at random. "Where did you find a healer?"

A green magic-user would never be anywhere near the ae'Magi's castle. Other than her, she supposed, but she was no healer—green magic or not.

Speaking had been a mistake. The dust of the road set

her coughing. He stopped, turning his head so he could watch her out of one dark eye.

When she could talk again she met his gaze and didn't like the worry in it. She was fine. "You got rooked if you paid very much; any healer worth his fee would have taken care of the ribs and cough, too."

Wolf twitched his ears and said in an odd tone, even for him, "He didn't have enough time to do much. Even if there had been the time, I wouldn't have trusted him to do more than what was absolutely necessary—he . . . didn't have the training."

Aralorn had an inkling that she should be paying more attention to the way he phrased his explanation, but she was in too much misery between her ribs and her cough to do much more than feel sorry for herself.

Then she had it. The conviction when she'd first heard his voice after waking alone in the little camp he'd set up. Of course Wolf had gotten her out and fixed her eyes so she could see.

But Wolf was a human mage. Son of the ae'Magi. And human mages might be okay at some aspects of healing— like putting broken bones together. But no human mage could have dealt with what had been done to her eyes.

———

Wolf kept to a walk, trying to make the ride as smooth as possible for her. He could discern that she was in a lot of pain by the way her hands shook in his mane when she coughed, but she made light of it when he questioned her. As the day progressed, she leaned wearily against his neck and coughed more often.

Worse, after that one, brief conversation, she'd quit talking. Aralorn always talked.

He continued until he could stand it no more, then he called a halt at a likely camping area, far from the main thoroughfares and out of sight of the trail they'd been following. As soon as he stopped, before he could kneel to make things easier, Aralorn slid off him, then kept sliding until her rump hit the ground. She waved off his concern, breathing through her nose, her mouth pinched.

Wolf regained his human form, then turned his attention to making a cushion of evergreen boughs and covering the result with the blankets, keeping a weather eye on his charge. By the time he finished, Aralorn was on her feet again—though, he thought, not for long.

"I'm moving like an old woman," she complained, walking toward the bed he'd made. "All I need is a cane."

She let him help her lie down and was asleep, he judged, before her eyes had a chance to close.

While Aralorn slept, Wolf stood watch.

———

The night was peaceful, she thought, except for when she was coughing. It got so bad toward the morning that she finally gave up resting and stood up. When she would have reached for the blankets to start folding them, Wolf set her firmly down on the ground with a growl that would have done credit to his wolf form and finished erasing all traces of their presence.

Dawn's light had barely begun to show before they were on their way.

Once she was sitting up rather than lying down, Aralorn's coughing mercifully eased. It helped that today they were cutting directly through the woods, which were thinned by the higher altitude. There was no trail dust to exacerbate the problem. When her modest herb lore identified some beggersblessing on the side of the road, she made Wolf stop so she could pick a bunch. With a double handful of the leaves stuffed in her pocket and a wad of them under her tongue, she could even look at the day's journey with some equanimity.

The narcotic alleviated the pain of her ribs and some of

the coughing, although it did make it a little more difficult
to stay on Wolf's back as it interfered with her equilibrium.
Several times, only Wolf's quick footwork kept her from
falling off.

———————

Wolf decided that the giggling was something he could
do without but found that, on the whole, he preferred it to
her silent pain. When they stopped, Wolf took a good look
at Aralorn, pale and dark-eyed from the drug she'd been
using. She'd refused food, because beggersblessing would
make her sick if she ate while under its influence.

The end result, he judged, was that she was weaker
than she'd been when they started that morning. He had
not transported them by magic because he was afraid that
his father would be able to track them and find where they
went. But if they continued at this donkey's pace, it was
even odds whether his father would find them before she
got too sick to ride at all.

He donned his human form once again, with his scars,
and after a moment's thought added the silver mask. It was
a difficult spell, and without the mask and scars, he was
uneasy. He didn't need anything distracting him.

"Wolf?" she asked.

"We're taking another way back," he told her, lifting her
into his arms—and took them into the Northlands.

Transporting people by magic was difficult enough that
most mages preferred travel on horseback or coach rather
than by magic, even in the spring, when the roads were
nothing more than a giant mud puddle. Transporting someone into the Northlands, where human magic had a tendency to go awry, was madness, but he aimed for the cave
where he had brought the merchant the day Aralorn had
joined them. That would leave them with only one day's
ride to the camp and only a few miles to travel before the

ae'Magi's magic would be hampered if he found out where
they had gone.

Concentrating on the shallow cave, he pulled them to
it, but *something* caught them and jerked them on with
enough force to stun Wolf momentarily . . .

He landed on his knees in darkness on a hard stone
floor. His instinctive light spell was too bright, and he had
to tone it down.

He was in the cave that housed his library.

Warily, he stood up and looked around—with his eyes
and his magic. Aside from the irregular oddness that had
become a familiar part of working his magic in the Northlands, nothing seemed wrong.

He laid her on the padded couch and pulled his cloak
over her. It would only take him a minute to let Myr know
he was back.

———————

In the castle of the Archmage, the ae'Magi sat gently drum-
ming his fingers on the burled wood of his desk. He was
not in the best of moods, having tracked an intruder from
castle to hold trying to discover who would be foolhardy
enough to trespass and powerful enough to get away with it.

And now he knew who it had been—and what he'd been
looking for.

The room that he occupied was covered in finely woven
carpets. Great beveled windows lined the outside wall
behind the desk, bathing the room with a warm golden
glow. On the opposite wall was a large, ornate fireplace
that sat empty in deference to the warmth of late summer.
In front of the fireplace, the pretty blond girl who was his
newest pet combed her hair and looked at the floor.

She trembled a bit. A month as his leman had made her
sensitive to his mood, which was, he admitted, quite vile
at the moment.

———————

Facing the desk was one of the dungeon guards, who held his cap deferentially in his hand. He spoke in the low tones that were correct for addressing someone in a position so much higher than his own. Though he was properly motionless, the ae'Magi could tell that his continued silence was making the man nervous. As it should. As it should.

Finally, the ae'Magi felt he could control himself enough to speak. "You saw Cain take one of the female prisoners? Several nights ago."

"Yes, Lord." The guardsman relaxed as soon as the ae'Magi spoke. "I remembered him from when he lived here, but I didn't realize who it was until he'd already gone. Last time I saw him, he were all scarred up, but I 'membered meself when he were a tyke he looked a lot like you, sire."

"And why did it take you so long to report this?"

"You weren't here, sire."

"I see." The ae'Magi felt uncouth rage coil in his belly. Cain had been here, *here*. "Which prisoner did he take?"

As if he had to ask. Dead, she'd told him. Cain was dead. And he'd believed her—so much so that when he found someone sneaking around in his territories, he'd never even considered it might be Cain.

"That woman Lord Kisrah brought in, sir."

There was a darned patch on the guardsman's shoulder. It had been so well done that the ae'Magi hadn't noticed it until he got closer. He would see to it that the guardsmen's uniforms were inspected and replaced when necessary. No one in his employ should wear a darned uniform.

This guardsman, the ae'Magi thought, enjoying himself despite his anger, wouldn't be needing a new uniform ever again. He took his time.

"Clean up the dust and leave me."

Shuddering, the sixteen-year-old silk merchant's daughter

swept the ashes of the guard into the little shovel that was
kept near the fireplace. She did a thorough job of it but wasted
no time.

After she had gone, he sat and ran his finger around one
of the burls on his desk.

"I had him," he said out loud. "I had the bait, and he
came—but I lost my chance. I should have felt it, should
have known she was something more." He thought about
the woman. What had been so special about her that would
attract his son?

Moodily, he took the stopper off the crystal decanter
that sat on a corner of his desk and poured amber wine in
a glass. He held it up to the light and swirled the liquid,
admiring the fine gold color—the same shade as Cain's
eyes. He tipped the glass and drank it dry, wiping his
mouth with his wrist.

"There are, however, some compensations, my son. I
know that you are actively working against me. You cannot remain invisible if you want to move to attack, and I
will find you. The woman is the key."

He whispered a minor summoning spell and waited
only a short time before he was answered by a knock
on the door. At his call, the Uriah who had once been a
Sianim mercenary entered the study. The mercenaries had
made fine Uriah. They were lasting longer than the ones he
made from peasants. This one might last years rather than
months. The old wizards had done better—theirs were still
functioning though they had been created in the Wizard
Wars.

He wished the second half of that book hadn't been
destroyed. He'd been looking for another copy of it for
years, but he feared that there were no more.

"You're that one who told me that you were familiar with the woman you took from Myr's campsite?" the
ae'Magi asked.

The Uriah bowed his head in assent.

"Tell me about her. What is her name? Where do you know her from?"

Another problem with the Uriah, besides longevity, the ae'Magi had found, was that communication was not all that it could be. Information could only be gotten with detailed questions, and even then a vital fact could be left out. They were good soldiers but not good scouts or spies.

"Aralorn. I knew her in Sianim," it replied.

Sianim. Had his problem spread beyond Reth?

"What did she do in Sianim?"

The Uriah shrugged carelessly. "She taught quarterstaff and halfstaff. She did some work for Ren, the Spymaster, I don't know how much."

"She worked as a spy?" The ae'Magi pounced on it.

"Ren the Mouse doesn't formalize much. He assigns whoever he thinks will be useful. From the number of her unexplained comings and goings, she worked for him more often than most."

"Tell me more about her."

"She is good with disguises and with languages. She can blend in anywhere, but I think she used to be Rethian." The Uriah smiled. "Not much use with a sword."

He'd liked her, the ae'Magi thought. *The man had liked her.* The Uriah was nothing more than a hungry beast, but he remembered what the man had known.

And then the Uriah said, "Ran around with a damned big wolf. Found him in the Northlands and took him home."

"A wolf?" The ae'Magi frowned.

"Those yellow eyes made everyone jumpy," the Uriah said.

The ae'Magi remembered abruptly that he'd recently had another escape from his castle. The girl had been aided by a wolf—or wolf pack—that had killed a handful of the ae'Magi's Uriah, who had inexplicably gone after it rather than after the girl they'd been ordered to chase.

He tried to remember what this Aralorn had looked

like—surely he'd have noticed if she were as exotic as his
Northland beauty.

"Describe her to me."

"She is short and pale-skinned even with a tan. Brown
hair, blue-green eyes. Sturdily built. She moves fast."

Not her, then, but still . . . green eyes. He'd bought that
slave because she had gray-green eyes, shapeshifter eyes.
Blue-green, gray-green—two names for the same color.

"You say she was good with disguises?"

―――――――

Aralorn was too tired to wake up when the covering was
pulled back, letting the cool air sweep over her warm body.
She moaned when gentle hands probed her ribs, but felt
no urgent need to open her eyes. She heard a soft sound
of dismay as her hands were unwrapped. A touch on her
forehead sent her back into sleep.

It was the sound of voices that woke her the second time,
a few minutes later, much more alert. The nausea that was
the usual companion to beggersblessing use had dissipated.

She noticed that she was in the library, covered with a
brightly colored quilt. A familiar cloak, Wolf's, lay carelessly tossed over the back of the sofa. Men's voices were
approaching.

She wondered how she'd slept through the trip to
camp—because he'd said that he couldn't have brought the
merchant all the way here.

She started to sit up, only to realize that the clothing
scattered on the floor was what she had been wearing.
Hastily, she pulled the blankets up to her neck to protect
her dignity just as Myr came around a bookcase.

"So," said Myr with a wide smile, "I see that you're
more or less intact after your experience with the ae'Magi's
hospitality. I must say, though, that it will be a long time
before I loan you any of my clothes again. I didn't bring
many with me." The pleasure and relief in his voice was

real, and she was surprised and not a little flattered that he cared so much about someone he'd known such a short time.

Aralorn smiled back at him and started to say something, but noticed that Wolf, who had followed Myr, was focusing intently on her hands. She followed his gaze to where her hands gripped the top of the blanket. Ten healthy nails dug into the cloth. The beggersblessing had left her wits begging, too; she hadn't even noticed that she didn't hurt at all.

Aralorn answered Myr absently. "Yes. Though he wasn't the best of hosts. I only saw him once or twice the whole time I was there."

Myr perched on the end of the sofa near Aralorn's feet and looked, for once, as young as he was. "And he prides himself on his treatment of guests," he said with a mournful shake of his head. "It doesn't even look like he left you any mementoes."

"Well," said Aralorn, looking at her hands again, very conscious of Wolf's doing the same thing. "You know he did, but I seem to have lost them. The last time I looked, my hands were missing the fingernails."

"How is your breathing?" asked Wolf.

Aralorn took a deep breath. "Fine. Is this your healer's work?" She wouldn't have asked, would have assumed that it had been Wolf, but he was looking particularly blank.

Wolf shook his head. "No, I told you that he was not experienced enough to do more than he did."

Wolf glanced at Myr. "I saw a few new people here, are any of them healers?"

"No," replied Myr, disgust rich in his voice. "Nor are they hunters, tanners, or cooks. We have six more children, two nobles, and a bard. The only one who is of any help is the bard, who is passably good with his knives. The two nobles sit around watching everyone else work or decide to

the invisible person could be seen. Wolf knew what she was doing—but there was nothing at the end of the sofa.

"Can you see him?" she asked Wolf.

When he shook his head, she directed her questioning to the man who wasn't there. "Who are you?"

"That's better," said the voice, and there was a distinct pop of air that accompanies teleportation.

That pop made Wolf confident enough to say, "He's gone."

"What do you think?" asked Aralorn, settling back onto Wolf, her voice husky from crying. "Was that our friend who gives us a hand with the books and healed me?"

"I can't imagine that there is an endless supply of invisible people here."

Wolf knew he should be more concerned, but he'd suddenly become aware that Aralorn was naked under the quilt. It hadn't bothered him before, when she'd been upset.

He started to shift her off him, with the end goal of getting as much distance on his side as possible. But as soon as his hands touched her hip—on top of the blanket—they wanted to pull her toward him, not push her away.

Self-absorbed, he only caught the tail end of Aralorn's question. "Say that again?" he asked.

"I asked how long you left me alone in the library."

"Not more than fifteen minutes. Less probably."

She made a sound of amazement. "I've never heard of anyone who could heal that fast. No wonder I feel like a month-old babe; by all rights I should be comatose now."

"Powerful," Wolf agreed.

Aralorn nodded. "It was odd in a voice that young, but he sounded a bit querulous, maybe even senile." She closed her eyes, and he couldn't make himself shove her away. More asleep than awake, she murmured with a touch of her unquenchable curiosity, "I wonder who Lys is."

When Wolf made no attempt to add to or answer her question, she drifted off to sleep.

Wolf cradled her protectively against him. He thought about shapeshifters, children, and refugees who unerringly found their way to Myr's camp. And he remembered the ae'Magi's half-mad son who wandered into these caves to find solace one night, led by a small gray fox with ageless sea-green eyes.

NINE

━━━◦◦◦◦━━━

From her station on the couch, Aralorn watched Wolf deposit another armload of books on the floor beside the worktable. The table, her chair, and most of the floor space were similarly adorned. He'd been silently moving books since she woke up, even less communicative than usual. He wasn't wearing his mask, but he might as well have been for all she could read on his face.

"Have you given any more thought to our invisible friend?" she asked, just to goad him. They'd worried and speculated for hours last night. During which time, Wolf had spent ten minutes lecturing her about how real invisibility was a myth, impossible to achieve with magic for a variety of reasons laid out in theories proposed over centuries.

She wasn't fishing for answers from him now; she was fishing for a response. Some acknowledgment that he was aware she was in the room.

He grunted without looking her way and went back into the stacks.

She might have been more concerned with their invisible—to all intents and purposes, no matter what Wolf maintained—visitor. But whoever it was had made no move against them; quite the contrary, in her opinion. If their visitor had meant mischief, he'd had plenty of opportunity. This was the Northlands, after all, full of all sorts of odd things.

It was Wolf she worried about.

He'd never allowed her to get as close as they had been last night. But always, whenever he'd opened up to her, let down the barrier that separated him from her, from everyone, he'd abruptly leave for weeks or months at a time. She thought this morning's distance might be the start of his withdrawal.

Having experienced the ae'Magi's touch firsthand, if only for a brief time compared to whatever he'd gone through, she finally understood some of what caused Wolf to be the way he was. It increased her patience with him—but it didn't mean she was going to let him pull away again without a fight.

"Did our apprentice write all of these?" Aralorn made a vague gesture toward the stacks before continuing to put a better edge on her knife.

Wolf turned to survey the piles. He let the silence build, then growled a brief affirmative before stalking back into the forest of bookcases. It was the first word he'd said to her since she'd woken up.

Aralorn grinned, sheathed her knife, and levered herself to her feet, still annoyingly weak. Scanning the nearby shelves, she found a book on shapeshifters and wobbled with it to the table, careful not to fall. Wolf had made it clear that he would rather that she stay put on the couch for a couple of days. She had no intention of giving in; but if she fell, there would be no living with him. So she'd save it for desperate measures if he didn't start talking to her. If she fell deliberately, it wouldn't be as humiliating.

She cleared off her chair and space enough to read. Now that the search had been narrowed to books that were likely to be trapped, Wolf had forbidden her to help. Aralorn decided if she couldn't be useful, at least she could enjoy herself.

Wolf balanced the books he carried on another stack and eyed her narrowly without meeting her eyes. He took her book and looked at it before handing it back.

"I thought human mages were supposed to keep their secrets close—not write down every stray thought that comes into their heads." With a tilt of her head, Aralorn indicated the neat piles of books he'd brought out.

He followed her gesture and sighed. "Most mages restrict their writings to the intricacies of magic. Iveress fancied himself an expert on everything. There are treatises here on everything from butter-making to glassblowing to governmental philosophy. From the four books of his I've already looked through, he is long-winded and brilliant, with the annoying habit of sliding in obscure magic spells in the middle of whatever he was writing when the spell occurred to him."

"Better you than me," said Aralorn, hiding her satisfaction in having gotten him to respond at last.

She must not have hidden it quite well enough. He stared at her from under his lowered brows. "Only because his books were considered subversive a few centuries back, and mages spelled them to keep them safe. Otherwise, I'd make you help me with this mess." He took a stride toward the shelves again, then stopped. "I might as well start with what I have."

"No use discouraging yourself with an endless task," she agreed.

He growled at her without heat.

She grinned at his familiar grumpiness—much better than silence—and settled in to read. It was fascinating, but not, Aralorn fancied, in the fashion the author meant it to be. In the foreword, the author admitted she had never met a shapeshifter. Regardless, she considered herself an expert. The stories she liked best were the ones that represented shapeshifters as a "powerful, possibly mythic race" whose main hobby seemed to be eating innocent young children who lost themselves in the woods.

"If I were one of a powerful, possibly mythic race," muttered Aralorn, "I wouldn't be bothering with eating children. I'd go after pompous asses who sit around passing judgment on things they know nothing about."

"Me, too," agreed Wolf mildly without looking up. Evidently the reading he was doing was more interesting than hers, because even his grumpiness had faded. "Do you have someone in mind?"

"She's been dead for years . . . centuries, I think."

"Ah," he said, turning a page. "I don't eat things that have been dead too long. Bad for even the wolf's digestion."

She snorted and kept reading. Aralorn learned that shapeshifters could only be killed by silver, garlic, or wolfsbane. "And all this time I've been worried about things like arrows, swords, and knives," she told Wolf. "Silly me. I'd better get rid of my silver-handled dagger—it would kill me to touch the grip."

He grunted.

The author of her book was also under the mistaken impression that shapeshifters could take the shape of only one animal. She devoted a section to horrific tales of shapeshifter wolves, lions, and bears. Mice, Aralorn supposed, were too mundane—and unlikely to eat children.

She shared bits and pieces of the better wolf tales with Wolf, as he waded through a volume on pig training. He responded by telling her how to train a pig to count, open gates, and fetch. Pigs were also useful for predicting earthquakes. Iveress had helpfully included three spells to start earthquakes.

Aralorn laughed and returned to her reading. At the end

of the book, the author included stories "which my research
has proven to be merely folktales" to entertain her readers.
After glancing through the first couple, Aralorn decided
that the thing that distinguished truth from folktale was
whether or not the shapeshifters were evil villains. Most
of the tales were ones she'd heard before. Most, but not all.

She read the final story, then thoughtfully closed the
book and glanced curiously around the room. Nothing was
moving that shouldn't be. Wolf had set the pig book aside
and was sorting through a pile near his chair.

"Once long ago, between this time and that, there was
a woman cursed by a wizard when she was young, for
laughing at his bald head." She didn't need to use the book
to help her memory, but kept her eyes on Wolf. "She was
married, and her first child was born dead. Her husband
died in an unfortunate accident while she gave birth to her
second, a daughter. When she was three, it became apparent to one and all that the second child bore a curse worse
than death—she was an empath. Upon that discovery, her
mother killed herself."

"A useless thing to do," murmured Wolf, pulling a book
out of the pile and setting it before him. He made no move
to open it. "You'd have gone hunting for the wizard."

Aralorn raised her eyebrow, and said coolly. "I'm not
finished."

· He smiled and lifted both hands peaceably. "No offense
meant, storyteller."

"The girl child was taken to a house outside the village and cared for as best the villagers could. Her empathic
nature meant that none of them could get too close without
causing her pain."

"I thought your book was about shapeshifters," Wolf
said, when Aralorn paused too long.

She nodded. "She grew up and learned to glean herbs
from the woods to pay for her keep. When she was sixteen,
a passing shapeshifter saw her. He took to following her

around in the guise of a crow or squirrel. But whatever shape he took, she knew him."

Wolf's eyes grew reserved. "Indeed?"

Aralorn frowned at him. "This isn't about you and me—and you would have found me the first time though if you'd thought about looking for someone who didn't look like me."

He looked away. She decided to ignore him and continued with the story.

"She knew when he fell in love with her, too. And he was able to guard his touch so she could bear it. When the villagers came to her home, he was her invisible guardian. She loved him and was happy.

"Once a month, the shapeshifter returned to his village to assure his people that he was well. They were not happy with his choice, and eventually his mother decided to solve the problem herself. She saw to it that a Southern slaver became aware of the girl and took her the next time the shapeshifter left her to visit the shapeshifter village. He returned to find the cottage empty, with the door swinging in the wind.

"The Trader was wary and, hearing that she had a magical lover, he took her through the Northlands, where no mage could follow. But her lover was no human mage, and he found them—too late."

A moaning sound echoed through the caves. Wolf tilted his head slightly so she knew that he heard as well.

"When the shapeshifter reached the slavers' camp," she continued, "he found nothing left of the would-be slavers except mindless bodies. The girl, terrified and alone, had evoked an empath's only defense, projecting her terror and pain onto her tormentors. She was alive when the shapeshifter found her, so he took her to a cave, sacred to his kind, where he tried to heal her. The worst of her wounds were of the spirit that even a shapeshifter's magic may not touch; and though her body was whole, she spoke not a word to him but stared through him, as if he were not there. Not entirely sane from his grief, the shapeshifter swore to keep her alive until he could find a way to heal her soul. And so he lives on, an old, old man tending his beloved from that day until this—and that is the story of the Old Man of the Mountain."

The moaning waned to a hesitant sigh that whispered through the library and faded to nothing.

Wolf raised an eyebrow at her. "I have never heard of a shapeshifter with the power that the Old Man is supposed to have."

Aralorn rubbed her cheek thoughtfully, leaving behind a streak of black dust. This was a secret—but she didn't feel like keeping secrets from Wolf. "The older a shape-shifter is, the more powerful he is. Like human mages, it is not unusual for a shapeshifter to live several hundred years. A really powerful shapeshifter can make himself younger constantly and never grow old. The reason that you don't see a shapeshifter much older than several hundred years is that they are constantly changing to new and more difficult things. It's hard to remember that you are supposed to be human when you change into a tree or the wind. An uncle of my mother once told me that sometimes a shapechanger forgets to picture what he is changing himself into, and he changes into nothing. There is no reason why our Old Man of the Mountain couldn't be several thousand years old rather than just a few hundred. That would make him incredibly powerful."

She stopped as something occurred to her. "Wolf, there was a snowstorm the night before the Uriah came. If it hadn't slowed them down, they would have come upon us at night and slaughtered the camp."

Wolf shrugged. "Snowstorms are unpredictable here, but I suppose that it could have been he who caused the storm. I suspect that we'll never know."

Wolf opened his book and went back to reading.

Aralorn found another book and managed not to show Wolf how unsteady she was. But when he'd checked it for her, and she opened it, it was difficult to concentrate as the little energy she'd regained dissipated. The words blurred in front of her eyes and soon she was turning pages from habit.

She dozed off between one sentence and the next. When Wolf touched her shoulder, she jumped to her feet and had her knife drawn before she opened her eyes.

"Plague it, Wolf!" she sputtered. "One of these days, you are going to do that, and I'll knife you by mistake. Then I'll have to live all my life with the guilt of your death on my hands."

Her threat didn't seem to bother him much as he caught her and lowered her to her chair as her legs collapsed under her. "You are trying to do too much," he said with disapproval. He started to say something else, then lifted his head.

She heard it, too, then, the sound of running feet. Stanis popped into the room at a dead run—he was one of the few people who knew his way to Wolf's private area. He was pale and panting when he stopped, looking as though he'd sprinted the half mile or so of cave tunnels that connected the main camp with Wolf's library. "Uriah," he panted.

Aralorn tangled with her chair when she tried to push it out of the way too fast, but kept from falling with the aid of a hand on her arm. She was firmly sat down on her seat.

Wolf, who had somehow donned his mask again, looked her straight in the eye, and said, "You stay here." His voice left no room for arguments. He shifted into the wolf and melted into the tunnel.

With the scary mage gone, the library felt safer than the outer cave to Stanis. But his mates were out there; he wasn't going to stay safely behind.

"Hey now," he said when Aralorn used the table to get to her feet. She looked like she weighed half what she had the first time he'd seen her—all pared down to bone and sinew. But she walked without limping to the little padded bench and shuffled under it until she came up with a sword and scabbard she belted on. He didn't miss that the scabbard was stained with blood—from the Uriah who'd killed Astrid.

"He told you to stay here." Maybe she hadn't heard the mage.

Aralorn glanced up as she sheathed the sword. "It says in my files—I know because Ren showed them to me—'Does not take orders, will occasionally listen to suggestions.' Did Wolf sound like he was suggesting anything to you?"

Stanis shook his head. "No." He shuffled his feet a little. "I don't follow no orders either, but if that one ever told me to do anything in that tone of voice, I can't help but think I'd be sitting where he wanted me until I was covered in dust."

She laughed. "Yes, he's a little intimidating, isn't he?" She checked the draw of the sword, adjusted it a little, and said, "But there's no way I'm sitting here while everyone else gets to fight." She looked at him. "You know your way to the rest of them? I might be able to find my way out, but I don't know how this cave connects into the rest."

Stanis squirmed.

She smiled. "No need to tell *him* that I couldn't find my own way there," she said.

"I'm not afraid of him," Stanis stated belligerently, though his mam had taught him better than that.

"Of course not," she said stoutly. "Nothing to be afraid of."

After about the halfway point, she put her hand on his shoulder. "Sorry, Stanis, we're going to have to slow down."

"No trouble," he said. "Why don't you lean on me a bit?"

She muttered something he didn't catch but put some of her weight on him. For a while that was all she did, but eventually her arm wrapped around his shoulders, and she honestly leaned on him.

"Good thing you're short," he said. "You should have

stayed. What would have happened if I weren't here to help you?"

"Then I'd have crawled," she said grimly.

He glanced up at her face, visible in the light of one of those little glowy balls Wolf had shown him how to make.

"Right," he said. She didn't look like a nice Lady right now, she looked like someone who could lick her weight in Uriah and then some. Maybe she was a match for that Wolf after all.

Aralorn swung a leg over the barricade erected to keep people—except for runners like Stanis, whose magic seemed capable of keeping them from getting hopelessly lost—from wandering the tunnels.

She listened for sounds of battle, but the tunnel was suspiciously silent.

"Where were the Uriah when you came running?" she asked, as the passageway floor took a steep upward bend.

"Don't know." Stanis shook his head. "Somebody spotted 'em outside and sprinted to the caves like an idiot. They're sure to have followed 'em here." He paused. "I don't hear nothin'."

"If they were inside our camp when Wolf came, you'd still be hearing things," she told him stoutly, finding that she couldn't quite believe it. What if they'd taken him by surprise? What if he hadn't had a chance?

"What if they took him by surprise?" asked Stanis, echoing her thoughts, his voice a bare whisper as they crept closer to where there should be a bunch of people fighting for their lives.

Her hands were sweating—from effort, she told herself. "No one takes him by surprise," she told Stanis. "He works things the other way."

And that was truth. She could breathe better, doubtless because the floor had flattened out again.

Stanis stopped. "Big cave's just around the corner," he mouthed. "The main one where everyone's camped. We should—"

"*Not* his wards?"

Oh, she recognized that voice. She stood up straight and strode around the corner, where the whole camp—as far as she could tell at a glance—was standing armed and ready. She couldn't see the owner of the loud voice, but she could hear him just fine.

"What does he mean 'not his wards'? Why didn't you ask him more? Do we expect them to come running in?"

She pushed her way through—not hard once people realized where she was going.

"It means that they aren't his wards," said Myr neutrally.

The big nobleman who stood in front of him was used to getting his way—with money or intimidation.

"Boy," he boomed. "You don't let that strippy bugger get away with half-assed answers. He's not in charge here."

She couldn't get there any faster without falling on her face, but . . . Myr hit him. A quick, decisive blow that dropped the ox like a stone.

Aralorn pulled her sword and held it to the downed man's throat, making sure he felt the sharp edge. A foot on his shoulder.

The fear that had held her since she realized that it was too quiet made her testy, and she would have been quite happy to put the sword all the way through the blasted man's neck and take care of the problem. But her father had been a canny politician when it suited him, and she could hear his voice in her ear.

So instead of killing him, she said coolly, "Do you desire this man dead, my king? I assure you it would be a pleasure. We could display his body on a stake just outside for the crows to eat."

"And attract every scavenger in twenty leagues," said Myr regretfully. "No. Not just yet." She couldn't read his voice and wouldn't lift her eyes from her enemy to look at his face.

She grimaced at the triumph in the eyes of the nobleman at her feet. He started to say something, then stopped. Maybe it was the weight of her heel on a nerve just in front of his shoulder, maybe it was that her arm dropped just a bit, letting the sword dig a little deeper.

"Permission to deal with him as my father would?" she asked.

"I recall the stake incident," said Myr dryly. "My grandfather told me about it. No one disobeyed the Lyon's orders for a few years afterward. Effective but extreme, you have to admit. We are a little short of numbers here—so I find myself reluctant to give you my unqualified permission."

The nobleman paled. "The Lyon?" he said.

Aralorn bared her teeth at him, but continued to talk to Myr. "Your Majesty, if you please. Haris?"

"Aye?"

"Haris, I think that you've been working too hard. You need an assistant."

"Don't need no nobleman to help me cook," said Haris grumpily.

"Haris," said Myr in silky tones, "I have no intention of allowing this man to interfere with your efforts. However . . . skinning, turning the spit, or taking out the refuse—how much could he hurt?"

"Oh aye," said Haris, sounding remarkably happier. "That I'll do, sire."

"Aralorn, let him up," Myr said.

She pulled her sword away after wiping the blood off on the idiot's shirt.

"Oras," Myr said. "A week of helping Haris is a gift. Do not make me regret it."

The nobleman swallowed. Perhaps he recognized, as Aralorn did, the old king in his grandson's face.

Myr turned his attention to Aralorn then, ignoring the man on the ground. "I need you to go out and find Wolf. Is this an assault we need to prepare ourselves for—or can I take people off alert?"

"What's going on?" she asked, sheathing her sword.

"The Uriah tried to come into the caves after our hunting party and were stopped by wards on the cave mouth. Wolf says they aren't his wards and sent us all back here to cool our heels and guard the narrow entrance."

Aralorn looked at the opening Myr indicated, where daylight shone through.

"Oras aside," Myr said, "it would be useful to have a bit more information. I'd like an update, and you're likely to get more information out of our wizard than anyone else."

———

Once in the tunnel to the outside, she drew her sword and held it in a fighter's grip. Someone had painted signs on the walls of the tunnels to facilitate travel, and it was a simple matter to follow the arrows to the outside by the magelight she held cupped in one hand.

The howls were louder as she turned into a cave marked "Door to Outside" over the top. She smiled at the awkward lettering even as the cold sweat of fear gathered on her forehead. Cautiously, she crept forward through the twisted narrow channel.

The Uriah were there, howling with frustrated rage at the wall of flame that covered the entrance. Someone, Aralorn noted with absent approval, had set up the wood for a bonfire where the tunnel began to narrow—it sat unlit, a good ten feet behind the magical fire that blocked the entrance. Aralorn couldn't feel the heat from the fire, but toasted bodies of Uriah lay twitching feebly just outside the cave as evidence of the effectiveness of the barrier.

Aralorn leaned against the side of the cave and watched

as another Uriah, incited by her presence just inside the barrier, dove into the flames. Nausea touched even her hardened stomach as she watched the hungry flames engulf it.

"I told you to stay in the library."

She'd been expecting him, knowing that the situation would mean that she probably wouldn't hear him. She didn't jump, didn't start, just turned to look at him a little faster than strictly necessary. It wouldn't have mattered except for the low spot in the roof of the cave.

"Ow," she said with a hiss of indrawn breath, putting her hand to her head where the rock had cut it.

He came out of the shadows and set his staff down—the crystals on the top blazed as soon as its clawed feet touched the ground. She shut her eyes against the light.

With a hand on her chin, Wolf used the other to explore the damaged area despite the fact that she squirmed and batted at his hand. In clipped tones, he said, "It seems like every time I've turned my back on you lately, you are getting hurt one way or another."

To her surprise, he bent down and pressed his cheek against hers. She hadn't experienced the healing of a green-magic user very often, barring her more recent experience. Generally she hadn't been in any shape to know exactly what it was that they did, but she knew enough to know that this was very different. This was not purely physical, there was an emotional link, too—a meeting on a more primal level.

It was over before she could analyze it further. Wolf stepped back as if bitten, and she could hear him gasping for breath beneath his mask. She looked at him in wonder—she knew enough about human magic to know that he shouldn't have been capable of doing what he had just done.

"Wolf," she said, reaching out to touch him. He backed away, keeping his head away from her and his eyes closed.

"Wolf, what's wrong?" When he said nothing, she took a step back to give him room.

He flung his head up then, and blazing yellow eyes met

hers. When he spoke, it was a whisper that his ruined voice made even more effective. "What am I? I should not be able to heal you. The other things—the shapeshifting, the power I wield—they could be explained away. But magic doesn't work this way. It doesn't take over before I can react and do things that I don't ask of it. I swore that I would never . . . never let anything control me the way my father did. In the end, even he could not eat my will entirely. This . . . does."

"It was you who healed my eyes." She wanted to give herself time to think. There was something that she should be grasping, a puzzle solved if she could just figure out how to look at it.

"Yes," he said.

"Were you trying to, then?"

He forced himself to adopt a relaxed posture, leaning against the wall as he spoke. "If you mean did I try to heal you with a spell, no. I just . . . wanted you to quit hurting."

She could almost see the effort he made to open up to her, this man who was so private. It was, she thought, maybe the bravest thing she'd ever seen anyone do.

He continued with his eyes on the mouth of the cave where three Uriah—none of whom resembled anyone she knew—stood motionless, watching them.

"I was so tired," Wolf told her. "I hadn't slept much since I found that you were gone." He looked at her. "You were getting worse, and I couldn't do anything about it. I do not recall what I was thinking, precisely. I had done all that I could for you and knew that it would never be enough and something made me lie beside you and this magic took over." He clenched his hands in what was very near revulsion.

"Who was your mother? Do you know?" asked Aralorn. "I've heard a lot of stories about Cain, the son of the ae'Magi, but none of them ever mentioned his mother."

Wolf shrugged, and his voice had regained its cool tones when he answered. "I only saw her once, when I was very young, maybe five years old. I remember asking Father who she was, or rather who she had been, for she was quite dead, killed by some experiment of his, I suppose. I don't remember being particularly worried about her, so I suspect that it was the only time I saw her."

"Describe her for me," requested Aralorn in a firm voice that refused to condemn or to sympathize with the boy he had been. He wouldn't want that. The Uriah weren't coming in anytime soon, she thought. She folded her legs and sat on the ground—healing or no, her legs had done as much as they were going to for a while, and it was sit down or fall down.

"I was young, I don't remember much," Wolf said. "She looked small next to my father, fragile and lovely—like a butterfly. The only time I ever heard him say anything about her was when some noble asked about my mother. He said she was flawlessly beautiful. I think he was right."

Aralorn nodded, her suspicions confirmed. "I would have been surprised if she had been anything else."

He narrowed his gaze.

"Your mother must have been a shapeshifter, or some other green-magic user—but the 'perfectly beautiful' sounds a lot like a shapeshifter. That feeling that the magic is taking control of you is fairly common when dealing with green magic because you are dealing with magic shaped by nature first, and only then by magician. You need to learn to work with it so that you can modify it. If you fight it, it will prove stronger than you."

He stared at her a bit and joined her on the floor without speaking. Maybe his legs wouldn't hold him up any longer either.

"I suspect," continued Aralorn, as blandly as she could manage, "if you hadn't been taught how magic should work, you would have discovered your half-blooded capabilities long since. You were told that you couldn't heal, so you didn't try."

Two of the Uriah stepped forward at the same time. The wards flared, and they burned. Aralorn caught a brief hint of burnt flesh, like cooking pork, then nothing.

"Your theory fits," said Wolf finally.

"I should have thought about it sooner," apologized Aralorn. "I mean, I am a half-breed. It's just that I've never met another half-breed. I could tell that you weren't a shape-shifter, so I just assumed that you were simply an extraordinarily powerful human magician." She hesitated. "Which you are."

Wolf gave a half laugh with little humor in it. "It sounds just like an experiment the ae'Magi would try. To a Darranian like him, it would be the ultimate form of bestiality. Just the thing to spark his interest."

Aralorn leaned over, pulled down his mask, and bussed him on the unscarred mouth with a kiss that was anything but romantic. "You beast, you," she said, and he made an unpracticed sound that might have been a laugh.

He got to his feet and pulled her to hers, his eyes warmed with relief, humor, and something else. Gripping her shoulders, he kissed her with a passion that left her breathless and shaken. He stepped back and returned the mask to its usual position.

"We'd better get back and tell Myr he can relax. It doesn't appear that the Old Man is going to welcome the Uriah into his cave anytime in the near future," he said, offering her his arm to lean on.

"You think those are his wards?" she asked.

"Someone has powered them up since I looked at them last. It wasn't me and no one else here has the skill or the power."

She caught her breath, smiled, and tucked her arm through his. "Do we tell the whole camp that we are being protected by the Old Man of the Mountain?"

"It might be the best thing, even if it scares a few of them silly. I have the feeling that we shouldn't push his hospitality by wandering around too much. The best way to see that it doesn't happen is to tell them the whole truth—if they'll believe it." Wolf slid though a narrow passage with his usual grace, towing Aralorn beside him.

"We are dealing with people who have some minor magic capabilities; are following a dethroned king who just barely received his coming-of-age spurs; who number among their acquaintances not just one half-breed shape-shifter, but two half-breed shapeshifters—one of whom, incidentally, wears a silly mask. We could tell them that we were in the den of the old gods and that Faris, Empress of the Dead, conceived a sudden passion for Myr and it probably wouldn't faze them," Aralorn told him.

Wolf laughed, and Aralorn pulled him to a halt. "Wait. Did you say that the ae'Magi is Darranian?"

"Peasant stock," he confirmed. "Apparently his master was very surprised to find a magician who was Darranian— used to tell jokes about his Darranian apprentice. My father smiled when he talked about how he killed his teacher."

"Not the first Darranian mage," Aralorn said.

Wolf grunted and started to walk.

Aralorn let her hand drop and followed thoughtfully.

Wolf was first in the tunnel that opened into the main chamber. He hissed and jumped back, narrowly avoiding Myr's sword.

"Sorry," said Myr. "I thought that you were one of the Uriah. You should have said something before you came in. Did you find out why the Uriah aren't coming in?"

"Is there a reason the King of Reth is guarding the door-way instead of someone more expendable?" asked Wolf.

"Best swordsman," said Myr. "Are you going to answer me?"

"Let's do this where everyone can hear," Aralorn said, continuing on so she could do just that. "The Uriah aren't going to be coming in here."

She stepped out into the main cave and saw that most

of them had heard her last remark. "Our guardian of the cave doesn't want them in." She was in her element, with a captive audience and a story to tell. She projected her voice and told them the story about the origin of the Old Man of the Mountain and finished with the barrier that was keeping the Uriah out.

———————

She made the tale sound as if it were part of shapeshifter history, Wolf decided, rather than a forgotten story in an obscure book. Usually, she did it the other way around—turning an unexciting bit of history into high adventure. He hadn't realized that she could do it backward.

As she had predicted, the refugees seemed reassured by her story, not questioning just how far the Old Man's benign stance would continue. Right then, they wanted a miracle, and Aralorn was giving one to them.

Responding to Wolf's look, Myr joined him just outside the cave, leaving Aralorn to her work.

"We may be locked in here for some time," Wolf informed Myr. "They might not be coming in, but there is no way to determine how long they are going to howl at our door. Do we have enough food to last us a week or so?" He should have been paying attention, but it was an effort to remember that he was supposed to care about these people. He was trying to be . . . something other than what he was. Someone Aralorn could be proud of. When she'd been hurt, he'd lost all interest in the extraneous details.

Myr shrugged. "We have enough grain stored to last us into next summer, feeding animals and people. We're short on meat, which is why I sent out the hunters this morning. They came back with Uriah instead of deer. For a week or two, we can do without. If it turns into a month we can always slaughter a goat or sheep to feed ourselves. Our real problems are going to be morale and sanitation."

Wolf nodded. "We'll have to deal with morale as it

comes. I might be able to do something about the sanitation, though. The blocked-off tunnel where you're storing grain leads to a cave with a pit deep enough that you can throw a rock into it and not hear it hit bottom. It's fairly narrow, so you should be able to put some sort of structure over it to keep people from falling into it." Solving logistic problems helped center him.

"That should relieve Aralorn," commented Myr, a smile lighting his tired face for the first time since he'd heard the Uriah. "She was really worried that before this was all over, she'd be pressed into digging latrines."

Myr laughed wearily and pushed his hair out of his face. "I should have asked this right away. Is it possible that the Uriah can find their way in here through another entrance?"

"Maybe," answered Wolf, starting to head toward Aralorn, who was swaying wearily as she finished her story. "The Old Man has been here a lot longer than we have. If this entrance is protected, I suspect that all of them are."

Outside, the Uriah quieted and sank to their knees as a rider came into view. His horse was lathered and sweating, showing the whites of its eyes in fear of the Uriah. But it had learned to trust its rider, and Lord Kisrah was careful to keep the Uriah motionless with the spells of control that the ae'Magi had taught him.

He dismounted at the entrance to the cave. He could see the runes just inside the entrance, but he couldn't touch them to alter their power.

In the air, he sketched a symbol that glowed faintly yellow and passed easily through the entrance. The symbol touched a rune and fizzled as a man walked into the cave and approached the mouth.

"You are not welcome, leave this place," he said. In

the light, the man was almost inhumanly beautiful, and
Lord Kisrah caught his breath in admiration. Abruptly, the
mouth filled with flames, the heat uncomfortably harsh on
his face.

Kisrah backed up and tried to push the flames down
again, with no effect. The third time he tried it, the Uriah
began stirring as his hold on them weakened. With a curse
he desisted. He led the horse back through the Uriah until
he had some space.

"You will stay here until the ae'Magi releases you," he
ordered briskly. "If someone comes out of the cave, you
will not harm them. Take them prisoner—you know how
to contact me if that happens." He mounted the horse and
let it choose its own speed away from the Uriah.

———

"Thank you, Lord Kisrah. I am sure that you did your best
with the warding—but the old runes are tricky at best, and
in the Northlands, they could easily be the work of one
of the races that use green magic." The ae'Magi smiled
graciously.

Lord Kisrah looked only a little less miserable in his
seat in the ae'Magi's study. "I got a look at some of the
runes there, and I'll look them up and see what can be done
about them. The magician had no trouble with my magic,
though. He's more worrisome than the runes."

"I agree, Kisrah," purred the ae'Magi. "I intend to find
out just who he is. Can you describe him for me again?"

Lord Kisrah nodded and set aside the warmed ale he'd
been drinking. "No more than medium height. His hair was
blond, I think, although it could have been light brown. His
eyes were either blue or green—the overall effect was so
spectacular, it was difficult to pay attention to the details.
He couldn't have been more than twenty-four or -five and
could have been younger except that he was so powerful.

His voice was oddly accented, but he didn't say enough that I could tell much about the accent other than that the Rethian he spoke was not his native tongue."

"There was no way that his hair could have been darker? His eyes golden? No scars?" queried the ae'Magi softly.

Lord Kisrah shook his head. "No. His eyes, maybe. They were some light color. But his hair was light." He yawned abruptly.

The ae'Magi stood and offered his arm for support to the other mage. "I am sorry, I have kept you up talking, and you are almost dropping from exhaustion." He led him to the door and opened it, clapping his hands lightly. Before he clapped a second time, a pretty young serving girl appeared.

"Take Lord Kisrah to the blue room, Rhidan, and see to his comfort." The ae'Magi turned to his guest. "Pray follow the girl—she will attend to your every need. If you want anything, just ask."

Kisrah brightened visibly and wished him a good night.

Alone in his study, the ae'Magi brooded, disliking the thought of yet another magician in his way. Who could it be? He'd been sure that his son was the last mage of any power who stood against him.

Abruptly, he got to his feet; all this worry could do no good. It was too late at night to try to think, and he was too frustrated to sleep. He motioned abruptly to the pale young girl who had sat in her corner unnoticed by Lord Kisrah. Obedient to his gesture, she dropped the clothes she wore and stood naked and submissive before him.

He cupped her chin in one hand and stroked her body gently with the other. "Tonight," he said, "I have something special in mind for you."

TEN

———— ∞∞∞ ————

Aralorn went back to work taking care of the children to give herself something to do since Wolf didn't need her in the library.

Keeping them entertained was harder than it had been before. There was no place for them to run and play, and they were restless with the Uriah just outside. To distract them, Aralorn taught them the letters of the alphabet and how they fit together to form words. She told stories until she was hoarse.

"So Kai bet the whole troop that he could sneak into camp and steal the pot of coffee on the coals with no one seeing him." Seated on a bump in the floor, Aralorn checked to make sure that most of the children were listening. "He and Talor were raised in a Trader Clan, just like Stanis. When he was little, he had learned how to be very quiet and to sit still in shadows so no one could see him.

"That night, their commander doubled the guard on the camp and assigned a special guard just to follow Kai around. Two men watched the coffeepot. But despite all of that, the next morning the pot was gone. The guard who was supposed to be following Kai around had actually been following Talor, who looked enough like his twin to be mistaken for him in the dark." Aralorn smiled at her intent audience. Stories about the twins were always guaranteed attention holders.

"Kai was not only good enough to get the pot, he also painted a white 'X' on the back of every one of the guards without their knowing it."

"I bet Stanis could do that," said Tobin. "He's sneaky." Stanis, with his inability to get lost, was more often to be found running errands than hanging out with people his own age. It gave him even more cachet among his followers.

"Aralorn." Myr put his hand on her shoulder.

He looked a bit pale. "What's wrong?"

"It's Wolf. Stanis ran a message to him in the library for me and came running back a few minutes ago. He says there's something up—I think perhaps you ought to go check."

The library was engulfed in shadows when she cautiously peered into it, and it felt warmer than usual. The only light came from the crystals in Wolf's staff, which were glowing a dull orange. Wolf sat in his usual chair, motionless, his face in the shadows. He didn't move when she came in, that and the scorched smell in the library suggested that the scene wasn't as ordinary as it looked.

Using her own magic, Aralorn lit the chamber. One of the bookcases was missing. Thoughtfully, Aralorn wandered over to where it had been and scuffed a toe in the ashes that had taken its place. The bookcase next to her burst into flames and was reduced to the same state before she even felt the heat. She winced at the destruction of the irreplaceable books.

"Wolf," she asked in calculatedly exasperated tones.

"Isn't this hard enough without losing your temper?" She turned to look at him. He wore his mask again.

"I have it, Aralorn," he murmured softly. "I have the power to do anything." Another bookcase followed the first two. "Anything."

Her pulse picked up despite her confidence that he'd never hurt her.

"If I didn't have so much power," he said, "I just might be able to do something with it. You see, I found it. I found the spell to remove the ability to use magic from a magician who is misusing his power. I can't use it. I don't have the skill or the control, and the spell uses too much raw power. If I tried it, we'd have another glass desert on our hands." His eyes glittered with the flickering orange light of his staff.

Aralorn went to him and sat on the floor beside him, resting her head against his knees. "If you had less power, there would be no way to take the ae'Magi at all. You would never have been able to free yourself from the binding spells that keep all of the other magicians bound to his will. There would be no one to resist him. Quit tearing yourself into pieces and winning the battle for the ae'Magi. You are who you are. No better certainly, but no worse." It was quiet for a long time in the library. Aralorn let her light die down and sat in the darkness with Wolf. No more bookcases burned in magic fire. When Wolf's hand touched her hair, Aralorn knew that it would be all right. This time.

Aralorn trotted up the tunnels at a steady pace, walking now and again when she ran out of breath—which she felt was far too often. Slowly, though, her strength was coming back, and she had to stop less frequently than she had the day before. Morning and night for the past four days, she had run the tunnels from the library to the entrance, trying to rebuild the conditioning that she'd lost. Also, not incidentally, building up her understanding of how to get from one place to another.

Her path was free of people for the most part. The library was quite a distance from the main caves, and most of the campers respected Wolf's claims that the Old Man of the Mountain wanted to keep them out of the tunnels. Aralorn was of the opinion that Wolf didn't want to spend his time searching for lost wanderers because she'd seen no sign that the Old Man objected to anyone's presence. Although the path to the library was carefully marked out and considered part of the occupied caves, in practice it was seldom that anyone besides Aralorn, Wolf, or Stanis went there.

Wolf said that they were waiting for the wrath of the Old Man to fall on them. Myr said that it was Wolf, not the Old Man, that they were frightened of—Myr was probably right.

Only Oras had ignored the ban on the inner caves. Twice. The first time Myr brought him back. The second time Wolf went after him. Wolf wouldn't tell Aralorn what he'd done, and Oras didn't volunteer the information, but he'd come back white-faced and had been remarkably subdued ever since.

As she came to the outer caves, Aralorn slowed to a walk. There were too many people around for her to dodge at a faster speed. When she started down the path that led to the entrance, the first thing that she noticed was the sound of her own footsteps. It took her a minute to realize that the reason she could hear them was because the Uriah weren't howling.

Sure enough, when she reached the entrance, there was no sign of the Uriah. The bonfire Myr had ordered laid near the entrance was still unlit.

She stepped out slowly, moving cautiously in case there were any lying in wait. After so many days in the caves, the sunlight nearly blinded her. The air smelled fresh and pure, without the distinctive odor that accompanied Uriah. Only the smell of burnt grass and other things marred the fragrance of the nearby pine.

It looked as if a ball of fire had been spewed from the cave's mouth. A wide blackened path in the grass and soil began from the entrance and traveled in a straight line a fair distance before disappearing. Within the blackened area were ten or fifteen bodies of Uriah, burnt down to the bone. There were some that were less singed, but something had chewed on them.

Aralorn followed the blackened path up the mountain and found that the trail abruptly stopped on a wide, flat area. She started back and was several lengths down the slope when she realized that she might be thinking backward. What if the fireball hadn't come *from* the cave but had been launched *at* it? Muttering to herself, she trotted back to where the trail stopped.

Tracking wasn't her specialty, but it didn't take her long to find what she sought. When she was looking for them, they were hard to miss—very large, reptilian footprints with marks beside them that could be trailing wings. Just like the ones she'd seen the day she'd been taken by the Uriah.

"Well, Myr," she said thoughtfully, going back to examine one of the half-eaten corpses. She hadn't looked too closely before, assuming that the Uriah had just been practicing their usual cannibalism. Upon closer examination, she could tell that something much bigger than a Uriah had been feeding. "I think I know what dragons eat when there aren't any virgins chained to rocks."

———

"Well, then," said Myr in dry tones after Aralorn related her discovery. The main cave was almost empty. Myr had sent out a party to look for the hunters who'd been missing since just before the Uriah had come, and a second group out to find provisions. He'd sent a few of the remaining people to keep watches from the best lookout stations.

He rubbed his eyes and looked at her. "So what now? We've exchanged the Uriah for a dragon. The question that begs is, of course, is this a good thing?"

"The dragon's quieter and smells better." Aralorn leaned against the cave wall and watched Myr pace.

"At least we knew *something* about the Uriah," Myr complained. "A dragon. There aren't supposed to *be* any more dragons." He broke off when the sounds of ragged cheers echoed into the cave, followed by the missing hunting party and the searchers—all of them looking cold and tired.

When the welcoming was done, Farsi, who'd led the party, told their tale. "We came upon a herd of mountain sheep and got two so we headed back. About halfway here we stumbled upon some tracks, as if an army were wandering around. We followed the trail, and pretty soon we could smell 'em and knew that they were Uriah. Since their path was the same one we were on, it was obvious that the things were coming here.

"Figuring that we were too late to make much difference, we worked our way up the side of the mountain until we could see the Uriah. We couldn't see the cave, but the way they were swarming around showed that you must have found a way to keep them out. We decided that there was nothing we could do but wait. Our vantage point was far enough away that the chance of the Uriah seeing us wasn't considerable."

Farsi cleared his throat. "Late last night—just after the moon had set—I heard a cry like a swan makes, only deeper. I was on watch, and it wasn't loud enough to wake anyone else up. Something big flew over us, but I couldn't quite see it. Afterward, I saw a flash of golden fire down here and heard the Uriah step up their noise. Then it quieted down.

I woke up a couple others, and we finally decided that we'd best wait until we had light to see what had happened." He frowned, evidently still unhappy with that decision. "It was just that whatever it was—from the quiet that followed—it had already happened."

Myr nodded at him. "Sensible and smart to wait until you could see, especially with Uriah running around."

Farsi looked like someone had pulled a weight off his shoulders. "This morning, it looked like the Uriah had left, so we started home. The reason it took us so long to get here is that there are still a lot of Uriah scattered about. We were dodging two parties of the things, when we almost ran into a third. It's a good thing that they smell so bad, or we wouldn't have made it back at all."

———

Over the next few days it became obvious that if the Uriah had been held in concert by the will of the ae'Magi, that was no longer true. It didn't make them any less danger-ous individually, but it did make it possible to kill them in small groups.

Wolf, when appealed to, produced a detailed map of the area on sheepskin, which was hung on a wall of the central chamber. Aralorn suspected he'd made it himself, either with magic or by hand, because it was accurate, with very specific landmarks. At Myr's command, any sightings of Uriah were recorded on the map, giving them a rough idea where the things were.

Each group of hunters had a copy of the map, and if they ran into a group of Uriah, they would lead them to one of the traps Myr had placed in strategic places. The Uriah were slowed enough by the cold of the deepening fall that the humans could outrun them most of the time, especially since they were careful to go out only when it was coldest.

Haris suggested an adaptation of a traditional castle

defense and created a tar trap that was one of the most
effective of their traps. The easiest way to kill a Uriah was
with fire, so pots of tar were hung here and there, kept
warm by magic. Ropes were carefully rigged so that they
would not easily be tripped by wild animals. When they
were pulled, the pots tipped over, and the motion triggered
a secondary spell—something Haris cooked up—that set
the tar on fire—dousing the Uriah with flaming tar. The
spells on the traps were simple enough that everybody,
except for Myr, could do them after a little coaching from
Wolf and Haris.

Aralorn watched the small group of refugees become
a close-knit community, the grumblers fewer. Every evening, they would all sit down and talk. Complaints and
suggestions were heard and decided upon by Myr. Looking
at the scruffy bunch of peasants (the nobles, by that time,
blended right in with the rest) consulting with their equally
scruffy king, Aralorn compared it with the Rethian Grand
Council that met once a year, and she hid a grin at the
contrast.

Having an enemy they could fight—and defeat—put
heart in them all. Even Aralorn, who understood that the
Uriah were in truth a minor annoyance. Their real enemy,
the ae'Magi, was out there somewhere—and he knew
where they were. She suspected he was biding his time.
The snow wasn't accumulating yet, but it had become common to see a white coat on the dirt most mornings. A smart
general didn't attack the Northlands in the heart of winter
but waited for spring.

Only Wolf was excluded from the camaraderie, by his
own choice. He made them nervous, with his macabre
voice and silver mask. Once he saw that they were intimi-
dated by him, he went out of his way to make them more so.
Sleeping somewhere deep in the caverns and spending most
of his waking time in the library, he was seldom with the
main body of the camp. Usually, he attended the nightly

sessions with everyone else, but he kept his own counsel in the shadows of the caves' recesses unless Myr asked him a question directly.

Most mornings Aralorn spent entertaining the children. Occasionally, she went out with a hunting party—or alone to exercise Sheen and check the traps. The afternoons she spent in the library with Wolf, keeping him company and reading as many books as she could.

The nights she spent in the library as well, for she was still having nightmares and didn't want to wake the whole camp. Night after night she woke up screaming, sometimes seeing Talor's face, alive with all that made him Talor, but consumed with a hunger that was inhuman and wholly Uriah. Other times, it was the ae'Magi's face that she saw, a face that changed from father's to son's.

Wolf didn't know about her nightmares, as far as she knew. She had no idea where he was sleeping, but it wasn't the library.

Late in the afternoons, Myr usually joined them, talking quietly with Aralorn while Wolf read through books on rabbit breeding, castle building, and three hundred ways to cook a hedgehog.

After discovering that the spell he'd been looking for wouldn't work for him, Wolf had continued to look through the old mage's books in the hopes of discovering a way to manage the spell more crudely. Most spells, he'd told Aralorn, were refined so they required less power. He had all the power he needed, and an earlier version might work for him. If he could find it.

His temper was biting, and he didn't rein it in for Myr, nor after the first few visits did he bother with his mask. Myr answered Wolf's sarcasm with cool control—and sometimes a hidden grin of appreciation. Aralorn rather thought that Wolf's lack of common courtesy was why Myr liked to visit the library. Here he was a fellow conspirator rather than the King of Reth.

"What's he doing?" asked Myr, setting his torch to sputter on the stone floor, where, with nothing to burn, it would eventually go out.

Instead of reading, Wolf had cleared the table of everything except a collection of clay pots filled with a variety of powders. When Aralorn had gotten there, Wolf had already been grinding various leaves in a mortar.

She waved a lazy hand at Myr, but didn't take her attention off what Wolf was doing. "He thinks he's found a way to manage the spell. We're going to try it outside when he's finished. No telling what would happen if he worked it in here with all of the grimoires, especially since we don't know the range of effect."

She caught Myr's arm when he would have approached the table closer. "He doesn't want us any closer than this," she said.

They both watched, fascinated, though neither she nor Myr could work this kind of magic or probably even understand half of what was going on. Wolf took a small vial from the leather pack on the table. Opening it, he poured a milky liquid into the gray powder mixture, which became red mush and gave off a poof of noxious fumes. He donned his mask and cloak, then, ignoring his audience, he put a lid on the pot and took it and an opaque bottle and strode toward an exit route that would take them directly outside rather than through the lived-in areas, leaving Aralorn and Myr to trail behind.

"Won't the spell be affected by whatever it is that restricts human magic in the Northlands?" asked Myr in a whisper to Aralorn, but it was Wolf who answered.

"No," he said. "It is a very simple spell—its complexity has to do with power management. It should work fine here."

He led them to the old camp in the valley, where they

were unlikely to have anyone interrupt them. Aralorn found herself holding the containers while, at Wolf's direction, Myr paced off circles, each bigger than the last until the dirt looked like an archery target. The ground was muddy with last night's melted snowfall and held the marks of Myr's feet well.

Wolf disappeared into the underbrush and reappeared, holding a handful of small stones. He set several of them in each ring Myr had shuffled off, though maybe "set" was the wrong word, because they floated about knee high above the ground.

"This shouldn't be a particularly powerful spell," Wolf said. "If I can get it to work, it doesn't need to be. If he doesn't know that it's coming, then he won't know to block it. All that I need it to do is to throw him off-balance for long enough to turn our battle from magic to more mundane means. Aralorn, stand behind me. It won't hurt Myr, but I don't know what this would do to a shapeshifter."

"If I'm behind you, I can't see what's going on," Aralorn complained. "How about if I stand over by the old fire pit?"

It was well off to the side, a dozen paces away from the target range that Myr had drawn out.

"Fine," he said. "This should be a straight, line-of-sight spell, with a limited range."

He sat on the cold ground in the middle of the innermost circle.

"How old is the ae'Magi?" asked Aralorn from the fire pit.

Wolf shrugged gracefully and gave her a half smile. "You aren't going to kill the ae'Magi the way that Iveress killed his master. His master was ill and near death, kept alive only by magic. As far as I know, the ae'Magi is nowhere near death, unfortunate as that may be—at least not from disease."

"What are our chances if the spell works as it is supposed to?" asked Myr. "Will you be able to kill him? I've seen him fight."

Wolf shrugged. "If the spell takes him by surprise, then the odds are about even. I used to spar with him often, and sometimes I beat him, sometimes not. This spell gives us a chance, but that's all it does. If he recognizes the spell, it is easy enough to counter. That would leave us with only magic."

He looked at Aralorn. "I've learned some things about what I can do that he doesn't know, but even so, he would easily best me that way. Without magic, at least we stand a chance of killing him. Perhaps." No one, not even Aralorn, could have told how he felt about it from his voice.

Aralorn and Myr watched as he emptied the contents of the bottle into the pot. He counted to ten, then poured the mixture onto the ground in front of him, where it gathered into a glowing pool of violet patterned with inky swirls. Dipping a finger into the pool, he used the liquid to draw several symbols in the air. Compliantly, the purple substance hung in the air as if on an invisible wall. Wolf repeated the procedure with his left hand.

He picked up the pool in both hands. It swayed and oozed, never quite escaping the confines of his hands. He held it up in front of his face, then blew on it gently.

Pain hit Aralorn hard enough to knock her to her knees. She fought to maintain consciousness for a moment, but she never felt herself hit the ground.

When she recovered, she felt the hard strength of Wolf's thigh underneath her ear.

"I don't know," said Wolf, sounding vicious.

She blinked cautiously, and when her head didn't fall off, she pushed herself up.

"Fine," she told Wolf. "I'm fine. My fault."

Sitting up, she could see what had happened. The spell was directional all right, but mostly in a forward and backward kind of direction rather than the direction of a loosed arrow. It had knocked down the floating stones in a wide "V" pattern, with Wolf at the apex. The stones directly to either side of where he'd been sitting were still floating, but every stone more than two feet in front of him was on the ground.

She had been sitting on the edge of the path of the spell, but apparently the fire pit hadn't been far enough away.

"How long was I out?" she asked, noticing that her ears were buzzing and her balance was off. Even sitting flat on the ground, her upper body wanted to sway.

She was propelled down again with a none-too-gentle hand, as Wolf answered, "Not very."

"How do you feel?" asked Myr, concern evident in his voice.

"Like the entire mercenary army of Sianim just got through marching over my head." She closed her eyes and let herself enjoy their concern. She loved sympathy.

"Not too bad, then," said Myr with evident relief.

"Not horrible, but not fun." Aralorn decided that her headache had subsided enough she could open her eyes again.

"You need to try some magic," Wolf said grimly.

She would have whined at him, but the hand on her shoulder was shaking a little. For Wolf's sake, she called a simple light to her hand, then dismissed it.

"Wolf," asked Myr, "do you think that the ae'Magi will let you complete the spell? It seemed to take a lot of preparation."

"I won't need to," answered Wolf, relaxing against the wall of Haris's former kitchen. His thumb ran over her collarbone, then stilled. "With a spell this simple, it'll be easy enough to re-create the effect."

His relief was more obvious in the amount of words that he was using to explain himself to Myr. "Once I see the pattern to push the magic into," he said, "I don't need the physical parts of the casting anymore. It really is something only a beginning magic-user would have created. Take all of the most common spell components mixed together, add the first five symbols learned in magic, and blow—poof: instant spell. What is really amazing is that it didn't blow up in the apprentice's face. It came uncomfortably close to doing that with me." He tapped Aralorn's nose in emphasis. "Next time I tell you to get behind me, get behind me."

"What's next?" asked Myr.

Wolf took off his mask wearily. In the bright light of the winter sun, Aralorn noticed the strain he'd been under written into the fine lines and dark shadows beneath his golden ambient eyes. "What else? I storm the castle of the ae'Magi and challenge him to a duel. Whereupon he engages me in best Aralorn-story-time fashion. Then either I win, and go down in history as the cruel villain who destroyed the good wizard, his father. Or he wins." Wolf's voice was coolly ironic.

"If he wins, what happens?" Aralorn spoke from her prone position and showed no intention of moving. "I mean, what is he trying to do? Why does he want everyone to love him?"

While he answered, Wolf played with a strand of hair that had worked its way out of her braid. "You asked me about that once before. I think I know the answer now."

Myr sat down beside Wolf. "What? Power?"

"I thought that might be it at first," Wolf said. "Maybe that was even the correct answer at one time. When I was his apprentice, that seemed to be it. He could link with me and use the power that I gathered for his own spells, much, I believe, in the same manner that he now uses the magic released by the deaths of the children he kills. But there was an incident that scared him." For Myr's benefit, Wolf briefly explained his destruction of the tower.

Myr whistled. "That was you? I'd heard a story about that, I've forgotten who told me. They said that the tower looked like a candle that someone forgot to blow out. The stone blocks looked like they melted."

Wolf nodded. "He started to try using control spells on me, after that. I left before he had much success. But what surprised me was that he continued to try and get me back under his control. He's been looking for me for a long time."

He looked down at Aralorn. "If all he wanted was to kill me, he could have done that easily enough. Or at least come close. If it were only my power he wanted, then he's wasted a lot more of it trying to find me than he could ever get from me. I am more powerful than most magicians, but Lord Kisrah is very strong as well, and the ae'Magi never attempted to tap into his magic. The magic that he gets from one of the children he kills is also probably more than he could get from me because my defenses are stronger."

"Revenge, then?" suggested Myr. "Because he thought that he had you under his control and you escaped?"

"So I thought," answered Wolf, "but then Aralorn told me that she thought that I was half shapeshifter and that some of the magic that I am using is green magic."

Myr started. "Are you? That's why you have so little trouble taking the shape of a wolf. I thought it was unusual."

Wolf nodded. "Most of the magic that I use is human magic. Since I found out that I could use it, I've been trying to work with the green magic. It is bound by much stronger rules than what I'm used to; so, except for shapeshifting, I find it much harder to work. Even so, it might give me an edge over the ae'Magi."

Wolf paused, then continued, "The question still remains, what does the ae'Magi want from me? He is a Darranian, and the animalism of having sex with a shapeshifter might appeal to him, but I couldn't conceive that he would raise the resultant offspring as his own. Not until I realized that it might be the green magic that he wanted. Green magic that I didn't use until I left his control."

"But why green magic?" asked Myr. "I can't imagine that he values shapeshifting that highly."

"Healing," said Aralorn softly—for the sake of her throbbing heart. Because the idea that Wolf had been leading them toward was terrifying.

Wolf nodded. "Exactly. As you told me, Aralorn, a shapeshifter can heal himself until he is virtually immortal. What I believe the ae'Magi hopes to do is to reestablish the link that he had with me and use green magic to give himself immortality. Until then, he can use standard magic to defeat the problems of aging, but that doesn't make him young."

"No point in ruling the world unless you have time to do it in," offered Myr.

"Yes," agreed Wolf. "There was another clue as well. Neither of you was particularly well acquainted with the Uriah as they were a few years ago. I was in the ae'Magi's castle when he created the first of his, using his own spell. The Uriah that I knew then were barely able to function. They could not even understand speech as well as a dog can. Now, from what Aralorn says, he has some that even retain the memories of the person that they once were."

"The Uriah in the swamplands were created during the Wizard Wars; they are close to being immortal," commented Aralorn.

Wolf nodded. "They don't die unless they are killed. If he could get them just a bit more pretty, he'd probably turn himself into one."

Soberly, Myr said, "I don't think that he ever intended to turn himself into a Uriah. I've known him for a long time, too. There is no way he would turn himself into something that by its very nature is a slave to its need for food—pretty or not. If a Uriah retains most of its personality, then it is possible that it also retains its ability to work magic. What if he wants to kill you, Wolf, and turn you into one of his Uriah, obedient to his command, but just as powerful as you have always been?"

"Oh, isn't that a lovely thought," said Aralorn.

Blank-faced, Wolf considered Myr's comment. "I hadn't thought of that. I'll have to make sure that it doesn't happen, hmm?"

There was a heavy silence, then Aralorn said in a bright tone, "Speaking of Uriah, do you realize what a mess we are going to have to clean up when the ae'Magi is dead and we have several hundred masterless Uriah roaming the countryside? Sianim is going to be making good money off this.

———————

Wolf worked at the spell for days, until he could direct it better, but the force of the spell varied widely. Wolf muttered and finally even went back to mixing the powders, but the spell still wouldn't stabilize. He told Aralorn he needed to try a few different herbs that might refine the reaction. He didn't have all that he needed, so he left to do some trading in the south.

———————

The sun was drifting toward evening, turning the peaks of the mountains red. Aralorn shifted contentedly on her rock near the cave entrance. Several days ago someone found a huge patch of berries, and the whole camp had spent the better part of two days harvesting the find. Haris had been adding them into everything and today had managed to cook several pies. Given that the only thing that he had to cook on was a grate over a fire, it was probable that he'd used magic to do it, but no one was complaining.

Licking her fingers clean of the last of the sweet stuff, Aralorn ran an idle gaze up the cliff face and caught something out of the corner of her eye. It was a shadow in the evening sky that was gone almost as soon as she saw it. She got to her feet and backed away from the cliff, trying to figure out just what it was that she saw, calling out an alarm as she did so.

The four or five people who were out milling about doing various chores started for the entrance at a run. Stanis and Tobin were coming up the trail to the valley with a donkey cart laden with firewood. Although they heard the alert, too, they weren't able to increase their pace much because of the donkey, and they weren't about to abandon the results of their labors.

Aralorn distractedly glanced at them, then looked back at the cliff, just in time to see the dragon launch itself. If she hadn't caught the moment of launch, she probably wouldn't have noticed it because it used magic to change the color of its scales until it blended into the evening sky. Aralorn headed for Stanis and Tobin as fast as she could. Seeing her, they abandoned the donkey and began running themselves. As she neared them, the shadow on the ground told her that the dragon was just overhead. She knocked both boys down in a wrestler's tackle and felt the razor-sharp claws run almost gently across her back.

The dragon gave a hiss that could have been either disappointment or amusement, and settled for the donkey, which it killed with a casual swipe of its tail. As it ate, it watched idly as Aralorn drove the two boys into the cave and stood guard at the entrance.

Aralorn met its gaze and knew that her sword was pitifully inadequate for the task, even had she been a better swordswoman. She had some hope that the runes that had kept the Uriah at bay would do the same to the dragon, but dragons were supposed to be creatures of magic and fire.

She heard the sounds of running footsteps behind her, then Myr's exclamation when he saw the dragon. He drew his grandfather's sword and held it in readiness. Aralorn noted with a touch of amusement that his larger sword looked to be a much more potent barrier than her own.

"How big do you think that thing is?" asked Myr in a whisper.

"Not as big as it looked when it was over top of me,

but big enough that I don't want to fight it," murmured Aralorn in reply.

The dragon paused in its eating to look over at them and smile, quite an impressive sight—easily as intimidating as Wolf's.

Myr stiffened. "It understands us."

Aralorn nodded reluctantly. "Well, if you have to die, I guess a dragon is an impressive way to go; maybe even worth a song or two. Just think, we are the first people to see a dragon in generations."

"It is beautiful," said Myr. As if in approval of his comment, a ripple of purple traveled through the blue of the dragon's scales.

"Watch that color shift," said Aralorn. "Magic, I think. If it wants to, it can be nearly invisible. Would make it harder to fight."

"It makes you wonder why there aren't more dragons, doesn't it," commented Myr.

Finished with the donkey, the dragon rose and stretched. No longer completely blue, highlights of various colors danced in its scales. Only its teeth and the claws on its feet and the edges of its wings were an unchanging black. When it was done, it started almost casually toward the cave entrance.

Myr stepped out from the meager protection of the entrance into the fading light, and Aralorn followed his lead. Something about Myr appeared to catch the dragon's interest: It stopped and whipped its long, swanlike neck straight, shooting the elegant head forward. Brilliant, gem-like eyes glittered green, then gold. Without warning, it opened its mouth and spat flame at Myr with an aim so exact that Aralorn wasn't even singed although she stood near enough to Myr to reach out and touch him.

Myr, being immune to magic, was untouched (although the same could not be said about his clothes). The hand that held his sword was steady, though his grip was tighter than it needed to be. He was no coward, this King of Reth. Aralorn smiled in grim approval.

The dragon drew its head back, and said, in Rethian that Aralorn felt as much as heard, "Dragon-blessed, this is far from your court. Why do you disturb me here?"

Myr, clothed in little more than the tattered remnants of cloth and leather, somehow managed to look as regal and dignified as the dragon did. "My apologies if we are troubling you. Our quarrel is not with you."

The dragon made an amused sound. "I hardly thought that it was, princeling."

"King," said Aralorn, deciding that the contempt that the dragon was exhibiting could get dangerous.

"What?" said the dragon, its tone softening in a manner designed to send chills up weaker spines.

"He is King of Reth and no princeling." Aralorn kept her voice even and met the dragon's look.

It turned back to Myr, and said in an amused tone, "Apologies, lord King. It seems I have given offense."

Myr inclined his head. "Accepted, dragon. I believe we owe you thanks for driving away the Uriah, sent by my enemy."

The dragon raised its head with a hiss, and its eyes acquired crimson tones. "Your enemy is the ae'Magi?"

"Yes," answered Myr with a wariness Aralorn shared.

The dragon stood silently, obviously thinking, then it said, "The debt dragonkind owes your blood is old and weak, even by dragon standards. Long and long ago, a human saved an egg that held a queen, a feat for which we were most grateful, as we were few even then. For this he and his blood were blessed that magic hold no terrors for them. For this deed of the past, I would have left you and your party alone.

"Several hundred years ago, after the manner of my kind, I chose a cave to sleep—waiting for the coming of my mate. I chose a cave deep under the ae'Magi's castle, where I was unlikely to be discovered. Dragons are magical in a way that no other creature is. We live and breathe magic, and without it, we cannot exist.

"I was awakened by savage pain that drove me out of my cave and into the Northlands. The ae'Magi is twisting magic, binding it to him until there will be nothing left but that which is twisted and dark with the souls of the dead. The castle of the ae'Magi has protections that I cannot cross, and the power that he has over magic is such that if I were to attack him, it is possible that he could control me. That is a risk I cannot take. Except for the egg that lies hidden from all, I am the last of my kind. If I die, there will be no more dragons." It stretched its wings restlessly.

"King," it said finally, "your sword is new, but the hilt is older than your kingdom, and token of our pledge to your line. If ever I can aid you, without directly confronting the ae'Magi, plunge the sword into the soil, run your hands over the ruby eyes of the dragon on the hilt, and say my name."

Aralorn heard nothing but the rushing of the wind as the dragon spoke its name for Myr. Then, in the deepening light of the evening, it reared back on its hind legs and fanned its wings, changing its color to an orange-gold that gave off its own light. Soundlessly, it took flight, disappearing long before it should have been out of sight.

"Beautiful, isn't he?" Wolf's familiar hoarse voice emanated from somewhere behind and between Aralorn and Myr. It comforted Aralorn that Myr jumped, too.

———

The herbs that Wolf brought back did work better. Once he got the spell just as he wanted it, he began working it without the props until he could direct it effortlessly. When he could drop the ensorcelled rocks in any pattern he chose, he spoke to Myr over dinner.

"I have what I need to face the ae'Magi. I will leave tomorrow for his castle."

"You aren't going alone," said Myr. "This is my battle as well. He killed my parents to further his plans. You will need someone at your back."

Wolf shook his head. "You are too valuable to your people to risk yourself in such a way. If you are killed, then there is no one to rule Reth. If I am killed, your immunity to magic may be the only weapon left against the ae'Magi."

"Wolf's right," agreed Aralorn, "but so is Myr. Wolf, the ae'Magi is not the only thing that you will have to face. He has quite an assortment of pets in the Uriah. They will tire you out before you even reach the ae'Magi."

Wolf frowned at her. "I know how to avoid most of the monsters. The ae'Magi will see that none of them kill me. Even if he wants me dead, he wants to kill me himself. If there is someone else with me that I have to worry about and guard, they will be more of a liability than an asset. I'll leave at first light." He turned on one heel and walked away, leaving the remnants of his dinner behind—without giving anyone a chance to argue further.

Aralorn finished her roll thoughtfully. If he thought she'd give up so easily, he hadn't been paying attention.

———

That night, as Aralorn half dozed on the library couch—she couldn't sleep without the risk of missing Wolf—she heard an unfamiliar woman's voice speaking from somewhere nearby.

"I'm worried," the stranger said. "There are too many things that can go wrong with what they're planning. I wish that they'd paid attention."

"I did what I could." Aralorn recognized the voice of the Old Man. He sounded a little petulant.

"It is up to them." The woman's soft voice soothed agreeably. "She's healed him enough that he might be able to carry it off. Can't you give them a clearer hint, though?"

"No. It isn't our concern. As long as he leaves you alone,

I don't care what the ae'Magi does." There was something off about his voice; he sounded more like a child than an adult.

"Of course you do, dear heart." The woman might have been shaking a finger at him from the tone of her voice. "Who was it that brought that young wolf to shelter here? Who gathered all of the people to hide from the human Archmage's wrath? It wasn't I."

"I've interfered too much." The old shapeshifter's voice sounded completely rational for the moment. "My time is past. I should have died with you, Lys. It is not right to be a ghost and not be dead. If I tell them what to do, it might cause more harm than good. I fear that I have let you talk me into too much." There was a pause, then he said in a resigned tone, "Ah well, once more, then. She's listening, isn't she?"

"You know me too well, love," she said. "Yes."

The Old Man's next words were so close to Aralorn's ear that she could feel his breath. "Then daughter of my brother's line, you must go with him to the ae'Magi's castle and take what is yours with you." Aralorn felt a hand on her cheek, then she heard the rush of air that signaled the shapeshifter's exit.

Once they'd left her, she sat up and waved on the lights. "Hearing voices now?" she said. "It is sad to say, Aralorn, but you have definitely lost whatever touch of sanity you once had. That bodes well for the coming adventure though—only an insane person would go to the ae'Magi's castle three times. Once was enough, twice was too many, but my little voices tell me that I'm going to make it three."

She shook her head in mock disgust. Knowing that she wasn't going to get any more sleep, she got up, strapped on her knives, and began stretching. By the time she had warmed up, she knew how she was going to arrange to accompany Wolf.

Before first light hit the mountainside, she snuck out on

four feet, following the tracking spell she'd set into the bottom of his left boot a couple of weeks past. It led her to a small cave Wolf occupied. She had never been in it and was distracted from her intended goal by the opportunity to see a different side to her mysterious magician. He kept a small magelight glowing to keep the room from the total darkness that was natural to the cave. Wolf himself was lying with his back to her on a cot against the far end of the room.

Although it was spartan and immaculate, she could tell by the smell that Wolf had occupied it for a long time—longer than the few months Myr had been hiding in the Northlands. Being a mouse had its advantages.

Fascinated, she wandered around, noticing that for all of its surface plainness, there were touches that showed an appreciation of beauty in small things: A small knob of rock reaching up from the floor was polished to a high gloss. A large clear glass vessel was placed in a secure nook; the tiny fractures that spiderwebbed the glass glittered even in the dim light.

Wolf moved restlessly on the bed. Aralorn waited to make sure that he was still sleeping before she crept into the pack that lay out of place near the entrance, trusting that its position signified that it was something he was going to take with him.

She made a place for herself among the various items and sat very still. She didn't have to wait long. Although he had announced that he would leave at first light, she wasn't at all surprised that he was leaving well before that. It had been obvious that neither she nor Myr had been particularly happy with his decision to go and face the ae'Magi alone.

To her relief, he swung the pack up and carried it with him when he departed. She hadn't quite figured out what she would have done if he'd left it.

She felt the roar of dizziness that signaled the magical leap from one place to another. When the sensation passed, she scrambled for a secure position in which the shuffling contents, which seemed to consist of nothing but hard angular objects, were not as likely to squish her. Even in human form, it seemed that Wolf's favorite gait was a ground-eating run.

Apparently he had arrived at a point several miles from the castle, as he ran for a long time. Battered and bruised, Aralorn was beginning to wish she'd figured out a better way to accompany him.

———

When Wolf opened the pack, the first thing that he saw was a bedraggled gray mouse, who looked at him with reproachful eyes, and said, "Would it have hurt to pack something soft, like a shirt or something?"

He should have been surprised. Or angry. He found himself, instead, absurdly grateful.

He picked her up out of the bag and held her at eye level in the palm of his hand. "When one comes along without being invited, one cannot complain about the accommodations."

"Oh dear," said the mouse, in a shocked voice. "I hope I am not intruding."

He took off the silver mask, and sat cross-legged on the ground—careful not to knock her off her perch on the palm of his hand. "I don't suppose that you would go back, would you? I trust it has occurred to you that it would be very easy for the ae'Magi to use you against me."

She ran up his arm and poised for an instant on his shoulder.

"Yes," she replied, cleaning her whiskers, "but it also occurred to me that my wolf was going off alone to kill his father. Granted that he is not the typical father, but—I don't think this is as easy for you as you'd like everyone to believe."

She hesitated for a minute before she continued. "I know how he is. How he can twist things until black seems white. His power is frightening, but it is not as dangerous as his ability to manipulate thoughts with words. I was only there for a short time; you were raised by him. It doesn't seem to me that exposure would make you immune to everyone; the opposite, I think. Perhaps having someone with you might make it easier."

Wolf was still. He didn't want to do this alone, but he wanted even less to have her hurt—or worse. Aralorn abruptly jumped to the ground.

"I couldn't have lived with myself if something happened to you and I was not with you." She shrugged and twitched her whiskers. "Besides, why should you have all the fun? He will see only a mouse, if he looks."

He wanted to send her away, not just for her safety, but because he didn't want her to know what he'd been before, even though he'd done his best to tell her himself. The feelings that she brought out in him were so painful and confusing. It was easier when he had felt nothing, no pain—no guilt. No desire.

His father had taught him how to be that way. When Wolf had understood that he was becoming the monster his father wanted, it had driven him to escape. It was easier when he had cared for nothing, easier when he'd been his father's pet mage. Much easier.

The desire that he felt to return to what he had left behind terrified him. No one who hadn't been raised there would understand the addiction of his father's corruption. Aralorn was right. He needed her to keep him from returning to his old ways, becoming his father's tool once more. The knowledge that she was watching might be enough to strengthen him.

"Stay," was all that he said.

Once he'd made his decision, he ignored her. Kneeling, he emptied the contents of the backpack, a motley collection of jars, which he organized in an overtly random fashion. He stripped himself of his clothes and began a ritual of purification, using the water from a nearby stream.

Aralorn watched for a while, but when he started to meditate, she went for a scurry—mice seldom walk. Once out of sight, where she wouldn't pull his concentration back to her, she shifted into her own form.

She stopped when she had a good view of the castle. It was funny how she always pictured it as black on the outside, the way it had appeared both times she left it. In the sunlight it sparkled a pearly gray, almost white. She could almost visualize the noble knight riding out to face the evil dragon. She hoped in this story the dragon (accompanied by his faithful mouse) would defeat the knight.

She clenched her fingers in the bark of the tree she stood next to and turned her cheek against the rough texture, closing her eyes against the very real possibility that this story would turn out like all the rest—the knight living happily ever after and the dragon slain.

When the shadows lengthened into dusk, Aralorn—once again the mouse—snuck back to where Wolf sat with closed eyes, the last light resting on his clean-shaven unblemished face with loving affection. The sight of his scarless face momentarily distracted her from his nudity.

Aralorn fought the chill that crept over her, knowing that if he looked just then, his all-too-discerning eyes would see her anxiety. It was unsettling to be in love with someone who looked like the face in her nightmares.

Ah well, as her stepmother would have said, at least he was handsome. And his face wasn't the only beautiful thing about him.

She leapt blithely onto his leg and ascended quickly to

his bare shoulder, feeling a slight malicious pleasure when he jerked in surprise. When he turned to glare at her, she kissed him on the nose, then began to clean her forepaws with industry. With a sound that might have been a laugh, he ran a finger lightly up her back, rubbing her fur the wrong way. She bit him—but not too hard.

He smoothed her hair and set her down on the ground so that he could regain his clothing. She noticed that it wasn't the same outfit he'd taken off. It wasn't like anything that she'd ever seen him wear. The main color was still black, but it was finely embroidered with silver thread. The shirt was gathered and puffed, hanging down well over his thighs, which was just as well, because the pants were indecently tight, from mouse height anyway. She could see the faint flickering of magic in the fabric and assumed that the clothes he wore were the magician equivalent of armor.

When he was dressed, he put her back on his shoulder and strode out of the clearing like a man who was at last within reach of attaining a much-coveted goal. He talked to her while he walked.

"I thought of confronting him in the castle itself, but it has been the center of so much magic that I really don't know how this spell would affect it. I suspect that at least some of the construction of the older parts of the building was done purely by magic. Without magic, it could collapse on top of us. I don't know about you, but I thought it might be interesting to survive long enough to find out just what the ae'Magi's loyal followers will do to his murderers. That is, if we manage to make it that far."

"I'd forgotten that aspect of it," answered Aralorn in the squeaky-soft voice that was the best her mouse form could manage. "Will his spells still be in effect when he dies?"

"Probably not, but people will still remember how they felt. We will remain the villains of this story." Wolf leapt easily over a small brook.

"Oh good!" she exclaimed, holding on tightly with her forepaws. "I've always wanted to be a villain."

"I am happy to please my lady mouse."

"Uh, Wolf?" she asked.

"Umm?"

"If we're not going to the castle, where are we going?"

"Well," he said, sliding down a steep section of his self-determined path, "when I lived in the castle, he had a habit of going out to meditate every night. He didn't like to do it in the castle because he said that there were too many conflicting auras—too many people steeped in magic had lived and died there in the past thousand years or so. There is a spot just south of the moat that he used to like to use. If he doesn't do it tonight, he probably will tomorrow."

Aralorn sat quietly, thinking of all the things she'd never asked him, might never get a chance to ask. "Wolf?"

"Yes?"

"Has your voice always been the way it is?"

"No." She thought that was all of the answer that she was going to get until he added, "When I woke up after melting the better part of the tower"—he pointed to one of the graceful spires that arched into the evening sky—"I found that I'd screamed so loud that I damaged my voice. It is very useful when I want to intimidate someone."

"Wolf," said Aralorn, setting a paw on his ear since they were on relatively smooth ground, "not to belabor the obvious, but your voice isn't what intimidates people. It could be the possibility that you might immolate anyone who bothers you."

"Do you think that might be it?" he inquired with mock interest. "I had wondered. It has been a while since I immolated anyone, after all."

She laughed and looked at the castle as it rose black against the lighter color of the sky. She had the funny feeling that it was watching them. She knew that it wasn't so, but she was grateful that she was a mouse all the same, and even more grateful that she was a mouse on Wolf's shoulders. She leaned lightly against his neck.

She knew that they were near the place Wolf had spoken of from the tension in the muscles she balanced on. A stray wind brought the smell of the moat to cut through the smell of green things growing. It almost disguised another scent that touched her nose.

"Wolf!" Aralorn said in an urgent whisper. "Uriah. Can you smell them?"

———

He stopped completely, his dark clothes helping him to blend in. His ritual cleansing had left no human scent to betray him, only the sharp/sweet scents of herbs. Even a Uriah couldn't track in the dark, so unless they had already been seen, they were safe for a moment. Wolf scanned with other senses to find where the Uriah were. It wasn't hard. He was surprised that they hadn't run into one before. His father, it seemed, had been busy. There were a lot of the things around, waiting.

Once, he had watched a spider at her web. Fascinated he had tried to see what she thought about, waiting for her prey to become entangled in the airy threads. He got the same feeling from the Uriah. He wondered if he were the victim of this web.

He thought about turning back. If the ae'Magi was aware that he was here, it might be better to return another time. After a brief hesitation, he shrugged and continued on with more caution. The ae'Magi knew his son well enough to know that he would be coming sometime; a surprise appearance would make no difference either way.

———

Aralorn buried her face in the pathetic shield of Wolf's shirt, trying to block out the smell. For some reason, the

smell of the Uriah was worse than the sounds that they
had made outside the cave. Hearing Talor's voice, seeing
his eyes on that grotesque mockery of a human body, had
made her want to retch and cry at the same time. It still did.

By the time she'd gained control, Wolf stopped for a
second time and set her on the ground, motioning her to
hide herself. He hesitated, then shifted into his familiar
lupine form before gliding into the clearing.

The ae'Magi sat motionless on the ground, his legs and
arms positioned in the classic meditation form. A small
fire danced just between Wolf and the magician. The newly
risen moon caught the clear features of the Archmage ruthlessly, revealing the remarkable beauty therein. Character
was etched in the slight laugh lines around his eyes and the
aquiline nose. His eyes opened, their color appearing black
in the darkness, but no less extraordinary than in full light.
His lips curved a welcoming smile. The warm tones vocal-
ized the sentiment in the expression on the ae'Magi's face.

"My son," he said, "you have come home."

ELEVEN

If Wolf wanted to believe that smile, Aralorn could see no sign of it from where she sat hiding under the large leaves of a plant that happened to be growing near the ae'Magi. She hadn't, of course, stayed where Wolf had left her. She wouldn't have been able to see anything.

Wolf lay down and began cleaning the toes of his front feet with a long pink tongue.

The ae'Magi's face froze at the implied insult, then relaxed into a rueful expression. "It was always so with you. Say walk, and you run, stop, and you go. I shouldn't have expected a joyous reunion, but I had hoped. It warms my heart to see you again."

The wolf who was his son looked up, and said, not quite correctly, "We have no audience here. Do you take me for a fool? Should I return as the long-lost son to his loving father? Let me know when you are through making speeches, so that we may talk."

Aralorn marveled at the perfect response the magician made. A hint of tragedy crossed his face, only to be supplanted by a look of stoic cheerfulness. "Let us talk, then, my son. Tell my why you are come if it be not out of love for your father."

Something was wrong, but she couldn't figure out just what it was. Something the ae'Magi said? Something he'd done?

"I pray you be seated." He indicated a spot not too near him with his left hand.

It was a power play, Aralorn saw. By politely offering Wolf a seat, the ae'Magi made him look like an unruly child if he didn't take it. If he did take it, it would give the ae'Magi the upper hand to have Wolf obey his first request. He'd reckoned without Wolf, who looked not at all uncomfortable and made no move to come closer to the ae'Magi.

The entire effect was lost without an audience of some sort, Aralorn thought. Was there someone other than the Uriah watching them?

"I do not play your games," Wolf said impatiently. "I have come to stop you. Everywhere that I go, I see one of your filthy pets. You are annoying me, and I will not put up with it." Wolf put no force behind his words; the grave-gravel tone carried threat enough.

The ae'Magi stood and stepped slightly to his left, so the fire no longer was a barrier between him and the wolf. "I am sorry if I have caused you bother. Had I known that the shapeshifter woman was yours, I would never have taken her. She didn't tell me about you until we were done, and there was nothing I could do about it. Did she tell you that she cried when I . . ." He let his voice drift off.

Wolf rose to his feet with a growl of rage and stalked toward the figure. Abruptly, Aralorn realized what it was that bothered her about the ae'Magi. He cast no shadow from the light of the fire. She noticed something else: Wolf's path would take him directly across the place that the ae'Magi would have had him sit at.

"Wolf, stop!" she yelled as loud as she could in mouse

form, hoping that he'd heed her. "He has no shadow. It's an illusion."

―――――――

Wolf stopped, muting the feral tones in his throat. Her voice broke into his unexpected rage. He did then what he should have done first. Sniffing the air, he smelled only the taint of moat and Uriah, no fire—no human.

Ignoring the pseudo–ae'Magi, Aralorn the mouse scampered to the space toward which Wolf had been baited. "There's a circle drawn in rosemary and tharmud root here."

"A containment spell of some sort," commented Wolf. She was exploring a little more closely than he was comfortable with. She needed to be more careful of herself. "It's probably best if we don't trigger it." His voice was calm, but his body was still stiff. He sketched a sign in the air, and the image of the ae'Magi froze.

"Is he directing the illusion, do you think?" asked Aralorn, bouncing away from the circle toward Wolf.

"I doubt it. He would not have to. The illusion spell can be given directives, and the trap requires no magic to initialize once it is set." He regained his human form and picked up Aralorn, setting her on his shoulder, where he'd gotten used to having her. "If I had triggered the containment spell, it would probably have alerted him then."

"Like a spider's web," said Aralorn.

"Just so," agreed Wolf.

―――――――

He stared at the illusion of his father and made no effort to move away. It wasn't a spell; she'd have felt it if something was actually affecting Wolf. Maybe it was something more powerful than magic.

"Where to now?" Aralorn asked. "Do we wait for the Uriah to attack, or do we look for the ae'Magi?"

"For someone who should be scared and cowering, you

sound awfully eager." Wolf stood staring at the silhouette of the ae'Magi: His voice wasn't as emotionless as usual.

"Hey," replied Aralorn briskly, "it's better than spending the winter cooped up in the caves."

Wolf made no answer except to run an absentminded hand over the smooth skin of his cheek as if he were looking for something that wasn't there.

Aralorn waited as patiently as she could, then said, "He knew that you were coming."

Wolf nodded. "He's been expecting me for a long time. I knew that. I should have been more alert for something like this." He bowed his head. "I should have asked before. What he said, I have to know. Aralorn, when he had you here, did he . . ." His voice tightened with rage and stopped.

"No," she said instantly. "I'd tell you that before a time like this anyway, so you wouldn't get upset when you need your wits about you. But look here, the first time I was in his castle, he was working on a spell and wanted to save his energy. I was disappointed, but then a slave must wait on the master's convenience."

He was listening. She was taking the right tack, then. "The second time, he was too interested in finding you to worry about it. You shouldn't let him pull your strings so easily." She curled her tail against his neck in a quick caress. "I would have lied under these circumstances, you have to know that. But I wouldn't have hidden something like that when you got me out of there—I don't think I could have." And that was as honest as she was comfortable with—but it did the trick.

The tension eased out of him. "You are right, Lady. Shall we go a-hunting sorcerers in the castle? Perhaps you would prefer a Uriah or two to begin with, or one of my father's other pets. I believe that there are a few that you haven't seen before. Would Milady prefer to be outnumbered a hundred to two or just by three or four to two? This task can accommodate your tastes."

"Then of course," said Aralorn, "once you have attained your goal, we can arrange to have the castle fall on us conveniently. That way we'll escape mutilation from the outraged populace that you have saved from slavery and worse. Sounds interesting—let's get to it." She thought that Wolf might have been smiling as he headed downhill and away from the castle, but it was hard to tell from her vantage point.

———————

The woods grew increasingly dense as Wolf walked farther from the castle. A hoot from an owl just overhead made Aralorn-the-mouse cringe tighter against his neck. "Lots of nasties in these woods," she said in a mouselike voice devoid of all but a hint of humor.

"And I," announced Wolf in a grim voice that was designed to let Aralorn know that it was time to be serious, "am the nastiest of all."

"Are you really?" asked Aralorn in an interested sort of tone. "Oh, I just adore nasties."

Wolf stopped and looked at the mouse sitting innocently on his shoulder. Most people cowered under that look. Aralorn began, industriously, to clean her whiskers. When Wolf started to walk again, though, she said in a stage whisper, "I really do, you know."

They emerged from a particularly thick growth of brush into a narrow aisle of grass. In the center of it sat a suggestively shaped altar dedicated to one of the old gods. It was heavily overgrown with moss and lichen until it was almost impossible to tell the original color of the stone. There was nothing unusual about finding the altar, as such remnants dotted the landscape from well before the Wizard Wars. However, the altar itself was flanked by a pair of unusually shaped monoliths.

"Oh dear," said Aralorn drolly, crawling halfway down

his arm to get a good look. "Look. Two of them. I suppose that it must have belonged to one of the fertility gods, hmm?"

The southern monolith was broken about halfway up, but the northernmost stood as tall as a man and almost as big around. When Wolf touched it, it slid sideways with a creak and a groan. He slipped inside the dark hole that was revealed and started down the ladder. Aralorn darted off his arm altogether and checked out the ladder.

"The ladder is a lot newer than the altar," she commented, flashing back to her post and tucking a paw inside his collar.

"I put it up myself when I saw that there was some kind of exit from the secret tunnels up here. There was no sign of another one, so I suppose it must have rotted completely away. Plague it, Aralorn, you're going to fall and kill yourself if you don't stay put!"

She'd darted back out to his arm to get a closer look at the tile work on the wall. He picked her off his wrist and set her firmly back on his shoulder. "Just wait until we get down, and you can have a better look."

Once on the floor, he closed the opening with a wave and a thread of magic. As soon as it was shut, he let his staff light the hall in which they stood.

———

Aralorn scrambled to the floor and took her own shape, sneezing a bit from the dust. She scuffed a foot on the floor, revealing a dark, polished surface. The ceiling was as high or higher than the great hall in the castle, and the walls were covered with detailed mosaic patterns of outdoor revelries of times gone by. The ceiling was painted like the night sky, giving the overall impression of being outdoors. Or at least that was what Aralorn assumed. The years had covered the tile on the walls with cracks and knocked down whole sections. The ceiling was badly water-damaged,

showing the stonework that held it up through gaps left by
fallen plaster.

Reluctant to leave the room without adequate explora-
tion, Aralorn dragged behind Wolf, who'd already ducked
through a gap in the wall leading to a drab little tunnel that
looked as if a giant mole had dug through the earth. Much
less interesting than the room they'd climbed down into, it
branched several times. Wolf never hesitated as he chose
their way.

"How many times did you get lost exploring this?"

Wolf shot her an amused look. "Several, but I found a
book hidden in one of the old libraries that detailed some
of the passages, and I found a copy of the master plans in
the library—my library. The passages are extensive; it's a
wonder the whole thing hasn't collapsed. There are only fifteen or twenty large rooms like the one we started in, most
of them about in the same condition. If we make it through
the next few days, I'll show you a library that makes the
one we have in the Northlands look small. I don't know all
of the passages. There are a lot of secret panels and hidden
doors, magical and mundane, that make it difficult to find
most of the interesting places. Like this one." Wolf waved
a hand, and a large section of the tunnel just disappeared
into a finished and ornate corridor.

When they stepped through, the opening disappeared—
leaving a blank wall in its place. The end of the corridor
widened into a huge room with a fountain at its center. The
floor had once been wood, which was mostly rotted away,
leaving a walkway that was uneven and hazardous.

He wanted to linger and watch her.

Aralorn stumbled and tripped forward instead of walking, because she was too busy staring at the frescoed ceiling
and the elaborate stone carvings on the walls to pick her

way through the debris that littered the floor. When she
started muttering about "where the fourth Lord Protector
of Such and Such Port met with the Queen to defeat the Sorcerer What's-His-Face," Wolf put a firm hand on her shoulder and led her patiently around the old traps and pitfalls.

He enjoyed her enthusiasm quietly, as any comment
on his part was likely to spark a full-blown story. He led
her through several other moldering doorways before they
came to one of the stairways that led up to the castle itself.
He chose that one to keep their path simple—it would take
them to a small closet in the dressing room of the master's
suite.

———

Aralorn didn't need Wolf to put his finger to his lips as he
opened the secret door that dumped them in a small closet
that led to a sumptuously appointed room where hand-
carved combs and mirrors sat next to brushes and jewelry
of every masculine type. She recognized a piece that the
ae'Magi wore and realized that they were in his personal
rooms.

The suite consisted of interconnected rooms, all hung
with tapestries of great age and richness, preserved through
magic that made her fingertips throb when she brushed by
them. The rooms were empty except for a girl who was
crouched sobbing in a corner.

Her nakedness made her look even younger than she
was. The white skin of her back was mottled with bruises
and lash marks. An arcane symbol whose meaning eluded
Aralorn, was etched into one shoulder in bright red.

Wolf grabbed both of Aralorn's arms when she would
have reached out to touch the girl. He pushed Aralorn behind
him with more speed than gentleness and gripped his staff
in one hand. Noiselessly, he drew his sword in the other.

"Child." The word was gentle, his tone sad—for him;

but he gripped the sword and held it in readiness. It was fortunate that he did so.

With a chilling cry and uncanny speed, the girl turned and leapt. Once her face had been uncommonly pretty, thought Aralorn, with a small tattoo next to her eye that marked her as belonging to one of the silk-merchant clans. Now the skin was drawn too tightly against the fine bones. Her china-blue eyes were surrounded by pools of bloodred. Her full lips were stretched over pearly teeth, the kind that all of the heroines in the old stories had—with a slight difference. The lower set of teeth were as long as the first two knuckles of Aralorn's ring finger. Her mouth gaped impossibly wide as she launched herself at Wolf.

He knocked her aside easily enough, for her weight was slight, and in the process he cut her deeply in the abdomen. He ended her suffering with a second cut to the back of her neck.

Death was no stranger to Aralorn, so examining the body didn't bother her—much. "One of your father's pets, I assume." It was a comment more than a question.

Wolf grunted an affirmative and touched the symbol on her back. "She'd have been a lot harder to fight if she hadn't been so new at it. She didn't even know how to attack."

Aralorn jerked the embroidered bedspread off the bed and covered the pathetic little body with it before following Wolf out of the room.

The study was a wonder in cultured taste, not that Aralorn expected anything else. Wolf walked to the desk and picked up a sheet of paper. He laughed humorlessly and handed it to Aralorn. It read simply, "I'm in the dungeon. Join me?"

"Apparently," said Wolf, "he *was* monitoring his little trap. He probably knows that you are with me. It is time for you to leave. Now."

She looked at him with due consideration. "I probably should tell you that I will, then just follow you in."

"You would, wouldn't you?" Wolf's voice was soft. He glanced at a decanter on the ae'Magi's polished desk. It imploded loudly enough to make Aralorn jump. "Plague take you, Aralorn, don't you see? He will use you against me. He already has."

Aralorn felt her own temper rise to the surface. "Do you think that I am some weak helpless *female* who can do nothing but stand around while you protect her? I am not helpless against *human* magic or anything else he's likely to throw at us." She made "human" sound like a filthy word. "I can help. Let me help, Wolf."

He was silent for a long moment, then he waved his hand with a haphazard motion and the decanter re-created itself, leaving the desk unblemished. He walked over and pulled the stopper. Taking a token drink from the neck of the bottle, he met Aralorn's glare.

"I owe you an apology, Lady. I'm not used to caring about anything. It's . . . uncomfortable."

She tilted her chin up at him, flags of temper still on her cheeks, then she took the decanter that he was still holding and took a mouthful herself. She set it on the desk and muttered something that he wasn't supposed to hear.

"What?" he whispered. Evidently, he'd heard her.

She put her hands on her hips and glared at him, tapping a foot impatiently on the floor. He didn't have to look like someone had slapped him.

"I said, 'It's a good thing that I love you, or you'd be Uriah bait.' Now that that's settled, why don't we go find ourselves an ae'Magi?" Without waiting for him, she stalked out the door into the hallway.

"Aralorn," he said, his voice a little deeper than usual. "You're going the wrong way if you want to find the dungeons." He sounded . . . almost meek.

She glared at him, and he held out his hand in invitation. So she followed him through the twists and turns of the castle halls that were almost as convoluted as the secret

tunnels. The dimly lit passages, which had seemed threatening and huge when she had gone through them alone,
were not as intimidating as she remembered them.

Apparently there were no humans in the castle this late
at night—at least they didn't see any. The Uriah standing
guard here and there paid them no heed. Aralorn was careful to keep her eyes from their faces, but she recognized
Talor's boots anyway. Wolf's grip was steady on her shoulder as they went by it. Not him. Never again. It.

When they passed the entrance to the great hall, she
couldn't resist the opportunity to look inside. The bars of
the cage were discernible in the moonlight, but the light
wasn't good enough to see if it was occupied.

The stairway that led down to the lower levels was well
lit and smelled of grain and alcohol from the storage rooms
on the first sublevel. Each storage room was carefully
labeled as to its contents. Most of them contained food-
stuffs, but other labels read things like weapons, fabric,
and old accounting records. The stairway down to the next
level was on another side of the castle.

The second sublevel seemed to be smaller, and here
there were several small sleeping quarters intended for the
use of apprentices; at least so Aralorn judged them by the
traditional sparseness of the cells. The only other rooms
were obviously intended for labs, but from the dust that
coated the tables, they hadn't seen use for some time.

The dungeon was on the third sublevel, Wolf told her,
as they went down another set of stairs. Like the caves, the
temperature was consistently chilly but not cold. The smell
was overpowering.

Aralorn felt the hair on her arms move with the magic
impregnated in the walls of the castle at this level. Count-
less magicians had bespelled the stones here to prevent the
escape of the inmates, and the half of Aralorn that wasn't
human told her that the spells had been strong enough to
keep some of the prisoners in even after they died. Sick as

she had been during her incarceration here, she remembered the feel of the dead weighing down the air.

It occurred to her that she was lucky that she wasn't a full-blooded shapeshifter—they could sense the dead almost as clearly as the living. A shapeshifter wouldn't keep his sanity for very long in a place such as this.

Without the fever that kept her from shielding herself from the human-twisted magic, she could block out enough of the emanations that the pain was nominal. She ignored the discomfort that remained and kept close to Wolf.

The guardroom was empty. By prearranged plan, and it took a strong argument to convince Wolf, she entered the dungeons first—because it was unexpected, and the more off-balance they could throw the ae'Magi, the better off they were.

The first thing that she noticed was the lack of sound. There had never been a cessation of the moaning and coughing—sometimes the noise had almost driven her crazy. Now it was still and silent. The light was dim, and Wolf's staff had stayed in the guardroom with him, so she couldn't see inside the cells. She crept carefully down one side of the path and hid in the shadows. Unlike her, Wolf made a showy entrance. His staff glittered wildly, lighting the room with his power. The illumination slid off the shield of Aralorn's magic and left her hidden.

It didn't slide off the ae'Magi, who stood at the far end of the room. Like Wolf, he, too, carried a staff, massive and elaborately carved, which he tilted as if it were a lance. It wasn't aimed at Wolf, but at her. She dropped instantly to the floor, which vibrated with the force of the explosion of the outside wall of the cell behind her. She was so distracted that she almost missed Wolf's countermove, designed to force the ae'Magi to deal with him.

It caused the ae'Magi to turn to Wolf. While he was watching his son, Aralorn pulled one of her knives and threw it at the ae'Magi. She hit him in the chest. She only had a moment to congratulate herself before the knife passed through him without effect and clattered harmlessly to the floor behind him. The ae'Magi didn't even glance her way.

With a philosophical shrug, she stayed on the floor and prepared to watch the fight. It would have looked odd to someone who was not sensitive to magic and could only see two men gesturing wildly at each other. Aralorn could feel the currents of magic moving back and forth, gaining momentum and power with each countermove, but the only gesture that her limited experience with human magic allowed her to recognize was the deceptively simple spell that Wolf had been working on.

She had a moment to consider the results of an antimagic spell let loose in the dungeon of the ancient seat of the master magicians. A dungeon steeped in the magic of centuries of spells.

Since she was already on the floor, all that she had to do was flatten herself tighter and hope that it was enough. Then the antimagic spell hit, and chaos reigned.

She didn't know if it knocked her out, or just blinded her: Either way, she lost track of time. The first thing she could see clearly was Wolf sitting on the floor and leaning awkwardly against a wall, his staff clenched in his right hand. She crawled to him on hands and knees.

"Are you all right?" She patted his arm anxiously, afraid to touch him without knowing where he was hurt.

"Yes," he said, holding his staff out to her, as if he needed both hands to stand up.

Aralorn heard the noise behind her and twisted her head to see the ae'Magi getting to his feet even as she reached for the staff. She turned back to Wolf to warn him, and noticed something she would have seen right away if she hadn't been so dazed—she'd been in enough fights to know a broken back when she saw it. She saw the same knowledge in Wolf's face.

He smiled at her with a haunting sweetness as she touched the staff. He said something that might have been "I love you, too" but a jolt of magic traveled up her arm, and she blacked out.

When she woke up, the floor she was looking at was bare stone, not cobbled as the floor in the dungeon was. Wolf's staff lay beside her, the crystals in the top smoky dark. The musky smell of the books told her where she was.

"*No!* You stupid son of a . . . Plague take you, Wolf!" Her scream was muffled by the rows of bookshelves in his library. Helplessly, she pounded a fist on the floor, letting rage keep back her tears.

"The sword." She didn't see anyone, but a firm hand pulled her to her feet. The Old Man materialized and shook her by the shoulders. Who else could it have been? His features were the too-perfect features of a shapeshifter.

"The sword, you stupid girl. Where is the sword?"

Aralorn had been through a lot. She had long since outgrown any patience with being manhandled. With a deceptively easy twist recently learned from Stanis, she freed herself and backed away.

With the distance between them, she could see the aura of age that clung to him despite the smooth skin on his face. He was only a few inches taller than she was and far more beautiful to look upon. At another time, she would have been more courteous to the Old Man of the Mountain, but Aralorn wasn't in the mood for politeness.

"What sword are you talking about, old man?" she spat. Hundreds of miles away, Wolf was fighting for his life—she refused to believe that he was dead. She had no patience left.

"The sword! *The* sword!" His arms swung widely in one of the overblown gestures that shapeshifters favored. He dropped into their language, and Aralorn had to struggle to understand the dialect he spoke. "You haven't let the ae'Magi get his hands on it, have you? Where is it? He mustn't have control over it."

"What sword?" Aralorn's voice was harsh with impatience; she needed to travel back to the castle, and a goose wasn't the swiftest of fliers. It would take her days. Too late. She would be too late. "Sir, you will have to explain yourself more clearly."

"Your *sword*, did you leave it there? Didn't . . ." He stopped and looked behind her.

Curious, she looked behind her and saw her short sword, the one that she had left in its usual place under the couch, floating gently in the air behind her. She could almost see the person holding the sword—it was like looking at an image in rough water, impossible to discern any specific features.

"You didn't take it?" The Old Man's voice was filled with disgust. "What is wrong with you? I *told* you. Told *you*. If it weren't for the fact that Lys cares about that Wolf, I would let you stew in your own pot."

He stalked to the sword and took it from the apparition that held it. He unsheathed it and swung it once. "*This* is the third of the Smith's great weapons. Ambris." He gave it another name, but Aralorn was too distracted to translate it. "If the ae'Magi gets his hands on her and realizes what he has, there will be no one who can stand against him. You were supposed to take her with you and use her. I take it that your silly little spell didn't work?"

He didn't wait for her nod, but continued, "I thought that he just might pull it off. Here"—abruptly the shape-shifter's voice lost its force and became querulous like that of a very old man—"take it and go back. I'm very tired—maintaining this shape is burdensome. Lys?" He shoved the sword at Aralorn and was gone with an abrupt pop.

Aralorn took the sword and looked at it. It looked no

more magical than it ever had, but still . . . it did match the description given for the Smith's sword.

And the sword gave her another idea. Sheathing it abruptly, she slipped it onto her belt. With Wolf's staff in one hand, she ran out of the library to find Myr.

TWELVE

―――∞∞∞――――

Myr was never difficult to locate. Aralorn simply had to look for the largest group of people and head in that direction. She found him just outside the cave entrance, giving knife-fighting lessons to a group of the younger refugees. He glanced up and saw her as he was avoiding a crudely wielded blade; the distraction almost cost him a slit throat.

He spoke for just a minute to his former opponent, who was white-faced and shaking. It was no light thing to come so close to killing a king. Aralorn shifted impatiently from one foot to the other as Myr dismissed the class and strode to her.

He took a long look at her, noting the scrape on her cheek that she'd gotten rolling across the floor; the filth that clung to her; and Wolf's staff, which she held clutched in one hand. He didn't demand any explanations, merely asking in a businesslike tone, "What do you need?"

"I need you to call the dragon to take me back to the ae'Magi's castle. I can't get there fast enough by myself."

She noticed with detached surprise that her voice was steady.

Myr nodded, gestured for her to wait for him, and ducked back into the caves. He returned carrying his sword in one hand, the belt dangling from its sheath, and led the way through a thicket of brambleberry to a smallish clearing.

Carefully, he unsheathed his sword and gave a rueful look to the blade that years of his grandfather's warring had left unmarred. Then he drove it into the sandy soil, trying not to wince at the grating sound. Another time, Aralorn would have smiled.

When he was done calling the dragon, he stood quietly beside her, not asking her what had happened. It was Aralorn who finally broke the silence.

"We made it into the ae'Magi's castle. He was waiting for us in the dungeons. I think that Wolf's spell would have worked anyplace else. There was too much old magic, and the spell wasn't strong enough and backlashed. I was on the floor already so it didn't hit me very hard. The ae'Magi was knocked out momentarily. Wolf . . ." Her voice cracked and she stopped, swallowed, and tried again. "Wolf's back is broken, he tricked me into touching his staff and sent me back here. I don't know how fast a dragon can fly. Even if it consents to take me to the castle, it will probably be too late."

She laughed then, though it could have been a sob, and clasped the staff tighter. "He may have been right, and it was too late when he sent me back."

Myr didn't say anything, but he put a comforting hand on her shoulder. A cold wind swept down the mountainside, and Aralorn shivered with impatience as much as chill. Even though she was watching intently, she didn't see the dragon until it was overhead. Silver and green and as graceful as a hummingbird, the great reptile landed and eyed them with interest—or perhaps hunger.

"I need you to get me to the ae'Magi's castle as fast as possible." Aralorn knew she was being too abrupt, but she was desperate and couldn't find courtesy when she needed it. The dragon tilted its head back in offense.

Myr's grip tightened warningly on Aralorn's shoulder, as he said, "Dragon, the only one of us who stands a chance of facing down the ae'Magi is hurt and fighting alone at the castle. We need to get there to help him, or the ae'Magi has won. You are our only chance of doing so in time."

Aralorn started at the "we," but decided not to protest as it was likely to offend the dragon even more.

The dragon hesitated a minute, then asked, "Speed is important?"

"Very, sir," Aralorn said carefully, keeping a respectful tone.

It nodded, once. "I can travel much faster than flying, but it means that because of your safeguards against magic, I cannot take you, King Myr. The shapeshifter half-breed I can take."

Myr looked unhappy, but he nodded his acceptance. When the dragon lowered its belly to the ground and folded its wings, Myr helped Aralorn up as she was hampered by the necessity of keeping the sharp claws at the end of Wolf's staff away from the dragon.

The scales on the dragon's back were slick, but otherwise it was no worse than riding a horse bareback—until he began moving. The wings beat steadily until they caught an updraft, then flattened and spread wide—letting the wind pull them south.

Abruptly, the dragon lurched forward, and Aralorn felt a familiar dizziness seize her and clutched the fist-sized scales reflexively. He'd transported them the same way Wolf had sent her back to his library. When she was able to focus her eyes again, the castle of the ae'Magi lay just below.

Shouting, so that the dragon could hear her past the sound of the wind, Aralorn said, "Land wherever you can find a safe place, Lord. I can find my way in." She still had that little follow-me spell on Wolf's boot. He'd changed his clothes preparing to face his father, but not his boots.

In acknowledgment of her words, the dragon changed its angle of flight until it was losing altitude fast. Aralorn's ears popped painfully, and she tightened her grip on the dragon's scales until they cut into her hand. When the dragon landed, the jolt loosened Aralorn's grip, and she landed with a thud next to an impressively armed forepaw.

She rolled to her feet with more speed than grace. She turned to face the dragon and bowed respectfully. "My thanks, sir, and apologies for my clumsiness." Without waiting for a reply, she shifted quickly into a goose and flew as fast as she could to the castle.

The moat didn't smell any better than it had before, and it took her some time to find an intact pipe that was not plugged with grime. Once she found one, maybe the same one she'd used before, she balanced precariously on it until she could turn into a mouse. Even in mouse form, she had trouble negotiating the tricky business of crawling into the pipe from the top, but she managed. All the while, part of her wailed that she was being too slow.

The corridor she entered was only dimly lit by wall sconces, and from what she could see, it was not one that she'd been in before. She considered staying a mouse but decided that she would have a better chance of recognizing something familiar if she were in human form since she'd been in human form while she was following Wolf.

When she took her own shape again, the staff appeared beside her (she hadn't been sure that it would). She wondered if it had changed with her, like the sword and her clothes, or if it was following her on its own. She remembered how Wolf would just reach out and it would be there, under his hand. She'd thought it was something Wolf had done. The idea that it had been the staff all along caused her to pick it up gingerly as she started down the hallway.

There were still Uriah posted in the halls. As before, they allowed her to pass without bothering her though they followed her progress with their eyes. She kept a steady, rapid pace, hoping that she would find a clue to where she was soon enough to be of some help to Wolf. The spell on Wolf's boot was harder to follow in the ae'Magi's castle than it had been in the caves. She could feel it, but it was a faint whisper instead of a call.

The castle was eerily silent, so that when she heard sounds coming from inside a room, she stopped impulsively and opened the door. Kisrah looked up, startled, from where he'd been eating breakfast in bed with a giggling young beauty.

"Lord Kisrah, you wouldn't be interested in showing me the way to the dungeons, I suppose?" asked Aralorn. She wondered if she should draw her sword or knife. She didn't have a chance to act. Something flashed at her out of Lord Kisrah's hands. Instinctively, because it was already in her grip, she moved to block it with the staff. When the flash hit the dark, oiled wood, the crystals on one end of the staff, which up to this point had been dull and lifeless, flared brightly, and Lord Kisrah's magic dissipated without a sound.

Unwilling to let him get another spell off, Aralorn attacked with the staff. Lord Kisrah, unarmed, not to mention unclothed, didn't have much of a chance against Aralorn, who was wielding her favorite type of weapon. Her first blow broke his arm and her second knocked him unconscious on the floor next to the bed.

Aralorn turned to his bedmate with apologies on her lips, but something about the girl made her tighten her grip on the staff instead. Focused intently on the unconscious man, the red-haired woman slithered out of the bedclothes, knocking the bed table with their food onto the floor.

Remembering the harpy that she and Wolf had met earlier, Aralorn tapped the girl's shoulder gingerly with the clawed end of the staff. She hadn't realized how sharp the claws were until they drew blood. She felt bad about it until the girl turned and Aralorn got a good look at her.

The girl snarled, and Aralorn jumped back and seriously considered leaving Lord Kisrah to his fate. As the girl moved, her shape altered rapidly into something vaguely reptilian, with a large spiked tail and impressive fangs, not the same as the silk-merchant girl, though maybe they were at different stages.

The thing, whatever it was, was fast and strong: When its tail hit the post of the bed, the wood cracked. It was also, thankfully, stupid—very stupid. It jumped at Aralorn with a shrill cry and impaled itself on the claws of Wolf's staff.

Dying, it changed back into its former beauty and the woman blinked her green eyes—shapeshifter eyes—and said softly, "Please . . ." before she was unable to say anything.

"Plague it," said Aralorn in an unsteady voice as she retrieved the staff in shaky hands. She backed into the corridor and had started down it when she noticed the hungry gaze of one of the Uriah focused on the bloody end of the staff. She thought of Lord Kisrah lying like an appetizer beside his bedmate's corpse; she went back and shut the door to the bedroom and locked it with a simple spell that Lord Kisrah would have little trouble breaking when he woke up.

Just as she was about to give up hope, Aralorn rounded a corner and found herself in the great hall. From there it was a simple matter to find her way to the dungeon, and the closer she came, the stronger her follow-me spell summoned her. She was concentrating so hard on doing so that the whisper took her by surprise.

"Aralorn," said the Uriah from the shadows near the stairway that led down to the dungeons.

She came to an abrupt halt and spun to face Talor. "What do you want?"

It laughed, sounding for a minute as carefree as he always had, then said in a harsh voice, "You know what

I am. What do you think that I want, Aralorn?" It took a step closer to her. "I hunger, just as your companion will shortly. Leave, Aralorn, you can do no good here."

Aralorn shifted her grip on Wolf's staff from her right hand, which was getting stiff and sweaty, to her left. "Talor, where is your brother? I haven't seen him here."

"He didn't make the transition to Uriah," it said softly, and smiled. "Lucky Kai."

Aralorn nodded and turned as if to go down the stairs; instead she continued her turn, drawing the sword as she moved. Smith's weapon or not, the blade cut cleanly through the Uriah's neck, beheading it. The body fell motionless to the stone floor.

"Sweet dreams, Talor," she said soberly. "If I find Wolf in your condition, I will strive to do the same for him."

With the sword in her right hand and the staff in her left, she started down the stairs. The lower levels were darker, but Wolf's staff was emitting a faint glow that allowed her to see where she put her feet. As she started down the third set of steps, it occurred to her that she didn't really know what she planned to do. Alone against the ae'Magi, she had no chance. Not only was he a better magician (by several orders of magnitude), but, if he was Wolf's equal with a sword, he was a much better fighter than Aralorn.

The smells of the dungeon had become strong, and the stench didn't help her stomach, which was already clinched with nerves. In the guardroom, she abandoned the staff because she didn't know how to stop the crystals from glowing.

She sheathed the sword and dropped to her belly, ignoring the filth on the cold stone floor. Slowly, she slid into the dungeon, keeping to one side. The voices that had been indistinct were now intelligible. She heard Wolf speaking, and the huge weight of grief lifted off her shoulders.

". . . why should I make this easier for you than I already have? This is a very easy shield to break through, most third-year magicians could do it. Would you like me to show you how?" Wolf's voice was weaker than she'd ever heard it, but there was no more emotion in it than it ever had. "It does have the unfortunate effect of incinerating whatever the shield is guarding."

"Ah, but I have another method of removing your protection." The ae'Magi's voice was a smooth contrast to his son's. "I have been informed that the girl that you so impetuously sent away has returned all alone. She should be here momentarily if she isn't already."

For an instant, Aralorn plastered herself motionless to the floor before her common sense reasserted itself. It really didn't matter if the ae'Magi knew she was coming, the element of surprise wasn't going to help her much anyway. What did matter was that somehow Wolf had managed to hold the ae'Magi at bay, and no matter how much Wolf cared for her, he knew that it was more important that the ae'Magi not be able to control Wolf's powers. He wouldn't give himself to the ae'Magi just to save her skin . . . she hoped.

She inched forward a few steps more until she could see Wolf revealed by the light of the ae'Magi's staff. He sat in almost the same position that he had been in when she left him. He had drawn a single orange line of power around himself, and there was something different about his position. She looked carefully and saw that he was cautiously moving his toes. She smiled; he had bought enough time with his barrier to heal himself.

Aralorn drew the sword and stepped into the light in front of Wolf. She expected an immediate reaction, but the ae'Magi was pacing back and forth with his back to her.

". . . you should not have crossed me. With your power and my knowledge, you could have become a god with me. That's all that the gods were, did you know it? Mages who had discovered the secret to eternal life, and I have it now. I will be a god, the only god, and you will help me do it."

All of the dictates of honor demanded that she call attention to herself before she attacked. Aralorn, however, was a spy and a rotten swordswoman besides, so she struck him in the back.

Unfortunately the same spell that had rendered her knife useless previously was also effective against the sword, which slid harmlessly through him and knocked Aralorn off-balance. She turned her fall into a roll and kept going until she hit a wall. Although the sword hadn't done the magician any harm, the metal grip had heated enough that she was forced to drop it on the ground.

It had something to do with hitting a magician with metal, she supposed.

"Ah," said the ae'Magi with a smile, "who would think that the son of my flesh would fall for a silly girl who is stupid enough to try the same trick twice."

He turned to Wolf and started to say something else, but Aralorn quit listening. She couldn't believe that the Archmage was just dismissing her. She decided not to question her luck and began to shapechange, trusting that Wolf would see her and keep the ae'Magi's attention long enough that she could complete the transition to icelynx.

"Don't discount Aralorn so lightly, you may be surprised," commented Wolf, stretching the stiff muscles of his neck. "Certainly I never thought that she could get back from the Northlands so quickly. Perhaps the Old Man of the Mountain sent her back."

The ae'Magi snorted in disbelief. "You could not have sent her so far; the Northlands would have blocked such transportation. I do not care where she was. As for the Old Man of the Mountain myth, there is no such person, or I would have run into him long since."

Wolf curved his lips in the dim light of the ae'Magi's staff. "If you are so sure that the old gods are real, why not a folktale as well?"

The keener senses of the icelynx made the smell of the dungeon worse, and she curled her lips in a silent snarl of disgust as she stalked slowly toward the ae'Magi. She crouched behind him and twitched her stub of a tail, waiting for just the right moment before she sprang.

Her front claws dug into his shoulders for purchase while her hind legs raked his back, scoring him deeply. But that was all that she had time for before the ae'Magi's staff caught her in the side of the head with enough force to toss her against a wall. As she lay dazed, her eyes focused on Wolf.

On his knees, Wolf carefully retraced the circle of power. Reaching out almost casually, he snagged his staff where it apparently had been waiting for him in the darkness.

"Father," he said, getting to his feet.

The ae'Magi turned and, seeing Wolf, brought his staff up and took up a fighting stance. It was quiet for a moment, then Wolf struck. Some of the fighting was physical, some of it was magical, most of it was both—accompanied by a very impressive light show.

Aralorn watched from her corner and got slowly to her feet. Anything that she could do as an icelynx was likely to do as much harm as good with so much magic flying around. She took back her human shape, from habit as much as anything else. She had started to lean against the wall to watch when she caught a glimpse of the sword, half-buried in the filthy rushes on the floor. On impulse she picked it up; the heat that had made her drop it was gone.

Atryx Iblis the Old Man had called it in an archaic dialect. *Atryx* was easy, it meant "devourer." *Iblis* took her a while longer, but when she understood it, she smiled and held it at ready, waiting for a chance to use it again.

Healing himself had weakened Wolf, and he was showing it. His blocks were less sure, and he lashed out in fewer and fewer attacks. The ae'Magi was also tiring; the blood he was losing to the deep slashes that Aralorn had made on his back was bothering him, but it was Wolf who slipped in the muck on the floor and fell to one knee, losing his staff in the process.

For a second time Aralorn attacked the ae'Magi's back with the sword, but this time she stabbed him with it instead of cutting him, and released the grip. The sword Ambris hung grotesquely from his chest, though it was doing no apparent harm. Without taking his eyes off Wolf, the ae'Magi swung the tip of his staff at Aralorn and said a quiet phrase.

Nothing happened, but the Smith's sword was glowing brighter than either of the staves, bathing the dungeon with pink. Wolf got to his feet and retrieved his staff, but made no move to attack. Frantically, the ae'Magi grabbed the blade and pushed the sword out, cutting his fingers in the process, although the blade slid out easily enough and fell, shimmering, to the floor.

Aralorn grabbed it, heedless of the heat, and sheathed it, as she said conversationally, "The Old Man says that it's one of the Smith's weapons. *Atryx Iblis*, he calls it—Magic Eater."

The ae'Magi's staff was dark, just an elaborately carved stick to his touch. The ae'Magi's hands formed the simple gestures to call forth light, and nothing happened. Turning to his son, he said, "Kill me, then."

Passionlessly, the predator the ae'Magi had created looked at him with glittering yellow eyes, then said in his macabre voice, "No."

Wolf turned to Aralorn and, gripping her arm tightly, transported them to the meadow where they'd faced the ae'Magi's illusion, leaving the Archmage in the darkness, alone.

Wolf stepped back from Aralorn almost immediately and stood looking at the magician's castle. Aralorn looked at his brooding face and wondered what he was thinking.

He spoke softly. "I am still what he made me, it seems."

"No," said Aralorn in a positive voice.

"Do you know what I just did? I left him bleeding, to face a castle full of Uriah that he no longer controls."

"A kinder fate than he had in mind for you," Aralorn reminded him, examining the burns the sword had left on her hand. "He has as much chance of escaping from the Uriah as Astrid did. More of a chance than Talor or Kai did." There was nothing wrong with her that wouldn't heal up in a few days.

"You also eliminated the threat that his faithful followers would attack us after we killed the ae'Magi," she told him. "He'll be found, mostly eaten by his former pets."

Wolf caught her hand, and the burns disappeared from it, along with much of the dirt. Aralorn laughed softly and wiped her other hand on his cheek, showing him the smudge on it. "This time, you are almost as dirty as I am."

"He's dead," Wolf said.

"Dead," she agreed.

He closed his eyes and shuddered. She took his hand and he gripped it tightly.

"I think," he told her, "that I have just enough magic to take us back to the library."

"Let's go find Myr and let him know what's happened. Then I have to get back to Sianim and let Ren know that there is going to be a plaguing awful mess of Uriah running around that someone's got to clean up. If he works it right, Sianim stands to make a lot of gold off this."

"Not that you care," Wolf said. "Since you gave up Sianim to follow Myr."

"To follow you," she said. "And I've had time to think a bit. Don't you think it was a coincidence that Ren sent me to an inn not twenty miles from where the King of Reth was hiding? And you know what Ren says about coincidence."

"Usually, coincidences aren't," said Wolf.

FINIS

The fifth baron of Tryfahr, Seneschal of the Royal Palace (also known as Haris the Smith) stepped into the kitchen to examine the food being prepared for the feast celebrating King Myr's formal coronation. Seeing the Seneschal slip into the kitchen, the Lyon of Lambshold, who currently held the title of Minister of Defense, decided to join him.

In the main kitchen, the cook who ruled sprawled asleep in her rocking chair near the dessert trays, a nasty-looking wooden spatula in one hand. The new court taster stood silently near the stove.

The new cook was a marvel; the fowl had never been so moist, the beef so tender, and her sweets were beyond comparison. More wondrous still was that she was able to maneuver her bulk around (though no one but the hulking taster who lurked in the corner had ever witnessed it) and cook.

"So," commented Haris, "the mercenaries have offered to help clean up the Uriah."

"Aye," snorted the Defense Minister, "for a discounted

rate, since their troops will be in the vicinity clearing the
Uriah out of Darran as well. They've already cleared out
the ae'Magi's castle." His hand crept out involuntarily to
hover over one of the lacy sugar cakes.

"I wouldn't," muttered the Seneschal to the Lyon, nodding at the massive hand that was tightening around the
spatula's handle though the cook's eyes had remained
closed. He cleared his throat and remarked in a louder tone,
"Likely they were hoping to find the ae'Magi in a state to
pay them, but I heard that they couldn't find a trace of him
anywhere." There was a note of satisfaction in his tone.

The Lyon snatched his hand back, and said absently,
"Eaten, most likely, poor man. Sianim'll probably make
the next ae'Magi pay them before they turn the castle over
to—" He was interrupted by a shout from one of the pages,
who seemed to be taking over the castle lately.

"Haris! . . . Uhm, excuse me . . . I mean, my lord. Myr . . .
uh, King Myr wants to know if the delegation from Ynstrah
is here yet? He can't find them anywhere, though the gate-
keeper says that they came in last night." The page stood at
the top of the stairs pulling at the velvet surcoat he wore.

"Tell him I'm coming, Stanis," grunted the Seneschal.

The Lyon gave a last look at the cakes as he followed
Haris up the stairs.

When they were safely gone, the small, bright sea-green
eyes of the cook opened, almost concealed in the folds of
her face. She shifted her amazing mass out of the chair and
waddled to the bakery trays. Taking a cake in her pudgy
hand, she threw it to the guardsman who served as taster.
He caught it easily despite the eye patch he wore.

"I told Ren that we wouldn't learn anything at an event
this size," she said. "There isn't enough privacy for any
good plotting. The only thing that ever happens at a state
occasion is an assassination attempt, but Myr has already
hired Sianim guards to stop that."

The guard nodded—he'd heard her complaint more than

once. He examined the little delicacy with his good eye before biting into it, saying, "You could have let him have the cake, Aralorn. They're easy enough to make." Another cake appeared in his hand as he spoke, and he tossed it to Aralorn.

"I couldn't undermine the authority of the castle cook," said Aralorn in a shocked voice, while catching the treat with a dexterity that was out of character. "Besides," she added, taking a bite of her cake, "this way they'll enjoy the two that Haris snitched even more."

Wolf sauntered to the dessert trays and saw that there were indeed three delicacies missing. "Should we tell Myr that his Seneschal is light-fingered?"

"Not unless he wants to pay for the information. We're mercenaries, after all, Wolf." Aralorn licked her fingers. "By the way, where did you learn to cook like this?"

Wolf bared his teeth at her, and said, his voice as macabre as always, "A magician needs must keep some secrets, Lady."

Turn the page for an exciting excerpt from
the all-new tale of Wolf and Aralorn

WOLFSBANE

by PATRICIA BRIGGS

Available now from Ace Books!

A winterwill cried out twice.

There was nothing untoward about that, the winterwill—a smallish, gray-gold lark—was one of the few birds that did not migrate south in the winter.

Aralorn didn't shift her gaze from the snow-laden trail before her, but she watched her mount's ears flicker as he broke through a drift of snow.

Winterwills were both common and loud . . . but it had called out just at the moment when she took the left-hand fork in the path she followed. The snow thinned for a bit, so she nudged Sheen off the trail on the uphill side. Sure enough, a winterwill called out three times and twice more when she returned to the trail again. Sheen snorted and shook his head, jangling his bit.

"Plague it," muttered Aralorn.

The path broke through the trees and leveled a bit as the trees cleared away on either side. She shifted her weight, and her horses stopped. On lead line, the roan, her secondary mount, stood docilely, but Sheen threw up his head and pitched his ears forward.

"Good lords of the forest," called Aralorn. "I have urgent business to attend. I beg leave to pay toll that I might pass unmolested through here."

She could almost feel the chagrin that descended upon the brigands still under the cover of the trees around her. At long last a man stepped out. His clothing was neatly patched, and Aralorn was reminded in some indefinable way of the carefully mended cottage where she'd purchased her cheese not a half-hour ride from here. The hood of his undyed cloak was pulled up, and his face was further disguised by a winter scarf wound about his chin and nose.

"You don't have the appearance of a Trader," commented the man gruffly. "How is it you presume to take advantage of their pact with us?"

Before she'd seen the man, she'd had a story ready. Aralorn always had a story ready. But the man's appearance changed her plans.

Though his clothes were worn, his boots were good-quality royal issue, and there was confidence in the manner in which he rested his hand on his short sword. He'd been an army man at some time. If he'd been in the Rethian army, he'd know her father. Truth would have a better chance with him than any falsehood.

"I have several close friends among the Traders," she said. "But as you say, there is no treaty between you and me; you have no reason to grant me passage."

"The treaty's existence is a closely guarded secret," he said. "One that many would kill to protect."

She smiled at him gently, ignoring his threat. "I've passed for Trader before, and I could have this time as well. But when I saw you for an army man, I thought the truth would work as well—I only lie when I have to."

She surprised a laugh out of him though his hand didn't

move from his sword hilt. "All right, then, Mistress. Tell me this *truth* of yours."

"I am Aralorn, mercenary of Sianim. My father is dead," she said. Her voice wobbled unexpectedly—disconcerting her momentarily. She wasn't used to its doing anything she hadn't intended. "The Lyon of Lambshold. If you delay me more than a few hours, I will miss his funeral."

"I haven't heard any such news. I know the Lyon," stated the bandit with suspicion. "You don't look like him."

Aralorn rolled her eyes. "I *know* that. I am his eldest daughter by a peasant woman." At the growing tension in her voice, Sheen began fretting.

His attention drawn to the horse, the bandit leader stiffened and drew in his breath, holding up a hand to silence her. He walked slowly around him, then nodded abruptly. "I believe you. Your stallion could be the double of the one cut down under the Lyon at the battle of Valner Pass."

"His sire died at Valner Pass," agreed Aralorn, "fourteen years ago."

The bandit produced a faded strip of green ribbon and caught Sheen's bit, tying the thin cloth to the shank of the curb. "This will get you past my men. Don't remove it until you come to the Wayfarer's Inn—do you know it?"

Aralorn nodded, started to turn her horses, then stopped. "Tell your wife she makes excellent cheese—and take my advice: Don't let her patch your thieving clothes with the same cloth as her apron. I might not be the only one to notice it."

Startled, the bandit looked at the yellow-and-green weave that covered his right knee.

Softly, Aralorn continued, "It is a hard thing for a woman alone to raise children to adulthood."

She could tell that he was reconsidering his decision not to kill her, something he wouldn't have done if she'd kept her mouth closed; but she could clearly remember the walnut-brown eyes of the toddler who held on to his mother's brightly colored apron. He wouldn't fare well in the world without a father to protect him from harm, and Aralorn had a weakness for children.

"You are a smart man, sir," she said. "If I had wanted to have you caught, it would have made more sense for me to go to Lord Larmouth, whose province this is, and tell him what I saw—than for me to warn you."

Slowly, his hand moved away from the small sword, but Aralorn could hear a nearby creaking that told her that someone held a nocked bow. "I will tell her."

She nudged Sheen with her knees and left the bandit behind.

———

She crossed the first mountain pass late that night; and the second and last pass before Lambshold the following afternoon.

The snow was heavier as she traveled northward. Aralorn switched horses often, but Sheen still took the brunt of the work since he was better suited for breaking through the crusted, knee-deep drifts. Gradually, as new light dawned over the edge of the pass, the mountain trail began to move downward, and the snow lessened. Aralorn swayed wearily in the saddle. It was less than two hours' ride to Lambshold, but she and the horses were going to need rest before then.

The road passed by another small village with an inn. Aralorn dismounted and led her exhausted horses to the stableyard.

If the hostler was surprised at the arrival of a guest in the morning, he gave no sign of it. Nor did he argue with Aralorn when she gave him the lead to the roan and began the task of grooming Sheen on her own. The warhorse was not so fierce that a stableboy could not have groomed him, but it was her habit to perform the task herself when she was troubled. Before she stored her tack, she untied the scrap of ribbon from Sheen's bit. She left the horses dozing comfortably and entered the inn through the stable door.

The innkeeper, whom she found in the kitchen, was a different man from the one she remembered, but the room he led her to was familiar and clean. She closed the door behind him, stripped off her boots and breeches, then climbed between the sweet-smelling sheets. Too tired, too numb, to dread sleeping as she'd learned to do in the last few weeks, she let oblivion take her.

The dream, when it came, started gently. Aralorn found herself wandering through a corridor in the ae'Magi's castle. It looked much the same as the last time she had seen it, the night the ae'Magi died.

The forbidding stairway loomed out of the darkness. Aralorn set her hand to the wall and took the downward steps, though it was so dark that she could barely see where to put her feet. Dread coated the back of her throat like sour honey, and she knew that something terrible awaited her. She took another step down and found herself unexpectedly in a small stone room that smelled of offal and ammonia.

A woman lay on a wooden table, her face frozen in death. Despite the pallor that clung to her skin and the fine lines of suffering, she was beautiful; her fiery hair seemed out of place in the presence of death. Arcanely etched iron manacles, thicker than the pale wrists they enclosed, had left scars testifying to the years they'd remained in place.

At the foot of the table stood a raven-haired boy regarding the dead woman. He paid no attention to Aralorn or anything else. His face still had that unformed look of childhood. His yellow eyes were oddly remote as he looked at the body, ancient eyes that revealed his identity to Aralorn.

Wolf, thought Aralorn. This was her Wolf as a child.

"She was my mother?" the boy who would be Wolf said at last.

His voice was unexpected, soft rather than the hoarse rasp that she associated with Wolf.

"Yes."

Aralorn looked for the author of the second voice, but she couldn't see him. Only his words echoed in her ears, without inflection or tone. It could have been anyone who spoke. "I thought you might like to see her before I disposed of her."

The boy shrugged. "I cannot imagine why you thought that. May I return to my studies now, Father?"

The vision faded, and Aralorn found herself taking another step down.

"Even as a child he was cold. Impersonal. Unnatural. Evil," whispered something out of the darkness of the stairwell.

Aralorn shook her head, denying the words. She knew better than anyone the emotions Wolf could conceal equally well behind a blank face or the silver mask he usually wore. If anything, he was more emotional than most people. She had opened her mouth to argue when a scream distracted her. She stepped down, toward the sound.

She was naked and cold, her breath rose above her in a puff of mist. She tried to move to conserve her warmth, but iron chains bound her where she was. Cool metal touched her throat, and Wolf pressed the blade down until her flesh parted.

He smiled sweetly as the knife cut slowly deeper. "Hush now, this won't hurt."

She screamed, and his smile widened incongruously, catching her attention.

It wasn't Wolf's smile. She knew his smile: It was as rare as green diamonds, not practiced as this was. Fiercely, she denied what she saw.

Under her hot stare, her tormentor's yellow eyes darkened to blue. When he spoke a second time it was in the ae'Magi's dulcet tones. "Come, my son, it is time for you to learn more."

"No."

Something shifted painfully in Aralorn's head with rude suddenness and jerked her from the table to somewhere behind the ae'Magi, whose knife pressed against the neck of a pale woman who was too frightened even to moan.

Truth, thought Aralorn, feeling the rightness in this dream.

The boy stood apart from his father, no longer so young as her earlier vision of him. Already, his face had begun to show signs of matching the Archmage's, feature for feature—except for his eyes.

"Come," repeated the ae'Magi. "The death you deal her will be much easier than the one I will give her. It will also be easier for you, Cain."

"No." The boy who had been Cain before he was her Wolf spoke softly, without defiance or deference.

The ae'Magi smiled and walked to his son, caressing his face with the hand that still held the bloody knife. Some part of Aralorn tensed as she saw the Archmage's caressing hand. Bits and pieces of things Wolf had told her coalesced with the sexuality of the ae'Magi's gesture.

"As you will," said the sorcerer softly. "I, at least, will enjoy it more."

Rage suffused her with hatred of a man she knew to be dead. She stepped forward, as if she could alter events long past, and the scene changed again.

The boy stood on the tower parapet, a violent storm raged overhead. He was older now, with a man's height, though his shoulders were still narrow with youth. Cold rain poured down, and Wolf shivered.

"It's power, Cain. Don't you want it?"

Slowly the boy lifted his arms to embrace the storm.

But that taint of wrongness had returned, and Aralorn called upon her magic, girded in the truth of natural order, to pull it right. She had no more magic than the average hedgewitch, but it seemed to be enough for the job. Once more, the scene shifted subtly, as if a farseeing glass were twisted into focus.

"It's power, Cain. Don't you want it?"

"It comes too fast, Father. I can't control it." Wolf spoke the words without the inflection that would have added urgency to them.

"I will control the magic." When Wolf appeared un-moved, the ae'Magi's voice softened to an ugly whisper. "I can assure you, you won't like the alternative."

Even in the storm-darkened night, Aralorn could see Wolf's face blanch, though his expression never altered. "Very well, then." There was something quiet and pur-poseful in his voice that Aralorn wondered at. Something that only someone who knew him well would have heard.

Wolf bent his head, and Aralorn was aware of the cur-rents of magic he drew. The Archmage closed his hands on his son's shoulders; Wolf flinched slightly at the touch, then resumed passing his power on to his father. Lightning flashed, and the magic he held doubled, then trebled in an instant. Slowly, Wolf lifted his arms, and lightning flashed a second time, hitting him squarely in the chest.

He called it to him on purpose, thought Aralorn, stunned. If he had been wholly human, he would have died there, and his father with him. For a green mage, whose blood comes from an older race, lightning contains magic rather than death—but he would have had no way of knowing that. He didn't know what his mother had been, not then.

For an instant, the two stood utterly still, except for the soundless, formless force Wolf had assembled; then a stone exploded into rubble, followed by another and another. The broken bits of granite began to glow with the heat of wild magic released without control. Aralorn couldn't tell if Wolf was trying to control the magic at all, though the ae'Magi had stepped back and was gesturing wildly in an attempt to stem the tide. Shadow was banished by the heat of the flames. Aralorn saw Wolf smile . . .

"No!" cried the ae'Magi, as molten rock splattered across Wolf's face, from a stone that burst in front of him. Wolf screamed, a sound lost in the crack of shattering stone.

The ae'Magi cast a spell, drawing on the very magic that wreaked such havoc.

A warding, thought Aralorn, as a rock fell from a parapet and bounced off an invisible barrier that surrounded the ae'Magi as he knelt over his unconscious son.

"I will not lose the power. You shall not escape me today."

The scene faded, and Aralorn found herself back in the corridor, but she was not alone.

The ae'Magi stepped to her, frowning. "How did you . . ." His voice trailed off, and his face twisted in a spasm of an emotion so strong she wasn't able to tell what it was. "You love him?"

Though his voice wasn't loud, it cracked and twisted until it was no longer the ae'Magi's voice. It was familiar, though; Aralorn struggled to remember to whom it belonged. "Who are you?" she asked.

The figure of the ce'Magi melted away, as did the corridor fading into an ancient darkness that began to reach for her. She screamed and . . .

———————

Awake, Aralorn listened to the muffled sounds of the inn. Hearing no urgent footsteps, she decided that she must not have screamed out loud. This was not the kind of place where such a sound would have been dismissed. She sat up to shake off the effects of the nightmare, but the terror of the eerie, hungry emptiness lingered. She might as well get up.

She'd begun having nightmares when Wolf had disappeared a few weeks ago. Nightmares weren't an unexpected part of being a mercenary, but these had been relentless. Dreams of being trapped in the ae'Magi's dungeon unable to escape the pain or the voice that asked over and over again, "Where is Cain? Where is my son?" But this dream had been different . . . It had been more than a dream.

She pulled on her clothes. Her acceptance of what she had seen had been born of the peculiar acceptance that was the gift of a dreamer. Awake now, she wondered.

It had felt like truth. If the ae'Magi were still alive, she would have cheerfully attributed it to an attack by him—a little nasty designed to make her doubt Wolf and make his life a little more miserable. An attack that had failed only because she had a little magic of her own to call upon.

But the ae'Magi was dead, and she could think of no one else who would know the intimate details of Wolf's childhood—things that even she had not known for certain.

It was a dream, she decided as she headed out to the stables. Only a dream.